When John Frum Came

BILL SCHROEDER

PUBLISHED BY FIDELI PUBLISHING INC.

© Copyright 2014, Bill Schroeder

All Rights Reserved.

No part of this book may be reproduced, stored in a retrieval system, or transmitted by any means, electronic, mechanical, photocopying, recording, or otherwise, without written permission from the author.

ISBN: 978-1502916372

Banner Publications
P.O. Box 321
Finksburg, MD 21048

Introduction

The following novel, *When John Frum Came,* is based on a subject few people know much about — the effect of Cargo Cults in the South Pacific prior to World War II. European coconut plantation owners, primarily British, had held the natives in virtual slavery for at least 100 years. It is not to be confused with *John Frum, He come!*, a 1974 non-fiction book by Edward Rice. The novel takes a satirical and humorous approach, making it "a good read."

Through extensive and detailed research I have preserved the historical accuracy of the time. I was ably assisted in understanding the native point of view by a South Pacific woman who married an American friend of mine who lived in the islands for a prolonged period.

The actual John Frum is an archetypal and somewhat mythical American who spread dissent and revolution among the original inhabitants of Tanna and the other islands in the vicinity of the Solomons. He urged the natives to "return to custom" and resist the Christian Missionaries who were the unwitting tools of the European exploiters.

I have used humor and irony to tell a tale of a growing crisis that was halted by World War II. It addresses the plight of Pacific Island natives tempted by dreams of wealth, and the white men who did not seem have the slightest notion a problem existed.

Two men from opposite sides of the globe come together in a cultural clash that neither of them fully understands. Yani is a shaman of a stone-age tribe

Bill Schroeder

and Moses McDuff is an inept and naïve Boston missionary who tries to bring the "benefits" of civilization to an island named *Christ's Despair*.

According to local history and legend, in the 1930s an American named John Frum tried to get the natives to ignore the missionaries, and "go back to custom." The British Government supposedly put a price on his head. To merely get caught saying the underground code words –"John Frum, he come!" — could earn a Pacific native two years in jail. Yani believes in a Cargo Cult that says John Frum will bring a shipload of canned food for his people and they will never have to work again. This story is a snapshot of life on one of the Solomon Islands just before the U.S. Marines arrived for WWII's famous Battle of Guadalcanal in 1942.

Yani and McDuff go through many adventures involving head-hunters, self-serving white men, the Imperial Japanese Army, and the U.S. Navy. The surprising outcome will amuse you and cause you to think about the nature of synchronicity.

Chapter 1

1934 — Chase Island, British Solomons

Twenty boys were herded into an enclosure. They were about to become men, and they knew some of them would die trying. Each was sponsored by a male relative other than his father. In Yani's case it was his mother's brother who provided him with a bamboo pole. No one got a shield. Ooma, the shaman, who was also the chief village elder, addressed them: "If you want to be *pooja*, you will have to prove it by capturing the spirit house from the guardians who defend it."

With these minimal instructions, the boys were led to a clearing in front of the spirit house, or *tambaran*, as it was called. On their behalf, Ooma issued a long, loud and boastful challenge to the defenders of the building. The challenge was followed by ten seconds of complete silence. No one flicked an eyelash.

Then with a shriek, four men in six-foot body masks ran from the darkness of the doorway and waved broom-like wands in the faces of the fearful initiates. They made a symbolic mark in the sand and challenged the boys to cross it. Yani was among the few with the nerve to move.

However, as soon as they crossed the line no less than forty warriors appeared from out of the crowd in full battle costume; spears, shields, clubs and wearing penis gourds. Their bodies were covered with the most frightening and outrageous yellow and red body paint imaginable. They bellowed their war cries and descended upon the terrified boys. The initiates charged toward the *tambaran*, and a furious mock battle followed.

The attackers were repeatedly driven off with ferocious howls and jabbing spears. There was no intention of doing the youngsters any serious bodily harm, but heads were rapped with hollow gourd clubs, and there were more than a few drops of blood drawn from minor flesh wounds caused by the spears and the general scuffling.

Yani's nose was bloody from a number of blows from spear shafts and shields, but he managed to land a few solid smashes with his bamboo pole in retaliation.

Five minutes of this wild melee ensued, until the old man shouted as loud as he could. A rapid beating of a hollow log drum brought everyone to a standstill. The defending *pooja* turned, ran to the entrance of the spirit house and disappeared inside. Several women began to sob, and a small boy screamed hysterically. He thought his father was being gobbled up by the spirits inside.

Ooma gathered his charges together again in the center of the clearing. Those who still had their bamboo spears began to stamp them on the ground as they sang a victory chant. They had routed the enemy and were now men enough to enter the sacred structure. A doorway, looking much like an oversized grass skirt, was the entrance through which they followed Ooma.

Now the real initiation would begin.

***

Boston, Massachusetts

Moses McDuff was filled with self-doubt. He was not sure he had the qualifications implied by his about-to-be awarded Doctor of Divinity degree. He feared first that he was not worthy, and second that his attitude was too liberal to be an authentic Guardian of the Faith. Boston's True Church of God Seminary was, indeed, a no-nonsense school for young men who wished to devote their lives to preaching the Full Gospel of Jesus Christ.

But what was the alternative? After Harvard, his father had arranged for him to work in a stockbroker's office, but his aptitude for finance was lacking. A stint with the Headquarters of one of the major railroads demonstrated, as the Vice President of Personnel wrote the elder McDuff that, "Young Mr. McDuff lacks his father's leadership qualities. I suggest that he look into teaching at one of the better preparatory schools." However, his scholastic record did not support a teaching career.

In desperation his father had a talk with him. "The church would seem to be an honorable way out of this dilemma for you," he said. "I think you will do the least harm to the family reputation in that role. I will not have you lying about the house, doing nothing. No McDuff has ever been a dilettante."

As a teenager, Moses' interest in religion centered about what was right or wrong on a personal level. More recently, at the seminary he found that at times he dare not ask the questions that bothered him most. He told himself that some of his thoughts were perverse, if not downright sinful.

***

Yani's eyes did not adjust immediately to the dark room. The thick smoke from the smoldering fire in the center of the room did not help. All the boys were made to sit in a circle around the fire, with their individual sponsors standing behind them. Ooma spoke again: "You have taken the first step to manhood, and have captured the *tambaran*. But you are not *pooja*. You have much to learn and must speak with the spirits."

He called them to their feet to form a dance circle. At first the flutes, gourds and drums were played at the tempo of a man's heartbeat. As the beat slowed down over the hours, one by one the boys became unconscious from exhaustion, intoxication, kava paralysis, pain or just plain fright.

Yani could make out huge figures of the spirits the shaman was gesturing toward. They were one and a half times the height of a man, each carved from a single tree trunk. They were painted with bizarre faces and adorned with decorations of all descriptions, often highlighting erect penises. These were the spirits who were to speak to the initiates. Each represented a spirit that lived inside it. Meeting these spirits and viewing the sacred musical instruments marked the high point of initiation rites.

"This is the trumpet of Baloo," Ooma told them, holding a conch-like shell above his head. "It calls the fish from the sea. We sound it on the mornings the village goes fishing." Yani had seen and heard it often and even knew its name, but now his knowledge was official.

The boys were shown an almost endless procession of sacred objects, and told their secret names. Women must never know these things, they were told, or the tribe would perish. The spirit voices Yani had often heard turned out to be bamboo flutes. After the introduction of each, men played a wide variety of gourds that had been turned into oddly shaped instruments. The wails and moans that issued from them were eerie enough to run a chill up Yani's spine in spite of the 100-degree temperature of the room.

"When we play the sacred and secret notes during the full moon, Pakwa, the spirit of fertility makes the garden grow. If we do not play the right notes, the taro roots will be small and dry. If a woman hums the notes while she is working in the garden it will be overrun by pigs within a day."

The old man had a small coconut in each hand and held them at arm's length to his sides. With all the force he could muster he brought them together, smashing them in front of him, shattering both. The sharp rap was the signal to begin the next phase of the initiation. Each sponsor gave his boy half of a coconut shell filled with kava, heavily laced with palm wine. The kava was made from the root of a local pepper plant, and was to be drunk down in one long draught. One half a shell of kava was generally enough to incapacitate a man for the night, but in this case the boys were given two coconut halves to drink. The net result for the boys, who had no experience or tolerance of the beverage, was almost total paralysis.

This was a great help during the circumcision rite, and blessed were those who had achieved total unconsciousness. The work was done with a knife made from a certain variety of razor-sharp bamboo. "This will rid you of your mother's blood," the sponsor chanted over and over until his work was done.

Wholly engulfed in the ceremony, Yani felt the effects of the kava and palm wine mixture. They brought on a kind of twilight sleep. He was in two places at once ... in the *tambaran* experiencing some pain, but at the same time having a vivid dream recalling the beginning of the day. He was there again.

The screeching birds in the jungle signaled the approaching sunrise. As he awoke, the first thing he noticed was that he had an erection of which he could be proud. It was the most favorable sign he could have had on *kook'mba*, the day of change, this day when his childhood ended. It was to be the first day of his manhood.

He got out of his hammock of closely woven vines where he slept. Covered with a layer of coconut oil mixed with the juice of flowers that killed insects, he looked like a sheet of human flypaper. He was dotted from his hair to his ankles with dozens of small bugs that had sought his blood, but found their own deaths.

In his dream, he broke into a run and plunged into the light surf at the edge of the beach. Bugs and oil washed away into the frothy waves. When he left the water, he was refreshed and ready to face the most important day of his life. He could hear some of the young boys crying about their nightmares foretelling the next day's events. But Yani regarded it as a great adventure to be looked forward to. If a man was not initiated he would go through life as a *rubbish man*, having no status in the community.

The dream gave way to a feeling of floating above the strand, higher than the treetops. He could see the back of the ceremonial house. It was breathtaking. A graceful triangular spire soared above the coconut palms, with a facade of painted bark panels. It had taken nearly a year to build, using the skills of virtually all the adult males of Chase Island. The outside was guarded by carved spirit figures, impassive as sphinxes and magnificently attired with headdresses, leaves, and shell ornaments.

Yani could see the entire village crowded into the clearing in front of the *tambaran*. The skulls of ten human heads were on display in the center of the village. They were relics of bygone days of glory, grisly trophies of some long-forgotten ambush. They stared with startled shell eyes. Clay, paint, cowry shells, and tufts of human hair created a semblance of the original features.

A chattering stream of women clustered in groups, balancing pots of food and net bags bulging with cooked yams and sleeping babies. Women had been barred from this area for months: now at last they crushed excitedly around the structure. They were there to allow the men to show off.

Everyone cowered as the voices of the spirits were heard coming from the spirit house. It sounded like the wailing of lost souls, accompanied by the pounding of drums. In the already sweltering midday heat, several men in long body masks roamed around the village frightening the women and children. Their job was to dispense terror, and the women played along with it. Many had helped their husbands make the masks and costumes of shredded sago and collars of fruit. These tribesmen dressed as spirits often broke into swaying dances, sending quivers of fear through the watching crowd.

Yani felt himself slip backward in time to the months before, during the construction of the spirit house. He and some of the other boys watched in secret from behind some large-leafed plants as the main supporting posts were installed amid sacred and solemn rituals. As always, the chants had to be said in a certain manner — voice inflections mattered. The boys watched in fascination as Ooma dropped a skull into a freshly dug hole. At the bottom of each post hole rested a skull of a tribal enemy — the braver that man had been, the more powerful was his spirit. The hand movements of the warriors reenacted the beheading of their victims. As with the hula in another part of the Pacific, hand movements were always vital. They needed to be done just so.

Valid trophy skulls were becoming scarce. The Australian patrol officers had imposed strange new laws over the old unwritten ones. But, the Chase Islanders still practiced headhunting when the opportunity arose.

***

For Moses McDuff, having his own pulpit was out of the question. He simply lacked any leadership skills. At this solemn ordination ceremony he idly listened to the music, trying to recognize some identifiable melodies. When the organist reached the end of "A Mighty Fortress is Our God," Dr. Macintosh, the President of the Seminary, mounted the lectern before the students, graduates, and families of the somber and grave young men being awarded their degrees. Without smiling he said, "This is a joyous day. We are very pleased this morning to have with us a world-renowned Christian leader who has been so

When John Frum Came

gracious as to visit with us here in Boston. He awaits passage on a ship that will take him home once more to Glasgow, Scotland, after fifty years of missionary work in the South Seas.

"Half a century ago he and his comrades went to the Island of Tanna, southeast of New Guinea. They went as friends to dispel the black clouds that darkened the minds of the natives of that region ... They went to bring the word of our Savior, Jesus of Nazareth. They were met with bows and arrows, spears, stones, and curses. No matter how good an example they set, the natives reverted again and again to the black ignorance of their savagery.

"I have had the opportunity to listen to his first-hand accounts of the incredible hardships he and his people faced and the sacrifices they made. They left behind families, loved ones, warm hearths, and the comforts of civilization to live and preach the Gospel of Jesus Christ on hostile, untamed shores."

He wiped away an unseen tear, and with his voice full of emotion said, "Ladies and gentlemen, I give you Dr. John G. Paton." Moses McDuff stifled an impulse to applaud. Such behavior was inappropriate in this particular house of God.

A gray-haired man, whose frame indicated that he had once been physically powerful and robust, took the pulpit. His face was very tired, and his skin was somewhat yellow from a bout with hepatitis, or worse. He looked around but was silent for a full half-minute while the audience waited on his utterances.

Finally, he broke the tension and spoke. "It was all for the love of God and Jesus!" His booming voice was still strong and resonant. "We put an end to their barbaric ways. We forbade circumcision, polygamy, sensuality, magic, cannibalism, and headhunting. There was no more feasting, dancing, kava drinking, singing, and drumming."

McDuff leaned forward in his seat to be sure he did not miss a word. The words and the message were compelling.

"Their barbaric figures toppled to the ground. We burned every pagan idol we could find. We destroyed their savage artifacts and prohibited any further production. Thus stripped of their savage ways, they were naked before the Lord — they could be clothed with Western ideas and be led serenely into the True Light.

"We established laws, courts, stocks, prisons and fines to proclaim to these naked savages that the ways of Christianity are superior to the chaos under which they lived. We clothed their naked bodies ... We cut their hair ... We shaved their faces. We discouraged the use of ornaments and paint, feathers and jewelry. We overcame their resistance. Where their chiefs clung to the old ways, the authorities replaced them with men more congenial to the Christian way. These more enlightened natives had the power of the Australian Government behind them ..."

***

The pain of the tattooing process drew Yani's spirit back into his body and he regained consciousness. His sponsor made a geometric design on the boy's back. The older man incised the youth's skin with scores of small cuts. Then the wounds were rubbed with ash and oil to raise permanent welts. The unique design consisted of a series of slits which were then packed with a natural dye, designed to create a life-long identifying tattoo. These were meant to simulate the pattern on the skin of the fearsome crocodiles that lived in the inland lake. Even if a man should literally lose his head in battle, his body could be identified by his body markings and claimed by his family for funeral rites.

Tight-lipped with pain, the boys underwent the grueling introduction to manhood. Yani was one of the less-fortunates in the group, and remained awake during the entire process. His relatively uncomplaining demeanor brought him the praise of Ooma. The elder singled him out for recognition by the spirits. Yani was selected as a future shaman, and spiritual son of Ooma. The elder himself inflicted the additional identifying marks on the young man's chest.

***

In Boston, Reverend Paton went on for a full hour enumerating the ways Christianity had made inroads in the Satanic lifestyle of the Godless Heathens of the South Pacific islands. Moses McDuff was entranced by the story and it struck him: *This is the way I can prove my worth to my family, to God, and myself — Most of all myself.* He needed to succeed in the kind of adverse circumstances the great Doctor Paton had endured. He would seek an audience with the retired missionary before he left Boston, and find out how he could qualify for such a noble calling.

***

The tattooing done, Ooma poured a huge net bag of white ashes atop the central fire, which was almost out. These were the ashes left from the fire that had consumed the previous spirit house of four years before. They captured the power of the old spirits for the new generation of *pooja*.

The men who had earlier defended the spirit house from the attack of the novices, now reappeared. They were somewhat unsteady from the amount of kava and palm wine they had consumed, but they knew their duty. One by one, each of the naked men urinated into the ash pit while he chanted a magic spell he had inherited from his sponsor at the time of his own initiation to manhood.

When they had all made their contributions, Ooma stirred up the mess with his hands, mixing it with local clay, until it had the consistency of a gummy paint. "This will make you *pooja*," he said. "From the top of your head to the soles of your feet, cover each other with the spirit paint." He started the action by taking a handful of the gray mixture and putting it on the top of Yani's head. It ran down his face, and trickled on to his chest. Ooma spread it out to cover every exposed inch of skin he saw.

The boys did the same to each other, until there was a room full of gray adolescents. The mixture dried to a white, chalky powder which symbolized the crocodile egg waiting to hatch. One of the men twirled a bull-roarer around and above his head. It was a flat piece of wood with a hole in the middle that emitted a low growling sound like a male crocodile's warning noise as it spun. Its low frequency grumble added an additional element of dread to the generally frightening atmosphere.

For the third and final time they were organized into a circle and given more kava and palm wine. Their body movements had become automatic. Dancing in a tight circle for hours, they waited for the spirits to speak to them. Ooma, the shaman, whispered magic words into each initiate's ear. This mantra was meant for him alone to chant over and over as he danced to the beat of the hollow log drums.

As the twenty adolescent boys fell one by one to the floor of the smoke filled spirit house, they were carried out the back of the building to the beach. Their bodies were covered lightly with sand to simulate the crocodile nest. Three had died. A few, like Yani, experienced visions, but most just passed out. These were no longer boys, but *pooja* — crocodiles about to be hatched into maturity according to the ritual passage of their totem.

Yani now needed to lie quietly in the sand and rest while he waited to hatch into a new life. He was soon unconscious and he heard the spirits speak to him. All the young men remained in the sand until the afternoon cloudburst of the next day. Then they were urged to rise up and run down to the ocean where they were held in the surf by the older men until the white shell covering was washed off.

That evening the new *pooja* stretched out on the sand with their first hangovers. Their mother's inferior blood, having been cast out, they could now form virile blood of their own.

Yani awoke cleared-eyed and talkative in spite of the near mutilation he had undergone at the initiation. Ooma prophesied great things for this unusual young man.

***

The old Scotsman did not have time for a long personal interview, but obligingly sold Moses McDuff an autographed copy of "*A Missionary in the New Hebrides*" by The Reverend John G. Paton. The young minister promised to study the tome faithfully.

But, after a brief discussion, which included Seminary President Macintosh and his father, they concluded that Moses would be better suited to the conversion of the Irish Catholic immigrants in the Boston area.

Chapter 2

1939

Life on Chase Island had changed little in the past 100 years. It could be considered a blessing that there was nothing of economic value there that the white man found useful. Commercial coconuts did not grow well; there were no minerals worth mining, and the beach was blocked by a thick coral reef. It was difficult for the white man's boats to even approach the island.

While nobody was rich, neither was anyone what could be called poor. Everyone did for himself what needed to be done. There were no hut-builders, or spear-makers or canoe-shapers. Everyone built his own hut and made his own spears. If someone decided he needed a canoe, he would persuade a few friends to help him hack one out of a fallen tree, and it would be theirs jointly. Every family had a slash and burn garden at the edge of the jungle which yielded sufficient taro to feed its members.

Yani was on an errand for Ooma. He had grown to his adult physique, and his hair was now somewhere between red and garish blond. He soaked it with a paste of certain ground seashells that bleached it from its natural black. It was one of the visual markings that identified him as an apprentice shaman. He was walking along the shoreline looking for shells that could be inscribed with symbols to improve the quality of fish living in the lagoon. The fish were countless, as usual, but lately had been on the small side.

Fishing was communal, and an activity requiring much cooperation. Both men and women participated, dragging wide nets toward the shallow end of the lagoon from the deep. Usually, enough fish and other creatures were caught that made the activity necessary only every second or third day. With no refrigeration, it was pointless to catch any more than the islanders could eat before spoilage became a problem. The need for long-term food preservation had never arisen.

This was a non-fishing day. There were other things that Yani needed to attend to. Suddenly, Jimay, one of the men Yani had shared the initiation rites with emerged from the brush, carrying a squealing piglet. He was taking it home to corral it and fatten it up for a half a year; then he would offer it to the family of a girl he wanted to take as his wife.

Yani was not interested in pigs or wives at the moment. His mind was elsewhere. Pigs were a measure of wealth and a source of endless problems. They were always changing hands. The most common method of getting new pigs was in compensation for being wronged. If your garden was ravaged by someone else's swine, some — if not all the pigs involved — might become yours. If another man shared sex with your wife, he owed you some kind of gift in return. The village elders consistently ruled that when sufficient damage had been done to someone, a piglet was satisfactory compensation.

As he was wading out toward an unusually large shell, Yani saw a strange boat come into view. It was clearly not a native outrigger. It was a derelict European-style sailboat. By pure luck it drifted through the narrow opening in the reef. The moon was full and the tides were at their highest, creating the margin of safety needed for its hull to clear. Had it been any other time of the month, there would have been only wooden splinters washing ashore.

Yani called to two other men sitting in the sand. "Look! Something that wanders the sea is coming for a visit."

He pointed to the breakers, and the three of them waded out into the surf to catch the boat by its trailing ropes. They swam along with it, laughing as the keel buried itself in the sand. It was a medium sized yawl with a retractable centerboard, like those found on the Chesapeake Bay in the United States. It allowed the boat to enter shallow water without running aground. Once the tide went out, it would rest essentially on its side in the sand, but for now it rode well in the water. At the time of its construction it had been an expensive craft, and its solid construction is what kept it from breaking up as it beached. Its name was *Salvation*.

When they climbed over the sides, they found eight men sprawled in various positions from the bow to the stern. None were conscious. Two had obviously been dead for a while. Empty liquor bottles told a clear story to the older islanders who joined Yani on board. Outside contact with Witmen for Chase Islanders was a rare occurrence. This was the first time in five years they had made contact with Witmen (Pidgin for anybody who was not a dark-skinned native islander. They made no distinctions among Orientals, Malays and Europeans — they were all Witmen). Any time they had come ashore in the past, it was always the same — trouble. They were arrogant, unruly, dangerous, and drunk. They wanted women, water and food — usually in that order.

Inland, others quickly became aware of the event, and large numbers of villagers came to see the shipwreck. Yani and his friends lifted the unconscious men over the side, and the villagers received the limp bodies. They were uncertain what to do with two dead men, so, as was their custom, four old women dragged them off the boat, and left them at the water' edge for the time being. The old women had nothing to fear from their spirits since their days were numbered anyway.

The bottles were also handed over the sides; even the empty ones were highly treasured in a place where glass was not made in any form. Fortunately, none of the bottles were broken; bare feet did not do well among broken glass shards.

Ooma arrived. He surveyed the scene and declared the ship taboo because of the dead bodies. From that point on no one dared climb aboard.

The six remaining men were carried to the shade of the jungle and rainwater brought in wooden bowls, was poured over their heads. When they started to show signs of coming-to, those who could took long drinks, only to pass out again. They were suffering from heat stroke and dehydration for the most part. All that could be hoped for was that they might recover on their own. Chase Islanders had no treatment for heat stroke because they seldom suffered from it. They knew well what a man on the other side of the world named Noel Coward had been telling London audiences: "Mad dogs and Englishmen go out in the noonday sun," but this group of maritime misfits never got the message.

The leader of this motley crew of men without a country was, in fact, quite British, calling himself Captain J.R. West. He became a Captain only by virtue of the fact that he owned the yawl. It became his as the payoff of a crooked card game in which the former owner died under "mysterious" circumstances.

Before he became a sea captain, he had been a copra plantation foreman on another obscure island further north, but his title would have better been described as "overseer." He treated the natives as little more than slaves.

The question now arose among the islanders as to what to do with these Witmen who were thrust upon them. To others in their own villages the people were congenial; the men scrupulously democratic. During debates any man could stand and air his views, no matter how unpopular. But these Witmen had no status. They were virtually un-people.

A meeting was called and one of the men of about 19, another who had been through the initiation with Yani, said, "I think their heads would make an excellent addition to the village's collection."

The shaman shook his head and waved his left hand in front of him as though he were sweeping away debris. "No!" he said emphatically. "These Witmen were not enemies. There was no battle. No fight. Their heads have no spiritual value. It would be the same as making a feast from a pig we found dead in the bush."

The rest of the men voiced their agreement. They looked to Ooma for a better ideas. He thought for a while, then said, "I believe that the decision should be made by Akambep, the Sun. We interfered with a trial by the elements when we took these men out of the boat. They were being tested by Akambep. Lay grass mats out on the sand and stretch the Witmen out on them." Essentially, they would let nature take its course.

Mats were spread out and the sailors were dragged out of the jungle again. Stripped of all their clothes, the most outstanding thing about them was that the lower portions of their bodies were white, or light tan in the case of the Asians, marking where they had all worn cotton shorts. Men, women and children walked among the prostrate forms, remarking on the anomaly. They wondered if these men were diseased with their ghastly white rumps, resembling a certain type of fungus infection sometimes seen in the form of white circles on the skin.

At the height of the curious display, a huge cumulonimbus cloud above the island reached a critical altitude and the skies opened up in a deluge. The temperature dropped twenty degrees, as the cool rain bathed the six men on the mats. It kept raining for at least a half hour. While the entire village watched from the cover of the jungle, curtains of water swept over them in a tropical cloudburst.

Flashes of lightning illuminated the beach with dazzling brilliance. A clap of thunder, loud enough to shatter any glass bottles left on the boat's deck, woke Captain West from his coma. He opened his eyes, only to have them rinsed thoroughly by the downpour. Turning his head to the side and lifting on one elbow, he surveyed the prostrate forms of the other five crew members. He said out loud, "I thought Hell was fire and brimstone, and here it is bloody, God-damned rain. It ain't no different than England," and allowed himself to fall back on the wet, sandy mat.

"Akambep speaks with a loud voice," Ooma said to Yani when he saw West stir. "When he returns to the sky we will take the Witmen."

Finally, the drenching rain stopped as suddenly as it had begun. Two more of the men proved to be dead, and they were dragged along with the first two into the jungle to be left to the elements. Such was the customary and unceremonious disposal of non-tribesmen. Ooma gave the signal to carry the castaways who were still alive to the village.

***

In a matter of days, the four Witmen recovered their strength sufficiently to walk around the village. Food was provided for them with no fanfare since there was no shortage. Ooma, proved his wisdom by providing the convalescents with an unlimited supply of kava. The pepper-root beverage had a tranquilizing effect on the patients, and kept them in an almost numb condition most of the time.

Yani was captivated by the visitors and the things they carried. Among the possessions that the dead crew members no longer had any use for were filthy, ragged shirts and shorts. Clothes made of cotton, linen or wool fabrics were owned only by people who had traded with the last visiting Witmen five years ago. They were worn only for ceremonial occasions, but these men wore cotton clothing all the time. Yani had rinsed the castoff clothing in the surf, and now wore a pair of khaki shorts, and a tattered shirt.

Best of all, one of the dead men he had removed from the boat had worn a steel knife in a sheath on a belt around his waist. To Yani this was a magic tool. His people knew no metallurgy, and such things as this knife were so precious as to be handed down within a family as heirlooms. There were no more than three or four iron tools on the entire island. Ooma, confiscated the other knives as his own before the sailors' carcasses were disposed of.

However, as his health returned, the leader of the Witmen became restless. The occasional ground tremor caused by the local volcano added to his anxiety. "Don't drink any more of the bloody kava," Captain West told the other three, "or we'll never get off the island."

"Why do we want to?" asked Gash, who was from Borneo. He got his name from a scar that ran transversely across his chest from an old knife wound. He was becoming very popular with the unmarried girls of the village. "This is better than home ... or any place we have been," he said quite innocently and honestly.

West barked back at him, "I don't plan to spend the rest of my days in a reed hut, eating sweet potatoes. I plan to breathe my last in a whorehouse in Sydney full of good Scotch whiskey."

The other surviving crew members were Shim-shi, a Korean; and Bano, a Filipino. They shared Gash's sentiments, but they were afraid of the Englishman. None of them understood a word of each others' native languages, so they all spoke Pidgin, the lingua franca of the South Pacific islands. With each island essentially having its own dialect, there were hundreds upon hundreds of separate languages in use. Even native traders from neighboring islands used sign language. But since the end of the 19th Century Europeans had been spreading Pidgin. It was mostly English, but also used French, German and island words.

By listening to the sailors talking with each other, Yani made a discovery that would change his life. He had a gift — he understood and learned any language very easily. Within a week he understood many of the things they said. At the end of the second week he began making up his own sentences. Before a month had passed, he knew the language almost as well as his teachers.

They were pleased with him. It became unnecessary for them to even try to learn the Chase Island dialect. All they needed to do was tell Yani what they wanted, and he either got it or told Ooma what they said.

The taboo imposed on their beached sailboat meant nothing to the sailors. They made frequent trips to it for things to trade with the girls for sexual favors. The natives, however, continued to refuse to set foot on its decks for fear of the spirits of the men who had died there.

"Let's establish a pecking order here," West said one day. "It's time we taught these filthy savages who's really in charge." The method he had in mind involved bringing back his rifle and a supply of ammunition during one of his visits to the boat.

"Yani," he called out in full view of the fishing party on the beach. "Set three of those coconuts on the big rock by the ocean."

Yani did as he was told, and while he was walking away from them, West got off a quick shot that made one of them explode. Yani jumped in the air, then fell in the sand, terrified. He had never heard a rifle shot before, much less seen the damage it could do.

The fishermen dropped their nets, and crowded cautiously around West and his men to find the cause of the exploding coconut. Yani recovered from his fright enough to join them.

When West had everyone's attention, he raised the rifle to his shoulder again. The remaining two coconuts were in line, so he decided to take them both out with one shot. He pulled the trigger, and both brown globes flew to pieces.

The natives grabbed each other for protection at the deafening roar. West told Yani in Pidgin to translate his words so they would understand them. "Tell them that Captain West can blow heads away as easy as coconuts, so don't get any ideas about having us for dinner any time in the near future."

The younger men and boys were impressed with the shooting demonstration but the village elders worried. They had seen what Witmen with guns could do from earlier encounters. The German traders hired mercenaries to "tame" the island when they were colonizing 25 years before. Scores of natives were killed before it was decided that Chase Island would be unsuitable for the plantations they had in mind.

The most exciting thing Yani found in the inexplicable treasure-trove from the boat was "tinkens" (Pidgin: tin cans) of corned beef. He could not get enough of it. He traded all manner of fresh seafood and fruit for even small portions. The sailors told him that the meat was put in the cans back in Australia, but even they had only a sketchy idea of the technology involved. Yani became preoccupied with the riddle of how the tasty, salted beef got into the can. It also laid the foundation for a lifetime pre-occupation with how the Witmen got the tinkens in the first place.

***

The fact that the Australian authorities classified the Chase Islanders as a Stone Age culture did not hinder them from developing a rather sophisticated philosophy about the nature of reality. Since life did not require a minute to minute struggle to get enough food while dodging carnivorous animals, certain members of the tribe had time to think about how things got the way they were. During the five years since his initiation, Yani had spent the greater part of his time in the company of Ooma, asking questions.

Knowledge fell into two categories — secular and sacred. "Everyone knows how to fish, grow taro, and hunt for wild pigs," Ooma explained to Yani at one of the daily kava-drinking sessions. "A boy copies his elders in daily work. He watches — he does."

Ooma used his fingers to pick up a burning ember from the fire without apparently burning himself. "A boy learns about fire by burning his fingers." The shaman ran the sharp edge of a steel knife along the back of left forearm. It made a mark, but did not bleed. "He learns about knives by cutting himself. This is nothing. Life is a learning experience."

They both drank some more kava. "Do you understand?" the old man asked.

Yani lacked the words in any language to express the idea that "Sacred knowledge is paramount." But he understood that to his people *real knowl-*

edge ... the knowledge of myths, reading dreams, and the mastery of esoteric formulas was *True Knowledge*. Knowing how to make a bow was elementary knowledge, very low on the scale of intellectual achievement.

"I want to be like Ooma," he told his mentor. "You are one who *really knows*. I wish to understand. The others do not know.

"Men say our blood is dying," Yani said. "We have not had a raiding party against the *kanakas* in the bush since I became a man. We pretend war in our dances, but the *kanakas* live on the far slopes of the volcano. We live by the lagoon. We grow fat and lazy eating fish. Do not our spirits need exercise?"

Ooma shook his head. "The Witmen took away our protective spirits when they killed so many. I have thought to strengthen our blood by sending you and ten men to the islands just beyond the horizon to the south. You could satisfy our spiritual needs if we had two or three heads."

War for the Chase Islanders had nothing to do with economics and territorial expansion. For the past ten years, the vitality of the tribe had been declining. In short, things had been pretty placid. The arrival of the Witmen was creating some deep stirrings. The young men were beginning to show anxiety.

Yani and Ooma sat in silence for a few minutes, then Yani said, "Why are the Witmen here, Ooma?"

"I have thought on this many days and nights. From the first day they arrived."

Yani did not expect him to blurt out all the answers at once. He knew that the answer would come in the form of a recounting of a myth. His people dismissed the principle of intellectual discovery. To figure something out logically was not the route to credibility. Accepted myths were the sole and unquestionable source of all important truth. Even when a man composed a new melody or dance, he had to authenticate it by claiming that it came in a dream from a deity rather than out of his own head.

"I have dreamed of Kilibob and Manup. Do you know the story?" the headman said, ready to reveal his enlightenment.

"No, Ooma. I have not heard it," Yani said. Any other response would have been disrespectful. Actually he had heard versions of it dozens of times. If he told Ooma he heard it, it would be a great insult and the conversation would

Bill Schroeder

be at an end. Saying he had not, would allow the old man to modify, add to, or completely change the story to fit the situation.

"Kilibob and Manup were brothers created by Anut, the first god. One day they quarreled about their wives. Manup killed Kilibob. Anut breathed life back into Kilibob and the brothers decided to leave their birthplace. Manup made a small canoe, while Kilibob built a ship with a bottom like the one on the beach."

Yani liked it when Ooma got down to the relevant details. He listened attentively.

"The two brothers launched their vessels. Kilibob's was so much better, that Manup departed in shame from the sunrise side of the island to find a new home. Kilibob then provisioned his own vessel. He stocked it with iron tools and food plants and tinkens. He created men and kept them below deck. When all was ready he left. He sailed from the sunset side of the island to find other places.

"At each of the big islands he put a man ashore. He offered him the choice between a rifle, like these Witmen have, and a bow and arrow. He let them choose between a hollow boat like the one on the beach and a native canoe. He offered them taro and breadfruit, or they could have tinkens. In each case, the man rejected the rifle. He would say, 'This is a short and useless lump of wood.' Then he chose the bow and arrow because it was lighter and easier to handle.

"He rejected the hollow boat with a round bottom because it rocked in the choppy sea. He accepted the canoe. With its outrigger it rode steady and firm. The man rejected the tinkens and chose the taro and the breadfruit plants.

"When all the men he created were placed on the islands, Kilibob sailed a long distance. He found a country where the Witmen lived. He gave them everything that was left in his boat. They took the rifles and the boats, and the tinkens which the islanders turned down because of their own stupidity."

Yani was spellbound. "Then the Witmen took Kilibob's gifts. Blackfella," he said using his new Pidgin word for native, "had to live with poor sticks and what he could find? Right?"

"More important," Ooma added, "Kilibob also taught them the ritual to get knives of iron," pointing to the one on Yani's belt. "He taught them the formula for making magic food in tinken. When they say the words, they get more food without a garden. They get metal tools just by asking."

"How can Blackfella get back Kilibob's gifts?" Yani wanted to know.

Ooma thought back to the slaughter his tribe had endured when the island was taken over by the German trading companies when he was a boy, and then humiliation at the hands of the Australian authorities. Almost from the beginning of their contact, the islanders had envied the material wealth of the white men. He had heard from island traders that efforts by black natives to get the things the Europeans had had ended in disaster.

He did his best to explain to Yani the stories he had heard, but the young man's own personal experience was too limited for him to truly understand. However, he did know that others had tried.

Ooma indulged himself in a bit of reading the future. "After a war with the Witmen, Kilibob and Manup will be friends again," he said. "They will return and bring a period of peace and plenty. At the homecoming of the two brothers they will provide us with the goods Kilibob took away before. We will have the rifles, not to fight each other, but the Witmen."

Yani was enthralled. He now had sacred knowledge of what lay ahead for the Chase Islanders, indeed, without realizing it, for the whole Pacific. Now he wanted to go to the Witman's island and find Kilibob. He must be persuaded to make up with his brother, and return to his people with the gifts that were due them.

Chapter 3

It was one month to the day since Captain West and the good ship *Salvation* had been deposited on the shores of Chase Island. The day started with Gash severely beating one of the men who had loaned him a wife. He had left the man with a scar like the one that had earned him his name. Afterwards, he ran down to the boat to get away from the injured man's relatives. Retribution was sure to follow.

The Englishman and the other two crewmen were putting the finishing touches on the yawl in preparation for their departure. They had loaded breadfruit, bananas, and coconuts aboard and filled the water casks themselves, since the boat was still taboo to the natives. West was aware of raised voices that carried from the village and a number of belligerent looking men, who were carrying war spears.

They were addressing the elders, and Ooma was trying to quiet them down. Yani sat with the men who were not involved and listened to the arguments. It was quite simple: it was clear the Witmen were getting ready to leave the island, but they had not cleared up their accounts. The sailors had had sex with the wives of these men numerous times. All they had received in return was some tobacco, and a small amount of whiskey that was left in some of the bottles that were stored on board.

"What is it you want from the Witmen?" Ooma asked.

"We have decided that we should each receive one pig," one of the self-appointed spokesmen said. "It is only fair. They have used our women for their pleasure for a full turn of the moon."

"They have no pigs," Ooma pointed out. "They had nothing when they came here, and are leaving with food we have provided. We are better off with them out of our village."

The same young warrior that made a similar suggestion when they arrived, again proposed "I am *pooja*. I must not be dishonored by 'trash men.' I say we should take their heads."

This time the reaction of the crowd indicated that they liked the idea. "We have not had a battle with an enemy in many years," an older warrior said loudly. "We have been dishonored, and their spirits deserve to be ours."

"I agree. Let's take their heads in payment."

"Then Kilibob's boat will become ours. We can go to their island and bring back all their gifts," said a man who had heard the story Ooma now told on a regular basis during kava sessions.

"They have a rifle," Ooma cautioned. "You have seen what it can do to coconuts. I have seen what it can do to a man."

"I have whispered my secret protection into the paint that covers my shield," one of the men said. "Their rifle will be useless against my spirit protection."

"Manup told me in a dream that we should kill them," still another voice said.

Yani got up and slipped away from the heated discussion. He headed down to the boat and went directly to West. "You owe men pigs. You not have pigs. They take your heads," he told him in Pidgin. "They will be here in a short time."

"Let them come," West boasted, slapping a cartridge into the chamber of the rifle propped against the side of the boat. "I'll shoot any bloody spear-chucker that has the guts to come out to the beach."

Gash, Shim-shi and Bano looked worried. They did not share West's confidence. "We only have a few minutes to get clear of the reef while the tide is high enough," Shim-shi said. "We go chop-chop."

Bano and Gash jumped down from the deck where they had been running up the main sail. They started shoving the hull of the boat up and out of the sand that held it. Shim-shi was waist-high in shallow waves and pulling on a rope in an effort to get the sailboat into deeper water.

West watched the edge of the jungle and saw the *pooja* were lining up with their spears and shields at the ready. A charge was about to be mounted.

"Yani! Get up here on deck with me," West yelled.

"Boat taboo. No can touch boat," Yani replied.

"Fuck the taboo. I said get up here." He fired a round into the sand next to where Yani stood. In fear, he fell to the ground, and from the jungle it looked as though West had shot him.

Ooma was shocked. He regarded Yani as a son. "*Pooja! Pooja! Pooja!*" he shrieked.

The warriors let loose a flight of spears that gave the impression of a flock of birds taking off from the jungle. They all fell short by a couple yards.

Pointing to the fallen Yani, West called out, "Gash, drag him over here to the boat. We'll use him as a hostage. We'll use him for a shield."

Gash was a large and strong man. He literally picked Yani up by the thick mop of red hair on the top of his head and handed the frightened youth to West. The Captain dragged him up on deck by the hair and forced him to his feet. He held the young islander in front of him as he fired a shot at the line of dark-skinned men slowly advancing toward the lagoon. One fell. They all stopped momentarily and looked. It was the man whose shield was covered with the bulletproof paint.

West kicked Yani's feet out from under him, and gave him a quick butt stroke with the rifle, knocking him out. This freed his hands so he could reload his rifle again. His second shot found a second victim.

However, it was also the signal for another hail of spears. Gash was just clamoring aboard when a slender, barbed spear pierced his arm and he lost his grip. But, at the same moment a breeze magically billowed the mainsail, and the *Salvation* briskly pulled out into the deeper water, and headed for the flooded reef. Shim-shi climbed up the rope on to the deck, where he found Bano already frantically working the tiller. In a surprising display of seamanship and luck, West headed his craft toward the shallow opening in the reef. He cleared it with only inches to spare.

The salt spray splashed on Yani's face, restoring him to consciousness. When he figured out where he was, he looked over the gunnels toward the shore. He could see Ooma waving something at the departing Witmen. It was Gash's head.

***

For most of his first day on the small boat, Yani just sat on the deck and looked at the water. He had been off the island on an outrigger, but never out of sight of land. He knew that to the south of Chase were islands with other people. They came on occasion to trade, and then paddled out of sight again. Being out on this magnificent, endless blue sea with no land on the horizon was frightening. He also knew they weren't going south; they were going toward the setting sun.

J.R. West paid little attention to Yani and when he did, no doubt gave thought to throwing him overboard to save on food and water. Shim-shi offered him a cup of water and a banana in the middle of the afternoon. Of his three shipmates, the Korean was the friendliest. He put his hand on the islander's shoulder and said things in his native language that had a reassuring tone.

"If you plan to keep him as a pet," West said sarcastically, you better teach him to do some useful tricks. This is too big a boat for just the three of us." Short of an emergency, the Englishman was too busy being Captain to do any physical labor himself. Bano was the helmsman, and Shim-shi wrestled with the ragged sails. Nothing had been done to improve the condition of the boat while they were on the island. For one thing, there was no usable material on the island to work with. From their conversations, Yani had determined that they had run out of water two days before he found the boat drifting into Chase Island's lagoon. Like fools, they had drunk large amounts of gin and whiskey with the net result of dehydration and heat stroke. The liquor had come from their last port of call where (Gash had boasted) they had killed a trading post operator and two native employees. In their hasty departure, they took all the food and liquor they could carry, but no water. Then, as now, they set sail for wherever the wind might take them.

At first the Chase Islander did not understand the theory or principles of sailing, but worked the ropes as Shim-shi showed him. In a matter of a few days he was quite at home and resigned to the new adventure that lay before him.

Bano taught him how to open the cans of food from the storage locker in the galley, which he did whenever he had the chance. He was disappointed to find that some of them contained vegetables and usually left those uneaten.

Aside from keeping the boat heading westward, there was little to do but talk. Yani liked his new-found language, a sing-song mélange of words from everywhere. He had a very strange introduction to the ways of the Witmen, and he found that he could convey ideas that were foreign to his native dialect.

For five days the little boat corrected its course each evening by steering into the setting sun. With its four-man crew it went from one small, uninhabited atoll to another. They were looking for anyone who could tell them where they were, and were ready to beg, trade, or preferably steal what they wanted.

Late in the afternoon they spotted a fairly large island on the horizon, and the crew members cheered. One that size had to have people on it — hopefully white people.

Chapter 4

At the same time the *Salvation* sighted the island, another boat was approaching the island's small harbor from the opposite direction. It was a medium-sized Australian Government steam cruiser which had once been a rich man's yacht. It had become the property of the Administration after the stock market crash in 1929, and its original name, *The Wombat*, was still painted on the bow and stern, just above the boat's official identification letters.

The two colonial patrol officers for the region, Robert Wembly and Leslie Gale, stood at the rail watching the outriggers paddling out to meet them.

"Well, there it is — Christ's Despair. No matter how often we come here, I can't get over the name," Gale said. "I hope our American missionary has more patience than Jesus. I give him three months. They don't generally last longer than that on most islands. What's an American doing in this part of nowhere anyway? He's kept pretty much to himself since we left Port Moresby, but what I have gotten out of him hasn't been too informative."

"Yes, I know," Wembly agreed. "One of two things — either he is so inept he had to take whatever post his church assigned him to, or he's so devoted to his faith that he welcomes adversity."

"He'll get it here." Gale changed the subject and said, "I wonder if Jeremy has had any luck in finding any more workers for his plantation. There's another one for you ... how much must they be paying him to stay here? Copra is valuable, granted, but selling your body and soul to the Company has to be akin to joining the French Foreign Legion."

Since the Germans cleared much of the island 20 years ago and planted coconut palms, nothing much had been added. Jeremy Thompson's job was to keep the trees from being choked out by the jungle. One of the most common problems in the South Pacific was: "How do you get the natives to work? There does not seem to be anything they want. How do you pay them?"

The Patrol officers knew the problem well. Wembly made a speculation, "I guess he thinks all those boxes on the aft deck are supposed to solve his problems. Knives, axes, and machetes. He plans to use them as payment for physical labor."

"I'll be dipped in shit if I'd want to arm the natives ... that's what he's doing, you know. I'd be afraid they'd use them on something other than underbrush — like my neck, for instance."

With that, the Reverend Doctor Moses McDuff, opened the door from the inner cabin, and joined them on deck. He was a clean-shaven man with light brown hair and bright green eyes. Rather than chubby, he might be described as well-fed. There was the beginning of a sag above his web belt. He looked to be in his mid to late 20s. "Good afternoon, gentlemen. Mr. Wembly ... Mr. Gale."

The junior officer later described him as "looking as though he were part of the Stanley and Livingston search party, and the safari had left without him." Beneath his neatly pressed khaki shirt he wore a clean white clerical collar and a black bib. A large, carved mahogany cross hung on his shirtfront. To complement his creased shorts, he wore knee-high, tan stockings. Unlike the sweat-stained headgear of the Patrol officers, his Abercrombie and Fitch regulation pith helmet was spotless, apparently just out of its New York box.

In the crook of his arm he held a Bible. "I'm ready to meet my congregation," he said with bubbling optimism.

"Have you ever been to one of these islands before, Dr. McDuff?" Gale asked cautiously.

"Quite frankly, no," he answered. "But I have virtually committed to memory the text of *"A Missionary in the New Hebrides"* by The Reverend John G. Paton. I have read every relevant word about New Guinea in the *Encyclopedia Britannica*. Furthermore, I researched all the *National Geographic* articles on the subject for the last 30 years. I feel quite well prepared."

Wembly bit his tongue and Gale had to turn toward the harbor to hide his grin. Reverend McDuff seemed not to notice, and moved closer to the railing to observe the approaching canoes. "I assume that's the welcoming committee," he said. "I see a white man in one of them."

"That would be Mr. Thompson, the copra plantation manager. His will be the only white face you'll see here for a couple months, Dr. McDuff. That's when the next supply ship will be here with whatever you ordered."

"Supply ship? I was given to believe there were trading posts on the islands where one could buy what he needed," McDuff said.

"Tell me you're joking, Dr. McDuff," Wembly said glumly. "You mean to say you haven't made arrangements with the Port Moresby Trading Company to deliver your needs on a regular schedule."

"Why, no," the minister said. "Is it too late? Can I give you a letter to take back to Port Moresby with you to make the proper arrangements?" He looked worried.

"They're not big on credit sales. You have to pay for everything in advance," Wembly explained.

The American looked bewildered. He truly had no idea how serious his situation was.

"Normally, I wouldn't do this, but you are a veritable 'babe in the woods.' I suggest you make a list of what you will need for a three-month period. Give me the cash to cover it and I'll drop it by their office when we get back into port."

"I hope you brought enough stuff with you to last you a couple months to start with," Gale said. "Like we told you, there aren't any stores on the island."

"The Home Church has provided me with a large amount of food and tools. The idea was that I should begin construction of a church as soon as possible. The parishioners generally will be expected to provide the pastor with food in return for his services," McDuff explained.

"I hope you like raw fish, Capricorn beetle grubs, and sago palm, Doctor," Gale said, teasing the clergyman. "That's what makes up the diet of most of these people on a daily basis."

He had McDuff worried. "I really had better get down to my cabin and make a list for you. This is very upsetting."

He made a hasty return through the doorway, and hurried down the companionway. The Australians looked at each other. Gale said, "Did I say three months? Make it three weeks!"

Jeremy Thompson climbed up the rope ladder from the outrigger, and hopped over the rail onto the *Wombat's* deck. With his right hand extended he said, "Hey, mates! Am I glad to see you. Where's the Scotch?"

They shook hands and went into the main cabin. Fully anticipating Thompson's needs, they had the glasses and whiskey waiting on a table. The plantation manager downed a four-ounce shot and allowed himself to sag into an upholstered chair. "Ah, civilization!" he sighed. "I hope there is a surplus of this nectar on board."

"Two cases, Jeremy. Just as we promised."

While the helmsman brought the boat into the primitive pier, the three men talked about Australia, Port Moresby, and the world in general for an hour. At length, Thompson said, "I thought I saw another white man on board with you while I was coming out. Who was that and where is he?"

"An American missionary name of McDuff. He's down in his cabin making a list of what he wants the supply ship to bring him. I think he's both *in* trouble and is going to *cause you* some," Gale said.

"He's totally unprepared for what's out there," said Wembly. "He'd have trouble adjusting to Brisbane. I'm afraid you might have to keep an eye on him."

"If he's a minister, maybe he'll understand me when I say, 'Am I my brother's keeper?' I've got enough bleedin' problems without having to baby-sit a fuckin' missionary," Thompson protested.

"Think of him as somebody to talk to in between our visits," Gale joked.

"And he's a Yank to boot? What can I talk to him about?"

Wembly was the senior of the two, so he undertook to explain what was planned. "The Commissioner thinks that one of the reasons the plantation owners have had so much trouble getting natives to work is that they don't see things the way we do!"

Thompson grimaced and downed another four ounces of Scotch. "Well, the Commissioner should get an award for brilliance. These bleedin' *kanakas* couldn't see things any more different if they came from the Moon. They live in a different world." His tone reflected his anger and his frustration. "What does his lordship propose to do about it?"

"Well, he believes that if they can be converted to Christianity, they can be made to see the reason for work. As long as they worship their pagan gods, and don't have a sense of right and wrong, they'll never see the value of work.

"However, none of our local people were willing to come here to Christ's Despair to set up a church, so they accepted this American ... this McDuff fellow, for lack of anyone else. I have my doubts as to how long he'll last."

"Wonderful," Thompson said. "And am I to be on hand to pick up the pieces? Why don't one of you fellows stay with him for a couple months?"

"Sorry, our territory is too big already. Too many places to cover. We weren't even due here for another three weeks, except that we were told to deliver Dr. McDuff to the island."

Gale added, "The Crown expects its administrators to civilize the natives throughout the Empire. We've done it before. Look at India, Ceylon. I understand they have done very well with the natives on the islands in the Caribbean."

"The Caribbean!" Thompson exploded. "You think there is any comparison between this and Barbados? If you will remember your history, Les, the original natives have been replaced with Africans who came as slaves. They're so domesticated now that those fuckers hound you to try to sell you souvenirs — These bastards want to kill you, roast you for dinner, and put your head on a pole in the middle of their town square."

As Thompson was finishing his description, Dr. McDuff entered the cabin, and the patrol officers stood up. Thompson remained slumped in his soft chair. "Dr. McDuff, I'd like to introduce Mr. Jeremy Thompson. He's the plantation manager on the island for Pacific Copra, Limited. You are going to see a lot of each other in the next few months."

Dr. McDuff reached out to shake hands with him, but Thompson did not get up or return the gesture. His civility surfaced somewhat, but his manner was cool. He gave McDuff an offhand salute, by touching his brow and saying, "Howdy, mate."

"Well it looks like you're going to have some competition for the title of Big Man on the island, Jeremy," Gale said.

"I'd say there was no contest," Thompson answered.

"You have nothing to fear from me, Mr. Thompson," Dr. McDuff put in hurriedly. "I have no intention of usurping any of your prerogatives. A servant of the Lord should have no aspirations for secular power ... certainly not to be a *Big Man.* That has a certain political ring to it."

The Australians all laughed. "You misunderstand the term, Doctor," Gale said. "That's what the natives call important people in their community. Rather than chiefs, they call the leader of their tribe a Big Man — at least that's the closest translation we can offer. In the case of white men, anyone who has any form of material wealth that they can share is also a Big Man."

"Well, I don't qualify on that score either," the missionary protested. "I don't have any wealth to share with them. I am here to save their souls, not to make them rich."

"If you don't have any beads and trinkets for them, Dr. McDuff, how the hell to you expect to get their attention?" Thompson said. "They couldn't care less about what we do if we don't come bearing gifts. And believe me, there's damn little they really want that we have. They don't understand what money is."

"Jeremy's mad because he hasn't found out what to pay them with. They don't want to work on his plantation. Working for somebody else just doesn't fit into their world. Self-sufficiency is the order of the day."

When no one else had anything to add, Wembly broke the awkward silence. "That raises a question, Doctor, have you prepared the list for the supply boat?" he said.

The missionary reached into his shirt pocket and produced a folded sheet of paper and a sheaf of Australian banknotes. "Yes, I think this should be what we will need. I expect to receive a bank draft from the Home Church in a month or two, and then we will order some more."

Wembly could not control the involuntary shake of his head. "Dr. McDuff, I still don't think you understand. Whatever mail you receive will be on the same boat. I think we will need to discuss this once more in the morning before we depart. You may want to return with us."

"Most assuredly not," McDuff said. "I am here to preach God's word. I will not worry about worldly, financial matters. I think my guiding star Reverend Paton summed it up in his book. If you will allow me, I will quote:

"'I continually heard the wail of the perishing Heathen in the South Seas; and I saw that few were caring for them. I saw them perishing for lack of the true God and his Son Jesus. But Jesus called. We set off for Tanna, an island of cannibals, where we feared we would all of us be cooked and eaten. We were but two devoted men set apart to preach the Gospel to those dark and bloody naked Savages. My salary was 120 Pounds per annum.'"

In a stage whisper Thompson said to Gale, "Please, Leslie, please ... tell me you're not gonna leave him here with me."

***

Captain West was delighted to see *The Wombat* tied up at the dock, but did not recognize it as a government boat. Speaking to Bano, he said, "Chances are they'll have liquor aboard — and good stuff at that."

He guided the *Salvation* along side, and called out. "Ahoy, aboard the *Wombat*! Ahoy, aboard the *Wombat*!"

One of the seamen looked over the side at the yawl. "What can we do for you, mate?" he asked. Informality was the watchword in the islands.

"Captain J.R. West requests permission to come aboard."

"I'll ask the senior officer."

The seaman knocked on the door of the cabin where the Patrol Officers and their guests were talking. Gale went to the door and opened it. "A sailboat's tied up alongside, sir. A Captain J.R. West requests permission to come aboard."

"Of course. Tell him to come aboard, and join the conversation," Gale said. He closed the door and said, "Looks like the word is out that we're having a party. The captain of a sailboat is about to join us."

A few minutes later, West entered the room, unshaven, and his ragged clothes smelling heavily from perspiration. He became immediately aware of the scrutiny of the others. "If you will excuse my appearance, gentlemen, I've just come from a month of being trapped on an island with a tribe of bloody savages. We barely escaped with our lives." Looking at the bottle of Scotch, he said, "Do you think you could spare a man a drink?"

Wembly hurriedly poured him a glass, which he drank down like rainwater.

"How did you get away?" Gale asked.

"We snuck back on our boat one night about a week ago, and we've been sailing westward ever since. I can't tell you how glad I was to see a white man's boat in the harbor." He then realized that his hosts were wearing Patrol Officers' uniforms.

"What's your name, Captain?" Wembly asked.

"J.R. West and my boat is the *Salvation*. Can I have another drink, please? It's been a long time." This time, without waiting to be served, he picked up the bottle and poured himself a full glass. The other men in the cabin were introduced in turn.

Dr. McDuff, who did not approve of drinking at any time, resisted his inner urge to give a lecture on the subject and addressed himself to West. "I'd be very interested to know what your life among the aborigines was like. I am here to convert the heathen to the understanding of the Gospel of Jesus Christ. I am anxious to know what I can about them."

West saw Thompson roll his eyes, and assessed the situation pretty accurately. "Well, you can start on Chase Island where I was held captive by a tribe of head-hunters. It's called Chase Island by the white men, but the natives call it something else you wouldn't want to try to pronounce?"

To the amusement of everyone else, McDuff asked," Did any of them speak English?"

"English? Of course not … They spoke Booga-booga like they do on all the other islands around here."

McDuff asked Thompson, "Does anyone speak English on this island?"

"Yeah," said Thompson, "…me!"

"How did you communicate with them, Captain West? Is this *Booga-booga* the language the Britannica refers to as Bughutu, or Bugotu? Do you speak their language?"

"Hell, no," West said. "At first we couldn't understand a bloomin' thing. As it turned out they had a smart kid who learned Pidgin from us, and in no time he became our translator. In fact, he stowed away on my boat since he was afraid they would kill him for being too friendly with us."

"How did you wind up there to start with?" Thompson asked.

"We got caught in a storm, and lost a couple hands. We ran out of water, and we all passed out. The next thing I remember is waking up in the middle of the worst typhoon I've ever seen. When we got our senses about us, there were only four of us left out of eight. I think they ate the others before we woke up."

"How come they didn't eat you?" Gale asked, thinking to himself that he was probably too unappetizing for any self-respecting cannibal to touch.

"I think they were saving us for a special feast. They caught one of the crew during the escape and killed him, but we managed to get away."

West did not notice, but while he was spinning his yarn for the attentive audience, Wembly left the cabin and went to the operations bridge. He read over some wireless messages that had been received nearly a month ago, and returned to the group.

"They fed us taro to fatten us up, and gave us Kava to keep us under control. I had to make my men stop drinking it, or they'd be in the soup ... so to speak," West was saying when Wembly returned.

"Captain West, did you say your boat is named the *Salvation?*" Wembly said.

"Yes."

"Where did you get her?" the patrol officer asked.

West knew something was up, but he remained calm. "Actually, I won her in a card game in Port Moresby. I have my papers to prove ownership."

Wembly surprised everyone by taking his pistol out of its holster and pointing it at West. "Unfortunately, we have reason to believe you took those papers off the dead body of its previous owner, Philip Honore, a French planter. Mr. Gale, make sure he hasn't any weapons."

Gale searched him and removed a knife from his belt. "That's all I see, sir," he said. West sat down in a nearby chair.

Wembly continued. "Do you recall a visit to an island known as Schyler's Delight? It used to belong to the Germans."

"I've been to thousands of islands. I don't remember that one."

"But they remember you quite well. A band of cutthroats killed the trading post operator there. They left in a boat named the *Salvation*."

"You can't take the word of a bunch of stinkin' natives. We was never there."

McDuff intruded. "I thought you said there weren't any trading posts in the islands," he said.

"Precious few, thanks to the likes of West here." Wembly almost stood at attention as he said, "The Crown hereby places you under arrest for murder and piracy. We'll take you back to the mainland with us. In the meantime, Gale, use the extra head in the bow for a brig, and put iron on his wrists and ankles."

"I will arm our crew so we can take his men into custody."

Chapter 5

The Australians commandeered the *Salvation* without so much as raising their voices. Shim-shi and Bano had no idea what they were being arrested for. They had just arrived, so how could they have broken any laws? The events at Schyler's Dream were all mixed up in their memories, with several other places where they had robbed whites and natives alike. Usually, they were so drunk details were impossible to recall. One thing they agreed upon, however, was that if there was any shooting it had to be West who did it. He never let any of his crew touch firearms — lest they use them on him.

The interrogations took place right on the pier where they were arrested. The Patrol Officers spoke Pidgin as well as they did English. Bano and Shim-shi told a story different from West's regarding Chase Island, and how they had gotten there. It was considerably closer to the truth. Yani was largely ignored until the other two had finished their tales. Most important, they verified that Yani certainly had not been with them at Schyler's Dream. Also, he did not stow away on their boat, but was, in fact, kidnapped by West.

Yani had never seen an Australian Patrol Officer before, but Ooma had described them from the time they had made the natives of Chase Island aware that they were under Australian rule and owed their allegiance to the King. Australian soldiers had shot a number of Ooma's *pooja* in a pitched battle, and while the white men were not aware of it, those deaths had not yet been avenged. The story was all part of the sacred knowledge of the tribe Ooma had passed on to the young man.

There was one thing of which Yani was sure — the *Wombat* was Kilibob's boat. In his wildest dreams, using the most potent image-inducing drugs, he could not have pictured anything so wonderful. The officers and men were so proud of their craft's panels of polished mahogany, scintillating brass fixtures, and white enamel paint, that they often used their own money to keep it looking like the pleasure yacht it had once been.

Poor Yani was terrified. He saw them leading his crew-mates on to Kilibob's boat, and they disappeared below decks. He wondered if they were being taken to see Kilibob himself.

"Well, Leslie, what do we do with our lost soul here?" Wembly asked in English. "I'm not about to take him back to Chase Island. I just want to get West and his assassins back to Port Moresby. Somebody there can hang them."

"It's going to knock hell out of our schedule. We're behind already. Maybe we should hang them ourselves in the interest of efficiency," Gale answered.

"I'm afraid his lordship would take a dim view of that. If West wasn't an Englishman, we might put them all ashore at Chase Island. That would solve the problem neatly, but we had better stick to the regulations.

"In the meantime, let's talk to this Blackfella here and figure out what to do about him."

"What is your name, boy?" Gale asked in Pidgin.

"I am called Yani," he said in the same.

"Where did you learn to speak Pidgin?"

"Shim-shi, Bano, Gash teach Yani speak sing-song."

"Who is Gash?"

"He Witman. Lose head on island. He throw me on Witman boat. West-fella take hair." After a few trials, he managed to demonstrate how West had dragged him on board by his hair.

While Yani spoke Pidgin as well as his teachers, he was limited by their vocabulary. The Patrol Officers had a wider grasp of the language, and had to narrow down their questions to very simple ones.

Yani's fear faded, and the white men found him cooperative and non-threatening. Jeremy Thompson stopped to say good-by and said a few words to Yani in the language of the residents of Christ's Despair. To their amazement, the language was similar enough for them to understand each other.

Considering the hundreds of languages spoken in the Pacific islands it was a minor miracle.

After Thompson left, Wembly said, "I have the germ of an idea. I first thought of giving him to Thompson as a laborer, but if he can speak the local *Booga-booga*, maybe we can let him be an interpreter for Dr. McDuff. He might be able to translate well enough to get him started. We'd be killing two birds with one stone, as they say."

"Bob, there's only one thing wrong with your idea," Gale said.

"Oh? What's that?"

"We don't know if McDuff speaks Pidgin."

"Well, he's a god-damned doctor. Let the son-of-a-bitch learn."

***

Pairing Yani up with Dr. McDuff was well within the plans of the Administration. It was clear that the missionary was not going to be very effective converting the natives on Christ's Despair unless he had some serious help. Thompson had made it clear that his priorities lay elsewhere, and the Chase Islander was better off with McDuff, since there was no predicting if the locals would work with him on the plantation. It cost an extra bottle of Scotch, but the plantation manager gave in on some points.

Wembly and Gale were standing on deck, next to the gangway, watching Thompson's native boys unloading the Scotch and other special supplies they had brought. McDuff's crates and boxes were stacked at the end of the pier in wild profusion. Anything that was not destined for the plantation was dumped on a huge pile.

The missionary himself appeared, carrying a number of sacks and a satchel full of hymnals and assorted church papers.

"Where are you planning to settle down, Dr. McDuff," Wembly asked, anticipating the answer.

"I thought I would get everything ashore, and then look about for accommodations. I have a tropical tent to live in when we locate a place to build our church, of course …"

Wembly interrupted him. "Dr. McDuff, it is my considered opinion that you should return with us to Port Moresby and do a great deal more planning. You are totally unprepared for the project you are about to undertake. There *are* no accommodations, just as there are no stores or trading posts.

"All the goods you have stacked at the end of the pier will be gone by tomorrow morning. The natives will remove every can of food you have brought with you. And when the boxes are empty they will find a use for every last splinter of wood."

McDuff was silent. He seemed to be piecing together how to best explain his situation. "I cannot go back. I have given my word. For me to return to Port Moresby would be the source of a great deal of personal embarrassment and would create problems I do not wish to discuss.

"My church is a small one, and getting me here has consumed most of our funds. I cannot go back to Boston until I have established a successful church here in the islands … Beyond that I can say no more. I will go ashore on the island."

The Australians had to respect his obvious resolve and integrity, if not his judgment. "In that case, Doctor, I have taken it upon myself to at least keep you alive until we return in a few months.

"Mr. Thompson has agreed to allow you to move into the Big House with him while you find a place to set up your church. I fear that you will not survive the week, unless you do so. I have never seen anyone so ill-prepared for a life and death struggle as you appear to be. And, as a white man and a Christian I can't abandon you to the wilds of the jungle."

Gale asked, "Do you speak Pidgin English?"

McDuff's face brightened. "*Me Churchfella. Come this place tell Blackfella Big Boss longa sky makum inside glad. Takem walkabout longa too much good fella. No more fright — Big Name fella longa me.*"

"Very good, Doctor. It seems you have been studying. Sounds like you could carry on a good conversation."

McDuff showed Gale a dog-eared sheaf of mimeographed papers, stapled in one corner. "I have been studying since I left Boston. That's why I have neglected the social amenities. I believe I am ready to preach the word of God in Pidgin."

"Yes ... too bad the natives only speak *Booga-booga*. Thompson learned their language since they wouldn't learn ours."

The minister was almost in a state of shock. "Then Mr. Thompson will have to teach me the native tongue. My mission depends upon it."

"I wouldn't count on it. He has a number of problems to solve, and he is not inclined to missionary work." When he saw McDuff droop visibly, Gale added, "But I think I have somewhat of a solution to your language problem, however."

"What might that be, sir, an English to *Booga-booga* dictionary?"

"Much better. When we arrested West and his crew last night we found that they had kidnapped a young native boy whom they taught to speak Pidgin. He is really quite good, considering his experience. I propose to give him to you as an apprentice ... what we call a *churchboy* in this part of the world. You can speak to him in Pidgin and he can translate into the native tongue. By a marvelous coincidence they speak pretty much the same language on his island and this one."

"Is he civilized?" McDuff asked.

"More so than many I've seen," Gale said. "He's young enough for you to train to do things your way.

"I will tell him that you are his Big Man from now on. You, in turn, are responsible for providing him with food, clothing and a place to sleep. But, if I know my natives he will be able to provide those things for himself even if you can't.

"As I see it, he should be your first convert. If you can't Christianize him, you had best come back on the next supply ship."

"Speaking of supply ships, Mr. Wembly, please be sure to make the proper arrangements with the trading company. I don't know what I should do if they don't bring me the material I will need to survive here and build a church."

Handing Gale an envelope addressed to a bank in Boston, he said. "Will you please post this as soon as possible. I have had to seriously alter my financial plans in light of what I have found out in the past 12 hours."

"Had you asked sooner, we could have told you the facts of life before we left Port Moresby. We thought you were experienced in this missionary work."

"Unfortunately, only among the Irish Catholics in the Boston slums. But there, I could go back to my family's home in the evening."

The three men descended the gangplank to the pier. Wembly pointed to the *Salvation,* which was tied up to the jetty, and said, "Had any sailing experience, Dr. McDuff?"

"I spent all my summers on Cape Cod, if you know where that is. And the McDuffs have been members of the Cambridge Yacht Club for three generations. The greatest disappointment of my college years was to *not* be selected for the crew of one of Sir Thomas Lipton's entries in the races because I was an American."

"Pity. That would have been an adventure."

Yani was not in the boat. Instead they found him looking over the stack of boxes that belonged to Dr. McDuff. Although he could not read, he was familiar with cartons of canned food from West's storage locker. He was literally salivating, at the thought of so much canned goods in one place.

Mr. Gale called to him. Then observing the island greeting ritual as much as he was familiar with it, he introduced the missionary. He told him McDuff was a Big Man and all these boxes were his. He was ready to share his wealth with this Blackfella if he listened and learned the Big Man's rituals and chants. He had much power and Yani needed to learn to have the powers of this Churchfella. Yani would be his churchboy.

McDuff got into the conversation, and by the time the Patrol Officers were ready to leave, Yani had a pretty good idea of what was expected of him. He understood that the Churchfella was to be his replacement for Ooma. He would learn McDuff's sacred knowledge, as well as his secular knowledge in how to build a church. In return, he would share in the treasure of *tinkens*. Judging from the quantity of boxes at the end of the pier, the Churchfella was richer by far than the West-fella.

As they turned to leave, Wembly remembered another piece of unfinished business. He handed a folded sheet of paper to Dr. McDuff. "These are the ownership papers for the *Salvation*. Fill in your name in the right places. If I tow it back to Port Moresby, it will slow us down by at least a day. Furthermore, I will have to do more paperwork than I wish to, just to turn it over to the Admiralty. I will leave it in your custody. You may find a use for it — to go fishing if nothing else."

Yani watched them go back aboard Kilibob's beautiful ship with mixed emotions. He would have really liked to meet one of the famous brothers, but maybe he would have a chance in the future when he learned the sacred knowledge that appeared to have done these Witmen a great deal of good.

Chapter 6

McDuff was anxious to get things started now that he was here. It had been more than a month and a half since he left Boston to travel on a cargo ship to Brisbane, Australia. It was more than a year since he had started negotiations through the mail with the Administration for him to set up a church. He left the selection of which island to them, feeling they knew better than anyone where the services of a new church were needed.

Judging from the way the crowd of islanders were eyeing his possessions, the minister realized that the Patrol Officers were right. Left in the open, everything would disappear into the village overnight. His first thought was the often discussed logic problem of the three missionaries and the three cannibals trying to cross a river with a canoe that only held two people. The idea was that anytime the balance was disturbed, the cannibals would kill the missionaries. He was not concerned with being killed in this case, since he believed that the natives regarded white men as inviolate. They wouldn't *dare* kill a white man — he was sure. But leaving his goods unprotected while he "arranged his accommodations," as he put it, was another question. The answer clearly lay in the services of his new churchboy, Yani. He would leave him to guard the stack.

He spoke to the young man in Pidgin, reinforcing their verbal contract to his satisfaction. It became clear that Yani expected his pay in *tinkens*. Indeed, there was nothing closer to the Chase Islander's heart than this mountain of cartons filled with tinkens of beef and other tasty delights.

When John Frum Came

"Yani no have food in bel-bel one sun-come-up past," he complained to McDuff, who understood. He had not eaten since yesterday and was looking for breakfast. The minister pried the lid loose on the nearest box and gave him a can of bully beef. Before McDuff could find his can opener, Yani had opened the top of the can using only his prized possession, the steel knife he carried at his waist. His speed and precision was amazing. The lid was hinged up and his fingers plunged into the boiled beef in less than 15 seconds.

The local natives watching were envious. They believed they were entitled to cans as well, and pushed forward behind one of the larger men. Yani was tall for an islander, but this man was taller. He addressed McDuff in a definitely aggressive tone of Booga-booga, not so much asking for a can as demanding one.

The minister did not know what to do. "Yani, tell him tinken bilong churchfella. Him no have."

The concept of a bodyguard was foreign to Yani's culture, but McDuff was his Big Man and he resented anyone treating him with disrespect. More important, his understanding was that he was a joint owner of this cache of food. He was not disposed to share it with these strangers.

Yani understood enough of the man's language to make him decide to act. The native shoved McDuff backwards and said, "Witman trash man. You have no scars of battle. You have no tattoo. I am full man." He swaggered back and forth in front of the crowd. "I have three heads before spirit house. I take *tinkens* from trash man. I claim all tinkens for my *tambaran*."

Yani put down his can of beef with his left hand, and held his knife in his right. Speaking in his own language, with a sprinkling of Pidgin, he said, "This Blackfella no trashman. This fella *pooja*." He pointed to the welts and tattoos on his well-muscled body. His chest markings were recognized by the other islanders as those of a shaman. With a flick of his wrist, his cotton shorts fell to the ground and he stepped out of them.

McDuff was shocked and embarrassed. Yani was standing there stark naked. Pointing to his circumcised penis, he said, "None of my mother's blood runs in me. I am full man of *tambaran*."

As far as the natives were concerned, this was a show-down. If their man backed away without a fight, he would be disgraced. He had to continue his bluff. He made a mocking noise and reached into the open crate to take out a can of beef.

The knife games Yani had played on the *Salvation* with West's pirate crew were not wasted. His knife glinted in the morning sun as it nailed the man to the wooden box. It went in through the middle of the back of his hand, just below the third finger, and buried itself in the soft pine. At the same time, Yani kicked the man's feet out from under him and he fell, causing the double-edged knife to slice its way between the knuckles and to freedom. He pulled the knife out of the wood, and jumped back as the big black man screamed in pain. Clutching the bleeding hand to his chest, he scrambled to his feet and ran away toward the village, with just about everyone following.

Dr. McDuff had difficulty believing what he had just seen. Someone could have been killed over a can of food. This was nothing like he pictured establishing a church would be. In its simplest form, his dream was that he would set up a makeshift church using his jungle tent. It would be in a clearing somewhere with benches made from palm logs. He had seen pictures of such churches in *National Geographic* — but they were in Africa. Obviously, things were different here.

The sight of Yani standing naked on the pier, finishing his can of bully beef without being the least self-conscious was disturbing. These people had no modesty. He was uncomfortable enough that the women were bare breasted, but men going about completely unclothed was too much. Besides, Yani's bravery deserved some sort of reward. There is no telling what might have happened if he had not been there.

McDuff looked over the crates until he came to one marked "clothing." It was packed full of castoffs, mostly donated by friends back on Cape Cod, and was intended for situations just like this. He opened the lid and took out two packages.

It was just as well that Yani had rid himself of the filthy, worn-out shorts he had been wearing. When he first saw the boy, McDuff commented to the Australians that his drawers were more decorative than functional and that they "covered everything and concealed nothing."

When the churchboy finished eating the contents of the can in the nude, and had licked his fingers clean, McDuff told him to kneel on the ground and receive his first gift from the true God. He did so without protest.

The minister held a neatly folded white shirt and khaki shorts over Yani's head and with his eyes closed said, "And Adam and Eve became aware of their nakedness and they hid their shame and took raiment unto them."

Of course, what Yani had no way of knowing was that not only could Dr. McDuff quote the sacred and magic scripture, he was equally capable of creating it to suit his own purposes.

The American handed the shirt and shorts to Yani and said, "God wants you to cover your nakedness with these clothes." Yani took the clothing and unfolded the shirt. Here he found the minister's secret markings that shielded him from danger and the evil spells from other gods. Emblazoned on the back, in bright embroidery was a golden cross and in red, "Massachusetts Youth for Christ Conference — 1934."

Yani was impressed and very happy. This God was not only generous, but had had an eye for beauty as well. He put the shirt on and then tried the shorts. He was clearly better dressed than any of West's crew had been, and certainly better than any Blackfella on Chase Island.

Dr. McDuff told him for the first of hundreds of instances to button up his fly. That seemed to be silly since the fly had to be unbuttoned so frequently. However, he allowed that perhaps this buttoning and unbuttoning procedure was one of the sacred hand movements this God required of his followers to insure the magic.

McDuff was sufficiently confident in his new assistant to leave him to guard the supplies, and began his trek up the dirt trail to Thompson's Big House.

In addition to the corned beef, stewed beef, and mutton, the other thing that Yani found fascinating was a bolt of cotton cloth. To him the red and white checkered material was as fine as silk might be to a European. Chase Island had no such luxury. People wore grass skirts because that was as close to fabric as nature made available. Cotton did not grow in the South Seas.

He cut off a length and made himself a headband, and thought how impressed Ooma would be if he could see him now.

When McDuff reached the house, his shirt was soaked through with perspiration. Thompson, sitting on a verandah with a drink in one hand and binoculars in the other, wore only shorts and an undershirt.

"That was quite a show your boy put on down there," he said. "I watched the whole thing through my field glasses. They'll think twice before trying to steal from you with that yahoo as a watchdog. If I were you, I'd make sure you keep him near you at all times until you learn your way around here."

Thompson was more friendly than he had been the night before. He decided that an American missionary was better to have around to talk to than no one at all. They spent the next hour or so getting acquainted, and McDuff deposited his bag of hymnals in his assigned room.

"I'll tell my boys to move your stuff up here, and put it in the storehouse along with the boxes Wembly brought me. Tomorrow we can look about for a place for you to start clearing the brush and set up your tent."

"What do I do with Yani, my churchboy? I don't imagine he is allowed in the house."

"Of course not. I have a few servants, but they all take care of their own living space outside. I'll tell Jeeves to show him a place near the house where he can build a lean-to."

"Jeeves?" said McDuff, raising an eyebrow.

Thompson smiled. "My little joke. I call him my butler, but what he is, of course, is really a houseboy. He affects to the white man's ways whenever he can. He even has learned a few words of English, believe it or not."

"I'm glad you mentioned that. I'm in a quandary about this language business. I understand that the natives don't speak anything but Booga-booga, as you call it. I had expected them to speak Pidgin, and that's what I have learned," McDuff said.

"Your boy speaks Pidgin, doesn't he?"

"To a limited degree. Not as much as the Patrol Officers seemed to think. However, I *do* manage to make myself understood."

When John Frum Came

"Well since he speaks the same language as the natives, and the only link you have in common is Pidgin, the path seems rather clear. Reinforce his Pidgin skills so he can explain the rules and regulations of the church to your would-be congregation."

"To be quite honest, Mr. Thompson, I had a different approach in mind," the American said. "I was thinking of teaching Yani to speak English, and it would eliminate a lot of this circumlocution business — which is all Pidgin seems to be."

Thompson's posture became somewhat more rigid. "Actually, Reverend, there really are a few things you should know about before you plunge into deep waters and find out you can't swim."

"What do you mean?" McDuff asked.

"I have a very strong feeling that you regard these natives as ordinary people who just happen to have dark brown skin."

"Of course, they're people. Whatever do you mean?"

"If you think about it, it's quite obvious that the closer your origins are to the Equator the stupider you are. These people would have to go north to get any dumber," Thompson said. "Take this cargo cult business that's been running rampant in the islands the past few years ..."

McDuff interrupted him, "Cargo cult? I'm sorry I am not familiar with the term. What's a cargo cult?"

"Good God, man, you *really don't* have any idea of what's going on in this part of the world, do you?" Thompson said angrily. "They see us as the 'haves' and themselves as the 'have-nots.' They look at what we call subsistence living here in the islands, and perceive it as vast wealth. They don't have the foggiest notion of factories or production or any kind of technology. Worst than that, they refuse to learn."

McDuff looked thoughtful. "I take it this causes some kind of problem."

"You're god-damned right it causes a problem. They're waiting for a messiah and I don't mean Jesus Christ. They are waiting for some fella named John Frum to bring all the White man's cargo to them without working. I can't get them to work for me on the plantation. They figure if they just wait long enough, we'll leave and everything we have will be theirs."

"I was unaware of that. I guess it is up to me to convince them that Jesus is the true messiah," McDuff said.

Thompson was not listening. He was too wound up with his own rhetoric. "The Cargo Cult couldn't exist in Sweden, England, or Germany, now could it? Not unless they were overrun with immigrants from some perpetual warm area. Temperate zones, like we have in Australia, or northern climes in Europe produce people that need to plan ahead for their survival. Equatorial climates produce people without a need to plan anything of a practicable nature. It's almost impossible to starve here and quite impossible to freeze to death. The brain coasts into neutral … there to remain for centuries."

"That's a very interesting theory, Mr. Thompson," Dr. McDuff said, "but what's it got to do with teaching Yani to speak English?"

Thompson jumped to his feet. His eyes blazed. "See here, McDuff, I suggest you forget that idea immediately. One of the rules we follow in this part of the world is — *Don't teach the natives English*. If you can't learn their language, teach them Pidgin, but under no circumstances should they be taught the King's English!"

McDuff was taken aback. He was bewildered. "Why on earth is that?" he asked.

"Quite simply, *Reverend* McDuff." He sneered the title. "Because once you teach them English, you will no doubt teach them how to read. If they begin to speak and read English, they are going to start to *think*. The last thing any of us wants here is a native population that bloody thinks for itself. Just watching most of them trying to think is painful."

"Surely that's not true of all of them," McDuff argued. "My man, Yani, seems quite bright. They can't all be so stupid that an occasional spark of latent intellect does not bloom forth to produce a marginally effective person."

"The reason you are here, Dr. McDuff, is to tell them *what* to think. Once you have finished teaching them *what* to think, it is my job to tell them what to *do*. The only thing we want them to do is work on the copra plantations. That's why we are bloody here! You can save their souls all you want, but their arses belong to me!"

Thompson stormed off the verandah, and headed for the pier. At first, McDuff's American democratic hackles were up, but as he reflected on what his host had said he decided to consult his Second Bible. The minister took out Reverend Paton's book and thumbed through it until he found what he was looking for: *"The Tanese had hosts of stone idols, charms and sacred objects which they abjectly feared, and in which they devoutly believed. They were given up to countless superstitions, and firmly glued to their dark heathen practices. Their worship was entirely a service of fear, its aim being to propitiate this or that Evil Spirit, to prevent calamity or to secure revenge.*

"They deified their chiefs, like the Romans of old, so that every village or tribe had some sacred men. They exercised an extraordinary influence of evil, these village or tribal priests, and were believed to have the disposal of life and death, through their sacred ceremonies, not only in their own tribe, but over all the Islands. Sacred men and women, wizards and witches received presents regularly to influence the gods, and to remove sickness, or to cause it."

McDuff had no idea that his churchboy was regarded in that light by the local tribesmen. He read on: *"Their whole worship was one of slavish fear; and so far as ever I could learn, they had no idea of a God of mercy or grace.*

"The natives, destitute of the knowledge of the true God, are ceaselessly groping after Him. Not finding Him, and not being able to live without some sort of god, they have made idols of almost everything: trees and groves, rocks and stones, springs and streams, insects and other beasts, men and departed spirits ..."

He put the book down and looked out over the lagoon. Perhaps it would be best if Yani did not learn standard English. It would do a lot in the way of putting them on an equal footing. The success of his religious mission depended on his being superior to the natives in every way, intellectually as well as spiritually. Thompson was right; if they could speak his language they might argue with him, or even develop thoughts of their own. It was important that they accept, not question.

If they were limited to Pidgin they could construct only mediocre responses and simplifications. The Home Church in Boston had provided him with a few mimeographed church services, prayers and hymns in Pidgin. McDuff made a conscious decision to observe this white man's taboo. He had enough problems with setting up a church as it was ... He would encourage his churchboy to see the Truth as he saw it. Anything else would only make things harder.

Chapter 7

A truce was declared between Thompson and McDuff, but there remained a cool gap between the two men. They took their meals together at the Big House where the plantation manager had trained several native women to keep things looking European — or Australian, depending on your point of view.

A suitable clearing was selected and McDuff put up his tropical tent. Yani loved it. By tacit agreement, he slept there and for all practical purposes it was his home. Yani proved to be a good pupil, and Reverend McDuff was a stern teacher. The boy improved his Pidgin very quickly and McDuff made no conscious effort to teach him English.

It was not difficult for Yani to learn carpentry skills since he regarded the steel tools with awe. He learned to use a handsaw almost with glee. Working palm wood was slow and laborious work with a stone ax, but a steel crosscut saw ripped through a log with hardly any effort at all. The Chase Islander drew a crowd of boys every day as he fashioned benches out of trees. When one of them picked up the saw while Yani was nailing two boards together he snatched it away from him and cuffed him smartly on the ear. "These are sacred tools," he told them. "Kilibob gave them to the Witman, and one by one Yani is taking them back. They are not to be touched, except by me." It was a message the children carried back to the village, raising Yani's stock even higher.

Hammering nails to join wood was another new experience. The steel hammerhead driving the iron nails truly gave him joy and a feeling of power.

When John Frum Came

Big Man Duff, as he called him, had to stop him from using too many nails. There was only one keg of six-penny nails, and they would have to wait a long time before any new ones would come their way.

The young native man thought constantly about the nature of the things he now saw around him: Steel tools. Nails. Tinkens. He wore his red-checked gingham headband all the time, and wondered if he might not make himself a matching sash. It was said among the natives that the red squares were made from the blood of men Yani had killed in battle back on his own island.

He wondered continually how he would get all of Kilibob's gifts back to his island. When would Big Man Duff teach him the sacred chants and ceremonies he would need?

When Yani felt he had enough nerve and mastered Pidgin sufficiently to phrase the question, he approached the minister one evening after they were finished working for the day. "How Witman get tinken? How Witman get cloth?"

McDuff had no idea how much time his churchboy had spent thinking about this subject. He had begun to plan how he would approach the islander's conversion, and decided this was the time to lay the groundwork. His answer in Pidgin was simplistic. "We worship God. We are his children. We do his will. We believe his son, Jesus Christ, died for our sins and he is gracious unto us. We receive his gifts because we follow his word."

Yani became an instant convert. Any God who delivered food in tinkens without having to wait long weeks for pigs to mature or the garden to yield vegetables from the dirt was worth following. All Christians needed to do, apparently, was learn the chants, prayers and significant hand movements McDuff used, and God would send *him* food and cloth ... not to mention the metal tools McDuff had taught him how to use.

On Christ's Despair, as it had been on Chase Island, it was customary for everyone to arise at first light, and complete most of their obligatory activities well before the sun got too high in the sky. On an equatorial island the temperature is always near 90 degrees at midday. By what would have been 10 a.m. in the white man's reckoning, whatever was going to be done was, indeed, done. Everyone returned to the shade of his hut to sleep, eat, drink, enjoy sex or just lounge. If you had planted your garden according to the proper family ritual, with the right chants, there was nothing else for you to do but wait for everything to ripen.

About three in the afternoon the almost daily cloudburst occurred when the rain clouds reached the right altitude. Once the storm was spent, the temperature went down and the humidity went up. At that point the social life began, women began preparing food. The day usually ended with the men consuming massive quantities of kava that induced a form of docile paralysis.

It was not until sundown that the island's only white men had dinner. Although he still ate at the Big House, Dr. McDuff now slept at his church-under-construction. He had strung a jungle hammock covered with mosquito netting in the tent. He got up each day at what he called sunrise, but actually it was a good half hour after everyone else had already been up and around. As soon as he washed his face, he called Yani to the makeshift altar they had built in the church tent. He knelt before the altar, bowed his head, and folded his hands. Yani did the same.

McDuff closed his eyes and brought his folded hands up to his forehead. Yani did the same, but kept one eye slightly open so he could mimic what was going on. Dr. McDuff made a face that made him look as if he were in serious pain. Yani did not master that behavior at first, but he worked on it. It was only after he discovered the minister's shaving mirror that he could practice looking dismal.

McDuff prayed silently, then recited the Lord's prayer out loud in English. Yani could not repeat the words, but listened carefully. This was followed by a rather loud recitation of what things the minister wanted God to do that day, such as send him glass windows for the church and to help him bring the living word of Jesus to the heathen who lived on the island. As time passed, Yani began to recognize some of the words but not the meanings.

At the end of the session, Reverend McDuff would spread his arms beseechingly toward Heaven and shout, "Amen, Lord, Amen!" Yani realized that this was an important part of the magic ritual and he enjoyed shouting and raising his arms to Heaven. This was repeated everyday for weeks.

The missionary had been told that the best way to make Christians out of pagans, was to allow them to ask questions on their own when they were ready. Early in his training Yani asked, "Where Witman come from?"

McDuff considered his answer. Using his best Pidgin phrasing and shared vocabulary, he explained the Creation as it appears in Genesis. He concluded with: "Witman and Blackfella both come from Adam-and-Eve-Fella. We are all brothers. We are all Adam-and-Eve-Fella."

This single source for all men did not sit well with Yani's knowledge of totems. There were Crocodile-fellas, and Shark-fellas, and even Bird-fellas. Everyone knew what animal his lineage was derived from, and they were not to eat the flesh of their totem. If they were Adam-and-Eve fellas, this meant no one could eat the flesh of other human beings. It struck him as an odd notion. He was sure the natives from Christ's Despair and his own Chase Island must not be Adam-and-Eve-Fellas. He was afraid his Big Man Duff had gotten that part of the story wrong.

The next day he asked, "Where God live?"

McDuff's answer: "He lives in Heaven with the angels and our loved ones who have died."

"Where is Heaven?"

"In the sky."

After that Yani frequently strained his eyes trying to see Heaven in the night skies. It was a better explanation than Ooma's who said that the stars were the fires of tribes who lived on far away islands. Now he knew the fires were those tended by the ancestors of the Witman.

That accounted for the Witman's ancestors all right, but he had a bigger question, "Where Blackfella go when he die?" he asked.

"If they believe in the teachings of Jesus Christ, they go to Heaven," McDuff explained.

Not entirely understanding the entry requirements, Yani assumed all his people's ancestors were also in Heaven. All his gods on Chase Island lived in trees, bushes, rocks, gourds and drums. He liked the idea of a god who lived in the sky better.

"What dead fella do there?"

"They praise and glorify God."

"What is praise and glorify?"

McDuff was growing tired of this line of inquiry. The questions were getting harder. "They sing hymns of praise and give prayers of thanksgiving." That was as far as the minister wished to pursue the conversation for the time being.

Yani made friends with some of the locals who had been acquainted with the previous missionaries. They confirmed that dead islanders were in Heaven, according to the other Churchfellas. They talked about it at length as Yani sat around the fire with them, drinking kava. He developed his own ideas. He was sure that the ancestors spent their time making knives, iron hatchets, and machetes.

He was also sure they spent a lot of time putting meat and vegetables in tinkens. There was clearly no way an island man could make a tinken. A man could cut a tree down and make wooden planks. He could cut a piece of wood and nail it to other pieces and make a bench. But where could anyone find a piece of metal except in Heaven? A mere man could not kill and cut up a pig into small pieces, cook it, and put it in a tinken. The ancestors could do this with magic in Heaven with no trouble, and send the tinkens to God's followers among the Witmen.

As he cut wood and nailed nails, he thought about it continually. God gave the ancestors His magic to enable them to make tinkens. Therefore, he reasoned, if one could find metal only in Heaven to make tin cans, certainly nothing short of divine intervention could produce a steel saw, knife, a hammer or an ax head. He was pretty sure that the ancestors who were in Heaven were too busy making things to spend much time singing and praying.

He came to a conclusion. He was obliged to become a Christian, considering all the trouble they were going through up in Heaven.

The division of labor was clear. Dr. McDuff planned how he wanted to build his church and Yani did the physical work. But to him it was not work. Yani's greatest contribution came from his knowledge of local building techniques and materials. The minister was far from being an architect, but common sense made the mission church grow rapidly.

Finally, the basics of the church were completed to Dr. McDuff's satisfaction. It was built along the same lines as the *haus tambaran,* the spirit house of

When John Frum Came

the male cult, not because of any similarity of function, but because there was just so much a limited imagination could do with palm trees, thatched reeds, and simple tools.

The most curious thing they found when they marked off the boundaries for the church walls were beer bottles buried upside down and in straight lines. Later, Thompson was able to explain the phenomenon. When the Germans started the coconut plantation many years before, this was the site of one of the wives' flower gardens. As they emptied the beer bottles, they made a decorative border with them.

The minister told his churchboy that they needed to get word out to the people. Both men and women were welcome at the new church. So, Yani went to the village and mentioned that his Big Man was going to have a feast at his new church. At that time he would tell the residents of Christ's Despair about his God who promised many good things for his followers.

However, the idea did not arouse much enthusiasm among the people. They had seen other Churchfellas hold what they called "prayer meetings," all of which proved to be dull and uneventful. One of the village elders said, "He has no pigs. How can he have a feast without killing pigs?"

Picking up the thread another added, "He has no garden. How can he make pudding for the people? He doesn't even raise taro."

Yani stood and retied his gingham headband to gain their attention. "Big Man Duff's God does not need pigs. He does not need a garden. All his food is made in Heaven. His God sends him tinkens full of food. He has powerful magic. He knows many chants and formulas for speaking to his God. Those who follow Big Man Duff's God will get tinkens and cloth and tools when they prove they are worthy."

The next morning was Sunday, and all were invited to attend. That was the end of the publicity. Conversation returned to local gossip and the demands being made by the plantation manager.

The Reverend Doctor Moses McDuff realized that Christmas was only about a week away. The first service should be a Christmas service — what better opportunity to "begin at the beginning." His logic was simple: if the natives were childlike in their understanding of things, then they should be introduced

Bill Schroeder

to Christianity the same way children were back home. He would use a Sunday School Christmas story approach.

His own favorite Christmas Carol when he was a child was "Away In A Manger." *This reduces the story of Jesus to its basics,* he thought. *If I can tell the story of how God was born as a child to human parents, then they will understand how he loves them.*

It was all very simple. He would even *sing* the carol. *Music hath charms to soothe the savage breast,* he reminded himself. He wrote down the words as he recalled them.

When he told his churchboy what he planned he realized that Yani had never heard the words before. The American translated them from English to Pidgin, but Yani still had no idea what they meant or how to translate them into Booga-booga. McDuff, for his part, just assumed the flow of ideas was natural.

Minister and churchboy arose earlier than usual on the big day. To the Chase Islander's surprise, the clergyman put on a white satin gown over his usual clothes and white collar. He had a less ornate, but similar, robe for his churchboy to wear. Much to Yani's surprise he also was given a clean shirt, much like the first one with the "Massachusetts Youth For Christ Conference" embroidered on the back, but this one had blue lettering and was dated 1936. In place of khaki shorts, he was given blue ones.

Yani's smile lit his whole face. The villagers would be overwhelmed when they saw the clothes he would wear at the first church service. McDuff helped him change into his new outfit and looked with pride on his churchboy in full regalia. His very dark skin stood out in sharp contrast to the white vestments.

"Well, Yani, what do you think of your new clothes?" McDuff asked. He looked over the minister and then himself. A frown crossed his face. His eyes were on the ground. "Yani not have shoes like Big Man. I can have shoes?"

McDuff rummaged through one of the clothes boxes and came up with a rather worn-out pair of size 12, brown and white saddle shoes. That they were without shoelaces did not matter to Yani. He put them on his feet and reveled in the sensation they produced. Feeling his feet enclosed in leather for the first time in his life, he knew these were special and sacred. He would only wear them to church. Nothing else justified such finery.

When John Frum Came

A few young women were the first to arrive at the new church site, and hung back at the edge of the clearing. Yani's palm wood and foliage altar was impressive. They were curious, but did not want to be the only ones to declare so.

Reverend McDuff had heard that the unofficial measurement of the success of missionaries on South Sea islands could be measured by the kind of muumuus the native women wore. The closer the hem line was to the ground, the more influential the Christian missionary had been. The ultimate was a muumuu that trailed in the dust, and whose sleeves reached to the wrists. The women of Christ's Despair wore only a sort of G-string made of woven pig leather.

Although they were practically naked, McDuff did not find them sexually stimulating, only shameful and embarrassing. He was aghast.

"They can't come to church naked," he whispered to Yani.

"Naked ?"

"With no clothes on."

Why not?" asked Yani.

"God doesn't like it. That's why. They need to cover themselves before they can enter a holy place. This is no longer part of the jungle. This is the dwelling place of God."

The only part of the explanation Yani really understood was that God didn't like it. That was good enough for him. After all, he had received special clothing to participate in the ceremony, it followed that the others should do likewise.

He picked up and carried the cardboard carton from which his shoes had recently emerged. In black crayon the words "Clothes for Mission" proclaimed the contents. He walked directly up to the girls and pulled out the first piece of clothing his hand touched. He handed it brusquely to the first girl, then did the same for the second. "You put on and come in church. Not wear clothes taboo in church."

They giggled and examined the clothes they had just been handed. They quickly figured out how to wear them. One wore a lady's pink rayon slip and the other a print housedress that was supposed to button down the front over her protruding pregnant belly. However, the buttons were taken for ornaments, their function not even imagined. Thus attired, they entered the holy church tent and sat on one of the palm log benches Yani had nailed together.

When the male would-be church-goers saw what the girls had received for coming to the church, they clamored around Yani for garments of their own. In spite of himself, Reverend McDuff could not help being amused. Neither Yani nor the other islanders recognized the distinction between male and female clothes, or that there were different sizes. It was a problem best left for another day.

At the very bottom of the box Yani found a treasure he could not believe — a pair of sunglasses with only one earpiece. He had seen the Patrol Officers and the plantation manager wearing them, and could not believe his luck. From then on, he wore them constantly during the daylight hours.

There had been no rehearsal. As soon as the natives appeared to be settled down Reverend McDuff began the service with an acappella solo:
"Away in a manger, no crib for his bed,
The little Lord Jesus lay down His sweet head.
The stars in the Heavens look down where he lay;
The little Lord Jesus asleep on the hay."

He then turned to Yani and said, "Yani, would you please translate that into Booga-booga?"

Yani tried to remember what the minister had told him the words meant, and after a few moments he took as stab at it. "On an island far from this, God took off his head and put it down where the animals eat. Lights we see in sky at night are eyes of God. He have Sheepy-sheep watch what Blackfella do."

The churchboy indicated that he had done his best, and the minister could proceed.

McDuff sang the second verse:
"The cattle are lowing, the Baby awakes,
But little Lord Jesus, no crying He makes.
I love thee, Lord Jesus; look down from the sky
and stay by my cradle 'til morning is nigh."

Yani warmed to his task, and said, "Big Man Duff is reciting the magic formula for calling God. He is not ready to tell us what those words are. He is asking God to give us tinkens, and steel knives, and cloth. You must sit still and listen to his magic words. If you leave you will get no gifts."

For the next twenty minutes McDuff explained the Christmas story in installments, and Yani delivered variations of the same message: "Stay put, be quiet and you will receive tinkens full of food."

Actually, the members of the new congregation saw nothing unusual in this. It was pretty much the way their shamans had been calling on the gods for hundreds of years. It violated nothing in their spiritual views to allow someone to try to call on a new more powerful god. Myths and legends explaining the nature of reality were always being changed and reinterpreted to fit changing situations.

At the end of the service, Pastor McDuff gave his benediction to the congregation, using a lot of the pageantry he had borrowed from the Roman Catholics. He had read that the natives in some places around the world preferred the mass celebrated by the Catholic Church because it was more colorful. He vowed that such petty jealousies would not keep him from winning the hearts of the native population.

Then, to McDuff's utter amazement, Yani lifted one of the sheets that had been used to cover the altar. He displayed several cases of canned goods which he had moved down from the Big House store room. Yani pried open the lids, and announced that everyone who had stayed for the entire service would receive a tin of beef, vegetables, or whatever happened to come up as the cartons were unpacked.

McDuff almost panicked. "What are you doing?' he yelled at Yani. "You're giving away our food."

"We tell Blackfella we have feast without kill pig. We no have taro. You ask God. He send more tinken. Plenty more tinken in Heaven."

McDuff could not get near the cartons to stop the whole-sale giveaway. Nor did he realize that if he did not give them each a food gift, no one would ever return to his church. He would have broken an unwritten contract with them. There were nearly 100 men and women who received cans, making a serious impact on his larder.

After the Great Giveaway, Yani was sought out by the church attendees. Most of them had no idea how to open the cans. They had banged

Bill Schroeder

them against rocks, stabbed them with sharp objects and had thrown them unopened into the fire. Yani used his knife to open lids until it became almost too dull to do so.

Moses McDuff was frightened. If the congregation expected free food each time they came to church, he would run out of supplies after two more services.

Chapter 8

Part of the reason Jeremy Thompson was more successful managing the copra plantation than his predecessors, both English and German, was his ability to go slightly native. If necessary, he could have lived on native food alone. He even had a small herd of pigs, but he drew the line at planting his own garden. That he left to Jeeves, the houseboy.

When Dr. McDuff first arrived, Thompson joined heartily with the American in eating dishes his housekeeper made, using the canned goods. However, as time passed certain items became less frequent, and finally disappeared from the menu. The other thing that changed was that supper was now the only meal McDuff ate at the Big House. He spent most of his waking hours working at the church.

One evening while they were sitting at the table waiting for dinner to be served, McDuff said, "I don't want to overstep my limitations, Mr. Thompson, but I am developing a craving for a piece of fresh meat."

"That's a generally scarce commodity on the islands. No refrigeration, you know. I'd love to have an ice cube in a cool drink, myself."

"I noticed that you have a small herd of pigs out in the back. If I may be so bold to ask, how often to you butcher one of them."

"Hardly ever," he replied. "A boar piglet once in a while for a festival day. Pigs are the closest thing to money you will find in the islands. You can buy practically anything with a pig — including a woman if you are interested."

Dr. McDuff blushed brightly.

The plantation manager continued, "You don't serve dollar bills for green salad back in the States, do you? Well, here we don't go around chopping up pigs indiscriminately"

"No offense intended," McDuff said.

"None taken," Thompson said, realizing that he had been a little rough on the minister. "I'm sorry. I shouldn't have jumped on you like that. It takes a while to get used to things here. Of course, since I was the last of eight kids on a station in the Outback, I never got used to any kind of fancy food. One thing you'll never see on this table though, is a piece of mutton. I gag at the thought. It's a wonder I don't 'baa' when I speak. It's all we ate." He thought for a moment and added, "The other thing is water."

"Water?" McDuff asked.

"I didn't take a tub bath until I was 14 and ran away from home. Talk about saving something for a special occasion, water was almost that bad at the station. We had only one well — and the sheep got first call. Here, there's no end to it. Water comes out of the sky every bloody day. It's marvelous."

"Thank you, Mr. Thompson. You're quite right. You just made me aware of God's abundant grace. I had been resenting the rain without realizing it. I thought it was a hindrance, now I see it as another blessing."

"Without it, Dr. McDuff, there wouldn't be no jungle. These islands would be little deserts in the middle of the sea.

"As to the meat, you'll get used to it," he laughed. "I'll tell the cook to see that we have some fresh meat on the table tomorrow."

The next day, back at the church clearing, the American clergyman became anxious in general, and decided it was time for an assessment of his situation. He constantly rejected Yani's offers of native fare, and was completely unable to make the cultural adjustment. He ate an almost exclusive diet of canned foods. A visual inventory showed that Yani's generosity with the tinkens at the opening of the church, combined with the young man's own appetite was leading to a crisis. Supplies were running low.

Of course he could not call the Australian Patrol officers to check on the progress of his replenishments of food and building materials. Thompson had a radio, but he said it didn't work properly and preferred to save it for emergency messages.

The bright spot was that Thompson had promised to kill one of the piglets for dinner, so he took heart in that. He spent the day developing sermons he felt would be suitable for his congregation. He had no idea how much the thoughts that migrated from English to Pidgin to Booga-booga lost in their translation. Although Yani hung on his every word, both men were operating from a different base of cultural understanding.

Toward evening when McDuff arrived at the Big House, Jeeves and the cook smiled at him. Dinner was apparently almost ready, he could see them rotating the carcass of an animal on a spit over hot coals. He had wondered during the day if it would be served with a mango in its mouth, in place of the traditional apple. He went over to the pit to inspect its progress.

Dr. McDuff never made it into the small dining room where his host awaited him. His stone crab salad went uneaten. In fact, Dr. McDuff never ate another meal at the Big House from then on. A closer examination of the barbecue revealed that the fresh meat being served for dinner was on his personal taboo list. He realized that the Australian dingo-type dogs that roamed the native villages were not pets, but livestock.

When their work on the church was finished for the day, McDuff and Yani had begun a recurring pattern. The Chase Islander still covered himself with the natural bug repellent every night, as he had since childhood. So did all the natives. In the morning everyone went for a swim in the lagoon to clean off. It was part of an important social exchange. It was customary for people to tell their dreams of the night before, and speculate on their meaning. It was an important form of community bonding. Yani was sought out because he was a good dream interpreter. He also always seemed to have interesting dreams of his own. Very often he dreamed about Kilibob and Manup, the brothers whose return was awaited by all the islands.

The effect of this communal bathing was that the people were exceptionally clean. They rubbed each other down with fragrant coconut oil when they came out of the water. This occasioned Yani to tell Big Man Duff that he had a case of "Witman stink." As he did not bathe first thing in the morning, he had the odor of stale perspiration about him. All Witmen did. The islanders found it uncomfortable to be around him.

But it was out of the question for him to undress in the presence of the natives and join them in the morning, so he opted for the next best thing. He cleaned up the *Salvation* and took her out into the lagoon each morning. When the white man felt he was out of view of the shore, he stripped down to his undershorts and went over the side for a swim. Afterward, he would tie up at the pier and practice throwing a net to catch fish, as his acolyte had taught him. It was this daily activity that helped McDuff hold on to his sanity when things got difficult.

By the time three months on Christ's Despair had passed, his canned goods were completely gone. The natives would not attend church without receiving tinkens. McDuff went into panic. When the last slice of bacon from the large supply of smoked pork ran out, the man was nearly in tears. Fortunately, all those summers on Cape Cod in his youth allowed him to at least consider a seafood diet. He and Yani collected stone crabs and shellfish in the tidal pools. He had eaten certain kinds of fruit since his arrival, but the sweet potato-like taro root stuck in his throat.

There was no way McDuff could know that the shipment of supplies from Australia was delayed because the island steamer developed engine trouble. That took her out of service for a month. Thompson knew. He had received a radio message to that effect. But since the two white men were not on speaking terms, he took cruel delight in keeping silent on the matter. The Australians were not really worried about the American since everybody knew that no one could starve to death on a South Pacific island.

Yani knew that his Big Man was upset with the food situation, although he could not imagine why. There was plenty to eat, and all he had to do was perform the ceremony that would bring a new supply of tinkens full of meat from Heaven. But the ways of Big Men were often strange, and the ways of white Big Men evidently even stranger. The young man was pleased when Big Man Duff addressed the problem one morning.

At the sunrise service the minister seemed more serious than usual. Yani watched carefully, still trying to learn the ritual. After McDuff had done the preliminaries of the Lord's Prayer and the meditation under painful facial expression, he prayed aloud and Yani listened.

"Lord we thank you for keeping us alive to serve you in converting the heathen of this island to understand your word. We have tasted the swill the natives eat, and we feel pity for them. I believe I have learned compassion for their sad state. Your church is almost finished but we need food to keep up our strength.

"We need glass for our windows. We need nails to join the walls together. This is not much, but it will be the first Christian church on the island. We beseech you, Oh, Lord, to protect the ship and send it to us with food and our needs for the church. Send us trade goods to help convert the heathen and establish civilization and plantations on the islands. We ask this in the name of your only begotten son, Jesus Christ. Amen."

"Amen," Yani echoed. Although the prayer had been in English, the islander found that he understood a good deal of it. The Big Man told God to send more tinkens and tools.

Since they were out of nails and other building materials Yani had little to do. But Dr. McDuff had an assignment for him. After he arose from where he had been kneeling on a prayer bench, he said in Pidgin, "You go top of mountain. Look out to sea." He put his right hand above his eyes in a sort of salute serving as a sun-shield. Then he cupped his fingers around his eyes like binoculars. "You look. Ship come. Bring food. You tell me when ship come."

Yani understood. He climbed the steep slope of the tall volcano peak that crowned the island. From the top he had a commanding view of the Pacific Ocean in almost every direction. Unlike the minister, he had little trouble living off the natural foods that surrounded him in the jungle and helped himself to snacks as he climbed — a beetle grub here, a piece of fruit there.

There was a path around the rim of the volcano that the tribal shaman used almost every day, so he walked completely around that. *Which direction will the ship come from?* Yani thought. *Since it will get its cargo in Heaven it will most likely come from the sky. If that's the case, will it descend slowly from the sky?* He remembered how Kilibob's boat, the *Wombat*, slowly disappeared over the horizon. *Will it come slowly toward us from the horizon like a canoe from another island? Or will it drop like a rock from the sky into the sea?*

He remembered McDuff's directions, and the minor (but no doubt important) ritual he had shown him for searching for the enchanted ship. He made a sun-shield over his eyes with his right hand. Then he cupped his fingers around his eyes like binoculars and looked around the 360 degrees of the horizon.

He stayed on the volcano's rim all day, watching the fishermen throwing nets in the lagoon, and listening for the *kanakas* or bushmen hunting for pigs. He busied himself by building a lean-to. He talked to the village shaman when he came for his daily circuit of the volcano just before the afternoon torrent of rain. As usual, Yani slept a good deal during the hottest part of the day, and made another circuit of the rim after the afternoon storm.

At nightfall he wound his way back down the slope to the church where he found Dr. McDuff eager for news.

"Did you see anything?" he asked.

"I see big water. I see fish-fella ... *kanaka* hunt pigs."

"But did you see a ship?" McDuff asked impatiently.

"No see ship."

McDuff fell to his knees before the altar and motioned Yani to do likewise. "Oh, most merciful God ... He who provided manna for the children of Abraham, hear our pleas. Send us the shipload of supplies we so desperately need. Help us to do your great work of conversion. We ask this in the name of Jesus Christ. Amen."

"Amen," said Yani.

McDuff spoke carefully to his churchboy. "When you go to bed, Yani, pray to God that the ship comes soon," and went off to his room at the rear of the tiny church building. When Yani laid down on his mat he tried to re-create the words of the magic chant, but could not get past the first few words —"Owa fada huartin Heaven..."

He gave up and went to sleep with his hands folded on his chest in the approved prayer position. He would have to leave the real work of the ritual of bringing a ship to the island to Dr. McDuff. He was afraid he might make the wrong hand movement or chant the wrong word making the spell worthless.

The next morning the sunrise service was performed again. McDuff did his chants and made his mystical body movements. Yani tried to learn what words were being said. He realized that getting tinkens from God wasn't as easy as he had thought. After the formal appeal for the arrival of the ship was completed, Yani asked, "Big Man Duff teach this Blackfella pray for ship?"

McDuff was surprised. He really didn't think anyone needed to be taught how to make a personal prayer. "You speak feeling inside heart," he told Yani. He thumped his chest lightly to show the location of his heart as he spoke.

"No. This fella speak 'Owa fada huartin Heaven…' like churchfella speak. Tell God need ship."

The missionary's response was negative. "Island fella no speak English. Churchfella make prayer in Pidgin for Blackfella. I teach churchboy tonight. You speak new prayer next sun-come-up."

The young man climbed the mountain with a new spring in his step. He liked it when McDuff called him a churchboy. It was a form of validation he needed to confirm that he was special. He was excited that he would learn a special prayer tonight. When he reached the summit he did his ritual for the scanning of the horizon for ships pretending to have binoculars. But there were no ships to be seen. He was sure one would come once he learned how to pray properly. Once the strength of his will was known to God, a ship would come for sure.

When he reported back after dark, the missionary was waiting for him. He reported his lack of success, and they repeated the evening service that followed much the same form as the morning's. McDuff outlined for God, just what it was He was expected to do. After the "Amen" Yani said, "I speak prayer now?"

During one of the daily downpours, some of McDuff's papers got wet. Unfortunately the Pidgin translation of the Lord's prayer was among them, smearing the ink to illegibility. However, he found a substitute, the Home Church's official Pidgin translation of the 23rd psalm. By the light of a candle, McDuff sat down with Yani. "Repeat after me," he said.

Yani did not understand. Pointing to himself and then to his student he said, "I speak … you speak."

The minister spoke in his deepest tones. "*Big name watchem Sheepy-sheep; watchem Blackfella. No more belly cry fella hab.*" Even McDuff had to admit to himself, that was a long stretch from "The Lord is my Shepherd I shall not want," but that's what the Home Church in Boston said to teach, so here it was.

They went through the whole psalm, and Yani recognized that this was the most powerful chant he had ever heard. It would take a long time to learn, but in its difficulty lay its power. Finally, McDuff reached the saturation point, even if his churchboy had not. When he called it quits for the night, he said, "You learn one line at a time. You speak *"Big name watchem Sheepy-sheep; watchem black fella."* all day tomorrow. He made the magic sign of folding his hands in prayer, and said, "Lord, I ask your help and guidance in making this ignorant savage a God-fearing Christian. Amen."

"Amen" said Yani.

More than a week passed with Yani going each day to the top of the volcano. Everything remained the same, except that Yani did his seafood gathering chores at daybreak each day to make sure the missionary had something to eat to get him through the day.

But one morning it was apparent that the monsoon season had suddenly engulfed them. It did not just rain in the afternoon, it rained continually all day. There was a shroud of mist when Yani started up the mountain. When he got to his lean-to he was literally among the clouds. Visibility was zero. There was nothing to be seen but fog in all directions. He knew there was no point in going back down the mountain just because he couldn't see anything. Dr. McDuff had nothing for him to do without building materials, so he would only send his churchboy up the mountain and tell him to wait for it to clear.

With the practicality of his people's long centuries of dealing with monsoons, he crawled into the relative dryness of his lean-to and lay on his woven-reed mat. At the foot of his bed he had made his version of an altar, a reed box, surmounted by jungle greenery woven into a cross. He stared at the palm fronds with his hands folded on his chest. He spoke the entire text of what he called the "Sheepy-sheep" chant over and over. The steady hypnotic patter of the rain on the leaf roof lulled him into a deep sleep.

When John Frum Came

His slumbers were suddenly interrupted by a horrendous noise. It was not thunder and not the wind. Yani knew those sounds. This was a long drawn out "Bwaaasppp!" in very deep tones. He rolled out of the lean-to and jumped to his feet. The sounds started again — "Bwaaasppp!" This time it was followed by a very high pitched: "Poot! Poot! Poot!"

It is the voice of God! was his first thought. *What else could it be?*

"Poot! Poot! Poot!" came the higher noise again.

Terrified, he looked down through the steamy jungle landscape. The fog had thinned slightly, and he could barely make out a huge black and white and red form sitting just outside the island's tiny harbor. It was barely visible, emerging from the haze.

A final "Bwaaasppp! Poot! Poot! Poot!" made Yani's thick black hair stand on end. He was thrilled with fear. If he had known the word he would have called this a miracle. He realized that this was the ship from Heaven he and Dr. McDuff had been praying for. This was the answer God had sent him for just reciting "the Sheepy-sheep" chant. He wondered what wonders he would be able to perform when he knew the whole thing.

He pushed through the underbrush and broke into a run down the mountainside. Surely Dr. McDuff had heard the noise and would be on the beach. As official churchboy he wanted to be there when God's gifts were delivered to the missionary.

As he ran, he began to be angry with himself. After all that waiting, he had been asleep when the great ship had dropped through the clouds from Heaven. He would have loved to have seen whether the huge ship made a splash when it hit the ocean. He was certain that it had not appeared on the horizon and come to the island gradually. It had obviously sailed down from Heaven on the monsoon winds and the incessant, heavy rain.

He was worried that God would be angry with him for sleeping through it all.

Chapter 9

Yani stopped by the church on his way to the pier, but as he expected, Dr. McDuff was already gone. He found the missionary at the water's edge, so excited that he looked like he might swim out to the steamer by himself. "It's here! The ship is here. Praise be to God Almighty, Yani," he proclaimed when he saw the young man emerge from the jungle.

In mixture of English and Pidgin Yani shouted, "He has answered our prayers. God hear churchfella. Witman's big canoe is finally here. God answer churchfella prayer. Amen."

Thompson's barge was already being paddled out to the freighter. They could also see that a small boat had been lowered from the ship and there were several men pulling at the oars.

Thompson had come down to the pier as well. The missionary was so excited that he forgot he wasn't talking to the plantation manager. "Is that as close as they can come?" he asked, nodding in the direction of the steamer.

"There's no channel in the lagoon. They'll off-load the cargo onto a barge, and then the boys will paddle it in to the pier. That'll be the purser coming toward us in the dory. He'll be wanting his money and the orders for their next trip," Thompson volunteered.

"My Lord. I gave all my money to the Patrol Officers when they were here. I hope they made all the arrangements I requested."

Thompson left the missionary and walked briskly out to the end of the pier to greet the purser when he stepped ashore. He produced a bottle of Scotch, from which they each took healthy swigs and then passed it to the two sailors in the boat. They spoke in a little huddle for a few minutes, took another heavy pull on the bottle and then Thompson slapped the ship's officer on the back. When they finished laughing together, the rowers secured the boat.

Dr. McDuff approached the purser and Thompson, who was holding the other man's elbow in a friendly manner.

"How do you do? I'm the Reverend Moses McDuff," he said to the officer, and they shook hands.

"I'm Jake Vogel, the Purser for the *Fenestra* — the pride of the Port Moresby Trading Company's merchant fleet."

"Not to mention the *only* ship in the Company's merchant fleet," Thompson added, laughing heartily.

"An what might a man of the cloth be doing here on Christ's Despair?" he said with a strong Australian accent, slurred a bit by its alcohol content. "Even its name tells you that they gave up on this island — savage and white man alike. Hell, even the Germans couldn't shake the natives out of the jungle, and get them to work like people are supposed to."

"I'm here to bring them the light of Christianity, Mr. Vogel. I really don't want to get involved in the economics of whether the Protestant Work Ethic is a universal good."

"Listen to him," Thompson said to Vogel, his growing inebriation becoming more evident.

"Talking about economics," Vogel said, "How do you support yourself on this island. Are you living off the land ... depending on the contributions of your parishioners? I took the last preacher off this place half crazy for trying that. I think he's still in hospital in Sydney, trying to get his health back."

"I brought a good deal with me, and I depend on whatever you have brought me on your ship," McDuff said. "I gave Major Wembly all my money, and a list of what I thought we would need when they brought me here."

Vogel opened his eyes wide and turned to Thompson. In a disbelieving tone said, "Did he really give his money to Wembly the Weasel?"

"That's what he did," said Thompson. "I didn't want to get in the middle. I depend on those fellas to keep me supplied with Scotch, so I kept my mouth shut."

"You mean he never gave the money and my list to you?" McDuff said, feeling his heart sink.

"You didn't think he keeps the *Wombat* looking like a luxury cruiser on a Patrol Man's pay did you? He's one of the biggest con artists and rum-runners in the South Pacific."

"Oh, Good Lord," The minister cried out. "That was all I had. I depended on him to contact you and place my order. What am I going to do?"

"Have a drink?" Thompson suggested. "That's what any real man would do." He offered him the bottle of Scotch.

McDuff brushed it away. "Solutions to problems don't come in bottles," he said with a manner that indicated that he had said it many times to other men. "I will need a little time to think," he told Vogel. "There must be a way out of this."

"Why don't you just get on the *Fenestra* and let Mr. Vogel take you back to Moresby or someplace," Thompson said sarcastically.

"No. I have promised the Lord that I would stay here, and bring his Word to the heathen. I cannot be released from that promise because of the first setback."

Thompson and Vogel looked at each other, and at the seamen who had moored their boat and caught up with them. Slowly, a grin spread across Vogel's face, and he burst out laughing. The sailors, who were also in on the joke all joined in. The purser put his hand on McDuff's shoulder and said, "Good show, Reverend McDuff. You've got balls. I've got to hand it to you."

"Hand what?" he asked, not sure what was going on.

"We've got your bloody supplies onboard. Major Wembly gave us your list and paid for everything."

McDuff was giddy. It was all a joke. He was so relieved he almost broke into tears. Instead, he joined in the laughter and playfully slapped Vogel on the arm. "You really had me going there for a few minutes," he said. "That was a nasty trick to pull on me. I believed you."

"Call it an initiation, if you like," the purser said. "I guess we must pull that one on all the new hands in the South Seas at least once."

Thompson's expression, however, turned sour. "Shit, I thought we were rid of him. Well, he ain't using my barge to bring his stuff ashore."

"Come on, Jeremy, it was just a joke," Vogel said.

"I'm not joking. Let him use his own boat to fetch his stuff. He ain't using my barge, and he ain't using my boys."

"I think that Yani and I will be able to manage for ourselves in the *Salvation*, Mr. Vogel. We have a little yawl we can take out to your ship. We will unload the crates into it, thank you."

The purser looked surprised, and said. "You can sign for your stuff here, and then go out and pick it up." He leafed through the papers on his clipboard, and handed the manifest to McDuff to sign. He gave a copy to the minister, and added, "Oh, another thing. Your church wired a letter of credit to our headquarters, so you can give me a new list of whatever you want us to bring the next time. Let me know when you have all your stuff off our ship. My men and I are going up to the Big House with Jeremy for a little shore leave. You'll find me there when you're ready."

The two men put their arms around each other's shoulders and walked up the long hill toward the plantation.

In addition to his daily solo bathing sessions over the side of the *Salvation*, Reverend McDuff had taken Yani out with him in the boat to catch fish. He did it often enough that the islander was comfortable with just the two of them managing the boat. They brought it alongside the *Fenestra* quite skillfully, and the crew lowered nets full of boxes and crates into the sailboat. Dr. McDuff expected his money would have bought a lot more than it did, but at least he now had considerably more than the small quantity of food he had arrived with.

Yani was thoroughly pleased with the amount of goods they received from the freighter. He wanted to climb aboard the huge iron-hulled vessel, but there as no ladder hanging down. If Kilibob wasn't on the *Wombat*, he certainly must be aboard this ship. It was the biggest structure he had ever seen on land or sea — it was even bigger than the men's spirit house on Chase Island.

The rain and wind from an approaching storm made the trip back rougher than they were accustomed to. McDuff was worried that they would capsize and lose all the precious cargo he had waited for so long. It was dark by the time they finally reached the pier, and they could see Thompson's barge being unloaded by the light of torches and bonfires. Even if the plantation manager were there, he certainly could not object to their taking advantage of the light from the burning palms.

They tied up the yawl and began the strenuous process of lifting the individual boxes from the deck of the small craft on to the dock. Yani said, "Them Blackfella help churchfella take boxes bilong church," meaning he would get Thompson's boys to carry the heavy stuff up to the church clearing.

"No. Them Thompson-fella," he explained.

"Blackfella churchfella. Serve God get tinken."

Before the missionary could stop him, Yani was talking to the work gang. He explained to the men who had been to the church that this was a shipment from Heaven. This was good cargo made by their ancestors in Heaven. Big Man Duff had said his magic chants and now all these gifts from God were here. If they wanted to share in "the glory of God" they would be well advised to help him and Big Man Duff to transport everything up to the clearing.

In a matter of minutes, there was a string of men toting bags and boxes from the beach to the jungle. Yani led the way, carrying a large torch. When everything that belonged to the church had been removed from the *Salvation* and the pier, Yani handed out a can of meat to each of the twenty-odd natives who had helped. He opened them with his knife, and a sheltered fire burned brightly, fanned by the storm breezes whistling through the brush. Everyone, including The Reverend Doctor Moses McDuff sat in a circle around the fire eating stewed mutton. He didn't even bother to wait for it to get warmed up by the fire — he was ravenous from the exercise.

McDuff told Yani that he wanted to thank the men for their help, and the two stepped into the center of the circle. The natives fell quiet and the minister said, "Blackfella makum Big Boss longa sky inside glad."

Yani translated into the local tongue: "Witman God happy with island people."

"Blackfella no sorry him sit down longa Big Name allatime," McDuff said. "You sit at Witman God's fire all the time. You receive more cargo."

There was an appreciative murmur among the men at the prospect. They liked the idea. "Churchfella thank Blackfella help move cargo to church. You come church Sunday. Blackfella praise god. I teach sing hymn-song."

Yani was not certain of the message to be conveyed, but he, too, was beginning to see that if they gave cans of food every Sunday to those who came to church, it wouldn't last very long.

He told them: "You come see Big Man Duff and Yani in ceremony clothes. Big Man Duff tell us magic words make more cans come from Heaven. You learn secret words, you get more tinkens."

When the storm abated some, Dr. McDuff decided to let Mr. Vogel know that the job was complete, and to deliver his long list of needs for the next visit of the *Fenestra*. As he walked past the pier, it was too dark to see anything, but he knew that Thompson's crates were being soaked by the rain since the natives had all abandoned the barge to work for him. There would be hell to pay in the morning, but he took perverse glee in knowing that the manager would be furious.

As he approached the Big House he saw that there was a campfire in the native living quarters. The tropical building was nothing more than a thatched roof supported by palm logs that kept the rain off the floor. However, the wind was blowing through the open sides, fanning a struggling fire like the one he had left at the church.

He could make out several figures dancing around the fire and singing. He did not approve of native ceremonies, since Dr. Paton's book said they were bad. But he did find them interesting from a theological standpoint. He approached in the dark, unnoticed. To his amazement two of the figures were white. They were the seamen who had rowed the dory ashore, and were waiting for Vogel to come out of the Big House.

They were drinking whiskey and prancing about clumsily with some of the native women. They were trying to teach them an English sea shanty. He was stricken with the absurdity of it all. Here, ten thousand miles from England, were two grown men who probably had families back home singing with black whores.

He listened to the words:

"What shall we do with a drunken sailor
What shall we do with a drunken sailor
What shall we do with a drunken sailor
Earl-lie in the morning!

Way hay and up she rises
Way hay and up she rises
Way hay and up she rises
Earl-lie in the morning!"

The native girls, who were also drunk, made some unintelligible response that captured the tune but not the words. He entered the open structure in the dim light of the fire and said, "What are you men doing?"

The two men stopped short in their dance and looked at him, dumbfounded. In the murkiness they couldn't make him out. Straining his eyes the taller of the two said, "Who the hell wants to know?"

"I am Dr. McDuff, the pastor of the church on this island. I want to know what you men think you are doing with these two young women?"

"Having a fuckin' good time, I'd say, until you stuck your nose in here. Who the hell do you think you are?" the taller sailor said. "Get your arse out of here before I bury my boot in it. We don't belong to your fuckin' church and neither do these girls."

The second man threw a nearly empty whiskey bottle at him that glanced off his shoulder. "The next one will catch you right in yer big mouth. Get the fuck out'a here."

The fire was between McDuff and the men and they started to come around it toward him. They were serious.

He turned and walked quickly toward the steps up to the Big House. "It's time I had a word with Mr. Vogel," he muttered as he walked through the now driving rain.

He could see the warm yellow glow of the kerosene lamps against the curtains on the French windows. He felt a longing stir within him to return to his family's summer home that looked amazingly similar to this house. He wondered if he would ever see it again.

He rapped on the small square panes of glass in the door, but no one answered. He rapped again.

It probably sounded like the wind rattling the door to the men inside, so he made the bold move of turning the little brass lever handle. The door opened and he entered quickly, turning toward the doors to close out the storm behind him.

His eyes adjusted to the room light and he saw Vogel and Thompson standing next to the wicker couches that furnished the room. They were both stark naked, and were — in delicate terms — in a state of active, hot-blooded manliness. At first he thought they were interested in each other, but his perception was not complete. Crawling around on the floor at their feet, vying for individual attention were the three native women who belonged to Thompson.

One of them seemed to be climbing up Vogel's leg, while the other two were on their hands and knees. They were making a show of covering each other with wet kisses.

As though this were a London drawing room and the parson had just dropped in from his walk on the moors, Thompson said, "Ah, the Reverend McDuff has decided to join us. Would you care for a drink, sir?"

Vogel was so drunk as to be speechless for the moment. He stood there smiling, as he lifted his glass in a toast to the late arriving guest.

"There are three sheilas, Dr. McDuff. Which one would you like? Or don't you think you can rise to the occasion."

The Australians laughed at the weak joke.

"I think Lucille, here, would be the most docile of the bunch. They're nothing like your reluctant white women, you know. They participate. White women are mattresses by comparison." Thompson said something to Lucille, and she began to creep toward McDuff like a big cat stalking its prey.

"I am shocked at you both," McDuff said. "I thought you were here to civilize the natives, not to lead them down Satan's path of sin. I'm especially surprised at you, Mr. Vogel. A ship's officer behaving in this manner."

Vogel did not take well to being criticized. "Where the hell does an American get off telling us how to run our lives here in the islands? You don't know anything about me. Why should you be surprised? We all take turns going ashore on these bloody, stinkin' islands. This happens to be one of the better ones for shore leave, thanks to Jeremy here. It was my turn at Christ's Despair, so who are you to criticize my behavior? Damned Yank."

"Does the Administration know that you turn the native women into whores? It's no wonder that you have trouble getting them to work for you. What kind of an example do you set?"

"I think you'll find the Patrol has more important things to do besides play pussy police, Dr. McDuff," Thompson said as his girl slithered up behind him and stuck her tongue in his ear. "They couldn't care less what we do, as long as we don't kill anybody and don't start any native uprisings."

"I demand you respect my position as the pastor of the church on this island, and curtail your vulgar language," he said.

"Pastor my arse," Thompson said. "You ain't even a British subject, and you set yourself up here as some sort of authority on what everyone is supposed to do."

Lucille was only three feet from McDuff's knees and was making purring noises. He took two steps backward, toward the door.

"They ain't Christians, Doctor. They're bloody headhunters, and you'll be lucky if you don't become part of their trophy collection. In the past ten years, we've had two missionaries just plain disappear, and lots more grab the first available transportation out of here after a month."

"The Administration has authorized me to set up an evangelical program on this island, and I expect the cooperation of any white man who lives here," the minister said. "I may not know what your official reasons are for being here, but I doubt if the government approves of unbridled debauchery."

Thompson, still making no effort to hide his nakedness, showed no change in his virility from the encounter. He sipped his drink, smiled contemptuously at the clergyman, and chose not to answer.

After a brief silence, Vogel voiced his thoughts. "Didn't you ever hear of the *White Man's Burden*, Reverend. We teach it in our schools. That's why Jeremy's here. That's why I'm here. There's many a bloke who can't remember the words to *God Save the King* who'll deliver the entire works of Rudyard Kipling to ya`."

Vogel started and Thompson joined him as though on cue. They pushed the girls aside, locked elbows and the two men recited together like school boys in a class pageant:

> *Take up the White Man's burden —*
> *Send forth the best ye breed —*
> *Go, bind your sons to exile*
> *To serve your captive's need;*
> *To wait, in heavy harness,*
> *On fluttered folk and wild —*
> *Your new-caught sullen peoples,*
> *Half devil and half child.*

They finished by clinking their glasses and downing the remainder of the Scotch in them.

"That's it, isn't it, Jeremy? It's our duty as citizens of His Majesty's Empire to teach the conquered races the joys of being British."

"Yes, but we don't want them to learn English," Thompson said, glaring at McDuff.

"The other thing we won't let them do, that's very British, is to get quietly drunk. They get loud and rambunctious when they get drunk. We maintain our gentlemanly dignity — even when we get thoroughly pissed," Vogel said. "Your average native reverts to his savagery, and picks up the first sharp instrument he can find and starts swinging — especially at us — the White Man.

"So you see, Doctor, we have no choice. As long as there's an Empire we are the chosen ones, who have to run it. In compensation, some of us get to screw the natives — who it turns out are more fun than our own women."

Thompson was not as mellow as Vogel and said, "Now you know, Reverend McDuff, why this is really all none of your God damned business. So go back to your little church in the Wildwood, or better yet, why don't you leave on the *Fenestra* tomorrow and go back to the States where you belong."

McDuff was burning with anger, but it was wasted on Vogel who said, "Do you know what the name of my ship means in Latin?"

"Yes," he said stiffly, "*window*."

"The people who launched it thought it would be a 'Window on the World.' But here it is bringing food and junk to these filthy islands, year in and year out. But we keep up our spirits because children around the world sing about us in their little music classes…"

He began singing to the two nearest girls, who were now lying on the floor making sensuous movements. The song was one that Dr. McDuff had learned in grade school himself. It was ridiculous that he should be hearing it now under these obscene circumstances.

"A capital ship for an ocean trip
Was the walloping window-blind.
No gale that blew dismayed her crew
or troubled the Captain's mind.

The man at the wheel was taught to feel
Contempt for the wildest blow,
And it often appeared,
when the weather had cleared,
That he'd been in his bunk below.

Sooooooooo, blow ye winds high ho,
Wherever you may go…
Many a stormy wind shall blowwww…,
Ere Jack comes home again."

Lucille was crouched in front of Reverend McDuff, ready to pounce, when she recognized the possibility that he might do her bodily harm with his knee if she moved another inch toward him.

McDuff's fury matched that of the storm, as he went back out through the French doors. He did not bother closing them behind him, nor did the people in the house seem to care. He put his head down and walked determinedly toward his church. But in spite of the driving rain he could hear the "best of His Majesty's breed" singing another chorus.

Chapter 10

At McDuff's request, Yani awakened him at first light. He needed to catch Vogel before he left. Therefore, he was on the beach when the islanders were taking their morning baths in the ocean. He was still disturbed that the native people made no effort to hide their nakedness, and were quite free in their touching each other's bodies when they washed off the insect repellent goo. More often than not, he spied sexual play among young men and women in the surf, and on the beach when they emerged from the water. He was on the verge of telling Yani what was on his mind, when he saw his churchboy frolicking in the waves with a nubile young woman himself.

As he approached the water's edge, however, he saw the figure of the ship's purser coming down the path from the Big House with his two rowers. His impromptu lecture to the swimming sinners would have to wait for another time. He had business to transact now or never.

"Good morning, Dr. McDuff," Vogel called affably. "Did you sleep well? What with all that wind and rain last night, it's a wonder my ship didn't blow out to sea."

"No, I did not sleep well, sir. I spent a lot of time tossing and turning after the shocking display I witnessed at Mr. Thompson's house last night," the minister said.

"Shocking display?" Vogel said. "Did something happen that I don't know about?" He turned to one of the seamen. "Were you two carrying on again?"

They both gave him "Who me?" looks and shrugged. "I'm sorry, Doctor, but I had a bit too much of Jeremy's Scotch, and I fear I passed out right after dinner. I didn't hear a thing. Sorry if the lads were a bit noisy. They've been at sea too long, and were probably letting off steam. You know how it is."

Dr. McDuff *knew* how it was. There was apparently going to be a conspiracy of silence with Vogel as a witness that there was nothing irregular taking place on the island.

Vogel looked around at Thompson's boxes still sitting in the sand. A few of them were even bobbing in the shallow waves. He called to a couple of Thompson's boys who were bathing and told them in Booga-booga to collect the boxes, and make sure they were brought up to the plantation.

"It looks like they quit in the middle of the job. The storm must have been worse than I thought. They don't usually do that," Vogel said. "How about your stuff? Did you get it all safely tucked away in your church?"

"Yes, thank you," he said, without commenting on Thompson's abandoned boxes. "I wanted to make sure I caught you this morning to give you my list of needs for the next time. When do you expect to stop here again?"

The purser accepted the list and read it over as he talked. "We take three months to make the circuit. We go to Port Moresby to reload the ship after we finish here. Then we hit a dozen little islands in between. I checked before I left the *Fenestra* yesterday, and we will be back here in ninety days … give or take a day or two."

The officer reached out and Dr. McDuff reluctantly shook hands with him. "I be back then," he said. "Don't let Jeremy get to you. He has a tough job, too. But, if you decide to leave with us the next time, I'm sure we can find a cabin for you on the ship. Good bye, Reverend."

Yani stood a good distance away from Big Man Duff and the Witman who came from Kilibob's ship. They were having a discussion, which he neither understood nor was interested in. The other Witman got into his small boat and his men rowed away from the pier.

Yani stood on the beach for a long time and watched the large ship steam toward the horizon with the same feeling of disappointment he felt when the *Wombat* left. This time when he heard the deep-throated "Bwaaasppp!" of the ship's steam horn he knew that it was the voice of Kilibob telling him he would be back another time with more gifts from Heaven.

***

Thompson turned in the direction of the ship when he heard its parting signal. He looked again at the letter from the Headquarters of Pacific Copra Limited that Vogel had given him, and re-read a part of it: "*The investors have a right to see a greater return on the money they have so generously provided you. Your promise to be able to manage the aborigines better than previous managers because you are fluent in their language is, indeed, being put to the test.*

"*The test results, Mr. Thompson, are expected to take the form of larger quantities of copra. The current market is at an all time high, and need I remind you of the old adage that one cannot do business from an empty cart.*

"*We have decided to extend your contract by one year from the date of this letter. That extension is based on our trust that you will be able to deliver on your promises and make the plantation profitable.*"

He had been miserly with the steel knives and hatchets that the Patrol boat had delivered to him, but he wanted to be sure he was getting all the work he could from his boys before he rewarded them. When the merchandise arrived he told the native laborers that if they put in three months of hard work as he directed them, each would receive either a knife with a 7-inch blade or a hatchet and handle cast in one piece. Of course, they were all made in Japan and cost next to nothing compared to European or American tools.

The time had come for the payoff. In addition to the obvious lunar calendar, the islanders had come to measure Witman time by the intervals between visits by the supply ship and the Government Patrol boat. They were anxious to get their blades and the status they represented.

Once the ship was out of sight, Thompson called everyone to the Big House. "You don't deserve anything!" he shouted at the native men in their own language. They were assembled below the verandah, looking up. "You left my goods laying on the beach last night to be washed away in the storm. I'm lucky half of it wasn't swallowed by the ocean.

"In return, it will be another month before you receive your knives in payment. I want every last piece of wood picked up from the beach, and put in my storage shed before noon."

His similarity in appearance to Benito Mussolini posturing and gesturing to the crowd below was wasted on the islanders. His attitude and style was much the same as the Italian Fascist leader. He fancied himself a powerful leader of men.

The laborers grumbled among themselves. The Witman had broken a contract, an important measure of honor in their tribal culture. The worst part was that they could not take the matter before the elders because the Witman had no responsibility to the tribe. Their response was to not submit. They would not shuffle down to the waterfront to pick up the wood as they were told. Instead, they glowered at Thompson and walked in small groups back to the village to talk about the situation.

***

While Thompson was castigating his employees, Dr. McDuff was reviewing his newly arrived supplies. Yani was still impressed with the quantity and variety of tinkens he took from the boxes. The cans had drawings on paper labels of the animals from which the meat inside had come.

Yani picked up a can of stewed mutton, packaged in Australia, and looked at the picture of a ram on the label. "What is?" he asked, showing Dr. McDuff the can.

Realizing that there were no sheep on Chase Island where Yani grew up, he smiled and told him in Pidgin. "Him Sheepy-sheep!"

Yani's face lit up with a smile. *So, this is the spirit the Witman God uses to know what Blackfella doing,* he thought. *I wondered what Sheepy-sheep looked like. Now I know.*

This in itself was a major spiritual event in terms of his earlier island training. Knowing what a spirit looked like gave you power over him. It was one of the key elements in his initiation to the *tambaran*.

Now I understand the magic chant: "Big name watchem Sheepy-sheep; watchem Blackfella." The Pidgin version of the 23rd Psalm had become his favorite prayer.

Big Man Duff says God always sees what the Blackfella does. God sends Sheepy-sheep to watch Blackfella. Sheepy-sheep tells God what Blackfella does.

When John Frum Came

Yani was smug in his newfound power, and felt a thrill run through his body. He tore off the label, and stuck it on a protruding nail above the cans. With an image of Sheepy-sheep, his mastery over this spirit was assured.

McDuff saw him place the picture over the mutton cans and said, "I think you have some real administrative ability, Yani. That way we will know what is on the shelf without having to examine the cans each time." Since the churchboy did not understand all the words McDuff spoke, he only knew that the minister was pleased with his progress.

When McDuff pried loose the lid of one of the heavier boxes he was surprised to find it was filled with hunting knives. A second crate held machetes; and a third had tools that were a combination of hatchets and hammers. When he checked the manifest he learned that he had left it to the distribution company's discretion to define "$200 to be used to purchase assorted tools." What he had in mind were construction tools, but there were only about a half-dozen each of shovels, picks, saws, and adzes. He had had visions of putting this congregation to work building a church and maybe even a parsonage.

I thought $200 would have bought a lot more tools than this, he mused. *The Port Moresby Trading Company may not be any more reputable than their Mr. Vogel ... taking advantage of people like myself who can't take their business elsewhere. I must talk to Mr. Wembly when he returns.*

What Dr. McDuff did not understand was that they saw in him an opportunity to unload a bit of merchandise that was overpriced for the general market. People like Thompson only bought the cheapest grade of tools they could get away with to trade with the natives. The higher quality, English-made knives and other implements had been sitting around their warehouse for a long time, waiting for someone with more money than sense to come along. He suddenly appeared in the form of the missionary on Christ's Despair.

Yani, on the other hand, recognized the merchandise as Heaven's finest. He had never seen a machete before he was taken onboard the *Salvation* by West's pirates, and there was a great deal of anger and foul language exchanged when one of them carelessly allowed their only machete to fall overboard. Its potential as a tool in the jungle and as a weapon of war was immediately apparent to the Chase Islander the first time he saw it. Now here were unimaginable numbers of them at his fingertips. Actually there were 24, but the island concept of mathematics was literally digital — quantities corresponded to the number of a man's fingers. A hand of coconuts, for example, was five, two hands of coconuts were ten ... anything beyond ten was simply *many*.

He told McDuff of his feelings. "Witman God most powerful spirit this Blackfella ever see. Big Man Duff speak best magic. Ooma no have same magic you," Yani said. He was gradually mixing English constructions into his sentences. If McDuff noticed, he said nothing, Pidgin was such a clumsy language, he was pleased every time he and Yani had a successful communication, regardless of the grammatical details.

"It is not magic, my boy. It is the power of prayer. We ask God in his infinite wisdom to provide us with the things we will need to do his work. When we pray he hears us, and answers our supplications in the best form he sees appropriate."

Yani liked it when the Big Man used magic words he did not understand. He knew that someday, he would know those words too, and he would have the power to call God to deliver all these wonderful things from the hard-working ancestors in Heaven. McDuff just spoke to Yani as he would to any of his colleagues back home, hardly aware that his vocabulary exceeded that of most white men.

After hours of work, all the boxes were opened and their contents arranged, with the exception of one. Dr. McDuff knew what was in it, and chose to save it for last. It was a direct shipment from Boston, and although it was six feet long, it was lighter than the rest. The two men lifted it onto the table at the front of the church and the minister used one of the new hatchets to carefully pry up the lid.

It appeared to be full of wood shavings, excelsior, and sawdust. McDuff swept the packing materials aside with his hand and the contents were gradually revealed. It was a stained glass window that he had selected himself in Boston before he left. The subject was Christ's Ascension to Heaven, in which the Savior was rising above the mourners at the cross with clouds at his feet, and a radiance streaming down from above his head.

The minister worked the frame loose from its packing material and dusted it clean with a cloth. Together they took it outside and placed it on a rock so that the sun could shine through it from the rear. It was a breathtaking piece of workmanship. Again, Yani was simply dazzled. There was no end to the marvels that Big Man Duff produced through his prayers to the Witman God.

"Let us pray," the pastor said to his churchboy, and they knelt before the stained glass window. "Oh, Lord God, we thank Thee for the gift of food and tools which thou hast bestowed upon us. We pray that You will continue to smile upon our efforts to bring Your Word to the lost souls here. With Your guidance we will change the name of this island from Christ's Despair to God's Triumph."

He stopped for a moment and looked at the stained-glass window. "This is one of the happiest days of my life. To see this wonderful piece of artwork here in the midst of the jungle, shining like a gem on a bed of green velvet. We thank You for Your grace in allowing this token of our faith to have come all this way from Boston without a crack … without a chip. Help us to make it the centerpiece of our church building that all may be inspired by it. We offer our deepest thanks for this recognition of our efforts to bring Your Word to these souls who have lived in the dark for so many years. Praise be to the Father and to the Son and to the Holy Ghost, Amen."

"Amen," said Yani.

McDuff got to his feet and walked over to the window. He touched the frame and said, "This is what it is all about, Yani. This is a picture of Jesus going up to Heaven after he died and was resurrected on the third day. He went to Heaven, where he sits on the right hand of God the Father. When he comes back he will judge the living and the dead. Those of us who believe on his name will be saved, and will live with him in Heaven for all Eternity."

"He come back?" Yani asked.

"Yes. He will come back at the Final Judgment of mankind. He will return to us. It says so in the Bible," McDuff said, holding the book aloft to underscore his words.

"We go Heaven, too?" the young islander asked.

"If we accept Jesus Christ as our savior, yes," the minister explained.

Yani thought about Dr. McDuff's words. Jesus would come back someday, just like Kilibob. He wondered if the Witmen might not have gotten the name wrong. Maybe Jesus and Kilibob were really the same person.

As for the promise, he liked the idea of going to Heaven someday.

Chapter 11

Word spread rapidly through the native population that the churchfella had received large amounts of tinkens, and wooden boxes full of mysterious gifts. While Dr. McDuff was praying with Yani, a small crowd had collected in the church clearing to see the stained-glass window. The minister was almost unaware of his curious visitors. When he finally noticed that he had company, he saw the opportunity to tell them what the picture was all about.

"Come, come. Gather around," he said, gesturing with his arms for them to form a circle about the picture. In Pidgin he gave Yani instructions to translate his thoughts about Jesus and told him to explain it in their language.

I had better start small, he thought. *I can get into the details later on when we establish a Sunday school.* He told Yani to say that God lived in Heaven, which is in the sky and a source of great enlightenment. God watches over the world. He pointed out in the glass picture the radiance falling on the figure of Jesus from above.

Yani did his best. "The Witman God is Big Man for all white fella. He live on the Sun." Remembering what he had learned from Ooma, he added, "Blackfella call him Akambep. He get up every morning and wake his people. He send Sheepy-sheep every day, watch, see what Blackfella do." Yani nodded to McDuff to continue.

McDuff said, "Jesus was killed and rose again from the dead. He intercedes for the people on earth to give them God's blessings. This picture shows Jesus going to Heaven to live with his father."

"What mean blessings?" Yani said.

"Tell them blessings are God's gifts," the minister said.

"Bad fella kill Jesus, maybe his brother, Manup. But Akambep angry with Manup and make Jesus live again. White fella call him Jesus, Blackfella know his name Kilibob. Witman God angry with Manup not give him gifts. He give Manup bow and arrow for Blackfella. He give Jesus rifle for white fella.

"Picture show Jesus go up through clouds to sky. Jesus go to Heaven see ancestors. Make knives … tinkens. He live with father. Big Man Duff say Blackfella who good friend of Jesus go to Heaven, too. Good friend of Jesus get gifts here now — tinkens, knives, tools."

Although he could not understand Yani's words in Booga-booga, Dr. McDuff was pleased with the natives' rapt attention. His message was attracting more attention than he had hoped for. He told Yani to invite the men to join them in building a new church with the stained-glass window.

"They get blessing for work on church?" he asked.

"Of course, God's blessings are upon all who help to build the church and worship him. I will teach them the proper form of worship — prayers, hymns. They will become Christians."

"Big Man Duff say you work on church. He give you God's gifts. I have seen big knives, hatchets, chop knife (he did not have a word for machete). He teach you magic words to say like him. Tell ancestors in Heaven send *you* tinkens."

There was almost a cheer that went up from the assemblage. "Blackfella say you speak magic words. They do what you want."

"They're not magic words, Yani," the minister corrected. "They're prayers and hymns. Tell them to be here tomorrow after swim time, and we will start building the Church of *God's Triumph*."

***

The morning dip in the lagoon, usually an extended social time, was one of the shortest ever spent by the men of Christ's Despair. Everyone was anxious to find out what kinds of gifts could be had from Big Man Duff in return for working on his church.

Pastor McDuff (as he now wanted to be known and addressed) had to get Yani's zeal under control, lest he give away all the implements during the first hour. The men who worked for Thompson were accustomed to checking out one steel tool at a time for the day's work, and then checking it back in at the end of the day. This was all done under the watchful eye of the plantation manager himself. When Yani gave the first few men shovels and picks with no strings attached, a thrill of excitement ran through the crowd.

"Are you a friend of Jesus?" Yani asked the first few men. If they said yes, he handed them a shovel, or a pick and said, "Then Jesus gives you a tool from Heaven to use in building the church." The natives read an implied promise that they could keep the tool even when the work was done.

Pastor McDuff watched and said. "I think we only need about three men each with a pick and shovel. What we need mostly is men to cut down trees to build walls. Open the box of hatchets, and give them out. I think two hands worth of hatchets will be enough."

Through a laborious process, Yani counted out ten hatchets by lining them all up on a table, and touching each one with a different finger. When there was a tool to correspond to each finger he knew he had enough. Now the competition among the potential workers became somewhat heated. It was clear to them that there would not be enough implements to go around. These were far more valuable tools than the shovels, so some of the friends of Jesus who were initially happy with their shovels wanted to trade them in or give them to someone else to get a cutting tool instead.

McDuff did not understand what the squabbling was about and asked Yani what was going on. When he explained the situation, the white man said, "Tell them everyone will get a chance to work on the church. Today we only need ten men to cut down trees, and six to dig a foundation. They can come back tomorrow."

"Pastor Duff say Jesus need two hands worth of friends cut trees. He give more gifts tomorrow," Yani said. Someone got hit with the flat side of a shovel when he tried to examine it too closely without the owner's permission.

"Jesus does not like fighting!" McDuff yelled. "Tell them there will be no fighting. They will be punished by God for fighting."

"Jesus says you cannot be his friend if you fight. Jesus like Blackfella work, not fight. When you bad fella God take gifts back." Pick and shovel owners almost hugged their tools protectively. They had no desire to part with these treasures under any circumstances.

Yani was left to decide who would get the tree felling equipment. McDuff assumed the selection would be made on the basis of who was the strongest or most physically fit. There was a lot of hard work to be done. While the pastor might have had misgivings, the natives were not surprised when Yani chose men who had young wives and would be willing to share them with him if they were given hatchets.

It made sense to everyone present, but it never occurred to McDuff that this was the situation. At this stage of his Christian moral development, Yani was not aware that the minister would have any problem with it.

Once the chosen few had their hatchets in hand, Yani and McDuff led the band to a section of the island where there were numerous coconut palms. McDuff lined up his workers and began to sing a hymn. He explained to Yani that on his signal the men would chant a sort of chorus as they marched through the jungle. He sang:

> *"Come to the Church in the Wildwood,*
> *Come to the church in the dell..."*

On cue they all sang, "Come... come ... come ... come..."

Not knowing the second verse, McDuff sang the first again, and pranced alongside of the single file of workers like an animated bandleader. The jungle resounded with "Come... come ... come..." as they entered the plantation portion of the island.

Since he had no idea of building or architecture, Pastor McDuff had visualized his "church in the Wildwood" as being built along the lines of a log cabin. The palms were relatively straight and could be felled by the men with the steel hatchets. They could be notched and stacked pioneer style as he had seen many times in books and magazines about the American western frontier. He did not see the irony in introducing to this equatorial island a method of construction believed to be invented by the Iroquois Indians in upper New York State to survive bitter winters.

McDuff surveyed the jungle and made an "X" with his own hatchet on each tree he thought would be suitable. However, the men did not fall immediately to work and complained to the churchboy. "What's the trouble, Yani?" he said.

"Big Man Thompson tell them no cut down trees. They afraid him," Yani said.

McDuff was annoyed. "Well, I'm sure Mr. Thompson doesn't own every tree on the island. You tell them I say OK. They cut trees I mark. Mr. Thompson does not tell me what to do. He is not Big Man to God.

"Yani, tell the men to kneel and I will say a prayer," he said almost defiantly.

"Pastor speak to God. Everybody on knees," Yani commanded. They followed the direction obediently.

"Oh, God, bless this forest of trees which Thou hast given life. Bless these men who are about to do Your work. Help them to achieve their labors in Your service to build the Church of God's Triumph. We ask this in the name of Your only son, Jesus Christ."

The minister made the sign of benediction over the kneeling men, and signaled them to rise.

Yani told them, "God says friends of Jesus cut down trees pastor mark. He speak magic words. Protect you from Thompson."

In a manner of minutes the tribesmen started hacking away at the tree-trunks like men possessed. They loved their new hatchets, and each selected his own tree. The din of the chopping did not go unnoticed by Jeremy Thompson who was walking through the jungle on a nearby path. He stopped and listened to the noise. Then, once he recognized what it was he broke into a run toward the hacking frenzy.

He reached the scene just in time to see the first large tree sag, then crash into the underbrush. The men all cheered, and shouted encouragement to each other. He was stunned ... He was speechless ... He was outraged. He unslung the double-barreled 12-gauge shotgun he was carrying and fired into the air.

The large gun's report echoed through the trees. Everyone stopped work, almost in mid-chop. All eyes turned to Thompson whose face was so distorted with anger; he looked as though he might explode with more force than his shotgun.

"What are you doing?" he screamed in English, then immediately repeated himself in Booga-booga. "Put down those hatchets, NOW!"

Several of the men who had worked for him allowed their hatchets to fall to the ground. But the one closest to Thompson was not one of his boys and clung to his. The white man turned to him and said, "I told you to put that hatchet down!" and made a move toward him to take the tool away from him.

Not intimidated, the native stepped backward and raised the hatchet above his head in a war-like stance, ready to use it on Thompson if he moved.

"Stop!" another voice called out in Booga-booga. "Jesus no like fight." It was Yani.

"Mr. Thompson, back off before he kills you. Don't be a fool," said McDuff.

The adversaries stood facing each other for a long minute, when the minister thought that discretion was about to overcome valor, Thompson took a step backward and fired his shotgun at the man's feet. One of the buckshot pellets caught him in the foot and he screamed and fell in a heap.

McDuff rushed forward to come to the man's aid. "What have you done? He was going to put the hatchet down."

"Bullshit! He was going to sink it into my skull," Thompson said excitedly. "Besides, if you ever back down to these bastards once, they'll never do what you tell them again."

McDuff examined the wound of the shrieking man, and found that it was a clean shot that went all the way through. Yani translated the necessary directions and a group of men took him back to the village where he could be treated.

Ignoring McDuff, Thompson addressed his boys in their native tongue. "You know it is taboo to cut down any of my trees. How dare you take an ax to one of my coconut palms?"

"It OK," one man explained. "We cut down trees for Jesus. Big Man Duff talk to God. God say OK."

Thompson turned his shotgun in the direction of McDuff. "What kind of cock and bull story have you been feeding these people ... You talked to God and he said it was OK to cut down my trees?"

McDuff was now angry also. "They're not your trees, Mr. Thompson. God put them here for all of us. I don't believe they were put here for your exclusive benefit."

"The hell they weren't! The fucking, bloody Germans put them here 20 years ago. They don't grow here naturally. They were planted by the Huns and purchased — every last one of them — by Pacific Copra Limited. As their representative here, I am responsible for them. Each is worth a fortune for the copra they produce, and you just did a few thousand quid worth of damage."

McDuff didn't know what to say. He feared that Thompson was perfectly right, and he had just committed another blunder. "Yani," he said, "Tell the men to stop cutting the trees. We will go back to the church and decide what to do next."

Yani evaluated the situation rather quickly and told the men, "Big Man Thompson not a friend of Jesus. Him say trees taboo. No cut down. Pastor go back to church talk to God. We go, too."

Thompson was gloating more than smiling now. "All my boys get out of here and go to my Big House. We have real work to do," he ordered.

The men were talking among themselves and picking their hatchets up from the ground where many of them had dropped them. "You better get your axes back from your boys, Reverend, or you'll never see them again."

"They're not my axes. I gave them to the men for helping me build the church," he said in a downcast manner. "I'm sure they will find other uses for them. I need to find out how to build in the native manner — without coconut palms."

Thompson's eyes were wide with shock again. "Do you mean to stand there and tell me that you *gave* them those tools just on a promise that they would help you build that church of yours?"

"Of course. They are the core of my new congregation. They're not employees. They are working with me, not for me. We are building a church out of the love of God," McDuff said.

"You *gave* them those hatchets?" he said again.

"That's what I said. I trust these people and they trust me. Together we will change the name of this place from Christ's Despair to God's Triumph."

"And just how do you expect me to get any of them to work for me? I have had a bad enough time coming up with something to use as payment to get their worthless arses to do anything but kill pigs and screw their women. I finally came up with hatchets and knives and now you give them away free for attending Sunday school."

McDuff cowered in the face of Thompson's rage. The angry man snatched the hatchet from McDuff's hand. "Let me see that damn thing," he said, and examined it more closely.

"Why this thing is industrial grade! Are all of them?" he said.

"They're all the same, if that's what you mean."

"That's exactly what I mean. They'll never wear out. I give them cheap Jap shit that breaks in six months, and won't hold an edge. That way they have to come back at some future date to work for me again to get a replacement. With these things, they'll be handing them down from father to son."

Chapter 12

When Thompson got back to the Big House he expected to find his boys all standing below the verandah, waiting to be chewed out for their misguided allegiances. But, to his dismay there were only six men standing in a group under the trees. They were all older men, and although he had no way of knowing it at the time, they were also ones who had not received any of the tools that had been given out.

He didn't bother mounting the steps to his house, but went directly to the small knot of laborers. He felt the occasion called for a few words of humiliation and sounded the depths of his Booga-booga vocabulary for insults. He told them they were all rubbish men, pig-fuckers, and catchers of dead fish. And without realizing it, he was right. After the tree-cutting episode in the jungle the elders of the village decided that only rubbish men would work on the plantation. Real men would become friends of Jesus and get food and tools from the Witman churchfella by going to his church.

Thompson was fuming after he sent his few workers out to collect coconuts for the day. He walked around the grounds surrounding the house, muttering and swearing to himself. One of the dingo dogs that should have known better began to run after him yapping and nipping at his heels. In a fit of anger, he turned and let the poor mutt have both barrels of the 12-gauge, leaving it in a bloody mess for the women to clean up.

Some of the shot bounced harmlessly off the petrol-driven electric generator in the shed behind the house. Suddenly his face lit up. "That's it," he said. "I'll show that Bible-thumpin' son-of-a-bitch."

He walked over to the rusty machine and cranked it over until it caught. He usually hated its noise, but this time it was music. Once he was certain it would stay running he went inside the Big House and sat down in front of the two-way wireless set-up.

He adjusted a few knobs, picked up the microphone and began transmitting. "Despair to Island Patrol," he said in a voice he reserved for such occasions. "Despair to Island Patrol. Do you read me?"

He kept it up for almost ten minutes before he got a crackling of static mixed with a voice. "Island Patrol to Despair. Island Patrol to Despair. We read you, but the transmission is bad. Can you hear me?"

"This is Thompson on Christ's Despair. Who's this?"

"Hey, Jeremy, this is Gale on board the *Wombat*."

"Howdy, mate. Bad static here too. Keep talking."

"We're headed toward your island, anyway. Big news."

"Big news?" he said, "What's going on?"

"The war in Europe is coming our way. Hitler has ordered British merchant ships to be considered warships. We're worried about the *Fenestra*."

Thompson was surprised. "Surely there ain't no German Navy vessels hereabouts?" he said.

The next few words were broken up by the static, but Thompson heard Gale say, "...Japs joined Axis ... give you details tomorrow. What's going on there? How come ... the wireless, anyway."

Before communication died completely, Gale heard Thompson say, "McDuff is arming the natives..."

When he lost contact he told Mr. Wembly, "It sounds like we are getting there just on time. I think he's got a serious problem with the natives."

***

Pastor McDuff and Yani returned to the church clearing and found that no work had been done on the foundation. Although the tribesmen were very happy with their picks and shovels, they had not been told what to do with them. They weren't sure how to use them, and Yani had never seen either tool before he found them in the packing cases.

When John Frum Came

Even McDuff's experience was second-hand. Members of the McDuff clan had ceased using picks and shovels a generation before his. Being friends of Andrew Carnegie, they had moved on to financial investment involving the railroads at the turn of the century. However, Moses gave a brief demonstration of what he had seen the Irish day laborers do with them in and around Cambridge, Massachusetts. But, after five minutes of working in the tropical sun, he remembered other obligations.

"You seem to have the idea, Yani," he said. "Have them make a hole for the foundation from here to there," he said marking the beginning and end with stones. "I need to be alone and pray over the problem with Mr. Thompson."

He went to his little corner of the unfinished church, and sat on his bed. He leaned forward and buried his face in his hands. In tears, he prayed silently for an answer to the situation that was overwhelming him a little more with every passing hour.

He heard a rhythmic beating of native drums from the direction of the village. An echoing answer came from a point halfway up the mountain ridge. It went up and down the shoreline, until there seemed to me drum messages everywhere.

The sounds triggered a now familiar response, and he reached for his worn copy of *"Missionary in the New Hebrides"* by John G. Paton. Next to the Bible, this was his only guide to dealing with the problems that surrounded him. He read:

"*When I first beheld these Natives in their paint and nakedness and misery, my heart was as full of horror as of pity. My heart bleeds for the Heathen, and I long to see a Christianized native from some other island such as Samoa or Tonga for every tribe and a Missionary for every island of the New Hebrides. We found ourselves face to face with black Heathenism. They were but children and full of superstition.*

"*The first visible difference betwixt a Heathen and a Christian is that the Christian wears some clothing, the Heathen wears none. When these poor creatures began to wear a bit of calico or a kilt, it was an outward sign of change, though far from civilization.*

"*Concerning my former flock in Glasgow, though chiefly working girls and lads in trades and mills, their deep interest led them to unite their pence and sixpences and to buy web after web of calico, print and woolen stuffs, which they themselves shaped and sewed into dresses for the women, and kilts and pants for the men in the New Hebrides. This continued to be repeated year after year, long after I had left them.*

The chiefs at both stations willingly sold sites for houses and appeared to desire Missionaries to live amongst them; but perhaps it was with an eye to the axes, knives, fishhooks, blankets and clothing, which they got in payment, or hoped for in plunder."

McDuff looked up from his book. *Somehow, dressing up the natives in western clothes does not seem to be the key to the problem,* he thought. *If I did not have Yani, I would not have gotten as far as I have. I have no idea what these people are saying, much less thinking. How do I convey abstract ideas to a bunch of Stone Age people who can't even figure out how to use a shovel? What do I do about a white man who wants to keep them the way they are?*

But Reverend Paton is right; their eyes are on the knives and axes. I wish I had thought to order some fishhooks.

He was musing on these points when Yani burst into the room. "All men go village. Elder give feast. Big Man Tomsin give one hand pigs. Him call coconut spirit. Make much sorry. You come see," he said in one continuous stream of words.

What would Reverend Paton do in a case like this? He said: *"... for the love of our Lord and God we put an end to their barbaric ways. We forbade dancing, feasting, singing, and drumming."* Dr. McDuff was thoroughly perplexed. *Fat lot of good it would do for me to forbid them to hold a feast ... or do anything. I fear they hold Yani in higher regard than me.*

Unfortunately, he was right.

"Spirit worship is sinful," he told Yani. "It would be wrong for me to take part in the feasting. I must be true to my church. We do not allow such goings on."

The Chase Islander looked at him with a quizzical expression on his face. He was not sure he understood what the missionary was saying. He had never heard of someone not going to a feast. What could possibly be wrong with it? "Pastor McDuff sick? Have pain in bel-bel?" Then he remembered that the minister did not like native food. "You no eat'em pig-fella. You come see. You dance."

Not knowing how to explain himself, McDuff gave in. *I guess I should witness the activity so I know what I am fighting,* he justified to himself. "OK. You ... me go. You stay with Pastor. Tell what happens."

"OK!" Yani said with a big smile.

***

When it got dark, Yani led the way through the jungle to the site of the big feast. Five fully-grown pigs were cooking in a massive bed of glowing coals and hot rocks and greenery. The smell of the roasting meat was almost more than McDuff could handle. He had been dying for a piece of fresh meat (anything but dog) since he arrived. Now here was more roast pork than he had ever seen in one place. He was almost drooling.

He was guided to a place of honor next to Thompson and several native Big Men before the huge spread. Apparently, they had not waited for him to begin. Someone handed him a coconut shell full of pineapple juice that tasted like it had been mixed with muddy water. When he was seated on the ground, Thompson arose and talked for ten minutes in Booga-booga. Even though McDuff did not understand a word, he could hear the contrition in the white man's voice.

"What did he say?" he asked Yani.

"Big Man Tomsin say Coconut Tree Spirits not angry with men who cut down trees. He has whispered magic formula to the hurt trees. They will grow another time. Tree cut down now burns in the pig fire. He give these pigs to the Coconut Tree Spirits and they accept them. One pig left in jungle where we cut trees. Everybody eat the rest."

McDuff was bothered. He called over the noise to Thompson, who sat diagonally to him. "How could you tell these people such claptrap. You are a white man, and I presume were nominally a Christian at some point in your life. It's outrageous for you to pander to their pagan beliefs!"

"What should I tell them, Yank ... That they'll go to Heaven if they learn to sing some hymns written by a bunch of Huns two hundred years ago?"

Thompson had already had a number of shells full of palm wine and said, "Hey, mate. When in Rome ... and all that shit!"

Before the minister could respond, the elder playing the role equivalent to Master of Ceremonies said in his own language, "Big Man Tomsin has a present for all the men who work for him — steel knife or hatchet. If he has more left over he will give them to the men who have none." He held one in each hand, waving them for all to see.

There was a flurry of approval, and Yani translated the statement into Pidgin.

"It's about time," McDuff said to Thompson, raising his voice again. "You have been exploiting these people long enough. You make paying their wages sound like some great act of kindness on your part."

"Is that so?" Thompson said somewhat unsteadily. "We'll see who is capable of the greatest act of kindness before the evening is over.

"By the way, Reverend, these people believe that eating specific body parts of the pigs has healing value. If you want to see better to strengthen your tracking skills you eat the eyes. If you want to be as brave as a boar, you eat the heart. I have my own special interests — I think you call them mountain oysters in your country." With that he used his knife to cut off the boar's gonads and made a special show of eating them with gusto amid approving cheers from the men next to him.

A totally naked young woman gave Pastor McDuff a large piece of roast pork on a banana leaf. He couldn't decide which was more disconcerting — the naked woman or the roasted pig flesh. He gave into his uncontrollable urge and grabbed the roasted meat. In spite of himself he attacked it with the gusto demonstrated by his fellow diners. The woman's bare body held no allure for him. He acknowledged her as a female, but not necessarily as a member of the same species. He found the chunk of partially cooked pig far more attractive.

"Father forgive me, for I am about to sin," he said and took a huge bite out of the piece of meat. He literally lost control. His eating style could not be easily distinguished from the savages around the pit. His meat hunger had overwhelmed him. He was totally ashamed, but could not do anything about it. Even Yani was surprised.

A few minutes later, his attention was drawn to the drums that had started. A man started to dance to the rhythm and did a sequence of intricate movements. He was joined by the woman who had served him his pork, and what they did together he could only describe as lascivious. McDuff looked away, too embarrassed to watch.

He drank another coconut shell full of muddy-tasting pineapple juice. In his obvious attempt to avoid watching the dance, he gladly focused on the juice. He drank it down, in spite of the taste, and it was refilled almost immediately.

When the dance was done Thompson stood up again and spoke to the group. He pointed at McDuff and said something that met with the crowd's approval. And sat down.

"Come on, preacher, they're waiting for you to make a statement." Thompson said.

"About what?" he asked.

"You are a Big Man at a feast. You are supposed to make some kind of contribution to the peasantry."

"I have nothing to give," the Pastor protested.

"Not so, Big Man Duff. I already told them that you would give them *all* your tools, knives, hatchets and the store of machetes I hear you have in large numbers," Thompson sneered.

"These are for my church members," McDuff protested.

"I warn you, Reverend, they don't take lightly to cheap bastards who go back on their promises ... and as far as they are concerned, you've promised."

"That was a low down trick, Thompson," McDuff said.

"Tough shit, preacher. The chief has men ready to go back to your storehouse and carry the tools here. You and your church-boy better get a move on before the natives get restless..." He laughed with a sinister cackle.

The chief's porters stood next to Yani, ready to get the tools. When he went to stand up, the minister discovered that his legs were numb. The pineapple juice had been heavily spiked with kava. All he really wanted to do was sit quietly. He leaned back and felt like Alice taking a tumble down the rabbit hole.

An hour later, when Yani got back to the feast after watching the natives take all the tools, he found McDuff asleep. Yani roused him up to report what happened, but McDuff awoke to another shock. There was Thompson doing a native dance with the girl to the accompaniment of the drums ... without a stitch of clothing on his pale white body.

Chapter 13

As the islanders were going down to the lagoon for their morning swim, the *Wombat* came into view. Its profile was now modified by the addition of a quad-50 — a four barreled .50-caliber machine gun. As soon as Yani saw the boat, he left the water and ran back to the church clearing to tell Pastor McDuff. The two of them were down on the pier by the time the Patrol boat tied up.

There was no sign of Thompson, who was assumed to be sleeping off last night's celebration.

As Mr. Wembly and Mr. Gale stood on the deck prepared to climb over the side, the missionary greeted them. They stretched across to the pier and offered a handshake. "Thank the Lord you are here, gentlemen. I was wondering how to get in touch with you. Now, God in His infinite wisdom has brought you to me."

"Didn't Jeremy tell you we were coming? We spoke to him on the wireless yesterday," Wembly said. "Apparently there are a number of problems with the natives according to him. And we have some very important news and changes of concern to both of you — and all of us, for that matter."

"I'm afraid he and I do not engage in civil conversations, Mr. Wembly. Our views of the world and the natives on the island are at opposite ends of the spectrum," McDuff told him.

"Oh?" said Wembly, pretending not to know. "Would you care to tell us about it?"

"I'm not one for telling tales out of school, but I don't know what else to do about it."

He was invited aboard the *Wombat* and climbed gingerly over the railing. At the same time, a large, muscular native with a shaved head and features similar to Yani's climbed in the opposite direction. He was wearing a patrol uniform without any insignia, or markings. He smiled and said, "Good morning, sir. I'd like to speak to your churchboy if you don't mind," in perfect English with an Australian accent.

"Good morning to you," McDuff answered. "Go right ahead," as the man headed toward Yani, standing a few yards away.

"Who is that?" the missionary asked, amazed at hearing a black man speak English.

"He is our head Policeboy, Percy. I'll tell you about him later. Right now he wants to talk your boy ... What's his name?"

"Yani."

"Yes, Yani. I remember now," Wembly said. "By the way, remember those pirates that kidnapped him? They hanged the lot of them back in Sydney."

The minister did not like to hear of any violence, even of the legal variety. He had hoped they would have put them in jail and persuaded them to change their lives.

The three men made themselves comfortable in the large living room-like main cabin.

"Well, how are you making out with your Christianizing program," Gale said. "Do you have any converts?"

"I think I am making great headway with Yani, but I have run into some snags with the local population, thanks to Mr. Thompson."

"What kind of snags?" Gale asked.

"I hardly know where to begin. He doesn't pay them. He takes sexual advantage of the women. He shot one of the men yesterday, and last night ... well, you wouldn't believe last night," he said shaking his head.

They listened to Dr. McDuff's tale of debauchery and dishonor without indicating how they felt about the matter. Then, at length Wembly said, "I think I had best go up to the Big House and talk to Mr. Thompson. We have a number of things to discuss in addition to the items you just described.

"Why don't you stay here and talk with Mr. Gale, Doctor. I propose we all have lunch on board the *Wombat* at mid-day. You may have noticed our increased armaments," he said, pointing to the anti-aircraft guns. "I will explain the wartime changes that are about to descend upon us."

***

Knowing what things white men missed most in the islands, Mr. Gale poured Dr. McDuff a tall glass of ice water. Had he been a drinker, he would have added a tumbler of Scotch. "We carry enough fresh water on the *Wombat* for you to take a shower, if you wish, Doctor."

"You can't imagine what that would mean to me, Mr. Gale," he said. "The endless stickiness that comes from bathing in the ocean is getting to be a bit much. Sometimes I just go out and stand in the rain."

"Believe me, I know," Gale said. "I was a cadet for six months on an island much like Christ's Despair. This one is just a little worse than the rest."

"I never did find out how it got it's name," McDuff said. "I wanted to ask Thompson, but our conversations have always been antagonistic. Do you know?"

"Some of it. It's not pretty. I'm not sure you want to know," he said in a way that made it all the more tantalizing.

"How am I to deal with the problems if I don't know what they are?" he argued.

Gale hesitated, thinking it over, then said. "The Germans brought the first missionaries here in 1900, when they got into the copra business. They were Lutherans. They did things in a big way. They didn't just send one man, like Thompson. They sent whole families to the islands. The managers brought their families. The German officials brought their families. So, naturally, the missionaries brought their families."

"That sounds like a strong basic policy for colonization," McDuff said. "How were they received by the natives?"

"Well, considering how they took over the island, they weren't very welcome."

"Why was that? What did they do?"

"They armed about 75 natives — mercenaries — from one of the other islands who were their traditional enemies. They gave them rifles, and paid them with liquor and tobacco and sent them in to shoot everyone they could — with special instructions to kill everyone under ten years of age. They just wanted adult males to work on the copra plantations."

"I can't believe that!" McDuff said. "No one could be so heartless."

"I think it's a piece of verifiable history, Doctor. It didn't make the Krauts too popular with the natives. You can be sure of that. They burned off much of the vegetation, so they could plant their coconut palms. They didn't grow here naturally. Practically all the trees you see now are left from the first plantation. I don't think Thompson has planted a single tree since he took over a few years ago."

"He told me that, but I didn't believe him," McDuff admitted grudgingly. "Don't the indigenous people own the land?"

"Yes, but it is standard practice to own the individual coconut trees, rather than the ground they grow on. It's possible to own a plot of land, but not have the rights to any fruit from the trees.

"Well anyway, burning the jungle left the people in a famine situation. They were starving. The island split up into groups, and they reverted to cannibalism. They were attacking each other's villages and cooking the victims. It was only a matter of time before they decided to add white meat to their diet.

"They say that in one week, at the height of the frenzy, every German man, woman and child was slaughtered and eaten."

Dr. McDuff made a face. "I have read about that sort of thing in a book I have, but I still find it difficult to accept it as really happening."

Gale was beginning to enjoy watching the look of horror and disbelief on the missionary's face, and decided to administer the coup de grace. "Have you noticed that there aren't any kids among the villagers between the ages of five and ten?"

"Now that you mention it, I think you are right," he said. "Plague? Measles? What did them in?"

"Supposedly about ten years ago, they suddenly developed a taste for 'baby-meat' according to one of your predecessors. That's why there's such a gap in the ages of the kids. Mothers began to eat their own newborn children, sharing them with their sisters..."

"Stop it!" McDuff yelled. "I don't want to hear any more. This is revolting. I can't believe it ... I don't want to believe it!"

"I warned you," Gale said. "I'm sorry if I have upset you. That's why no one would take a missionary post on the island for the past five years, until you came along. There's a rumor that the last one killed himself at the hospital."

The Boston-bred minister was sweating profusely. He looked like he was going to be ill. "I'd like to take you up on that shower now, if you don't mind Mr. Gale," he said.

***

The four men sat around a dinner table in the main cabin, while a Papuan cook and mess steward served them a baked fish dinner that might be found in a better Sydney restaurant. Dr. McDuff had recovered from his encounter with the truth about the island, and was reveling in the civilized atmosphere of the meal. If he overdid anything, it was the ice water.

Wembly had talked with Thompson briefly about his behavior with the natives. He explained it all away by telling how he had to gain their confidence through participation in their feasts. As far as the shooting was concerned, the Patrol Officer was fully aware of the policy of not backing down in any confrontation with a native. He simply shot him in the foot to keep him under control.

As they ate, Senior Patrol Officer Wembly conducted his promised briefing on what was going on in the larger world. "As you are well aware, we are at war with Germany in Europe, and I fear things are not going well. I have brought you some newspapers that will fill you in on that element of world history. As we told Jeremy on the wireless yesterday, Hitler has given his navy orders to regard all British merchant ships as warships. In simple terms it gives them license to sink our freighters whether they are armed or not.

"I sincerely doubt that there are any German Navy ships in our waters, but what does concern me is what the Japs are up to. They have officially joined the Axis powers, along with Italy. The Japs may be planning to adopt the same policy of sinking unarmed freighters, so we are on alert. We know they have a large fleet of submarines, and they are probably cruising in the vicinity."

Thompson asked, "Do you think there is any chance of their invading New Guinea or Australia?"

"The Japs have already invaded Indo-China," Gale said. Then, indulging in his morbid fascination for ghastly events added, "I hear that there are so many Jap casualties that they are actually cutting off the right hands of the corpses to aid in later identification of bodies."

Wembly gave him a chilling look. "If you don't mind, Mr. Gale, we are eating our lunch."

"Sorry, sir," he said, looking down at his fish.

"British Forces have already abandoned Shanghai to the Japs," Wembly said. "But enough of the war news. What you gentlemen need is to be brought up to date on the changes in the administration of your island."

Dr. McDuff looked alert. "What changes are those?" he asked.

"It is vital to the war effort that we maximize the production of copra to strengthen our economy. There is even the chance that the Japanese might make a move to take over the islands that produce it. But more about that later.

"Dr. McDuff, one of the key problems we have had with the copra plantations on the part of the natives has been their lack of interest in working on them. We had hoped that Christianizing them would awaken their latent 'work ethic.'"

"*Latent!*" Thompson laughed. "That implies that there once was one and it is only asleep. These people are born retired. They won't do anything more than they need to do to stay alive."

"Well, we think we have the solution," Wembly said.

"What might that be?" McDuff asked earnestly.

"Taxes," Wembly announced.

Both Thompson and McDuff were wide-eyed. "Taxes?" they each said in turn.

"How terribly British," Gale wise-cracked.

"How are taxes going to make those lazy bastards get their arses up into the coconut trees?" the plantation manager said.

"Each adult male over the age of puberty will be assessed a head tax of five pounds a year. It must be paid in Australian currency — *no pigs, no taro, no shells and no dog teeth.* The only way they can get money is to work on the plantation. You will pay them five pounds for six months of work."

"Are you serious about this?" the missionary asked.

"Couldn't be more," Wembly said. "The plan is being introduced on all Crown-controlled islands throughout the South Pacific — effective immediately."

"That's virtual slavery," McDuff said.

"Dr. McDuff, need I remind you that you are an American and are here at the convenience of His Majesty's Government. Strictly speaking, your opinion is neither sought nor noted in this matter. It is a matter under the jurisdiction of the Exchequer. As a foreign national I am simply informing you of our laws," came the frosty response.

"How is this plan going to be implemented?" Thompson asked. "Are you going to collect the taxes when you get here every couple months?"

Wembly smiled a wicked smile. "Under the Wartime Powers Act you are hereby appointed Acting Governor of the island known as Christ's Despair. The salary for that position to be announced at a later date."

Thompson's face reflected mixed emotions. The announcement took him by complete surprise. He had just been awarded absolute power over this dismal place, and no longer had to put up with the Reverend McDuff's criticisms. But at the same time he just inherited a bureaucracy he had no idea how to manage.

The missionary was bewildered. He hardly knew what to expect. He looked to the Patrol as a source of justice, and they had just installed his main antagonist as Supreme Ruler.

"There's more," Wembly said. "We still have not resolved this business of arming the natives."

"Arming the natives?" McDuff asked.

"Yes. I saw no less than four men with machetes swinging them recklessly on the beach when I went ashore earlier. I also noticed that there is an abundance of knives and hatchets."

Thompson spoke up before the minister could say anything. "The good Pastor, here, gave them out at last night's feast as inducements to come to his prayer meetings. I've been using them as payment for work performed, myself. However, Mr. McDuff had a little too much kava last night and gave everything away before he fell asleep at the dinner table."

"See here," McDuff said sharply. "You know you drugged me and gave away my possessions without my being able to do anything about it."

"I suggest you take it up with the island's governor," Thompson grinned.

"Gentlemen, if you please. There is no point in arguing about this now. I, for one, would not want to try to recover any of those items from one of the men. But all is not lost. As I pointed out earlier, we may have a possible Japanese invasion to contend with at some time in the future. Providing the natives don't use the machetes on you, it may be to our advantage for them to be able to defend their island from the Japs. I suggest you think about that for a bit."

Chapter 14

In spite of the incongruous Island Patrol uniform, the large black man coming toward Yani from the *Wombat* was very familiar. Yani thought he knew him, but how could that be? He knew only people from his own island and those he had met since he came to Christ's Despair.

The man smiled at him and studied the tattoo on his chest. In it he read Yani's shaman status, and knew immediately where he was from. "You are my brother," he said in the Chase Island dialect, and placed his open hand on the tattoo. Yani was taken by surprise at this greeting — it was reserved for only "one who really knew."

After a moment of feeling Yani's heartbeat, the stranger unbuttoned his uniform shirt and revealed an almost identical marking. He took Yani's right hand and held it against his heart.

"I am Negeb, son of Ooma," he said proudly. "Who are you?"

"I am Yani. Also, son of Ooma," he answered. The two men stood with their hands on each other's chests smiling for a full minute.

"We must talk," Negeb said. "Let us clear a circle and build a fire." They left the pier and went to the edge of the jungle, but stayed on the beach. Without speaking they collected a large amount of shells, and arranged them in a pattern. It was a circle, but there was a sequence in the types of shells and the order in which they appeared.

Yani brought some dry driftwood to the center of the circle, and stacked it. He began to work at making a fire in the traditional manner, but Negeb

When John Frum Came

grinned mischievously, produced a match, and said. "Don't bother. I have the Witman's magic."

Once the fire was self-sustaining, they sat cross-legged in the sand, facing each other. "How is it that you are here?" Negeb began.

Yani answered, not with an account of his adventures, but with his spiritual quest. "I am searching for Kilibob. I want to go to the Witman's island and bring back Kilibob's gifts to our people. I have learned much about the Witman's ways. He has strong magic, and I wish to take it back from him."

Negeb said, "I have been away from our island many seasons, and I have learned much of the Witman's magic. But I am no longer sure it is good for our people."

"I think tinkens are better than gardens." Yani said. "Steel tools are better than rocks and wooden spears. You come in Kilibob's boat ... you know it is better than our log canoes." He wanted to ask if Kilibob was on board, but thought it best for Negeb to mention it first.

Negeb went deep into thought. Yani waited for him to return to the conversation. At length he said, "Do you know John Frum?"

The younger man knitted his brow. "Jonfrum? Jonfrum ... hmmmm. Sounds like a Witman name."

"It is," Negeb said. "He is from an island called America. It is far from here. It lies beyond the sunrise."

"My Big Man Duff is from America. Maybe he knows him. Is Jonfrum a churchfella? Big Man Duff is a churchfella." Yani said.

Negeb became aware of how sophisticated he had become. Although this young man was a son of Ooma, he was still a child in many ways. "He is no churchfella? He does not like churchfellas."

"Big Man Tomsin does not like churchfella either. He is not a friend of Jesus." Yani said.

"Are you a friend of Jesus?" Negeb asked worriedly. "Are you a Christian?"

"I am a churchboy," Yani said, sure that it would impress Negeb. "Big Man Duff speaks Pidgin. I understand. I tell kanakas what he says in Blackfella words."

"You are a translator," he said in English, since there was no word in their language for the concept. "Do you speak any English?"

Yani did not answer.

"English! The words the Witmen speak to each other," Negeb said. "Some words are the same as Pidgin."

"Yes. Sometimes I can say a whole piece of English." He recited a bit of what he had learned. "Our father huartin Heaven…"

"Don't let the Witman know you understand any of his language. He will beat you and tell you to speak only Pidgin," Negeb warned.

"Big Man Duff does not get angry when I speak Witman language. He says all his magic formulas in Ing-lish. I am trying to learn his words, so I can do the same magic."

"What magic?" Negeb asked.

"He gets tinkens from God in Heaven. He keeps no garden. God sends him food in tinkens when he says his magic words. I have seen it work."

Negeb smirked. "The tinkens come from Australia, Yani. They make them in a place in Sydney."

Yani had heard Witmen refer to Australia and Sydney. Negeb had just cleared it up. These were other names for Heaven.

"Australia is the name of the place where the Witmen come from. I have heard that we will take some island fellas there to teach them how to be Policeboys." Police was also another word with no equivalent in any island dialect.

"What is Policeboy?" Yani said, astounded at the number of new ideas this circle talk was bringing to him.

"I am a Policeboy," Negeb said. "I am allowed to speak English to tell the Patrol Officers what islander's say. Patrol Officers speak Pidgin, but some islanders speak only Booga-booga. They gave me a Witman name — Percy — and taught me some English. They do not know how much I understand, and I pretend I do not know everything they say."

Yani realized that he was doing much the same. He brought the conversation back to an earlier point. "What is Jonfrum?"

"Two words — John Frum," Negeb explained. "He comes to islands and tells the Blackfellas not to try to be like the Witman. He tells them to stay with custom. He says change will kill the Blackfella. Witmen have only one

When John Frum Came

reason to bring churchfellas to islands. They destroy the old way of living, and make the Blackfella a slave on their coconut plantation."

He was about to explain what a slave was when Yani said, "Yes. Big Man Tomsin makes slaves out of rubbish men on this island. True men will not work for him."

"That's why Patrol Officers are here. I am supposed to teach some of Tomsin's men how to be Policeboys. They give Policeboys big sticks. Everybody must pay taxes." He stopped. There was no native word for taxes, and he wasn't sure how to explain them.

"Anyway. They have to work on the plantation to pay taxes. If they don't, they beat Blackfellas. Then they go to the calaboose."

Yani looked mystified.

"Jail!" Negeb said.

Yani had never heard of jail either ... nor had any of the tribesmen on Christ's Despair.

***

Coffee was served as the after-dinner conversation aboard the *Wombat* devolved to gossip about topics familiar only to the Australians. McDuff was thinking about how his mission would function in light of the new rules. If he objected, he would be deported. If he stayed, he felt he was guilty of complicity in enslaving the people of the island.

"Excuse me, Mr. Wembly," he asked during a lull in the conversation. "What will you do if the natives just refuse to pay the tax, or work on the plantation? Who will be the enforcer of these tax laws?"

"Remember that tall Blackfella you saw when you came on board this morning?" Wembly said. "That was Percy. He is going to organize a unit of Policeboys. Generally, we pick out underdogs in the local population ... men who have been abused by the village. We train them to use truncheons to keep the others in line. They have no allegiance to the others because of the way they have been treated.

"Percy will supervise the construction of a jail house or a stockade. They call it a calaboose in Pidgin. These people hate confinement, and it hardly takes more than a few days in the calaboose to make them willing to work on the plantations."

"Can we trust this Percy-fella? Any chance of his sympathizing with the locals?" Thompson asked.

"He's from another island — I forget which. But, as I'm sure you know, they have no feelings of nationalism or unity, as we know it. If you are from another island you might as well be from another planet. It's like putting a German in charge of a bunch of Frenchmen."

"I know you are not interested in my view, gentlemen, but this all sounds rather brutal," McDuff said.

"We are at war, Dr. McDuff. The effort of all his Majesty's subjects is needed — black natives included," Wembly concluded. With that he pushed his chair away from the table, indicating that the luncheon was over, as was the briefing session. "Mr. Thompson, I will need to discuss your new responsibilities with you. Please remain on board." Which was another way of saying to the missionary that he was expected to leave.

McDuff started to leave, and then signaled Mr. Gale he would like to speak to him on deck for a moment. Once they were outside, he said, "This is really quite embarrassing, but since you have whetted my appetite for civilization with the shower, I have one other small request to make."

"Surely," Gale reassured him.

McDuff blushed and said, "Do you think the government would miss a package or two of toilet tissue?"

***

As McDuff walked down the pier, he could see no sign of Yani, and wondered where he went. It was unusual for him not to be around. At the same time he felt rather strange — he was having a chill. He hadn't experienced the sensation of cold since last winter in New England. *I guess I overdid the ice water*, he thought. *Even the shower was cooler than the usual dip in the ocean. Enjoy it while you can, Moses,* he told himself, *you'll be wet with sweat again before you get to the edge of the jungle.*

The fleeting remembrance of Massachusetts in the wintertime led to thoughts of his graduation from divinity school — The True Church of God Seminary. It was so long ago and so far away. Although it had only been a couple years since his graduation, it was a very much younger Moses McDuff who had committed to memory the words of his missionary inspiration, John G. Paton. He recited them aloud as he walked toward the church clearing: "We established laws, courts, stocks, prisons and fines to proclaim to these naked savages that the ways of Christianity are superior to the chaos under which they lived."

Is this what Reverend Paton was talking about? he asked himself. *Am I missing something here? How can I talk to these people about the love of Jesus Christ when my fellow white men see them as beasts of burden?*

***

Negeb asked numerous questions about Chase Island and about Ooma. He also asked him about the situation on Christ's Despair, making mental notes of the conflict Yani described between McDuff and Thompson. Under the rules of the circle Yani was obliged to tell Negeb everything he knew. But the same responsibility was also upon his partner. They meditated together for a long time, then Negeb said: "I tell you within the circle that I think John Frum is right. When the Blackfella tries to be like the Witman it hurts his spirit. You can appear to be a churchboy, but it must be with the plan to take back the Witman's magic to our people. When you get back to our home island you must cast away the part of the Witman's behavior that is bad. Keep what is good for our people.

"John Frum says all Blackfellas are brothers in matters of custom. Churchfellas drive our spirits out. The collecting of so many coconuts is a foolish Witman ritual. We have always collected only what we needed since the days of Manup. It does nothing to help us "*know.*" Picking and crushing coconuts is a job for rubbish men.

"Tomorrow I will teach Tomsin's rubbish men to look like Policeboys. Real men will not follow them. Yani *must not* become a Policeboy. You stay with churchfella now. You go to Sydney with me next full moon. Pretend you are friend of Jesus. Do what Churchfella McDuff wishes."

Negeb had laid a heavy load on Yani's shoulders. He did not really understand everything he was told, but a son of Ooma had told him truths while they were within the circle. He dare not do otherwise.

Chapter 15

Wembly and Gale went over the tax plan with Thompson, who liked the idea as a way for him to meet his contractual obligations to Pacific Copra. But, in reality, he was worried about the implementation of it.

"Percy will take some of your boys tomorrow morning, and teach them how to be Policeboys. For starters, he'll give them shirts and shorts and a six-foot truncheon. They're actually quarter-staves like Robin's Merry Men used, if you recall Little John and that lot. Percy will show the boys how to use them to keep the other natives in line.

"We have to take a hop over to one of the other islands, tomorrow evening, but we'll come back in a few days to check on their progress. I know it won't be easy, but you're an old hand with these people, so we have faith in you."

"What about McDuff? If ever there was a pain in the arse, it's him. How about taking him back to Port Moresby with you?" Thompson suggested.

"The Commissioner wants a missionary on all the key islands. I'm not supposed to say why at the moment, but it will be important if the Japs start giving us trouble. Trust me. It will give us some extra eyes. We know what we're doing," Wembly reassured him.

Thompson grimaced and said, "How is this plan working out on the other islands?"

"We won't know for a while," Gale said. "You're the first to try it. If it will be successful anywhere, it will be on Christ's Despair, mainly because you're here."

"The problems we're having on some of the other islands are with this John Frum business," Wembly said.

"Is that nonsense still about? John Frum, indeed. Who do you think he works for?"

"He doesn't work for anyone, except maybe the Japs. We think that he's an American, but no reliable white man has ever seen him," Gale said. "He stirs up the natives."

"He sounds like a spook. At least he's not another missionary like McDuff. There can't be two of them."

"Quite the opposite," Wembly said, lighting his pipe, and leaning back in one of the comfortable chairs. "Remember, even if you don't like the missionary, theoretically he's on your side. Frum goes around trying to get the natives to resist the missionaries. He tells them that they weren't meant to follow the white man's ways. He is trying to start sort of a 'Back to Nature' movement."

"Don't worry, there's no talk about him among the *kanakas* on my island," Thompson said.

"Well, we're cracking down on his followers. On Tanna you can get a one-year jail term — or longer — for talking about him. We figure that since he depends on word of mouth publicity, the best way to deal with him is to discourage the natives from discussing him."

"The other problem is just the opposite — the Cargo Cults," Gale said.

"Are they still around? What now?" Thompson said. "I thought they died out."

"No," Wembly said, "They're a perennial problem. You practically have one right here with Dr. McDuff and all his steel tools. I actually saw one of your natives digging shellfish with a steel shovel. What else has he given them?"

"God knows," Thompson said, "If you'll forgive the pun."

Gale, as usual, had a story to tell. "Did you ever hear of the 'Vailala Madness?'"

Thompson downed a couple more ounces of Scotch, and said with a laugh, "Sure, but that was before our time ... ten or more years ago."

"Well, it's broken out again ... in Rigo this time."

"Why do I have the feeling that you are going to tell me about it whether I want to know about it or not?"

"Because you are starved for news, and want to hear about it," Gale said.

They refilled the glasses all around and Gale unfolded a copy of the *New Guinea Weekly Times* and found the story he was looking for.

"July 10 — Colonel Angus MacKensie, Chief Agent for Inter-Island Trading, Ltd., reported to Constable Arthur Dennis yesterday that he wanted to have one of his employees restrained and held for observation. He reported that many of the natives were behaving strangely, but this one, named Kari, was the most extraordinary.

"According to Col. MacKensie, the natives at Rigo were saying that the spirits of their ancestors had appeared to several of them. The message of the deceased spirits was that all flour, rice, tobacco, and other trade goods belonged to the New Guinea people. The white man had no right whatever to these goods. They predict that in a short time all the white men will be driven away. Then everything will be in the hands of the natives.

"Furthermore, a large vessel will also appear shortly, bringing back the spirits of their departed relatives with quantities of cargo. All the villages are supposed to make ready to receive them.

"'It's not just idle talk,' MacKensie said, 'They're building platforms in several villages, and these are being loaded up with presents. Self-appointed "big men" seem to be running these preparations.'

"Readers of the *Weekly Times* may be familiar with the story of how Col. MacKensie runs his organization much like the Army unit from which he recently retired. He has taught his boys how to 'fall in' when he blows his whistle, and to perform close order drill. He is annoyed that one of the 'big men' has obtained a whistle and also makes the other natives 'fall in' and makes them salute. The real problem is these bosses are also instructing the natives that they are not to sign on with the white man any more.

"Constable Dennis reports that Kari, the native afflicted with the 'Rigo Madness' is well known as being of a very quiet disposition. He is not the least inclined to be impudent. At about midday yesterday he was sent to Col. MacKensie's house to help Mrs. MacKensie. He walked in smoking a cigarette, and wearing one of the Colonel's kilts. Although unable to read or write, he had a book in his hand, and also a pencil and paper. He scribbled a number of marks on the paper and told Mrs. MacKensie that it was a letter he had just written.

"When he began trying to sing, and do a Highland fling like the Colonel has been known to perform in public, she ran from the house screaming. She explained she was afraid to stay there, as the boy seemed to be mad.

"She sought out her husband, and he found Kari acting like a lunatic. He brought him straight to the Police office. When ordered to be quiet he came to his senses somewhat, but could give no explanation for his conduct. All that could be gotten out of him was, 'I no savvy. God he savvy.' He was not considered a fit and proper person to be at large, and was detained for a time at the station to be under observation."

Thompson and Wembly thoroughly enjoyed the story, and the plantation manager asked, "Well, was it just the one? Or did the rest of the village go mad, too."

"They were all acting strange, so the constable went to the village the next day to take a look. Here's what his report said:

"In open spaces throughout the village were to be seen ornamented flag poles, long tables and benches. The tables were covered with sheets of cotton cloth. They were usually decorated with flowers in bottles of water in imitation of the white man's dining table. At one of the forms a large number of men were seated with their backs to the table. They were all dressed in new clothing, some in shorts, others in new suits of European garments. They sat quite motionless and never a word was spoken for the few minutes I stood looking at them.

"A tall flag pole was painted with native paint. This is a very typical medium of communication between the shamans and the souls of the dead. There are certain individuals who claim to receive messages from the dead through its use.

"Several natives kept watch for a large ship which is to bring back their ancestors in the form of white men. The old nine o'clock curfew was in full vogue, though no doubt its stringency is modified by the fact that no one is in a position to tell the time."

"Dr. I. Proteus of the B.S.I.P. Medical department said, 'They believe that their expectations will be realized if they can generate "ahea" or heat. This calls for the taking of large amounts of ginger, which acts like a stimulant while at the same time giving the impression of heat being generated in the stomach. In my opinion the taking of excessive amounts of ginger would be consistent with the symptoms of the cult members."

"So what the doctor is saying is that the native population is suffering from a severe case of heartburn," Wembly said.

"I guess you could say that," Leslie Gale said. "As I think about this story, what strikes me is that we must look just as peculiar to them as they do to us."

***

By the time the *Wombat* was ready to shove off for Aku, the next leg of its journey, Percy had completed Phase I of establishing a group of Policeboys on Christ's Despair. Thompson had given him the same six "rubbish men" who came back to work for him after the village elders decided not to send anyone.

They were delighted to be given some kind of status after a lifetime without it. Before doing anything else, Percy gave them each a khaki shirt and a pair of shorts like his own. Around their waists a leather rope served as a belt. The clothes alone would have been enough to induce them to do anything that needed doing. The clothes were brand new, and better than the fancy items that Big Man Duff gave out to wear in his church. Most important, these were the kinds of clothes the Patrol Officers and Big Man Tomsin, himself, wore.

While they were getting into the official uniforms, they eyed the large poles Percy had brought with him. It was obvious to everyone that these were intended to be used as weapons. He called them truncheons, but they looked like heavy spears without points. Except for the machining, they would have, indeed, been very familiar to the merry band of men in Sherwood Forest. The island's war clubs were usually much shorter and heavier, mostly made from gourds filled with sand.

When Percy gave them out, everyone liked the heft of them. They were made in England of oak, a material the islanders had never felt before. With the help of Mr. Gale, Percy demonstrated how they could be used to attack, thrust, parry, and block. He made it look easy, but he neglected to tell them that he had been practicing with the staves for five years, and was the acknowledged champion among the Australian Policeboys in their use.

Percy left them in the afternoon paired off in practice skirmishes that resulted in a number of head bumps, bruises and scraped knuckles. He promised them he would be back in two or three days to see how they were doing, and to teach them more policing techniques.

That evening the new Policeboys began strutting about the village in their khaki clothes and threatening women and children with their new weapons. One made the mistake of provoking one of the warriors who was mastering the art of handling his English-made hatchet. In a fit of anger the man seized the quarter- staff, and with three swift blows turned it into two sticks three-feet long.

The Policeboy was devastated. Everyone in the village witnessed his humiliation and he ran into the jungle to a chorus of laughter. Life for him had not changed with the acquisition of a title.

Pastor McDuff's chills gave way to a fever the evening after he lunched with the Patrol Officers. He was able to diagnose his own symptoms — he obviously was suffering from malaria. He sent Yani to the *Wombat* to get whatever medicine they might have to help him fight the disease. Mr. Gale, who served as the public health officer, returned with the churchboy and took charge.

"Quinine is still the only stuff we're using. Nothing seems to cure the damned illness, but I understand it keeps the symptoms under control. I'll give you a bunch of these pills. Take them three times a day. Stay in bed until you feel better. Let your boy here wait on you hand and foot. Save your energy and drink lots of water."

"Is it fatal?" McDuff asked.

"It is for the natives if it goes untreated. The quinine seems to hold it in check. I guess we all get it sooner or later. Just rest. We'll be back in a few days. I'll look in on you to see how you're doing when we get back from running up to Aku. We're leaving within the hour."

When John Frum Came

The missionary drifted off into a fever dream. He heard the voice of that stalwart champion of the Christian Way, Reverend Paton, talking as though he were the "voice over" narrating a bad travelogue. McDuff's overheated brain provided the screen for a grainy black and white movie:

> *"We've got two kinds of people here: clothed (the Christian) and unclothed (the heathen)" the narrator said. "We have to rule with a rod of iron. The natives only understand an iron hand in an iron glove. We have used the mailed fist of evangelism to teach the love of Christ in the Pacific.*
>
> *"We've got our courts and policemen. Everybody's subject to them, white as well as black. But the whites have to stay on top to run things. Drinking kava gets you put in calaboose. Singing gets you put in calaboose. Dancing and just about anything you do means the calaboose... the calaboose... the calaboose... the calaboose."*

The words went on over and over, like an old cracked record. The fever dream did not have a shut-off switch.

Every once in a while McDuff would regain consciousness during a chill, and shake in uncontrollable spasms. Yani always seemed to be at his side when he awoke. The young man would place his hand over the missionary's eyes and say something rhythmic in Booga-booga. Whether the chill ran its course, or Yani's touch had suppressed it he could not decide. In his fever dream, Yani was replaced by Leslie Gale, for whom he felt a great deal of affection. Perhaps it was just the touch of another human being who apparently cared. Whatever the reason, the contact quieted the ravages of the malaria.

***

The next day was Wednesday. Not that it made any difference on Christ's Despair. Although he observed the Sabbath himself, Pastor McDuff had not yet gotten around to discussing the concept of it with Yani. In his fiery torment, followed by dreams of being stuck in a crevasse on a glacier somewhere, the minister heard someone calling to him.

"Dr. McDuff. Can you hear me? Dr. McDuff! Wake up."

He opened his eyes a crack and saw Jeremy Thompson standing next to him with his huge shotgun resting on his shoulder. "How did you get to Switzerland, Mr. Thompson? Who's minding the coconuts?" he said.

"You're delirious, McDuff. You're dreaming. You're here on the island with me," Thompson said in a loud voice.

The minister focused on the reality for a moment. "Oh," he said. "You're sure we're not dead. It's awfully warm all of a sudden."

"I'll see you in Hell, McDuff, but not yet. I just came by to tell you that I want your boy to be one of our Policeboys. But I can wait until he's finished playing nursemaid to you," Thompson said.

McDuff thought about the remark for a minute and said, "I don't know if he wants to be a Policeboy. I think we better ask him first."

"I don't care a rat-fuck if he does or he doesn't. As Governor of this island, if I tell him he's a Policeboy, he'll damn well be a Policeboy."

Yani spoke up and said, "Yani is churchboy. I work for Big Man Duff. No want to be Policeboy."

Thompson was taken aback. Addressing himself to the minister, he said, "This bloody bastard speaks English! Have you been teaching him English? You know that's against the rules. We warned you about that.

"You just wait 'till Wembly hears about this. He'll be back in a couple days, and I'll let him know what you've been up to. It's back to the good ol' U.S.A. for you, mate."

Thompson was leaving the hut and turned back to say, "If he's goin' to speak English, then he damn well better be a Policeboy. That's all we need, a subversive among the natives."

McDuff had passed out again and heard none of it. Yani realized that he had violated Negeb's instructions. He allowed the Witman to find out that he could understand English. Yani needed to talk to Negeb when he got back to see if there was some way he could save the situation.

Chapter 16

After Thompson left the church, Yani took it upon himself to take the stained-glass window of the *Ascension of Christ* out of its crate. The slot had been prepared in the earthen wall to receive the frame rather snugly, but it would take two people to lift it into place. The churchboy was sure that Jesus could work his magic better if he was out in plain view, rather than trapped in the wooden box. The pallet of palm leaves on which he had placed the pastor was in just the right spot for him to see the picture standing on the altar when he awoke again.

He wondered why the friends of Jesus had not come by to help them with the church. Maybe they realized that there were no more tools to be had, but since they enjoyed using them he doubted that was the reason.

One of the women who had taken a liking to Yani edged around the clearing, watching him position the window. When he finished, she said, "The picture of Witman God looks like it has much power. Can Big Man Duff go up through the clouds, too?"

"Yani and Pastor Duff will go through the clouds to Heaven when it is the time."

She was impressed.

"Where are the friends of Jesus?" Yani asked. "I thought everyone would come to work with me. Pastor is sick from bad spell. I think Big Man Tomsin is *bis*" using the local word for sorcerer. "He use *simka* on him," Yani said.

"Big Man Tomsin called all men to Big House. Everyone is there. He came to the village and told them to go there," she said, her words showing her obvious fear of the white man.

Yani saw that McDuff was sleeping well at the moment. "You stay here," he told her "Give him water if he wakes up. I go hear what Big Man Tomsin says."

When Yani reached the Big House, he stayed around the outer edge of the crowd. He did not want Thompson to see him. In his usual style, Thompson stood up on the verandah, bullying the natives in their own language.

"The Japanese are coming. They have big ships. They have soldiers with guns." He held his shotgun over his head. "They will shoot the Blackfella if he does not work on the copra plantations. The Witman chief in Sydney does not want the Blackfella to be shot."

The natives did not believe Thompson's words. They were more inclined to believe that the Japanese were their friends and were going to drive the Witman off the islands. However, no one dared to give voice to those thoughts at the moment.

Then he got to the sticky part. "Because we are at war with the Japanese, everyone will have to pay a tax of five Pounds a year." No one understood what he meant.

"All men will work on the Plantation for six months every year. I will give you knives, hatchets, steel tools, tinkens, cotton cloth, and clothes. I will also give you Australian money. Enough to pay the tax. I will give you five Pounds every six months."

The islanders looked at each other to see if anyone understood what Thompson was telling them. No one did.

There was a general grumbling that went through the crowd that Thompson interpreted correctly. They had no intention of working on the coconut plantation. The assemblage began to break up. They had no intention of hearing any more of Big Man Tomsin's nonsense, and drifted away.

His first reaction on seeing that he was losing his audience was almost automatic — he fired the double-barreled 12-gauge into the air. As always, it got their attention.

"I have not finished talking, yet!" he screamed. "I have been appointed Governor of this island. You are all British subjects, and will follow the regulations I set down.

"I have six Policeboys who will make sure you obey the laws." He called them up to join him on the verandah. They were wearing their uniforms and were carrying their six-foot quarter-staves. But when he counted them, there were only five — he was one short. He saw that most of the tribesmen wore smiles. They knew something he did not, but it seemed best not to call attention to the missing Policeboy.

Thompson pointed to one of his copra drying buildings, and said, "That is the calaboose. Anyone who does not report to work on the plantation and collect coconuts or do what I tell him will be held inside that copra shed in the dark. He will stay there until he decides to cooperate."

More islanders were beginning to go back to the jungle, and Yani decided that it was time for him to leave as well. Thompson picked three men to start work immediately. Again, waving his shotgun in the air, he said, "I will select the rest of the workmen as they are needed. We have to husk the coconuts already in the shed starting now."

Everyone knew that it was a particularly arduous and difficult process. No one wanted to do it. To say that the mood of the men was ugly, would be a gross understatement.

Yani found McDuff still asleep, and he dismissed the girl. Placing his hand on the minister's head, he closed his eyes and whispered the word formula Ooma had taught him to undo fever spells. *It is* simka *of Tomsin's doing that gives him hot skin,* Yani thought as he touched the sick man. *The Witman's pills are OK if Big Man Duff's magic calls for them. But I think the old way is better in this case. The Witman doesn't know anything about spells, and the work of* bis. *Tomsin is a strong* bis*, but I am stronger.*

The young shaman kept his eyes closed, and visualized McDuff active and working in his usual manner. He held on to this thought until the patient awoke 15 minutes later.

Dr. McDuff lay on the palm leaves, his clothes soaked in perspiration; a piece of wet gingham cloth across his forehead. His eyes opened and he gazed up at the stained glass window. He recited a series of prayers focused on helping him recover his health. He asked to be shown the way he could fulfill his mission. As he prayed, the noise from the village began as a low murmur, but grew steadily in volume as more of the men picked up the chant. Yani had heard it from its beginning, and McDuff noticed that the churchboy was acting strangely. He had placed a number of tinkens in a box, along with the Bible and "*A Missionary in the New Hebrides*"

"What are you doing, Yani?" the bleary-eyed American asked, pointing feebly with his shaking hand at the box. "Why are you putting my books in the box?"

The young man filled a large, hollow gourd from their rainwater cistern, and stuck a makeshift cork of palmwood into the neck. "You sleep. Yani tell you when time wake up," he said in his best English. He did not want to risk being misunderstood. "I go now. Come back soon. You sleep." And with that, he slipped into the jungle carrying the box and gourd.

"Come back!" McDuff called after him. "It's time for my quinine pills. I can't reach them myself..." But Yani was gone.

He slowly rolled over, and fell off the pile of palm leaves onto the floor, winding up on his stomach. From this position he was able to work his way into a kneeling position, and finally stood up shakily by holding on to the altar. He misjudged his sure-footedness, and his knees gave out from under him. He grabbed at the altar-cloth as he went down and caused the stained glass window to pitch forward. He sat down hard on the ground, and was quickly crowned by the falling window.

The broad surface of the window crashed down on the malaria-weakened man and shattered on impact, covering him with dozens of razor-sharp shards of colored glass. He was struck on top of his head by the heavy metal frame of the window, which rendered him unconscious almost at once. His head went

When John Frum Came

through the leaded glass joints and he received numerous scalp wounds that bled profusely. He fell against the altar in a sitting position and the window frame hung around his shoulders like a huge necklace.

McDuff had not been unconscious for more than ten minutes when four of the tribal elders crept up on the church clearing, weapons in hand. They all wore oversized *nambas* or penis gourds. The men wondered at the silence in the little compound. The Witman was known to talk almost incessantly, and Yani was also unusually verbal for an islander. On a signal from the head man, they all sprang to their feet and ran into the back end of the church swinging their recently acquired machetes.

The churchfella, Big Man Duff, was not stretched out on the floor, sick and delirious as the woman had told them. Instead he was sitting at the front of the church, facing them. His head and face were a bloody mess, protruding through the window, and was not moving.

The lead man raised his hand and signaled the others to stop where they were. He looked for a long moment, then shared his assessment of the situation. "Yani has already killed the Witman. But he had a strong spirit. If we go near him now, he can still make powerful *simka* against us. Leave the way we came in. Don't touch him." Slowly the four men backed out of the crude building, and hastened back to the village.

Yani did not take the pathway back to the church. He moved carefully from tree to tree, not revealing himself in case anyone was watching. Suddenly, he saw the four elders returning from the direction of the church, and he feared he was too late. Once they were out of sight, he hurried through the bush.

He found McDuff just as the natives had, but ran right to him. Seeing that the missionary was still alive and breathing, he carefully lifted the splintered window off the injured minister and threw the frame to the side. The jewel-like shrapnel lay strewn around the foot of the altar, so Yani lifted McDuff up and out of the danger zone.

He laid him back on the palm leaf bed and poured water on the man's head. The cool liquid revived him and he reached instinctively for his nose to keep the water from entering. He coughed and slowly opened his eyes. Fortunately, there was no glass around his eyes, but his face and scalp had numerous slits and cuts.

"Blackfella do this?" Yani asked him.

"Do what?" McDuff said, knowing that something had happened, but really having no idea what. He looked at the hand he had just touched his nose with. It was covered with blood. "What the …!

"What happened? How did I get this blood on my hand?" Then he became aware of the pain and discomfort on the top of his head and around his ears. When he reached up he gathered a new collection of blood on his fingers."

"Blackfella do this?" Yani asked again. "I see them run through jungle. I think maybe they kill you. I find Jesus hit you on head." He pointed to the ruined picture of the Ascension.

McDuff touched his hair and felt the tiny glass particles. It took a few minutes to compose himself. "I think I know what happened. I fell against the altar and the picture fell on top of me. What a shame it's ruined. We'll never be able to repair it," he lamented.

He tried to sit up with little success. Yani helped him. "Night time come quick," Yani said. "We hide in jungle now. We go down beach. No moon this night time."

"What on earth are you talking about, Yani?" the pandanus leaf walls of the church seemed to swirl around him. "Why do we want to hide in the jungle?"

"Blackfella kill Witman. Kill Tomsin. Kill Big Man Duff. Wait for Japfella come. Japfella Blackfella friend. They bring tinken, guns for Blackfella. Kill Witmen," Yani rattled off quickly. "Percy say so."

"You say they're going to kill Thompson? We've got to warn him. We've got to get down to the Big House."

"Yani think you head-sick. Yani put tinken, water, books in Captain West boat. Night time we go boat. We go Yani's island. See Ooma."

Those were the last words Dr. Moses McDuff heard within the confines of the Church of God's Triumph. He had passed out again. Yani draped him over his shoulders and carried him into the bush. He headed toward the strand, and hid his patient among the palm trees while he waited for the right time to race out onto the pier.

A bright light caught his eye at the other end of the lagoon. The Big House had just started to burn. It grew in intensity, and finally took on magnificent proportions when the drums of petrol for the generator blew. The natives were in a frenzy of joy at their liberation.

　　The island had again lived up to its reputation among white men as Christ's Despair. Yani took advantage of the blazing distraction, and carried McDuff out on the pier. He safely placed him on the deck of the *Salvation,* untied the moorings, and quietly put to sea.

Chapter 17

As dawn broke, the mists surrounding Christ's Despair began to dissipate. Wembly was on the *Wombat's* deck early and saw that there was a pall of smoke hanging over the lagoon. As Gale joined him he said, "Uh, oh. I think Jeremy's had some trouble."

He reached into the wheelhouse and picked up his binoculars. Scanning the shoreline, he said, "Stop the engines!" He handed the glasses to Gale and said, "look two fingers right of the pier on the water line."

Mr. Gale did as he was told. "Oh, my God," he said, and lowered the binoculars. "I guess we better not go ashore." Wembly focused the glasses again. He counted the heads of the six Policeboys, and that of Thompson. Five of the Policeboys' heads were mounted atop their quarter-staves. The sixth seemed to be on one of the truncheons broken in half. Thompson's head was at the end of a mangrove stick generally used for shucking coconuts.

They heard a muffled blast of a shotgun. On the pier stood one of the natives with Thompson's 12-gauge. He fired the second barrel, but the Wombat was well out of range. It was followed by more shots from two of the plantation manager's 30.06 hunting rifles. They were not out of range of those.

Wembly mounted the gun turret and turned it toward the pier. The chatter of the four .50 caliber machine guns was earsplitting, but the result was devastating. The shooters on the pier were virtually blown into the water by the wall of lead that engulfed them. After a couple minutes of raking the beach, Wembly stepped back down onto the deck.

"I had been waiting for an opportunity to try that thing out," he said on an ironic note. "I don't think we need to go any further than this into the lagoon."

Hearing the noise, Percy came on deck to find out what was happening. He picked up the binoculars and surveyed the scene without revealing his distress.

"The *Salvation* is missing," Gale said with a hopeful note in his voice. "Maybe Dr. McDuff got away." He scanned the horizon. "The question is which way did he go? He was pretty sick. He can't do much by himself with a boat that size."

"Well, we came from the west and we didn't pass him to our knowledge," Wembly suggested. "Although we might not have seen him in the dark."

Percy pointed toward the sun rising in the east. "They go that way. Chase Island that way — Yani's home."

"He's probably right," Gale agreed. "Due east. He'll sight on the sun. I think we better start looking for him."

***

Dawn found the *Salvation*'s prow lined up with the sun. Yani had a kind of built-in dead reckoning that told him which way was north. The cloud cover had obscured the stars, so the Chase Islander just followed his instincts. If they had sailed five days toward the sunset to get to Christ's Despair, then sailing five days toward the sunrise would seem to be the thing to do. His destination was home, and with him was a prize of sorts — Big Man Duff. He would make him comfortable on the island, and then persuade him to use his magic to have God deliver tinkens and tools. If he could do it on Christ's Despair, there was no reason to think it would not be just as easy on Chase Island.

Ooma would be proud of him. He had not brought Kilibob back home, but he had done the next best thing. He would be bringing someone who "knew" how to get Kilibob's gifts.

McDuff began to stir as the light of day became stronger. He opened his eyes and became quickly aware of where he was. The boat's only remaining sail was billowing and the yawl was moving at a fair clip. His fever had abated somewhat and he lifted himself up on one elbow. "How did we get here?" he called to Yani who was holding the tiller on a straight course.

The young man smiled broadly and answered, "You much sick. Thompson make strong *simka*. Try kill you. Yani's magic stronger. Pastor McDuff sleep ... I carry him on boat. Him sleep all night."

"What happened to Thompson? Did he get away?"

A serious expression crossed Yani's face. "Big House — big fire. I think Big Man Tomsin he cook."

The minister chose not to pursue the matter further. His imagination was sufficient. He leaned back, and shielded his eyes from the sun. "Where are we going? Do you know where we are?"

"We go my island. Witman call Chase Island. We stay there. Yani tell Ooma you my Big Man churchfella. You friend Blackfella."

Well, McDuff thought, it sounds more congenial than Christ's Despair. Any change would have to be an improvement. If the people are all like Yani, my chances of success sound an awful lot better.

The gourd full of water was within reach, and he took a long swallow from it. He was weak as a kitten. He propped himself up against the gunnel and took a drink of a different kind. This time it was the beauty of the scintillating blue water. Deep down he felt a wish to be free of his missionary vows, and have nothing to do but enjoy the splendor God had created in this part of the world.

His eye caught something moving swiftly through the water from the direction of the sun. "What is that, Yani. A sailfish? A shark maybe?" he asked.

Yani strained his eyes. "Him no fish," he said. He made a motion with his hands indicating that it was moving too fast.

To McDuff's second look, it appeared to be a strangely shaped motorboat. It was heading straight in their direction, and closing fast. *Thank God, we're saved*, he thought.

As the boat drew near, all too quickly the rest of the behemoth broke the surface 100 feet in front of them. It was like no fish Yani had ever seen. It had no scales, no fins, no eyes. It was metal. It was a Japanese submarine.

Yani's eyes almost bulged out when he saw the top of the conning tower open and three men emerge. To him this was a huge fish which had swallowed men, and they were now escaping. However, he was too astonished to do anything but look. McDuff was terrified. He guessed quickly what the encounter meant ... It meant that they were *not* going to reach Chase Island, and would be lucky to live through it.

Two sailors clambered down the outside ladder and ran forward to the single gun that was mounted on the sub's narrow deck. They removed the sea plug from the barrel, and loaded a shell one was carrying into the breech. The Japanese officer gave them some brisk commands, and the weapon was pointed at the sailboat.

McDuff drew on all the strength he could muster and rose to his feet. He staggered forward to the mast and yelled, "Ahoy, on the submarine. We are Americans. We are Americans."

The officer in the conning tower brought his right hand down sharply and shouted something unintelligible. Yani and McDuff heard an ear-shattering blast. The starboard bow of their boat disappeared in an eruption of wood and metal fragments, knocking both men to the deck.

The sailors, deck gun, and submarine were all new, making this the first time the gun had been fired at sea. The shell hit the boat, but not where it was supposed to hit. Water rushed in and the *Salvation* began to capsize. Before they had a chance to fully understand what was happening, the minister found himself and his churchboy submersed in the exquisite aqua-colored water of the South Pacific he had been admiring only minutes before.

***

The *Wombat* was heading east at flank speed. At most, the Salvation had a five- or six-hour lead on them. Diesel engines would eat up the sail-powered time and distance pretty quickly if they were going in the right direction.

Percy was perched on the forward railing, scanning the horizon, which might be a little more than two miles viewed from sea level. Suddenly he heard a noise that came from a point out of sight, but definitely straight ahead. "Mr. Wembly," he called, "You hear? Big noise." He pointed eastward.

Wembly turned his binoculars toward the direction Percy was pointing. "I think I see something, but I can't make it out." The former yacht was going as fast as it could, and the distance to the apparent horizon was closing fast.

Wembly almost did a double take when the image took shape in his glasses. "I think it's a submarine!" he called to Gale. "Most likely a Jap sub. H.Q. was right; they are operating in these waters, the bloody bastards. I think the *Salvation* has rolled over."

"I'll fire the quad-50. That'll get their attention," Gale said in a fit of excitement.

Before Wembly could remind him that they were not equipped to take on the Japanese Navy, the junior officer was firing volleys of six rounds in the direction of the submarine.

The Japanese officer in the conning tower heard the shooting, and saw the silhouette of the patrol boat. Thinking it was an Australian torpedo boat, he ordered his men back inside. They scrambled back up the ladder and into the vessel. They submerged as quickly as possible, and were out of sight in a matter of minutes.

The *Wombat* found Yani and McDuff clutching the hull of the yawl, which had gone belly up but still had air trapped inside. Percy jumped overboard and swam to the aid of Yani, who was trying to keep something from sinking. It turned out to be the wooden box of tinkens and the missionary's books. He held his sunglasses in his teeth, and refused to let go until Mr. Gale reached down and took the box from his hands.

"You take magic books," Yani called.

Yani climbed up a rope ladder dropped over the side and Percy towed McDuff away from the sinking sailboat. Between the Patrol Officer and the Policeboy they managed to get the white man onto the deck. Nearly unconscious, both from the exhausting experience and the malaria, he was lifted onto a blanket and carried to a bunk in one of the converted staterooms.

When John Frum Came

"Did you see the number of cuts poor McDuff had around his face and ears? The natives must have tortured the hell out of him," Gale said to Wembly. "I've never seen anything like it."

"Neither have I. It's not the sort of thing they do. But Christ's Despair has always earned its name," Wembly said. Then he turned to the two black men who were sitting on the deck talking in their own dialect. "Percy, ask him what happened back there."

Yani was still too excited to talk anything but his native language, and related the story to Percy, who in turn told the Patrol Officers in simplified English. He let the older man explain what happened to Thompson, but Yani tried to describe what happened to McDuff on his own.

Forgetting Percy's admonition about speaking English again. Performing many of the actions, he said, "Jesus in Heaven come down from altar. Make Big Man Duff bloody — look like dead. *Kanakas* come see him. They afraid him have too much *simka*. They go home.

"Yani come. See pastor. Take him boat. Go back Chase Island. See big tinken fish. You come."

"But how did he get all those cuts on his head?" Gale persisted, making lines on his own face with his fingers. "Jesus cut head. Cut ears. Yani throw Jesus away. Save Big Man Duff," he smiled.

Percy shrugged. "Forget it for now," Wembly said. "You speak English pretty well for a Blackfella, Yani."

Yani gave Negeb a guilty look. He wondered if he would now get the beating he was led to believe would follow.

"How would you like to go to Australia with Percy and some other boys? We'll give you some new clothes, shoes and teach you how to be a Policeboy."

Wembly was doing fine with his enticements, until Yani remembered how much the natives disliked Thompson's Policeboys. Negeb had told him how they wound up on the beach. It was not a very pleasant prospect, as far as Yani was concerned.

"This is different," Negeb reassured him in his own tongue. "The Policeboys on the island are the first ones I ever lost. That was because they put the evil Witman in charge. I will go with you to Brisbane."

"After you finish, we'll send you back to Chase Island. You like that?" Wembly promised.

Negeb reinforced the words in their own language just in case Yani did not fully understand the English.

"Yani go," he said. "You send Big Man Duff, too?"

"Big Man Duff very sick. We take him to Port Moresby until he is better. I don't know what he will do now. There's a war on, and he's not British. I'm afraid he'll be going back to America."

Yani was disappointed. He had really hoped to take McDuff back to Ooma as a gift.

Chapter 18

When McDuff came to, he realized that he was on board a ship and was lying between clean white sheets for the first time in six months. All his clothing had been removed and he had been bathed. The first word that came to mind to describe the bed was "delicious." He had not realized how much he longed for the finer points of civilization. It was just about sunset, but in the gloom he could make out the figure of Mr. Gale sitting next to his bed.

"Ah, you're back with us," Gale said. "I think you better catch up on your Quinine, old boy. I was afraid to give you anything while you were unconscious for fear you'd choke."

"Thank you, Mr. Gale," he lifted his head from the pillow to accept the pills and the water glass. He gathered his thoughts and asked, "Why do you think they did it?"

"Who knows how these natives think? I guess they just got fed up with Thompson's ways. The Head Tax must have been what pushed them over the edge."

"You're right there, but I was talking about the Japanese. I tried to tell the officer on the submarine that I was an American. I'm sure I said it several times, but they just fired at us point blank. He didn't even ask us to surrender."

"First off, he most likely didn't speak English. Then, my guess is they figured you had seen them, and would report their presence. The only way they could be sure you wouldn't alert us was to blow you out of the water. You're just lucky we were hot on your trail, or they would have finished the job."

McDuff's teeth began to chatter. "Could I trouble you for a blanket. When the chills hit, I feel like I have fallen in the snow on the slope of some ski lodge. I went to Switzerland when I was sixteen. I think that's what I keep dreaming about."

Gale unfolded a blanket over the bed. "I went to school in England, but I never got anywhere on the continent beyond Paris. Some great times there," Gale mused. "Marvelous place. I hope to get back there someday. So open. So free. Much more tolerant."

"I have no desire to go anywhere, now. I botched things up pretty badly here. I don't think my family will finance another attempt at missionary work," McDuff said in disgust.

Gale bit his lip thoughtfully, then said, "I don't mean to pry, Reverend, but why would an American, a man of means, ever want to come to these islands — other than as a tourist?"

McDuff was silent, evaluating how honest he should be with this man. He made his decision. "I perceive you to be a man who would understand my problem," he said, curling up in the blanket. "I chose the ministry because it seemed to be the most genteel way for me to go through life, without the usual hounding and harassment of one's family to marry and settle down. I didn't have the interests in the sports and pastimes my older brothers demonstrated.

"I expressed a desire to devote my life to the service of the Lord, and even volunteered to come here as soon as I received my Doctorate. However, the missionary board did not think I was suited for the life, and recommended me to work on a domestic project. They were determined to convert newly arrived Irish Catholic immigrants in Boston."

Gale laughed. "I can see where they could use some converting. We have a bunch of them in Sydney, too."

"Well, at least I didn't have the language problem I have here. They spoke a semblance of English if you listened really close," the minister joked. He hesitated, but then went on. "The problem was I fell in love with one of the students in my Bible class. I mean I was hopelessly in love, and it became clear the emotion was returned."

Gale smiled knowingly. "And your family didn't approve of you wanting to marry a Catholic girl, right?" he suggested, "And one beneath your station, as well."

McDuff did not answer right away, "No, Mr. Gale. Not exactly right, but close enough."

Gale did not respond.

"The Catholic priest in the neighborhood heard about it when my lover went to confession."

"What? I thought that was strictly confidential — a secret between the priest and the penitent."

"It is, but he found a way to get the message to my father, and to the President of my seminary. My father cursed me soundly, and disowned me. The head of the seminary agreed that the only way I could expiate my sin was to take the worst mission he could find."

"Well, I'd have to agree you did that. No sane British missionary would take Christ's Despair."

"My father gave me a cash settlement on the grounds that I never return to the U.S., and made an arrangement with the church in which he would pay all my expenses to get me established here."

"Well, you can be thankful for that," Gale said. "He might have just tossed you out on your ear."

The chill passed, and the fever returned. In an effort to cool off, McDuff threw back the blanket in response. "So there you have it, Mr. Gale. The shame of Moses McDuff. I truly have nowhere to go."

Mr. Gale leaned toward the bed and said, "I want you to know that I am your friend. Mr. Gale is so formal. I'd be pleased if you would call me Leslie." With that he placed his cool hand on the fevered skin of Moses McDuff's thigh.

***

Yani was not comfortable on a bunk, so Negeb had strung a hammock for him on deck. The two Chase Islanders talked for a long time about Yani's probable trip to Australia. Negeb told Yani he could learn much to help John

Frum. Finally, Yani got bored and fell asleep. He did not stir until the following morning.

"Mr. Wembly wants to talk to you," Negeb said waking him gently. "He will meet us in Dr. McDuff's bedroom. The churchfella is still too sick to go up on deck."

They found the door to McDuff's stateroom open, and the Patrol Officers already seated around the minister's bed. "Good morning, Yani," McDuff said. "I'm so glad you're all right. I want to thank you for saving my life — several times it would seem."

"Good morning, Pastor McDuff," Yani said with genuine happiness. "The Lord be with you," he added as he had been taught.

McDuff beamed at the greeting. It showed the other white men in the room that he had been successful in converting at least one native. "I especially want to thank you for saving my Bible and my missionary book. I heard how you held on to them when the boat was sinking."

"Yani save God's tinkens, too," he added.

"Yes, and the tinkens, too. But, I want to give you this cross as thank you."

McDuff gave him the mahogany cross he had been wearing around his neck since his arrival in the islands. Yani slipped the leather cord over his head and clutched it tightly. He could feel its magic sink into his heart.

Wembly spoke. "Pardon me, doctor, but do you feel up to talking about how you got those cuts all over your head? What did the natives do to you? They must have been brutal."

"The natives didn't do anything to me. It was an accident," he said. "A stained-glass window of the *Ascension of Christ* fell on me from the altar, and knocked me out. It was really a providence that I was not more seriously injured."

"Yani said that Jesus came down from Heaven and cut your head and ears. We didn't know what to make of it," Mr. Wembly said. "I think it might do us all some good if we taught him to speak English a little better."

"I thought the policy of the government was to discourage that very thing," McDuff said. "Why the change?"

"It seems the standard answer for just about everything these days is 'because we are at war.' But in this case it is a direct cause. We have a plan and a proposition for you Dr. McDuff. Mr. Gale tells me that you do not wish to return to the United States at this time..."

The minister's eyes flashed to Gale's face. *What else did he tell you*, he wondered. Gale's expression indicated that their little secret was safe.

"Missionaries and planters on all the British-protected islands are being asked to cooperate with us in starting a vital program. That Jap sub you ran into is a good example of what we fear. I've reported your run-in with the sub, and I have received a great deal more information on the subject. We have reason to believe that there are a number of Japanese ships and small tactical forces sprinkled throughout the islands. Little by little they will be taking over strategic islands they can use as bases of operations in preparation for an invasion of New Guinea, New Zealand, and Australia."

Dr. McDuff interrupted. "I no longer have a mission, Mr. Wembly, as you well know. Even if I did, what could someone like me do against the Japanese Navy? It's a bit out of my line don't you think? We're non-combatants. I think the Japanese will respect our religious positions."

"Not so, Dr. McDuff. Missionaries in Indo-China, Shanghai, and Singapore were among the first foreigners to be imprisoned. In many cases they were simply shot on the spot. The Japanese are not very fond of Christians. We are religious enemies to their way of thinking. As with the submarine commander, your chances of explaining that you are an American are not very good. Just because they are not at war with your country at the moment, don't discount the possibility that things couldn't change."

"But I still can't see what I can do."

"We propose to make you and Yani a team. We want you to be Coast Watchers," the Patrol Officer said.

Negeb had been whispering a running translation of the conversation into Yani's ear, just in case he did not follow it on his own.

"Coast watchers?" McDuff said.

"When we get back to Port Moresby we will put you in Hospital until you have recovered from your malaria. As soon as you are up to it, we will teach you a number of things. Primary among them will be the operation of a two-way wireless. The other part of your training will be provided by the Royal Navy, who will teach you how to identify the silhouettes of ships and aircraft — what's theirs, and what's ours.

"Yani, in the meantime, will be sent to Brisbane for some military training and English language instruction. He will take a sort of basic training for a few weeks. Actually, it will be training in our ways since he already knows how to be a warrior by virtue of the fact that he grew up on a jungle island. Percy, here, will be in charge of taking him and a few other island boys through their paces."

In spite of himself, McDuff was interested. "Then what?" he asked.

"We will take you and Yani to Chase Island ... Which is where you were headed when we found you ... and you will set up a camp on the side of the volcano there. It will allow you to have a commanding view of the sea for miles around. When you see a ship or an airplane, you'll send us a message over the wireless telling what it is, and where it's going. That's all there is to it."

McDuff laughed slightly, with an ironic note. "You're recruiting me into your armed services. That's quite a career jump — preacher to soldier."

Wembly lit his pipe and said, "We can't make you do it. Are you interested?"

"What's my alternative, if I don't accept your proposal?"

"You hang around Port Moresby until you decide to seek your fortune elsewhere," Wembly told him.

The minister addressed Yani. "What do you say? Do you want to learn the white man's ways? Do you want to go to Brisbane? Do you want to go back to Chase Island with me and work for the Patrol?"

Negeb made sure Yani understood his options. "Yes. Yani go Brisbane. Be Policeboy on Chase Island. Only if Big Man Duff come, too."

McDuff reached out his hand to Yani to seal the bargain. "We'll do it, Mr. Wembly. We'll be Coast Watchers," the erstwhile clergyman agreed.

Yani shook his hand and thought, *Now I'm sure Kilibob is on this boat and we will make Ooma very happy.*

Chapter 19

"I can't believe it, either," the High Commissioner said, picking up one of the telegrams on his desk. "But there's no doubt. The message says it was *The Fenestra*. A German raider steamed alongside her, looking to all the world like a Dutch freighter. Then they uncovered the guns on the deck and let the poor *Fenestra* have it broadside at the water line. They didn't even pick up survivors."

"How many men made it?" Wembly asked.

"About a dozen. One of our cruisers picked them up the next day. Sharks tore hell out of them though," the official said.

"How about my friend, Jake Vogel, the purser? Did he make it?"

"He was one of the lucky ones. At least I saw his name on the list of survivors. I don't know what condition he was in, though."

Wembly began pacing the office. "You know, your Lordship, that we were planning to send our native boys to Brisbane on the *Fenestra*. We need to get the Coast Watcher program running as soon as possible to prevent just such mishaps as this. The sailboat belonging to that American missionary we brought in the other day was sunk by a Jap sub. We need some way of knowing when they're around, besides following the trail of devastation they apparently plan to leave."

"We don't have any other ships going to Brisbane for the next few weeks, so far as I know. What else do you suggest?" asked the official.

"You know, the Americans owe us one since I saved one of their people from certain death," Wembly smirked.

"What are you getting at, Wembly?"

"Have you seen that big flying boat they have moored next to the Navy yard? I think they call it a PBY. I wonder if we could persuade them to take a flight to Australia."

The High Commissioner laughed. "You show me a sailor who has spent a week in Port Moresby who isn't ready to take a trip to the mainland. I've been entertaining their Commander. His orders are to just sit tight until some more of the U.S. Navy catches up with him. We could offer to pay for the petrol, if that's a problem."

"I'm willing to bet they will jump at the chance to spend a week in Australia. Let's give it a try," Wembly declared confidently.

Yani was living with Percy in a hut in the native community adjacent to the official buildings. Percy had a wife and three children in a building that was, like the man himself, halfway between the two cultures. He had a table and chairs. On it was a calico tablecloth, and a wine bottle with flowers stuck in the neck. The Vailala Madness was not wasted on him. He had acquired the very things many of the natives identified as "living like the Witman."

Nevertheless, Mrs. Percy, as she was known to the residents of the neighboring white enclave, still kept a taro garden, and had two pigs. She knew a number of English words and was highly prized as a housekeeper for the High Commissioner.

The Percys were the social lions of the native community.

Yani enjoyed all of this. He displayed his shaman tattoo the first few days, so everyone knew he was not a *kanaka* they brought back from one of the islands. He wore a Policeboy uniform, and carried a homemade baton, similar to the ones British Officers were seen carrying. He learned quickly.

The other four native boys were not so well respected. They were boarded out with working class black families. They spoke a variety of dialects — none of which were understood by the local people. Fortunately, they all spoke Pidgin, which was the reason they had been selected for their new jobs. It was also the language they used to communicate with each other.

When John Frum Came

The English Lieutenant in charge of the Coast Watcher's Program assembled the black half of the future teams on the steps of the Government Office Building. He made an eloquent speech, telling them about the war with Japan, and how they would each be paired off with a white man. Said white men were being trained in the use of two-way radios as he spoke, and would be ready to take on their new duties in a few weeks. In the meantime the black men would be sent to Brisbane for a week of special military training and enhancement of their language skills. He told them he had complete faith in their ability to perform their duties as subjects of the British Empire. He assured them that their behavior was consistent with the oath of "One king, one cause, one flag" in the prosecution of the war against the Axis.

When he finished, Percy snapped to attention in full British military style, and had his new troops do as close an imitation as possible. The Training Officer saluted and returned to his office in the building. Not wanting to spoil the noble moment, he chose not to inform the Lieutenant that since he spoke in English, his men did not understand a word of it.

Once back in the native quarter, Percy told the boys, "We are going to Brisbane today. Bring all the clothes and other things you own with you."

For the most part, the boys were wearing everything they owned, and had the rest of their worldly goods in kit bags Percy had gotten from the Army depot. They were left from World War I and were in rough shape. This made no difference to the boys who had never owned any kind of manufactured item, besides their ever-present knives.

"The boat we were supposed to take to Australia has been sunk by the Japanese," Percy told them in Pidgin. "We will fly there in the belly of a big bird." Since none of them had ever seen an airplane, and Percy had never been in one, he had no words to describe the event in any other manner.

"How do we keep from dying inside the bird?" one of the boys asked. "We will be bird shit when we get out!" he cried, since he was quite familiar with the natural processes of life.

"I think we will be safely inside an egg," suggested Yani.

They all breathed a sigh of relief. That made more sense. There was no point in sending them to Australia if they would be dead when they got there.

Everyone was delighted when they were loaded into the back of an open government lorry for the ride down to the plane. This, too, was a first for most of them.

"There is no end to the gifts Kilibob made to the white man," Yani said to Percy. "We can have all this, if we can get Kilibob to return."

Percy was puzzled by the remark, and then realized that all things mechanical were virtually unknown to Yani and these boys. How would he ever be able to explain any of it to them? The answer was simple — he couldn't possibly. He barely understood it himself. The best he could do was teach the boys to pretend to understand what was going on. No one could figure out the mind of the Witman.

Even Percy was frightened when the lorry pulled up on the wharf next to the huge U.S. Navy PBY seaplane. It bobbed on the choppy water like an albatross with immense wings extended. A gangway had been connected to make it easy to board — except none of the natives wanted to be the first to cross the little bridge.

On an impulse, Yani bounded across the gangway, and into the passenger cabin. He felt the floor of the plane bob like the deck of a boat and looked at the rounded interior of the fuselage. He went back to the entrance and said, "It is an egg, just like I said it would be."

Percy cautiously came across and told the others to follow. Finally they were all inside the "egg." An American petty officer made them sit down and secured each of them with a seatbelt. "No walking around until we are airborne," he said. No one made a move to do anything. There was a glint of terror in each man's eye, as the hatch was slammed shut. When the engines were cranked and then roared to life two of the boys peed in their new Policeboy khaki shorts.

Yani had a seat next to the window. Percy sat on the other side of the plane. The plane skimmed across the water like a hydroplane, feeling the thump of each wavelet. Then suddenly it was smooth and airborne, and entering into a steeper angle of ascent.

Yani could see the small harbor at Port Moresby getting further and further behind them. This was like being on the volcano's rim at Christ's Despair without having to make the long climb up the side. When the plane banked, he could see much of the mountain range that backed up the island port.

The plane leveled out and then began a gradual climb. He could see them approaching the strato-cumulus clouds just above them as they neared 5,000 feet. His heart quickened as they entered the fluffy clouds and there was a complete white out on the windows. He waited for what he knew must come, and within ten minutes it happened — they broke through the top of the cloud bank and he was looking at the bright sunlight reflecting of the tops of the clouds beneath him.

The rays of the sun took a myriad of shapes as they sailed through wispy cloud formations. He strained his eyes and scanned the immense horizon, even looking out the windows on the other side of the plane. Yani wished Big Man Duff were here with him now. If the pastor were with him, Jesus would surely reveal himself. There was no doubt about it. It was just like the stained glass picture back at the church. Yani and his friends were now on their way to Heaven.

Chapter 20

A few hours later, the PBY circled an airfield, and spotted the prepared landing place on the water near the Navy installation.

During quiet moments back on the island, Yani and McDuff had had many discussions about Heaven. Now below him lay the City of God that the missionary had talked about. It was grander than anything Yani could have imagined. Port Moresby was the first Witman town he had seen, and this exceeded that by far. His heart throbbed wildly.

When they had landed and the "egg" was opened again, the boys were anxious to get out. They did not necessarily share Yani's passion for this trip. No one had ever promised any of them that they would go to Heaven, so the idea was more foreign than exciting.

They were met by one of the strangest sights any of them, including Percy, had ever seen. In addition to the usual military officers, whom they accepted as normal, there stood a black man whose facial features were clearly Papuan, but his hair was cut short and he wore a white shirt and a tie like an Englishman.

There was complete silence among the black islanders as they walked in a circle around the Papuan looking him over from head to toe. He wore khaki shorts, which were ironed, knee socks, and shoes. Even the American Navy Commander had to look twice. He had seen Negroes in "Sunday-go-to-meetin'" clothes in his native South Carolina, but a South Sea Islander in such an outfit took him by surprise.

When John Frum Came

The Papuan introduced himself. "How do you do. Commander Henry, I presume." He offered his hand to shake, which Henry reached for hesitantly. "I'm Reggie, the Indigenous Liaison Officer."

"How do you do," Henry said cautiously.

"I can see you're surprised. That's the usual reaction I get from both Blackfellas and white men alike."

"Well, you're the first colored fella I've seen here who speaks English ... and dresses like a white man," Henry confessed.

Accustomed to explaining the situation, he said, "I was taken in by the wife of the former Governor General of the Island Territories when my real mother died in childbirth. I was raised and tutored with her own child while they lived in the islands. When they moved back to Australia, she refused to leave me behind and I have lived here ever since."

"You must be worth your weight in gold in dealing with the natives since you speak English so well."

"Would that it were so, Mr. Henry. I can hardly speak any of the native dialects, and have to get by in Pidgin like anyone else."

"Well, here are the boys I promised to deliver. My crew and I are ready to go into town as soon as our plane is secured. I'll be back in a week to fly them back to Port Moresby. Meanwhile, they're all yours."

Reggie looked over his charges and said to the man in the Policeboy uniform, "You must be Percy. I'm Reggie. I will be in charge of your group while you are here."

"I am pleased to meet you," Percy said, showing off his own knowledge of English. "I am the head Policeboy in Port Moresby, and these are my boys."

"You speak English very well," Reggie said. "Where did you learn?"

"From the Patrol Officers," he said. "Yani, here, speaks some English also. He learn from churchfella. Others speak Booga-booga. All speak Pidgin."

Reggie addressed the rest of the group in Pidgin from then on, and used English only to convey things to Percy he felt the boys did not need to know. "We are at war with Japan. Do not believe that the Japanese are friends of the Blackfella. They will kill you as easily as they will kill a Witman.

"You are going to be big men on your islands. You will work with a Witman who will watch for Japanese ships from the mountains on your islands.

"Does anyone know what wireless is? Radio?" he asked.

When Percy nodded his head, Reggie said, "Can you tell the boys what it is?"

Percy said, "Witman magic. He speak in box. Man in other box he speak too. We have on Patrol Boat — talk to Headquarters on other side of sun."

"Close enough," Reggie conceded. "The Witman will have box on your island. He will talk with other Witman on Patrol Boat. Say when he see Japfella boat."

"What Blackfella do?" Yani asked.

"Blackfella make sure Witman O.K. Get food. Water. Make sure island fellas friends of Witman. Not friends of Japfella. You go back to your island tell your Big Man that Witman help Blackfella after war."

Yani thought of how helpless he had been in protecting McDuff from the angry natives on Christ's Despair. *But this will be Chase Island. This is my island,* He thought. *I tell Ooma this churchfella, O.K.-fella.*

During the next few days Reggie took the boys to a section of the Army training grounds. He taught them how to fire a rifle and a pistol. With the help of Percy, he taught them to come to attention, and to march. They thought it was great sport and called each other to attention repeatedly just for fun. They would snap to, render a salute, and all would burst out laughing.

Yani was fascinated with Reggie. He had replaced Percy as his personal role model. Percy was dignified, but Reggie was elegant. He sought him out during spare moments and the man would talk with him in English.

Reggie warned him in much the same way Percy had. "You know, there are many Witmen who do not like Blackfellas to speak English. I am made fun of by many of them, but I have the protection of my white family. You do not. Be careful."

"I have a good reason to learn English," Yani told him one day. "My Big Man Duff knows all the Witman magic. He is churchfella. He teached me to say magic formulas — called prayers. But I learn Pidgin words. Not have the power his English words have. He made to happen very good things. He ask for knife — God send iron axes, knife ..." He was unable to remember the word for machete. He drew one in the air with his finger and made a hacking movement with his arm. "... chop knife."

"Oh, you mean a machete?" Reggie asked.

"Yes, machete." Then he added mournfully, "Blackfella on island use chop Big Man Tomsin head. We leave. Japfella try to kill us with tinken fish."

Eventually Reggie pieced together the story by consulting Percy. But Yani got around to his favorite topic: "Big Man Duff, he ask God for food — tinkens come. Tinkens come from Heaven."

Reggie laughed. "Tin cans are made right here in Brisbane. There is a canning factory only a mile from here. I'll take you there tomorrow. I want you to see where tinkens really come from. I want you to be better educated than the other people on your island." He laughed to himself as he left the trainees and went to the headquarters to make arrangements.

The next morning Reggie had the boys line up and march up the road to the cannery. He made arrangements with the man at the gate to allow them to walk around. Reggie had been there before and knew the factory.

According to the prevailing beliefs in the islands, people's spirits turned white when they died. This was one of the reasons many shamans covered themselves with ashes when doing certain rituals. The canning factory employed only white people to work on their manufacturing lines. Yani was pretty sure he had it all figured out, and explained it to the other boys. These hundreds of white people were ancestors who had died, turned white, and went to work for God in Heaven, doing what they were obviously doing — making tinkens for their people on the islands.

When they went into the tuna packing section they were processing several fish that were larger than any that had ever been trapped in the Chase Island lagoon. All the boys were duly impressed, as they watched a bandsaw slice the monster fish into workable sized pieces.

From a huge hopper thousands of cans rolled down an assembly line. Ah, they are coming from another part of Heaven where tinkens are made, Yani deduced. Since metal did not exist on his island, all things made of that material had to be made by God himself. He wished he could go watch God making them, but was satisfied to get this close.

When they reached the shipping department, everything was stuffed into wooden and cardboard boxes. Yani observed one of the men making certain marks on the boxes. He had a stencil and an ink brush. With this equipment the man placed the shipping addresses on the cartons. However, while he was there an error had been discovered, and while the first man went to lunch, his supervisor came through with a paint brush and painted out all the addresses on the boxes.

It was then that Yani's suspicions were confirmed. He saw the second man put new addresses on the boxes. He had seen it with his own eyes. The first man, an ancestor, addressed the cartons of tinkens to the Blackfellas on the islands. The second man came through and covered up those addresses and sent them to a Witman somewhere. All the tinkens that were rightfully the property of Chase Islanders were being diverted to somewhere else.

He toyed with the idea of raising the question with Reggie, but decided against it. It might get Reggie in trouble, and that would never do.

When they left the factory and were marching down the road back to the Army base, they passed a farm where a large number of animals were grazing along the road. Yani became animated. His excitement was unbounded. He broke ranks and ran over to the flock to touch one of them.

Reggie went over to him, and said, "What's the problem, Yani?"

Yani was grinning like a fool. He was almost jumping up and down, pointing at the animals. "Sheepy-sheep. Sheepy-sheep. Now I know I am in Heaven for sure. This is where God keeps his Sheepy-sheep."

***

On their last full day in Brisbane, Reggie took Percy and the native boys downtown to the business district of the city. The sights and sounds of the strange environment turned out to be more than they could handle. Along with automobiles, it was not uncommon for men in business suits to be found riding horses to work. On their home islands these strange, huge beasts were unknown and were thoroughly frightening to the young men. One of them thought that the man on horseback was one animal — a centaur of sorts. After less than two hours, most of the islanders were on the verge of a nervous breakdown — with the exception of Yani. He did not know when he would visit Heaven again, and chose to make the most of the opportunity.

Seeing the boys virtually huddling together as they moved from place to place, Reggie decided that the cultural shock was too great for them and started loading them into the open lorry that brought them.

Yani was disappointed. He was ready to spend the day in Brisbane, and told Reggie how he felt. "Yani in Heaven first time. Maybe not come again for long time. I not want to go back to Army house and sleep. I stay here."

"Well, I can't very well leave you alone in the city now, can I? There's no telling what would happen to you here. I could lose you anywhere and not have you ready to fly back to Port Moresby," he said.

Yani had been eyeing a large building. "Maybe we go in that place," he said pointing.

Reggie looked across the street. "That's the Queensland Natural History Museum," he said. Then, after a brief moment added, "Maybe you fellas would be happy in there, after all. They've got lots of things you're familiar with." He stopped the loading procedure and said, "Percy, let's take them into the Museum. I think you'll enjoy it, too."

Inside, Reggie got a real kick out of watching the boys approach the stuffed animals. They stalked a kangaroo that stood frozen in flight in a display at the center of a great hall. They approached slowly, surrounding it from three sides, and could not figure out why it did not flee when they were almost within tackling distance.

"He's dead," Reggie said in Pidgin. "Him spirit gone."

Percy reached out and touched the stiff animal. "He has turned to wood. He has no life. No meat. He feels like wood."

The others got up their nerve and also put their hands on the animal's rigid, lifeless body. "Him spirit gone," they agreed.

A glass display cases exhibited hundreds of shells that were common to the Coral Sea area of the South Pacific. Some of them had great value to their various tribes. In some cases, they agreed on their value, but each had a different name for the mollusk in question.

The boys were soon at ease, asking Reggie a hundred questions about what they saw. Whenever he could, he gave them an answer.

When the group entered the room with the sign that read, "Anthropology of the South Pacific Islands," they stopped as still and stiff as the kangaroo they saw when they entered the museum. In the center of the room was an oak-framed cabinet with plate glass windows on all sides. It was about 20 feet long, and 12 feet wide. It was crammed with mannequins of Pacific Islanders wearing all manner of tribal garments.

Some wore loincloths, some nambas, others had full body costumes made from jungle vegetation. They carried spears, bows and arrows, warclubs, and shields. Strewn about the ground where they did not belong were sacred musical instruments made from gourds, bamboo, and logs. There were flutes, bull roarers, drums and notched rhythm sticks.

Behind them were spirit figures carved out of single palm trees. There were full body masks. Every one of the black islanders had seen variations of virtually everything in the glass case back home. In most cases the items shown were sacred to the men's spirit house, brought out only during the initiation ceremonies or for other spiritual occasions.

Reggie walked right into the hall, but quickly became aware that he was alone. The entire group stood in the doorway transfixed. They were as frozen as the figures in the display. Their silence was stone-like. They barely breathed.

First they were not sure if the mannequins were real — or perhaps stuffed like the animals they saw earlier. Second, they all knew that the artifacts shown were sacred — if not to their tribes, certainly to somebody's. This was taboo. This room was overflowing with *simka*. A powerful *bis* had turned these Blackfellas into wood.

"Him spirit gone," Yani said to Percy, who nodded agreement. This was all new to him as well.

They edged backward toward the hall from which they had come. None of them would turn his back on the display. They would all dream of this event for the rest of their lives.

Once they reached the hall, they all broke into a run, with Reggie in hot pursuit, calling to them to stop. "Wait," he called, "I can explain."

They did not come to a halt until they reached the front room where they had entered. A number of the guards had joined them as they passed, not knowing what the excitement was all about. The museum guards, who did not know Reggie, were almost as surprised as the islanders when the Papuan spoke in clear English.

"Sorry about this, gentlemen," he said. "They were frightened by an exhibit in the Anthropology hall. Can any of you help me to explain what it was about?"

One somewhat leery guide said, "Those are all things that missionaries have brought back from the islands."

As he described the items, Reggie translated into Pidgin how churchfellas had brought the items back. The figures were not men turned to stone, but were very well carved figures of men.

Yani listened carefully. He did not believe anything the Witman said about the display. He saw it all as a missing piece of the puzzle. Witman churchfellas captured all the spirits on the islands and took them here. They are holding them prisoner in the glass cage. All the sacred spirit instruments are on the ground for all to see, and are now worthless. With all the Blackfella spirits kept in the glass cage, Jesus and the Witman God have all the power on the islands where the churchfellas build churches. Now he was sure he understood much about the source of McDuff's power.

As Reggie and Percy led the way out, they were so busy talking to the guides neither of them noticed that Yani was not among them. He had slipped away from the group and found his way back to the display of sacred instruments. The guide for that room was still seeing the rest of the group into the lorry out in front of the Museum. A few minutes later, Yani came running down the steps to get into the vehicle.

It was a full ten minutes before the guide for the anthropological exhibit discovered that someone had thrown his chair through the glass of the island display. He was angry beyond words, but did not realize that in an act of bravery and heroism Yani had set free the imprisoned spirits of his ancestors.

Chapter 21

A month had passed since Yani and Percy came back from Australia. The other boys were quickly paired up with their white partners in the Coast Watchers Program within a few days of their return to Port Moresby. However, Dr. McDuff was still recovering from his malaria, and the doctors thought it best to wait until his condition was closer to normal before he left the hospital. Leslie Gale came to visit him as often as his brief shore leaves would allow.

When he succumbed to the boredom, the minister pretended that he no longer had any symptoms, and he was given clearance to go to Chase Island. Whenever he was up to it, he sat in a white wicker chair in the Malaria Ward and studied his Morse code book, doing the exercises in the manual to sharpen his skills. Voice radio would not be used. It was felt that by varying the code, based on a different chapter of the Bible each day of the year, the Japanese could be kept confused. But, it precluded the native islanders from manning the equipment in an emergency if something happened to the white operator.

As soon as he passed the transmission and receiving tests given by the Admiralty, the former missionary and his churchboy were put aboard the *Wombat* with their necessary gear. With the *Fenestra* out of the picture, they had to limit the amount of baggage they could bring. They had to be more precise in their estimates of what they would need to survive beyond contact with Western Civilization. In the hospital, McDuff spent a lot of time with a couple "old hands" learning what could be eaten in the jungle once one overcame his initial squeamishness. The American surprised even himself in the mental turnabout he had accomplished. He was turning from priest to warrior and found that he warmed to the task. Now, actually looking forward to leaving his Boston existence behind, he began to think of himself as something like a South Seas version of Lawrence of Arabia.

The course for Chase Island was charted, and everyone settled down to a few days of skimming the seas, sharing a rotating watch for Japanese Navy vessels, especially submarines.

"I hear you caused some mischief while you were in Brisbane, Yani," Mr. Gale said to him the first morning out.

Yani looked to Percy. "Mischief?" he asked, seeking a translation. Although the last month had included intensive practice in speaking English, there were still quite a few words he had trouble with. Percy told him in their native language what the word meant.

Ignoring the original question, he said, "Yani like Heaven." He smiled. "I not expect to go there for long time. I be happy to go back again."

"Well, I have to agree. Brisbane is Heaven compared to Port Moresby. With luck I'll get assigned to the training command there myself. But if I were you, I wouldn't plan on going there again for a long time. The Government is not likely to pay for another trip in your lifetime."

"No problem," Yani said. "I go to Heaven with Big Man Duff when we die. He promise we visit God and sit on his hand."

The minister entered the cabin just as Yani was saying these mysterious words, so Gale deferred to him. "What have you promised your man, Moses? He seems to have some great expectations."

"I think he means that when he dies he will sit at the right hand of God, along with Jesus."

"Yani did not see God this time, only his Sheepy-sheep. Next time I go with Big Man Duff. He will in-tro-doots me to God," he enunciated carefully.

Wembly entered from the radio room, and said: "It looks like things are heating up, gentlemen. I just got this over the wireless. '3 November 1941: The Japanese Government has announced that General Hideki Tojo, the Minister of War, has assumed the position of Premier.'

"Now there's trouble looking for a place to happen. He already has Singapore and Shanghai. Last month he moved on Indo-China," Wembly recounted. "Next is Hong Kong, and then, gentlemen, is us. Naval Intelligence is keeping an eye on a Jap Carrier force that is building up in the Sea of Japan. When it leaves its base and moves eastward we better have all our Coast Watchers in place."

"I, for one, am ready, sir," McDuff assured him. "Yani and I will be in position, ready to report anything we see." He gave in to an impulse to give a snappy British salute. Everyone laughed.

Wembly found his enthusiasm amusing, but reminded himself that this was deadly serious. He may not have been too well prepared for his missionary job, but he felt this time the man was sufficiently trained and equal to the task he had agreed to undertake.

"We've been out to sea and out of touch, island-hopping as usual, Moses, what do you hear from the grapevine? Sitting there in hospital all that time, you were in a prime spot for picking up all the gossip and rumors making the circuit," Mr. Gale said.

He thought for a moment, and said, "I hear my countryman — the infamous and elusive John Frum is at it again. He's stirring up the natives on Tanna again."

"What's he doing now?" Wembly asked, on a note of exasperation.

"Reportedly, he is telling the Tannese to throw away their British money ... abandon their efforts at trying to emulate the white man. As I understand it, he wants them to stop going to the missionary churches and to stop working on the plantations."

"Well, that's what he's been doing all along," Gale said. "I wonder if he isn't an agent for the Japs. He's trying to undo everything we've done to try to pull these people out of the Stone Age. He wants them to go back to worshipping rocks and carved palm trees."

McDuff was smiling. Ever since he had stopped wearing his clerical collar, and his intense friendship with Leslie Gale had developed, his manner was considerably more relaxed and informal. "The funny thing is the natives don't understand his message. What they are doing is tearing up their gardens, killing all their pigs, and having food orgies. They think the reason he is telling them to throw their money away is that the millennium is at hand. They expect him to come to the island with a shipload of all the things the white man has. They expect to receive food, and knives and what-not from John Frum. The whole idea of going back to nature is lost on them."

They laughed uproariously at their own jokes about the native mentality, with no regard for two very intelligent, English-speaking black men sitting on the floor, taking it all in. After a while the white men went onto the deck for a smoke before lunch, and left Percy and Yani alone.

At first neither spoke. Finally, in the Chase Island dialect, the younger man said, "I think Negeb has thoughts to share with Yani."

Negeb's face was serious. He had listened to the conversation, but found no reason to laugh. In English he said earnestly, as a statement of obvious truth, "John Frum, he come."

Yani toyed with the phrase in his mind. He liked the sound of it. Then he too, said, "John Frum, he come.

"Is he a Witman or Blackfella?" Yani asked.

"Some people say he is white. I speak to Blackfellas who say he is like us. Some say he is a spirit and has no skin color. Maybe he is even Japfella, and he come to drive the Witman out."

"You think he will?" Yani asked.

Negeb nodded his head affirmatively. "John Frum, he come."

***

The next day Yani waited until McDuff was alone on deck, and approached him. "Big Man Duff, sir," he said. The "sir" was something they taught him in Brisbane to be used as a mark of respect with all white men. McDuff was uncomfortable with it, but no amount of correction had any effect. "I wish to learn the Lord's Prayer."

McDuff's eyes brightened. "That's wonderful, Yani, but you already know it. I've heard you say it a hundred times."

"No. Not half Pidgin. Yani want to say the Lord's Prayer like Big Man Duff — in English."

"In English!" McDuff echoed. *Well*, he thought, *he's officially been given permission by the government to learn the language, so I guess it can't hurt. It's wonderful that his conversion has stirred such zeal in him.* "Certainly, Yani. Come; let's sit in the main cabin. I will help you learn."

They went inside and sat at a small round table. "I will teach you sentence by sentence. If you have any questions about what the words mean, you ask."

Yani leaned forward to hear every nuance of speech.

Dr. McDuff ran through the whole prayer one time: "Our Father who art in Heaven, Hallowed be thy name. Thy kingdom come, Thy will be done …" At the end he closed with an emphatic "Amen."

"Amen," said Yani reflexively as the result of long training.

"Why don't you see how much you know, Yani?" the minister urged.

Reciting from rote memory, Yani sounded out what he heard. "Our fadda huartin Heaven, Hallow-head be thy name. Thy kingham come …" he stopped. "What means 'Thy kingham come?'"

"The words are 'Thy *king-dom* come," he corrected.

To Yani the words had a familiar ring. He thought of the words Negeb had said the day before: "John Frum, he come." Magic formulas were tricky. He wondered if there was any connection — Kingdom come … John Frum, he come.

Dr. McDuff misunderstood the question in his disciple's eyes. The last thing he would have guessed was that Yani was thinking about John Frum. Instead, he said, "When Jesus comes back to earth; there will be a day of Judgment. When we say 'Thy Kingdom come' we tell God we believe that there will be a terrible day when he will judge men for their sinful behavior."

"Terrible day?" Yani frowned. "I think you say day Jesus come back a wonderful day."

"It will be wonderful for the true believers who have accepted Jesus Christ as their savior. But for those who have rejected Jesus it will be a truly terrible day. The Bible tells us so." McDuff opened the Bible which had been laying before him, and the clergyman searched the pages for a reference.

Yani knew the book was powerful and full of magic chants, and stories about strange places. Reverend McDuff had read to him from it often, even though at the time he understood little English.

"In our prayers we ask God to send us the blessings of Heaven. We pray that the goodness of Heaven will be known on Earth," McDuff said.

To Yani that meant tinkens, knives, cloth and all the other things he saw on his marvelous trip to Heaven.

"Here it is in Isaiah. 13.6." He read those passages he thought Yani would understand, and skipped those he didn't feel he could explain.

"Howl ye; for the day of the Lord is at hand; it shall come as a destruction from the Almighty. Therefore shall all hands be faint, and everyman's heart shall melt;

"And they shall be afraid; pangs and sorrows shall take hold of them ... For the stars of Heaven and the constellations thereof shall not give their light; The sun shall be darkened in his going forth, and the moon shall not cause her light to shine.

"Therefore I will shake the Heavens, and the earth shall remove out of her place. Their children also shall be dashed to pieces before their eyes; their houses shall be spoiled...

"And the wild beasts of the islands shall cry in their desolate houses ... and the time is near to come."

Rather than be terrified at the prospect, Yani thought the whole thing sounded exciting. Leaning close to McDuff, he asked, "God make Sun and Moon go away? Make ground shake?"

"Yes. It is going to be the greatest demonstration of God's power man has seen. Here, let me read you what it says in Revelation 16. Verse 18." He found his place and read: "And there were voices, and thunders, and lightnings; and there was a great earthquake, such as was not since men were upon the earth, so mighty an earthquake, and so great.

"And there fell upon men a great hail out of Heaven, every stone about the weight of a talent; and men blasphemed God because of the plague of the hail..."

To clarify the language McDuff said, "When the day of the Lord comes it will rain stones from the sky."

"No," said Yani. "How this can happen?"

"All things are possible in the Kingdom of God…" Dr. McDuff assured him.

There was a pregnant pause, and Yani added, "And John Frum, he come?"

The minister did a double take. The comment was totally unexpected. "Yani, that's ridiculous!" he said.

Chapter 22

Much to McDuff's initial satisfaction, Yani practiced reciting the Lord's Prayer endlessly on deck, but by the end of the second day, even *he* was tired of hearing it. It occurred to him that he had traveled to the opposite side of the world to convert one man, and now his ministry was over. The ways of the Lord did, indeed, "passeth human understanding."

The other factor that forced Moses McDuff to acknowledge that he could no longer teach the Word of God was his intimate relationship with Leslie Gale. At first he was worried that Mr. Wembly would be suspicious about the amount of time he spent in Gale's cabin. But when he expressed his fears to his lover, the Australian said, "Don't have any fear of Bob. He understands the pressures of long isolation from civilization. He's equally at home with a Sheila or a John, but while we're on Patrol he virtually becomes a monk. Has nothing to do with either sex."

However, McDuff was still unable to discuss his feelings freely. Proper Bostonians simply didn't talk about sex, even with the people with whom they were sharing it. Hesitantly, he asked, "Have you ever been…" He tried to think of a way of saying what was on his mind. "…involved with him?"

Gale downed his third Scotch and said, "Ha! Wouldn't think of it. It would definitely get in the way of our work out here in the islands. You just learn to put your feelings aside until you get to port."

McDuff blushed and turned away. "I know what we are doing is sinful. And I feel like such a fool and a hypocrite,' he said.

Leslie laid a gentle hand on his arm. "For what? Our lives are our own to do with what we wish. We're certainly not alone in our preferences..."

"That's not what I'm talking about," he said. "I was part of a terrible scene back on the island with Thompson and a guest of his. I saw myself as an avenging angel of God, not tempted by the gross behavior of men like Thompson."

"What happened?' Gale asked.

"They were having an ... an orgy with the native women Thompson kept at the big house. I broke in at the height of the excitement and made a scene."

"You didn't!" Gale smiled. "You tried to save the damsels in distress?" He started to laugh lightly but it grew in volume. "I can't believe it," he chuckled and spilled some of his drink. "You're lucky he didn't kill you. Those women were his! He paid two pigs apiece for them."

"But that's slavery, Leslie. One person can't own another person. That's contrary to God's law."

"Get a hold on yourself, Moses," he said getting more serious. "Remember where you are. It may be against the law in Boston, but you're in the middle of the bloody Pacific Ocean, man. On these islands one man can do anything he damn pleases to another man if he is stronger. God's laws notwithstanding, might makes right. And mind you, The British Empire is not winning these people over with benevolence, Moses. It's telling them they better damned well get into line or suffer the consequences."

"Does that include raping the natives?"

"If you ask me," Leslie said, "the ones that only get raped are getting off easy. I've heard stories about whole populations getting annihilated. I'm sure they're true."

"How so?" McDuff asked.

"Sea Captains have been known to send their sick sailors ashore, not for treatment, but to spread the illness among the islanders. I've heard that Samoa went from 150,000 inhabitants to 15,000 courtesy of four sailors with the measles. It made the Samoans a lot easier to subdue; I guarantee you that."

"I can't believe white men could be so heartless. There must be some mistake. They wouldn't do that. I would have to assume that these ships' captains are from Christian countries," McDuff argued.

"You know, Moses, for an educated man you make some terribly rash assumptions. Look at your own country ... your people killed all the natives who got in your way. From what I understand, all your aborigines are allowed to do is sell blankets to wealthy tourists on holiday. You're a Christian country, I've heard. How to you justify having done in all the Indians so you could build bloody railroads?"

McDuff immediately became defensive. "It's my understanding that we have federal agencies that administer the Indian reservations, and make sure they are taken care of..."

Leslie Gale cut him off. "Have you ever heard the theory of 'The Superior Savage?'"

"'The Superior Savage?' No, I can't say that I have. What is it?" McDuff said warily.

"When I was in Paris as a student, there were some archeologists and anthropologists who were having a raging academic battle about the Neanderthals. If you remember, they were the race of men who preceded our own species."

McDuff wanted to show off the equality of his New England education, and said, "Yes, we're *Homo Sapiens*. As I understand it our ancestors were a little more quick-witted, and mastered the skills of civilizing themselves more easily than the ape-like Neanderthals. Our ancestors were able to hunt better and learned how to plant seeds and become farmers."

"Granted," said Gale, "but what one faction of the argumentors maintained was that Homo Sapiens was the 'superior savage.' The reason our species won out was that we were better at the art of warfare and survival — better killers, if you will. The reason we became the dominant species was the fact that we successfully slaughtered all the stupid Neanderthals."

"What a dreadful thought," Moses McDuff said. "I have always believed that they were absorbed into the evolving population. Leslie, I fear you dwell on dark thoughts. You're a born pessimist."

"Well, I have lots of company. Our 'friend' Adolf, up in Berlin, has whole teams of people proving the purity of the German people ... all that Aryan People nonsense. But I've read where some of his anthropologists have come up with some convincing arguments for one thing."

"What's that?"

"All these dark-skinned natives — both here in the Pacific and those in Africa — are descendants of the Neanderthals. While the white race, on the other hand are true *Homo sapiens*.

"Thompson said something along those lines when I first got there. You folks aren't as democratic as you would have the rest of us believe," McDuff said.

"Hell, man, you lived on Christ's Despair. You've seen them first hand. They kill and eat each other. I assume that you got out of there before you had a chance to see Jeremy Thompson's head stuck on a pole on the beach. We've outgrown that behavior. Do you think you belong to the same species of man as these bloody, fucking *kanakas*?"

"Please watch your language. I don't know what I think. I'm still sorting it out. I haven't quite recovered from my experiences on the island," McDuff said.

"Well, I think we — the white race — are Homo sapiens. We have continued to evolve. We have made progress. We've managed to civilize ourselves. They've stayed the same over the past million years.

"But here's the ironic part —" Gale paused for another sip of Scotch. "We're still the 'superior savage.' We don't kill and cook each other, but we are still engaged in the same battle we were fighting 30,000 years ago. We've let them keep their jungles for the most part, but the time has come to tell them to straighten up and fly right. If they can't handle the joys of civilization then, as I said, they will have to suffer the consequences."

"You sound amazingly like Thompson's guest. He wasn't kidding when he said you people take this White Man's Burden business seriously. They even recited Kipling," McDuff said.

"Then you must be talking about Professor Vogel. Old Jake used to be a professor of literature before he went to sea. He recites Kipling wherever and whenever he gets drunk," Gale said.

"That's who it was, all right. He had me believing that everybody knows the poem but me. But I'm an American, so I guess I have to settle for "Listen my children and you shall hear, of the midnight ride of Paul Revere…"

When John Frum Came

Leslie Gale poured Moses McDuff about three fingers of scotch and offered it to him saying, "Take up the White Man's burden — Send forth the best ye breed — Go, bind your sons to exile to serve your captive's need..."

The Australian Patrol Officer's smile was disarming. Moses McDuff sat down next to him on the bed, and accepted his first drink — but not his last. They talked for a long time, clarifying the American's picture of himself. He realized that he had truly left his former life behind him and was about to do something Jake Vogel had described as "very British." He was going to get quietly drunk.

After his third Scotch, Moses McDuff went out on deck and dropped *"A Missionary in the New Hebrides"* by The Reverend John G. Paton, off the stern into the churning wake of the *Wombat*.

Chapter 23

Mr. Wembly was coming up from the engine room when he found Yani peering anxiously down the stairwell. He was trying to see past the door that concealed the roaring diesel engines. "What are you up to, Yani, old boy? Is something puzzling you?" he said, reading the expression on the young man's face.

"Yani try to see Kilibob," was his simple answer.

Thinking the name was a Booga-booga word for a power source, Wembly said, "Only authorized people are allowed in the engine room. Sailor-fella and Captain only ones go into ... what did you call it? ... Kilibob room."

"Can Yani see Kilibob?" Yani asked, eagerly.

The restrictions on who could enter the engine room were intended to prevent accidental sabotage of the engines by people who knew nothing about them. *Well*, thought the Patrol Officer, *if the boy has developed an interest in mechanics, it can't hurt to let him see how things work.*

"Okay, Yani," he smiled, "just this one time. But you no go in when I'm not here."

He led the way to the door and opened it to the din of the churning twin-diesels. He raised his voice over the noise, and said, "These engines make the *Wombat* fly across the water."

The racket hurt Yani's ears, and the vibrations frightened him. This noise was worse than the Witman's big egg that carried them to Heaven. He watched the two crewmen doing mysterious things to the behemoths, like wiping them

When John Frum Came

and turning valves. Looking around at the cramped quarters he finally asked, "Where Kilibob?"

Believing he understood the question, Wembly responded, "This Kilibob!" With a grin, he pointed with pride at the mammoth engines.

Yani was amazed, and thought, *Wait until I tell Ooma that I have seen Kilibob in a magical shape like nothing anyone has ever seen before on the island. There is no end to the power Kilibob has and the things he can do. I wonder if Manup is able to become such a wonderful creature.*

The Chase Islander addressed the diesel engine in his native language, and asked if he planned to stay on the island when they got there. However, the motor continued to drone on without changing its pitch, indicating it did not wish to communicate with Yani at this time.

When Yani recognized the situation, he thanked Kilibob for his attention, and went to the door. Once they were in the relative quiet of the stairwell, Yani observed, "Kilibob have much power."

"Yes," said Wembly. "They were made in Germany and are fine-tuned machines. We're not sure what their actual maximum horsepower is."

***

"Chase Island off the starboard bow, Mr. Wembly," Gale announced in British naval style. "According to the charts there's no way the *Wombat* can enter its lagoon."

"Percy!" Wembly called to the stern where the two natives were talking. "Would you come forward, please? We're in sight of your island, but we need your advice on how to get ashore."

The islanders came onto the bridge where a rather crude, hand-drawn chart of Chase Island was unfolded on a table. Yani had only a passing acquaintance with Witman maps, but Percy seemed to understand them very well. He explained the map to his young friend, who quickly learned the correlation between the island's volcano, the lagoon, and the fresh water lake that covered the interior of the flat plain on which the tribe lived. In all, the island was ten miles across from east to west, and slightly longer on the other axis.

The key to landing was breaching the coral reef that created the three-mile-long, shallow lagoon, which ran roughly north and south. The two natives discussed the projected location of the opening in the coral reef, with Yani having a more recent recollection of its whereabouts. Percy had not been home in ten years but felt not the least apprehensive about returning. A shaman was always welcomed back to his island, regardless of how long he was gone.

"Entrance here," Percy said, pointing to a spot on the sketchy outline of a reef. "The *Wombat* cannot fit through. We put dinghy in water and row to shore."

"Well, let's start loading our supplies into the dinghy and get going," McDuff said, his exuberance getting the best of him.

"I think not," Gale said. "We had better send Yani and Percy in first to pave the way."

"Leslie's right," Wembly agreed. "Don't forget that Yani was kidnapped by white men, and they might attack us before we have a chance to explain what's going on. What do you think, Percy?"

"I think Mr. Gale is correct," he said again exhibiting his English vocabulary to emphasize his status in this situation. "Sun is past the high point now. It is better to begin changes when the sun rises tomorrow. It is island custom."

"Yani and Negeb go now in boat?" the younger man said.

"Who?" said McDuff.

"That's his island name," Gale said. "We call him Percy as his English name. It's best for him to reestablish himself with the tribe today, before we go any farther."

"Sort of the Prodigal son returning," McDuff commented. Wembly went out on deck to direct the lowering of the small boat by the natives. Once they had it in the water, Yani and Negeb stripped naked. They took nothing with them. It was another island custom. In spite of himself, McDuff found his thoughts dwelling on the question of whether their prominent sex organs were indicative of a Neanderthal heritage. If so, Homo sapiens had been short-changed by evolution.

***

When John Frum Came

The approach of the *Wombat* was detected almost as soon as it appeared on the horizon. No one had visited Chase Island since the *Salvation* had carried Yani away. A wave of uneasiness spread among the people, remembering the last unpleasant visit of the Witmen. A quickly assembled council of elders determined that no one would go down to the beach to greet the visitors. Instead, a war group armed with bows and slender, barbed arrows would hide itself at the jungle's edge. Anyone who stepped onto the beach would be a perfect target for the warriors in the bush.

Ooma and the reception party stayed in the dark shadows of the palm trees. He was surprised to see the little boat go directly to the break in the reef, alerting him that there was something slightly different in this arrival.

Out on the lagoon, in the dinghy Yani and Negeb discussed their situation. "No one comes to the beach," Negeb said. "That is not good. They are afraid that the Witman has come to do them harm. Maybe Ooma no longer lives. Maybe they cannot see we are sons of Ooma," he said pointing to the shaman tattoos on their chests.

"I think I see movement among the trees at the edge of the beach. They are waiting to see who we are," Yani said.

Negeb thought for a bit, then said, "When we beach the canoe, each of us will hold the paddles above our head. This will show them we have no weapons. While you hold the paddle over your head, I will gather shells to make a circle in the sand with them."

"Yes," Yani said. "When you finish the circle, you hold the paddle over your head and I will gather driftwood for a fire in the center..." Suddenly, Yani faltered and looked frightened. "We have no means of making fire."

Negeb laughed. "Have no fear. If we are not already dead, they will bring a torch from the village fire to signal their willingness to talk with us."

Ooma and his men watched the two men beach the boat. Their actions were the proper ritual requesting a conference with the island's Big Man, and Ooma's heart beat a little harder than normal. Crazy notions ran through his head. *No. It cannot be. It is clear that the men are not Witmen, but how could they be whom they appeared to be. It would take unbelievably strong magic to bring one of them back, but two of Ooma's sons at one time would be impossible. It must be one of the Witman's tricks.*

When the circle in the sand was completed, driftwood was stacked in the center. Within the circle of shells, the two men sat cross-legged and motionless facing the jungle. Several very anxious warriors calculated that they could hit both of them with arrows in a matter of seconds if Ooma gave the signal.

Ooma worried that these were evil spirits who had gone to a lot of trouble to take the form of two of his sons. If they captured his spirit, then they would make short work of the rest of the village. After watching them sit without moving a muscle for half an hour, Ooma finally shouted a command. "Bring fire from the village, and light the center of the circle."

The tension broke and a cheer went up from the crowd, but no one dared to advance to the beach until the protective firebrand arrived. Ooma took the torch and walked boldly to the circle. It took all his willpower to keep from smiling as he entered the circle and set the stack ablaze.

Negeb and Yani stood up as soon as the fire was lit, and Ooma threw the torch into the flames. They positioned themselves in front of the old man and he put each of his hands on their chests. When he felt their hearts beating, he knew they were not spirits. All three men fell into a group embrace and burst into tears. Their joy was so great that they continued weeping for a good fifteen minutes before anyone spoke. Meanwhile, the entire village gathered around them, respectfully observing the ring of shells and staying outside.

Once the initial emotions subsided, the three men sat at the cardinal points, leaving North vacant as a seat for benevolent ancestral spirits to protect the circle. Ooma was the first to speak. "How is this possible?" he asked.

Yani was quick to explain how he had been dragged on board the *Salvation* by Captain West, and proceeded to recount all of his adventures as any son might to a beloved father.

Ooma asked him, "Did you find Kilibob?"

"He is on the Witman boat," Yani reported, with a nod out to sea. "I spoke to him this morning, but he will not come to the island."

Negeb's eyes widened. It was against all custom to speak anything but the truth within a talking circle, so Yani must have had an experience he had not discussed with him. Furthermore, it was not their practice to deny what another said in the circle without a life and death challenge. He let it pass as a spiritual experience Yani had not mentioned but was certain he would have seen Kilibob if he were on board.

"I have not brought Kilibob home, but I have brought a powerful *bis* with me. His name is Big Man Duff. He is a Witman, but we have nothing to fear from him. I am able to control him. I learned two Witman languages. I have learned many powerful word chants from him. One is called 'Sheepy-sheep' and the other is 'Our fadda.'"

Ooma was very interested. "What can one do with such magic chants?"

"One can call Witman ships full of the blessings of Heaven," Yani boasted.

Yani had used English words in his response, and the old man wasn't sure what he meant. In an effort to clarify his meaning he said, "When the Witman says 'the blessings of Heaven' he means steel knives, axes, and tinkens. I have learned from the Witman *bis* how to call ships. I helped him to bring one to the island where we lived. It was full of blessings. The magic chant is more powerful than anything even Kilibob or Manup can do."

Negeb bit his lip. His knowledge of the Witman's world in his persona as Percy was struggling greatly with Yani's accounts. He knew that there was more to getting manufactured goods than just praying for them. He wanted to argue the point, but did not dare dispute Yani's perception of the Witman's power under the circumstances.

The younger man's description of his adventures in Brisbane, calling it Heaven, were painful, but Negeb did not want to create any disturbance because he had his own message to deliver to Ooma when it was his turn.

Finally, Ooma turned to Negeb and asked him for an accounting of his years of absence. His ten years away from Chase Island were full of the usual abuse black islanders experienced virtually everywhere they went. However, through a series of unlikely events, he wound up as the head Policeboy in the Patrol and now had more status with the Witman than any other native.

Ooma was not sure he was impressed. Negeb's stories of how he had gained the Witman's confidence seemed to be through the oppression and betrayal of his black brothers. Ooma knew that while the South Sea Islanders did not see themselves as being united, they did share a common enemy — The Witman.

"Then if he is our enemy, how can you be so friendly with him?" Ooma questioned. "If he is our enemy, then you must kill him."

"I have learned much about the Witman and his ways. If I kill any Witman, I will be killed. It takes planning to defeat an enemy as powerful as the Witman. Like Yani, I can speak his two languages. The Witman will believe almost anything I tell him. He does not believe Negeb can think. He calls me Percy, and thinks I am a fool. In my Patrol uniform I can go anywhere, speak to anyone. I tell my island brothers that a great day is coming, when we will have all things the Witman has and we will have guns, too."

Both Yani and Ooma were riveted by his tale. Yani never suspected that there was such a dark side to Negeb's nature. "I have been saving my message for our father, Ooma," Negeb said somewhat sternly.

"And what is that message, my son, Negeb?"

He leaned toward the fire and said in English in his best conspiratorial tones, "John Frum, he come."

Chapter 24

Wembly, Gale and McDuff watched the pageant unfold on the beach through binoculars. The Patrol Officers recognized the absence of anyone on the beach at first, as a danger sign and were concerned that their emissaries might go down in a shower of spears at any moment. They were fascinated by the construction of the circle and then the final lighting of the fire by Ooma.

"It's amazing," McDuff said, "that without any written documents or rules, Yani and Percy knew exactly what to do. They must have a very deep understanding of their people's oral history."

"On the other hand they might have made it all up as they went along," Gale said.

Wembly smiled and said, "I think Reverend McDuff is probably right. All of which should be a warning to you, Doctor, that you are going to be in their territory. Tread lightly. I think you might have learned that from your experience on Christ's Despair."

"Amen to that. One grows up quickly in this part of the world, as I have found out the hard way. You can't afford to make the same mistake once — much less twice."

"You are going to be truly the only white man on this island," Wembly said. "Before West and his pirates, I don't think they ever even had a white trader stay longer than it took to transact business. He must have left them wary of anyone with pale skin. Long before West, I believe they have had run-ins with the authorities over the years."

"The best thing to do is pay attention to what Yani tells you, Moses," Gale added. "We don't want to lose you."

McDuff blushed slightly at the implied emotional attachment, "Yes, I'm sure Coast Watchers are not going to be easy to find." They were quiet for a few minutes as they watched the circle on shore.

To break the silence, McDuff said, "You know there was one thing that happened just before the natives went on a rampage on Christ's Despair. If I had known more about their customs I would have left the island with you fellows. Yani explained to me later how he knew trouble was brewing."

"Oh, how was that?" Wembly asked.

"I assume you know what a namba is. You know, those outrageous sheathes made from gourds the natives wear on their sex organs."

"You'd have to be blind not to notice," Gale laughed. "I saw one with a hollow gourd almost two feet long, that needed a vine attached to his shoulders to hold it upright."

"Exactly," McDuff said. "Do you know the reason for wearing them?"

"I'd guess it was a form of advertising," Gale chuckled, "but of course delivering the product might be something else entirely."

"That's what I thought. But as it turns out they normally just wear small ones woven out of leaves, more as a sort of athletic protector than anything else. When they start wearing the gourds you had better watch out," McDuff said with surprising frankness.

"What happens then?"

"They get mean. If you think your average headhunter is ill-tempered under normal circumstances, imagine how vicious he could get when his private parts are in pain."

"Pain?" said Leslie.

"They are not smooth on the inside. Yani tells me that for three days prior to a battle or going to war, they put the gourds on to keep them from having erections, or being tempted to dissipate their strength in having intercourse with their women. Any swelling of the male member only makes the warrior more angry. The constant source of irritation puts them in a supremely foul mood.

"If I had known all this beforehand, I would have warned Thompson that they were getting ready to go on the warpath — or whatever you call it here in the islands. Everyone was wearing one of those gourds."

Wembly drew heavily on his pipe, thought a bit, then said, "I never knew that, either. Your story is really quite informative. I can't wait to hear Leslie tell it in more colorful language at the Officer's Mess after he has had three drinks!"

***

Negeb repeated his statement. "John Frum, he come."

"What is jonfrumycum?" Ooma frowned, never having heard the words before, and not understanding any English.

"It is the name of a big, big man. I have spoken with men from Tanna, an island many days sail from here," Negeb said. "There a Blackfella can be put in the calaboose for a long time just for saying John Frum's name in public."

Seeing the old man was having trouble with that statement, too, Yani explained that a calaboose was a sort of dark house with no windows — a thoroughly chilling thought to the elder who had spent his whole life outdoors in the sun.

Negeb went on. "But that does not stop him. John Frum can walk through the walls of the calaboose, and talk to the men inside. He tells them he will come in a big ship. It is filled with cloth, and tinkens, and guns, and wood to build houses like the Witman has."

Yani added, "He comes from the same island as my *bis*, Big Man Duff — America. They know the magic formula for calling ships. If Big Man Duff can do it, maybe John Frum can also. America must be an island full of sorcerers."

Novelty and change could not be accepted in the Chase Island culture through personal adventure. It was necessary for new ideas to come through the participants' dreams or trances. Ooma became aware that these men had been too long in the Witman's world. They had forgotten the nature of their people's reality.

He held up his hand for his sons to be silent. Looking at the setting sun he said, "It is time for us to drink kava. The spirit of the kava will give us greater understanding of the many strange things you have both told me. I am so full of your experiences I must stop and make my mind better able to receive such wonders."

A half dozen coconut shells were brought to the circle, and all the women were told to return to the village. The three shamans each downed two full shells of kava, and settled back while its mind-altering effects seeped into their brains.

***

The white men were still taking turns watching the seaside parley. When Gale saw that the coconuts were brought to the conferees, he said, "Gentlemen, since they have just observed the local equivalent of the sun going down over the yardarm, I suggest we retire to the salon for cocktails. They have just begun the kava portion of their deliberations, which means this is going to be an 'all-nighter.'"

"An 'all-nighter'?" McDuff asked naively. "Do you mean they will sit on the beach all night and get drunk?"

"You don't get drunk from drinking kava, Moses. You get peaceful. We don't have anything quite like it."

"I know. I was drugged with it by Thompson at a native feast and I fell asleep. I couldn't move as I recall," McDuff said. "But on the other hand, never having been drunk on alcohol until last night, I had nothing to compare it to."

"It sounds like we have really led you down a path of dissolution," Wembly said. "How's your head?"

"It's returned to its normal size, I believe. I'll pass on the cocktail hour, if you don't mind."

"I find that the first thing you feel with kava is your tongue and your lips getting numb. A silence overtakes you, and you become quite content," Wembly said. "When your legs don't respond, it's a good idea to stay seated or lie down where you are. Trying to walk can cause severe embarrassment."

"That's true. I thought I was suffering from some kind of jungle disease that induced paralysis," McDuff said.

"You're both wrong. Kava is liquid poetry," Gale suggested. "My own experience was that my thoughts became a hundred birds — each flying off in its own direction. They swooped and soared like a flock of graceful seagulls. I remember ideas rushing forward and rising to mental treetops. Then they tumbled to the ground to nestle in the soft grass."

Robert Wembly laughed out loud. "Very poetic, Leslie. So that's what goes on inside your head ... In case no one has ever told you, on the outside all you do is flap your arms and give weird birdcalls. I hear someone usually has to throw a net over you to quiet you down!"

The three men laughed heartily and went into the main cabin to prepare for dinner.

***

Food was brought to the men in the circle. They ate yams and a pudding made of taro and coconut milk. They had changed posture so that they were all sitting on their haunches, deep in thought. Ooma stood erect and went to the edge of the circle, facing out toward the sea and gave a loud yodel in a falsetto voice. He was clearing the air of jealous spirits. It was a ritual his predecessors had performed for hundreds, maybe a thousand years.

The thin veneer of the Witman's ways was gone from Negeb and Yani. Silence, peace, and the quiet of the jungle settled on them. They were again in the Stone Age, where they belonged.

Inevitably the conversation came back to John Frum and the Witmen. "John Frum says the Pope in Rome is building an Army to drive out the English-speaking missionaries."

"Who is Pope?" Yani asked, thinking it was a personal name.

"He is the leader of the Catholics. They are white missionaries who do not have sex with women. They do not like the missionaries who do," Negeb said.

Yani considered the description. "Big Man Duff must be a Catholic. He is never interested in women. He will never talk about them. Strange people. How do they have sons?"

Negeb did not want to talk about that aspect of Catholics. "I don't know," he said bluntly. "John Frum says the Pope's army will give the Blackfella guns. They are friends of the Japfella. The Japfella will free Blackfellas from their Australian masters — like Big Man Tomsin.

"We talk to John," said Negeb. "We drink kava and talk to John." Negeb picked up two cockleshells of nearly the same size from the sand. He placed one inside the other, and said, "This is me and John Frum. We are the same. His spirit is upon me."

In a mild trance he began speaking. "The Witman is killing custom. He sends us churches and schools. The Witman tells us what we do is wrong. They call us 'heathen' which is a bad name in English. We use what God gives us on our islands, and they tell us it is wrong."

Yani added, "They have a strong God named Jesus. I think he is the same as Kilibob. He gave the Witman food and guns. Jesus will return. Kilibob will come back. I think Kilibob is Jesus."

Ooma listened. He tried to absorb what Negeb was telling him, but he reserved judgment. "I will come back, too," the channeled John Frum spirit said. "There is a big fight coming. Many Witmen cover our island. The Japfella will give the Blackfella guns. Blackfellas will drive the Witman out of islands.

"Some men think I look like a Witman, but I am a Blackfella like you. I will come back in an iron boat. I will give your people tinkens, guns, and clothes, just like the Witman has. No more gardens. No more hunting pigs in the jungle. I will bring everything that the Blackfella needs to live. I will bring canoes like the one my friend Negeb came in.

"Do not trust the Witman. He wants to take the Blackfella's island."

Yani began to worry about what he should do with Big Man Duff. He was not personally angry with the Witman. Who was this John Frum spirit that wanted to kill the Witmen? Yani had brought home a great prize to his people — a *bis* who could call ships — but he was white.

When Negeb seemed finished, Yani spoke. "When will John Frum bring us this ship full of tinkens and guns?"

"First there will be a big fight," the spirit of John Frum said. "Then I will come in my ship and give the Blackfella all he needs."

Yani argued, "We have a ship outside the reef now that already has tinkens and guns on it. Big Man Duff can call ships with his formula. He has taught me to call ships. We do not need a fight. Big Man Duff will give us tinkens now."

When John Frum Came

Had it not been for the soothing effects of the kava, Negeb would have been moved to strike the younger man. However, one of the peculiar qualities of the beverage was the harmony it produced. The spirit of John Frum left Negeb since it felt it was not wanted, and his host fell over asleep or unconscious as abruptly as if he had been clubbed.

Ooma mediated the dispute. He joined Yani in sipping another half coconut of kava. "The spirit in Negeb has departed. I think he was my ancestor, Fuma, who is always looking for ways to make trouble. We will bring your Big Man Duff in from the Witman ship when the sun comes up. Now we will enjoy the peace of the kava." He took another deep draught from the coconut, passed it to Yani, and both shamans stretched out to await the sun's return.

Chapter 25

It was nearly 9 a.m. by McDuff's new waterproof watch by the time Yani and Percy had loaded the radio, military tent, and even a rifle into an oversized lifeboat. In addition, there were enough food and medical supplies to last them at least three months. Both natives wore new Policeboy uniforms, but Percy's was decorated with various insignia, and military ribbons he had acquired in his travels. This time when they went to the island, they were dressed "to the eyeballs," as one of the *Wombat*'s sailors put it, and were even wearing shoes. Their roles had changed.

"Are you sure you shouldn't come along with us, to make my position official?" the American said as he climbed over the rail into the small boat.

"We'd only confuse the issue," Wembly said. "Besides, with all the stuff you've brought along, there's no room for us in the boat." Wembly gave him a casual military salute.

Leslie Gale leaned over the side, and shook his friend's hand. "Good luck, Moses," he said, giving his hand a gentle squeeze before they disengaged. "I wasn't kidding about listening to Yani. Do what he tells you, and you'll stay out of trouble."

Percy pushed the boat away from the larger craft and they rowed for the break in the reef.

***

Their arrival on the beach was quite different from the day before. Everyone in the village had come down to see the great wizard that Yani had brought back from the Witman's island. Whereas the nakedness of the two younger shamans yesterday was regarded as a sign of humility and obeisance to Ooma, today, their Witman's clothes were now objects of great curiosity and awe. It was their shoes (which, in fact, were only canvas deck shoes) they found the most fascinating. Percy took his off and helped Ooma put them on. The old man would wear them from then until they were torn to tatters by the sharp coral of the island.

McDuff was somewhat annoyed that he had not become the immediate focus of attention. He had planned to make a small speech of self-introduction until Yani reminded him that none of the residents of Chase Island spoke Pidgin besides him. Also, their memories of West and company were not too pleasant.

McDuff realized that he had no idea of the protocol involved in meeting the chief of the island's tribe. He turned to Percy and said, "What should I do? Should I give the chief some kind of gift?"

Percy's persona had returned largely to the one known to the Witmen. "It is best to let me introduce you to my father, Ooma."

"You are the chief's son? Good Lord, we never guessed. Why didn't you tell us?"

His answer took McDuff by surprise. "Yani is also a son of Ooma, but that means nothing to the Witman. We are churchboys, Policeboys, or houseboys to the Witman," Percy said with some satisfaction in his voice. "We are important only to our father."

Without further discussion, Percy raised his hands above his head and stood before Ooma. In the island dialect he said, "My father, Ooma! The Witman, who Yani calls Big Man Duff, wants to be known to you. He will be living here on our island for a long time."

The pot-bellied, old man focused his eyes on the white man who was dressed somewhat like a Patrol Officer. His face was expressionless as he asked, "Why?"

"His people have sent him here. He has magic boxes. He can talk to the Witmen on the boat through his magic boxes. He will go up the side of the volcano and make a place to live." Percy showed Ooma the big package containing the waterproof tent, which Yani had just unloaded from the lifeboat.

"How can he live in that?" the old man asked, touching the rubberized fabric.

"It is like a giant banana leaf, stretched out on bamboo poles," Percy said. "You will see. They have strange ways."

When he saw the rifle in the boat, Ooma became angry. "Does he bring that to kill our people? If he does, we will kill him now and save us the trouble later."

Although he could have answered himself, Percy directed his question to Dr. McDuff. "He wants to know why you have brought the rifle with you. Do you plan to kill his people when they don't do what you say?"

"No, no, no," he answered excitedly. "Tell him that we are at war with the Japanese and I bring these with me in case I have to defend myself. In fact, tell him I'm not even sure I could shoot a Japanese person in battle. I am a man of peace. I am a trained clergyman. I am a servant of the Lord, but now I must help my friends, the Australians, keep the Japanese out of the islands."

"The Witman says he needs it to kill the Japfellas when they come," Percy said.

Yani recognized this conversation as getting remarkably close to the one that took place in the circle the night before. "Big Man Duff will not kill anyone," Yani assured his spiritual father. "We will go up the mountainside, and set up our camp. We will look out over the ocean…" As he had been shown by McDuff many months ago, he shaded his eyes with his right hand and mimed a scanning of the horizon. Then he circled his eyes with his fingers, as though they were binoculars. "…We look. When we see Japfella ship, Big Man Duff sends message to Kilibob's boat with magic boxes. We will not shoot anybody. No Japfellas are on this island."

The old man looked over the Witman and his boat full of supplies. "I want to see the magic boxes that talk to Kilibob," Ooma said. Yani translated the request and McDuff dug through the stack for the radiotelegraph sending equipment until he found the crate.

"Yani, tell Ooma that I have to set it up after we unpack everything. He can come for a visit to our camp, and I will give him a demonstration. Meanwhile, give him some tinkens to show him that we are friends."

Yani said, "Big Man Duff has to do his magic with the boxes when we climb the mountain. You come later and he will show you the talking boxes." He looked through the food stores and his face lit up. He came across some cans with a color drawing of a large tuna fish on the label. He tore the paper label off and presented it to Ooma with great ceremony.

The old shaman would have been pleased to get the label alone, he was so stricken by its life-like quality. He was sure it would be useful in attracting large numbers of fish into the lagoon if used properly. However, Yani startled all the people within earshot when he said, "In this tinken is the fish in the picture."

"How can that be?" one of the disbelieving onlookers commented. "No one can get a fish in a tinken." The others laughed in agreement.

"Not only is there a fish in this tinken," he announced in a loud voice, "I was in Heaven and saw our ancestors cutting up the fish." He pointed to the sky. "I saw them put the pieces of fish into the tinkens. Now I have brought those tinkens from Heaven to our island."

"Heaven?" asked Ooma, prepared for more revelations of the kind his sons had been spewing forth since yesterday. "Ancestors?"

Yani was very proud of himself. He had captured Ooma's attention, and that of the entire village. He turned to McDuff and said, "They want to know about Heaven, sir. You talk and I tell them the story in Booga-booga."

McDuff was delighted. He told Yani to have everyone sit down on the beach and make themselves comfortable. The minister could not walk away from his old profession as easily as he thought. He climbed onto the prow of the boat so all could see and hear him. Yani stood next to him and did his best to translate his words.

"In the beginning God created Heaven and Earth..." he began. Negeb who recognized that the Witman was reverting to being a churchfella, settled down as well. He made himself comfortable, thinking of the warnings of John Frum. He knew his people loved nothing as much as a good story, and this was going to be a long one.

Back on the *Wombat*, Mr. Gale was watching them through the binoculars. "Well, I'll be God-damned," he said. "I do believe he's giving a sermon!"

***

It was almost sunset by the time McDuff's equipment was unloaded from the boat and the villagers carried it up the worn path on the side of the volcano. Near the top there was a natural clearing where the soil was too thin to support jungle plants on a tabletop of basalt. Nothing but small tufts of vegetation sprouted up in the cracks.

In earlier times, this had been the site of violent human sacrifices and the islanders refused to set foot on the exposed rock for fear of misplaced and angry spirits who still wandered about. The best McDuff could get them to do was stack his boxes and cartons in the high grass that surrounded the platform.

It gave a commanding view of the Pacific Ocean, especially in the direction of New Guinea. It was the movements of ships in that direction that especially interested the military authorities. McDuff peered down on the *Wombat* just in time to see Percy steering the lifeboat alongside.

A realization hit him. "I almost forgot," McDuff said to Yani. "They are waiting to see if our radio-telegraph works. They can't leave until we send a test message. Quick, get it out of the boxes and set it up."

Back on the *Wombat* Yani had set up the sending equipment no less than 25 times in practice drills. He knew how to connect the hand-cranked generator up to the radio blindfolded. In fact, just for fun the Witmen had him do so several times with his red calico headband around his eyes. In a matter of minutes they were on the air.

Ooma arrived on the scene shortly after the boxes had been stacked. As the spiritual leader of the tribe, he had no compunction about entering the taboo area. The spirits were under his control. He watched with pride as Yani seemed to be running things. The Witman just stood around with a strange headdress that covered his ears. He held a mysterious looking box, and was awaiting Yani's nod to tell him the conditions were right.

Everyone was focused on the two-handed, manually cranked generator that Yani sat in front of. He began to turn the bicycle pedal handles slowly and it gave forth a low grinding noise that built up to a high-pitched squeal. A flywheel picked up momentum and it spun along as though it were in high gear. No one paid any attention to the Witman picking out little clicks with his instrument. Yani was the big show, making humming noises that echoed those of the generator.

"Dash dash/ dash dash dash/ dot dot dot/ dot/ dot dot dot," McDuff quickly tapped out. It was International Morse Code for "MOSES" — his call sign (which would later be abbreviated to two dashes, followed by three dashes — just plain "MO"). "We have established camp. Please acknowledge signal."

Over the earphones there came a rapid series of beeps and buzzes, which read: "Do not forget why you are there. You can save souls for Jesus after the war. Wembly"

"Satan never sleeps," he answered.

Gale answered, "Then stay awake in case he passes in the night. Les."

Ooma was not impressed. The generator was noisy, but he did not see any magic being performed. He had no idea of any conversation transpiring through the magic boxes. Yani told McDuff that Ooma wanted some kind of a demonstration of the magic boxes.

McDuff relayed the message to Wembly for a suggestion. A few minutes later he had one.

"Keep turning your generator, Yani. Tell Ooma to come over to me at the magic box."

The old man did as he was told. "Now tell him to put his finger on the place where the wire is connected." Again he did so, and felt nothing. McDuff put his left hand on the other terminal and extended his somewhat sweaty right, offering it to Ooma. The shaman understood and the Witman grasped his fingers. The jolt was painful to both men, but the American was expecting it. The Chase Islander jumped back and broke the circuit, but it was long enough to make him aware of the power in the box.

The clincher was aboard the *Wombat*. The moment Wembly heard the static of the touch, he pulled down hard on the ship's fog horn, giving it a full 30-second blast. Gale fired the quad-50 machine guns out to sea, and Percy turned on the powerful searchlight mounted above the bridge. He shone it about in the deepening twilight until he zeroed in on the spot where everyone was gathered.

The word "stunned" was inadequate to describe the response of the islanders looking down on the patrol boat bobbing outside the reef.

***

The next day the Coast Watchers were settled in. "Looks like we're here for the duration, as the Aussies say," McDuff told Yani. "I think we should establish some kind of shift and routine for ourselves. We need to look in all directions, not just the one on our front porch."

"Front porch?" Yani said.

"Just an expression," the American answered. "Does the trail we came up go to the top of the volcano? Is there any place to get a view of the other side of the island?"

"All island have walk-about on top of volcanoes. People live in volcanoes. Negeb said on Tanna there is cargo in their volcano. A Witman came to visit their volcano — it is called Yasur — but they would not let him go down inside it. They say the Witman knows what is in it. He wants to take it.

"They have a place like this," Yani said, gesturing to the plateau on which they stood. "On the top of the volcano. Spirit people live there — both Blackfella and Witman."

McDuff pointed to his head and tapped his right temple. "I think Percy has an imagination. He listens to too many stories." He was trying to be gentle in his criticism. As they climbed along the trail he asked how anyone could live there.

Yani did not respond with any rational explanation, but continued with what Percy had told him.

"On the far side of the volcano they say there are holes. Two women fell into them. They are still there. They want men so bad they will ... how you say ... *ra-pay* any man who gets lost."

"Rape is the word," McDuff said somewhat reluctantly. *Judging from the women I have seen*, he said to himself, thinking back to the spectacle at Thompson's that seemed like years ago, *I don't doubt that is impossible in this part of the world. After a few more steps he thought, "Lord, how I miss Leslie."*

Yani continued talking as they climbed. Much of what he said was irrational, and McDuff missed much of it while he was lost in his own thoughts.

"...A fellow told Negeb that he saw the ground open up. A snake or lizard spoke to him. It held up its hand and said John Frum is going to bring Cargo..."

The name John Frum caught the Witman's attention, and a red flag went up. For lack of something else to say, he argued, "How can a snake have a hand. He was making it all up."

Without breaking stride, Yani said, "O.K., then it must have been a lizard. But he said, 'John Frum, he come!'"

"And just what will John Frum do when he comes, Yani?"

"He will bring Cargo for the Blackfella ... just like he does for the Witman."

McDuff's inappropriate thoughts of Santa Claus were interrupted by a sudden shaking of the ground. He fell to his knees, and grabbed a nearby bush.

"People in volcano say hello!" Yani announced, not in the least worried. He had grown up with earth tremors on this island. A minor "wake up call" like this was nothing to fear.

***

Moses McDuff looked out at the aquamarine seascape that spread to the horizon. From his perch on the stone shelf near the top of the volcanic mountain, he could just barely make out the presence of another island in the distance. What made it visible was the cloud formation that arose from the temperature differential of the land being surrounded by the cooling effects of the ocean.

For the first time in his life the American felt able to relax. The White Man's Burden was something he had decided not just to cast aside, but to walk away from. He was not a subject of the British Empire and had no desire to be a part of the system of Anglicizing or civilizing the brown-skinned people who lived in these islands. Yani had woven two hammocks from the reeds and weeds he found near the lake at the center of the island. Each was spread between two tree trunks, and turned out to be quite comfortable. At this level there were few insects to cause them any problem.

I wonder if the malarial fever affected my brain, he thought. *I seem to have left all responsibility down at sea level. Here I am an ordained minister of the Gospel, lounging in the sun on a tropical isle not giving a rat's footprint for anything. Meanwhile, my family is no doubt battling the slush and wet winds of December. I have abandoned my missionary calling and feel no obligation to persuade these simple people that my point of view is any better than theirs. Their ancestors have lived on this island for hundreds — maybe thousands of years. They've learned that some behaviors would keep you alive and others would end in disaster. They probably had things figured out for this part of the world while we were killing Saracens in the name of Jesus during the Crusades.*

Maybe Leslie was right. We're just superior savages. Maybe after all this trouble with the Japanese dies down we can do something to really help these people. Maybe Western Civilization isn't what these people need.

His reveries were interrupted by the ringing of a wind-up alarm clock. It was noon — time for him to make his daily radio contact with Port Moresby or the nearest British ship. As usual, he had nothing to report. There were no ships of any flag visible from Chase Island this quiet Sunday afternoon. Still mindful of the Sabbath, McDuff had conducted private worship services for Yani and himself at sunrise.

Over the weeks that he had been there, Moses McDuff had fallen into the habit of using the shorthand telegraphers around the world worked out among themselves. He signed on: "Mo/Isaiah 20," giving his call sign and the code of the day. He tapped it out three times, and waited for a response. He had barely clicked in the final letter, when his receiver all but buzzed frantically. It was almost going too fast to follow, but he concentrated and wrote down the letters as they came through.

"Mo. Japs attacked Hawaii at dawn. America is in the war. Les. 7Dec41 12:05 p.m."

McDuff could not believe what he had spelled out on the code pad. He flashed the signal meaning. "Please repeat message."

The second time, the message read the same. Leslie Gale added. "Looks like you are no longer lend-lease. Things are really critical. The Japs are massing to invade the Philippines."

He and Leslie talked back and forth about the heightened tension that would grip the island. After a while they slowed down to a conversational level. "Lousy maps," Moses said. "I can see an island to the north but no name on the chart. What is it called?"

A few minutes later Gale said, "One nearest you has no name. Keep going in a far northerly direction and you come to one called Guadalcanal. Nothing much ever happens there."

Chapter 26

"Well, boy, didn't anybody ever tell you that the U.S. Navy doesn't accept colored recruits," the petty officer smirked.

"No, sir. I just assumed that we were all Americans and you wanted to get as many good men to join up as possible. There's no reason I can't fight Japs like everybody else," the tall black youth answered.

"Have you ever seen a colored sailor?"

"On freighters," he said. "I have two uncles who sail between Boston and France on a regular basis. I imagine we could do just as good a job on Navy ships."

"Well, don't imagine too much, boy. The Navy doesn't like people with imaginations. We like people who do as they are told. The only colored sailors are mess stewards. Got that?" the petty officer glared.

The young man did not answer.

"This must be your lucky day, boy. I just got orders this morning to accept Negro recruits. The U.S. Navy will actually take applications from Negroes. That's a first in Naval history. I don't think too much of the idea, but like I said — the Navy likes us to do what we're told."

He shoved a clipboard with a sheaf of papers on it toward him. "Can you read and write?"

"Yes, sir," he said quietly, avoiding raising the petty officer's anger any further. He accepted the application forms.

"Go sit at that table over there, and fill these out. Then bring them back to me," he said, biting the corner of his lip in frustration. "I can imagine how you'll look in dress whites."

John Bartlett was not ashamed of his very dark skin. He could not resist returning the comeback, regardless of the possible consequences. "It doesn't come off, sir. It's not shoe polish."

When Bartlett got home later that afternoon, he went directly into the kitchen. His mother, Rose, was polishing a huge silver coffee urn. "Johnny, where have you been? There's a million things to be done. We have twenty-four people coming for dinner, and the table hasn't been set yet. Bessie is late and your father is trying to do it all himself."

"I'm not going to serve dinner, Mama. I'm going out with my friends."

His mother almost dropped the urn. "What? What do you mean you're goin' out with your friends?"

She stood in stunned silence. Johnny was a good boy. He had some crazy ideas about becoming an entertainer or something, but she was sure he would outgrow that. He spent all his money and his days off at the movies, and talked about wanting to go to Hollywood. He even told her that his dream was to make a Cowboy picture with nothing but colored actors.

But she figured he would meet a nice girl and settle down to real life. He always did his work around the mansion ... he helped his parents out any way he was needed.

"Jason!" she yelled. "Jason! Get in here."

Neither mother nor son moved as they looked firmly into each other's eyes. The door from the dining room swung open and an older black man in a butler's uniform came in.

"What are you shrieking about, woman. The Lady will hear you. You know she likes to take a nap this time of day," he said.

"Johnny says he's not going to serve dinner. He's goin' out with his friends, he says."

The older man asked, "Why are you setting your mother off like this? You know better. Get the silverware out of the breakfront, and start wiping it down."

"I mean it, Daddy. I'm not going to be here this evening. It's my last night, and I want to celebrate with my friends."

"Last night? What the hell are you talking about, boy? What are you celebrating? We have a dinner to put on." The old man started to fold napkins while he talked.

"I joined the Navy, Daddy. I have to be down at the train station tomorrow morning," he announced.

All activity ceased. It was as though he had said something in Chinese and they were trying to figure out what he meant. When he found his senses, the elder Bartlett said, "You enlisted in the Navy? They don't let Negroes into the Navy. Somebody is pulling your leg, boy."

"No," John said. "I read it in the *Boston Globe* yesterday, so I went down to the Navy Recruitment booth at Scully Square and volunteered. They gave me a hard time at first, but they accepted my application. Tomorrow I leave for Boot Camp."

The two older people reached for each other and embraced. They both cried like they never had before.

Like everyone else, John Bartlett had seen a number of war movies. It was during an English film about a valiant destroyer that he decided to join the Navy. He wanted to be one of the courageous gunners on any kind of ship. They were the ones who gave the Nazi U-Boats hell when they surfaced after attacking a convoy. Like any kid of 19, he had no fear of death. He saw only the glory of carrying the day for the good guys.

***

The Chase Islanders were very curious about the strange equipment Yani's Witman had brought with him. Every day they would squat around the edges of the clearing and watch McDuff operate his radio equipment with Yani's help at the generator. A cross member had been nailed to a tall tree at the rear of the camp to act as an antenna. It gave the impression of being a giant cross, erected at the highest point on the island beside the rim of the volcano. McDuff liked the effect. He had not given up Christianity, just the official teaching of it.

Since most of those present had seen Ooma get an electrical shock from the wires coming off the generator, they were anxious to know more about the phenomenon. Yani told McDuff of their interest and he spoke to a group of men who watched him make his noontime transmission.

"Yani turns the wheel, and it causes electric power to flow through the wires to the radio," he said. He held a terminal in each hand and demonstrated how a tiny blue spark jumped across the gap. "This power goes into the telegraph key, and I can send and receive messages from Port Moresby." He turned to Yani and said, "Try to explain that to them, if you can."

Yani stopped cranking the generator and said, "My machine makes magic power. The magic power goes through these..." he sought a word in the local language, but there was none. Since metal did not occur naturally on the island, copper, steel and iron became tin, as in tinken. "Magic power goes through tin vines. Big Man Duff gets messages from other Witmen through tin vines."

"I want to feel magic power like Ooma did," one of the bolder warriors said, taking the wires in his hand. He was adamant about it, and McDuff understood without an interpreter.

Let him feel it," he said to Yani with a slight smirk. Yani saw the amusement in it and began rotating the pedals slowly, gradually stepping up the power. But much to his surprise, the warrior held on as long as he could. Finally, he let go with a yell. But, it was one of triumph, not of pain or fear.

"Now I will also get messages from spirits," he said, strutting back and forth along the pathway. He spied the roll of copper wire from which the aerial had been made and said, "I would like a bracelet made from the tin vine."

Yani relayed the message to McDuff who saw no harm in humoring the man. He snipped off a length of wire, wrapped it loosely around his wrist, and pinched it in place with his pliers.

The warrior was delighted, and led the column of native men down the path to the village. There everyone marveled at his new-found spiritual gift. But it was only the beginning. The next morning practically every man in the village was lined up at the camp to receive his electric shock and spirit bracelet.

***

Bill Schroeder

When they arrived at the Great Lakes Training Center, Bartlett found that he and six other black recruits were pulled out of the formation and marched to the barracks they would occupy. It was separate from the buildings occupied by the white boys who had arrived with them from Boston.

A tough-looking Seaman First Class called them to attention, and proceeded to explain how they were to respond to the various commands — Attention! At ease! Present arms. He marched them to a supply depot and everyone drew the uniforms and equipment they would need. After that he told them to clean up the building they would be living in. He would return in an hour to see how they were doing.

As soon as the sailor in charge of them left, one of the men in the group, Sam, said, "You know, I was afraid it would be like this."

"Like what?" Bartlett said.

"Segregation, boy. Didn't you ever live down south? I left South Carolina because I was sick of Jim Crow, and I think we are in for more Crow than we can stand," he said.

The others agreed. John Bartlett naively said, "Hell, they can't do that. This is the Navy, man. That's just in civilian life."

Larry, a street-wise hustler who joined to get away from a police warrant said, "Johnny. You is about to find out what it feels like to be the first nigger on line. They don't know what to do with us, so they gonna give us lots of shit."

***

It was a very small dinner party by the standards of Francis X. Bartlett, III; only six couples. The men had retired to their customary drawing room in the spacious Marblehead mansion for their obligatory cigars and brandy. They were all executives of Xavier Shipping Enterprises, and all related to each other in one way or another.

Jason, the butler served the brandy, and melted into the woodwork while they talked. The eldest member of the family, and Chairman of XSE raised his glass in a toast: "Gentlemen, to our leader in the fight against the Axis Forces, Franklin Delano Roosevelt." Amid a few "here-heres," they all sipped their drinks.

Francis held up an official looking document. "In case you have never seen one before, this is a direct commission naming yours truly as a Rear Admiral in the United States Navy." He paused for a moment, and added, "Those of you who thought we were pissing our money away when we backed him for a third term, please take note."

"Christ, Francis, you were unbearable when they made you Commodore of the Marblehead Yacht Club," his brother called out. "I hope they don't put you in charge of any ships named The Bounty. The Navy will have its first mutiny in a hundred years." Everyone laughed.

"Don't worry, Ed," Bartlett said good-naturedly. "They're sending me to Australia as Chief Liaison with the British Forces. The only ship I have anything to do with directly will be the one that takes me to the South Pacific. You just make sure that there's an excess on the books for XS Enterprises when I come back."

"We'll do fine, providing your friend, Roosevelt remembers to compensate us properly for all our Lend-lease arrangements," the XSE V.P. of Finance answered.

"I can't say that I envy you, Francis," said one of his cousins. "From what I hear, those islands out there are the armpit of the earth. Where will you live?"

"We don't have the details all worked out just yet," he said, "but I assure you that Flag Rank Officers manage to live like white men, regardless of where they are assigned. I will be putting together a cadre of my own staff of officers during the next few days. Now that Frankie, as if you didn't know, has graduated from the Academy, I hope to have him assigned to work for me as soon as possible."

Bill Ryan, vice president of XSE's planning, said, "I've already worked up a list of things I think you'll need that the Navy might be a little slow in getting out there. With luck, it will arrive at Port Moresby before you do."

Francis threw him a thank-you salute.

***

The waters around Chase Island were undisturbed for weeks, until suddenly one morning the rising sun revealed a flotilla of Japanese Navy ships steaming in the direction of the island Leslie Gale had identified as Guadalcanal. McDuff spotted them as he walked to the edge of the clearing where the stone shelf dropped off as a sheer cliff above the ocean. He ran back to his tent to get his binoculars.

"Yani," he called. "Look to the North. Can you see all the Japanese ships?"

Without intending to be comical, he circled his fingers a round his eyes and looked toward the far off island. "Yes, sir, I see them. I think there are two hands of them," he said, using the native method of counting ten. "Maybe more."

The Witman looked intently at the silhouettes on the water, and made notes on a small lined pad. "Fire up the generator. I have to get this to Port Moresby as soon as possible." In a few minutes he was on the air reporting three battleships, one aircraft carrier, four destroyers and at least four freighters — probably troop carriers.

To the utter amazement of the Chase Islanders, a squadron of Japanese fighter planes from the aircraft carrier crossed over the island. They flew at an altitude of about 300 feet, engines roaring. The people were terror stricken. They had never seen an airplane before, not even off in the distance. These were without a doubt Hevehe, demons that had sprung from the depths of the ocean — which everyone knew was the nest of monsters.

Ooma led the delegation to the Coast Watchers' camp, to seek answers from Yani and Big Man Duff. "What kind of monsters are these," Ooma asked. "How do we keep them from carrying off our people?"

"These are airplanes," McDuff said. "They come from those Japfella ships out there on the horizon." He pointed to the ships, which were now just dots. In frustration, he said, "Yani, you were on an airplane. You flew to Australia. You tell them what they are. I don't know where to begin."

Yani had grown to love being a fountain of knowledge. Everyone realized that he had become a powerful shaman while he was away from Chase Island, maybe even smarter and stronger than his father, Ooma. He mounted a boulder and encouraged the group to fill what had been a taboo area until recently. His ease and familiarity with the formerly sacred clearing had put most of the younger members of the village at ease. They gathered around him now.

"When I was on the Witman's island I went to Heaven on one of the strange creatures that flew over us today," he said. They had heard about Heaven from the Witman the day he arrived.

"Did you ride on its back?" someone asked.

"No. I was inside. They are like big bird's eggs. They climb up through the sky and past the clouds. They live in Heaven with Jesus. I went with Negeb and some Blackfellas from other islands. When it got to Heaven the egg hatched and we all got out."

He had told of his visit to Heaven on many occasions, but had never told of this aspect before. They had not seen an airplane before, so he had not gone into detail.

"So they are birds," Ooma said.

"Yes," Yani agreed, "but only the Witmen knows how to catch them. Only the Witman can tame them. I think the ones that flew over us were wild ones. Big Man Duff says they come from the Japfella boats, but I find that hard to believe. I think he does not know and does not wish to say so."

"Can we catch one?" Ooma asked.

Yani relayed the question to McDuff, who was amused. He had not understood any of the preceding discussion, and facetiously answered, "I don't know. Maybe we could put out decoys to attract them."

"What are decoys?" asked Yani.

Sorry he had gotten into this tangential discussion, McDuff proceeded to explain the finer points of duck hunting in New England. He told his protégé how the decoys were carved out of wood, and placed where flocks of migrating waterfowl could spot them.

While Yani roughly translated the explanation, McDuff decided it was time to climb to the volcano's rim to get a better view of the disappearing naval task force.

Chapter 27

At breakfast one morning Rose Bartlett, the cook, was serving bacon and eggs to Rear Admiral F.X. Bartlett, III, USN.

"Good morning, Mr. Francis," she said. "I see you're wearing your new uniform. I can't believe you're a full-fledged Admiral. It's so exciting."

"Good morning, Rose. Yes, it is sort of exciting. Don't tell anybody in the family, but I am glad to dump the company on Ed. He's always wanted to be in charge, anyway."

"But now you're gonna be responsible for something bigger than just a shipping company. Like they say, 'There's a war on.' I hope you will come back safe to us after it's all over."

"No fear. I'm really only just trading my desk in Boston for one on the other side of the world. When all is said and done, it's still only a desk job."

She poured his coffee and said, "You know my boy, Johnny, up and joined the Navy, too."

"Is that right? I guess I haven't seen him around here for a while. I wondered what became of him. Where is he?"

"Well, he's out at the Great Lakes Training Center, but he's not too happy," she said.

"I hear that boot camp can be tough for some of the young kids. He'll get used to it. What is he training to be?"

"Well, that's the trouble, Mr. Francis, they're not training him to be anything. He's been in the Navy for a month and he hasn't even started Boot Camp."

The Admiral looked up from his eggs. "In fact, I have a letter from him right here," she said, reaching into her apron pocket. She didn't wait for his response; she read:

Dear Mama:

The other fellas and I just finished another detail in the mess hall, mopping down the floor. That makes 16 times we have pulled that detail in one week. I really prefer to get on the painting details, since they are a little more interesting.

Still no word when we will begin our training. Joe Boznik, the sailor who is in charge of the colored detail, says he has no idea what they have in mind. There are not enough Negro sailors to start a training company, and he also says that even if we get trained, where will they assign us? None of the ships have separate quarters for colored sailors, and they sure as heck aren't going to let us bunk with the white guys.

I wanted to be a gunner, but I'll be lucky if I ever set foot on a ship of any kind...

Rose folded the letter and said, "The rest is personal stuff."

"That's too bad, Rose. But I doubt that I can do anything about it. I'm an Admiral, all right, but I have nothing to do with that part of the Navy," he said between sips of coffee.

She was not done. "I hear that you arranged for Frankie to be assigned to your staff out in the Pacific Ocean."

Bartlett read her message at once. "Yes, he's an Annapolis graduate, and has been made a Second Lieutenant in the United States Marine Corps. I hope to have him as my Operations Officer."

"Wouldn't it be wonderful if the boys could serve together, considering how they grew up together and all." She was referring to the unusual arrangement under which Johnny was included in Frankie's private tutoring sessions. A group of Boston College students had served as teachers for Frankie and his sisters. At Frankie's insistence, Johnny, although the son of the cook and butler, was included in the lessons. This made it unnecessary for him to attend public school until Frankie went off to Prep School before the Academy. As a result, Johnny's education was better than that of an average white child, much less a black one of the 1930s.

Admiral Bartlett was beginning to feel ill at ease. He didn't like a servant trying to wheedle a favor out of him. "I don't think it would work too well, Rose."

She played her trump card. "You mean about the confusion in names? There might be too many Bartletts? Well it seemed like a good idea 80 years ago, when my husband's family named their children after your family. Being slaves and all that, they had no other family name to assume. Your Grandfather thought it was a good idea then. I guess times have changed."

Francis X. Bartlett III, gritted his teeth. This was all code for *"We haven't forgotten that my husband's father and you may have the same paternal ancestor. Letting the children assume the Bartlett name was a concession to that possibility."*

***

Seaman First Class Joe Boznik called out the names of the men in his permanent work detail. In twos and threes they were marched away by sailors from various departments on the base to the locations where they would be working for the day. After about ten minutes, the last of his friends marched away to the cadence of "Drip-po, drop-po, wring out the mop-po. Left, o right, o left."

"Well, Johnny Boy, it looks like it's just you an me left. I got orders to bring you back to the C.O.," Boznik said, wrinkling his forehead. "What the hell did you do to get called to the Old Man's Office?"

John Bartlett did not know either. He had learned quickly that it was not a good idea to let anybody get used to your name. Whenever they had something miserable that needed to be done you didn't want yours to be the first name they called out.

Boznik marched him to the headquarters section, and gave him a quick review of how to stand at attention, and respond to meeting the commanding officer. He was told to sit on a bench in the outer office until the yeoman told him he should go in.

After two hours he finally got the nod, and entered the office of a Lieutenant who looked like he should have retired after the last war. "Seaman Recruit John Bartlett reporting as ordered, sir!" he said.

"At ease, Bartlett." He looked over the young man in front of him and smiled. "I think we have a mix-up here, sailor. I have a set of orders here promoting one Seaman Recruit John Bartlett to Apprentice Seaman. Then it goes on to order the immediate transfer of the man to the Navy Base at San Francisco as part of a special group being formed under Rear Admiral Francis X. Bartlett, III.

"I've got a suspicion that Washington has fu— fouled up here," the aging Lieutenant said. "I'll bet this was supposed to send some relative of the Admiral." He looked down at the orders again, "I've never heard of him — to some cushy job out in the California sunshine."

John said nothing.

The officer started laughing to himself, and built up in volume. "I'd love to see their faces when they get some nigger boy instead. What do you say to that, Apprentice Seaman Bartlett?"

John took it as a direct question. "I think the Admiral might be my cousin, sir."

The answer sent the Lieutenant into such a spasm of laughing that he almost couldn't get his breath. He finally managed to get out one word: "Dismissed!"

Chapter 28

McDuff had been making daily trips to the top of the volcano during the past few weeks. He walked along the footpath, always looking north to see if his range of view could be improved. Some points on the lip of the crater were higher than others. If he remembered his physics and math, the higher up he got the further away the ocean's horizon would be.

He loved the relative silence of the place. It was different when he came here without Yani, who talked constantly. It was truly the quietest place on the island that he had seen, but somewhat frightening in its aspect. There were no birds or insects chattering and buzzing. Vegetation was sparse and selective. Every once in a while he would smell the distinct rotten eggs stench of sulfur compounds that pervades all high school chemistry labs. He also remembered that Professor Kraus, his chemistry teacher, gave an hour-long lecture about the toxicity of well-intentioned chemical jokes. McDuff made it a point to take a deep breath of clean air each time he sniffed the foul odor.

As he reached the summit of the highest pumice hill, he saw not only the Japanese ships he had been reporting, but others that were coming in from other angles. *Good Lord*, he thought, *I wonder if the Admiralty knows how big this fleet is getting. The whole blasted Japanese Navy must be there.*

As he looked behind him he got a new perspective of the interior of the volcano. *It's like an abstract painting by one of those outlandish European painters from that new school of art — whatever they call it*, he observed. Through his binoculars he could see that the lake on the floor of the volcano was not made of water, but thick, boiling mud. It bubbled and popped like a neglected pot of butterscotch pudding about to burn on Grandma's stove. From cracks in the side of the sheer walls of the cone, fumaroles emitted clouds of yellowish steam.

No wonder no one ever comes back from their visits to the other side of the volcano, he concluded. *They're not being held captive by love-starved women, they've been cooked into that primordial soup down there.*

Looking back at the portion of the Pacific Ocean called the Coral Sea, he did his best to count the ships he saw, but could not distinguish the types at this distance. *With the size of that Armada,* he told himself, *I don't think it makes any difference what kind they are.*

An hour later when Dr. McDuff reached his camp, he was surprised to find that Yani had left with all the men. He wondered where he might have gone, since he needed his generator man to send his new observations to Port Moresby.

His question was soon answered. As he began to descend the incline toward the village, he met a large number of men and boys coming up from the lowlands. They had obviously been down to the lake since everyone was carrying bamboo poles, vines, or reeds that they had cut there. Everyone was in a happy mood and he wished he could appreciate the jokes that were being bandied about among the men during their steady climb toward the top.

Finally, Yani appeared. He was carrying some of their steel tools with help from beaming pre-teenagers. They had saws, hatchets, knives and tin snips (the latter having been found perfect for cutting tough reeds and vines).

"What on earth is going on, Yani?" he asked.

Yani grinned brightly. "John Frum, he come! We help."

That was all the explanation he got as Yani pushed past him with his entourage. They laughed and talked their way to the top of the volcano from which he had just come.

McDuff caught one of the straggling boys, about 10 years of age, and motioned to him to come with him into the camp. He had nicknamed the boy Pee-wee when he first started to hang around the camp. He showed him how to turn the generator, and waved a small can of fruit salad at him. Pee-wee understood, and with no hesitation he began to spin the wheel while Moses McDuff transmitted his additional information across the airwaves.

For the rest of the day Dr. McDuff stayed near his wireless equipment since the base at Port Moresby called him almost every half hour to see if there were any changes. At 4:17 p.m., to the Coast Watcher's amazement, a Japanese destroyer passed Chase Island, coming from the south — a direction in which he had not been looking. The ship was so close that he could see the sailors along the rail and the white-uniformed officers on the bridge. The reality of the situation hit home. McDuff had to admit to himself that he was scared ... suppose they opened fire on the island? Innocent people would die.

Only minutes later Yani came down the path from the top of the volcano, thoroughly excited. "John Frum, he come!" he shouted. "You see, Big Man Duff? John Frum, he come!" Yani was pointing at the Japanese destroyer and jumping up in down, as though he were running in place.

The other natives followed Yani into the camp. They were yelling something similar to "John Frum, he come! John Frum, he come!" but had only matched the rhythm not the words.

Yani was ready to lead everyone down to the lagoon to greet the ship, until he realized that it was passing them by. He stopped jumping and became silent. His disappointment was evident. The others gradually recognized the change and the chanting stopped.

"Why did John Frum not come to Chase Island?" Yani asked his American wizard.

McDuff reached out with both hands and grasped the young man's shoulders, looking into his eyes. "That wasn't John Frum, Yani," he said. "That was a warship that belongs to the Japfella. It's just like all those ships we saw out to sea. This one just happened to be close by. I think he is on his way to join the other ships."

Yani was crestfallen. McDuff could not understand the words, but the tone of what his friend said to the other men had a melancholy note to it that could not be mistaken.

They left the camp and headed down the mountain toward the village without much discussion. Yani took the place of the ten-year-old at the generator while McDuff transmitted his latest observation.

***

When John Frum Came

All the other sailors had a pretty good idea of what kind of jobs they would have once they processed through San Diego. John Bartlett's future was as much of a mystery to him as it was to everyone else. They had all received some kind of school training in addition to basic at Boot Camp. He hadn't even been to Boot Camp.

When he reported to the personnel section in San Francisco, they sent him to one of the big office buildings marked Allied Liaison Command. No matter where he went, heads turned. Navy people were not yet accustomed to seeing sailors with very dark skin wearing dress white uniforms. There were Filipino mess stewards galore, but no American Negro sailors had yet found their way onto major Navy bases.

As usual, he was told to wait in an anteroom until someone could see him. So, he sat down with his seabag and a large manila envelope that contained his papers and his most recent orders. As he watched the steady stream of officers of all ranks he suddenly spotted a familiar face coming toward him, talking with a yeoman with an armload of official looking papers.

Without thinking, he jumped up and called out, "Frankie! Frankie! Hey, man, over here." He waved his right arm above his head, so he could be seen in the crowd.

The man he was calling looked up, and focused on him. For a long minute he seemed frozen to the spot. There was a look of disbelief on his face. He pushed his way through the crowd of sailors in the waiting room, made eye contact and said, "Are you speaking to me, sailor?"

"It's me, Frankie ... Johnny Boy. I'm in the Navy," John Bartlett said.

"Come to attention, sailor," the Marine officer said.

"But, Frankie..." John tried to say.

"Do you know what attention means, sailor? It means your eyes are straight ahead, your body is straight and rigid, your hands are at your sides, and your mouth is shut. Do you understand?"

John had played this game often enough at Great Lakes to know he was in trouble. He hit a brace worthy of a cadet and looked straight ahead. The Marine officer stood directly in front of him.

"Do you see the insignia on my collar, sailor?" he shouted in John's face from only inches away.

"Yes, sir!" he shouted back.
"Do you know what rank I hold in the United States Marine Corps, sailor?"
"Yes, sir!"
"And what is that rank?"
"Second Lieutenant, sir."
"What is your name and rank, sailor?"
"Apprentice Seaman John Bartlett, sir."
"I am Second Lieutenant Francis X. Bartlett, the Fourth. In the future you will address me as Lieutenant Bartlett, sir. Is that understood?"
"Yes, sir."
"Now go into my office and wait for me until I return."
"Yes, sir."

By this time they had the attention of the entire office. A hush had fallen over the previously noisy scene. All eyes were on Lieutenant Bartlett as he left the office area and proceeded down the hallway.

Apprentice Seaman John Bartlett continued to look straight ahead and went into the office marked, Operations.

Fifteen minutes later, Second Lieutenant Bartlett returned to his office, visibly more agitated, and closed the door as he entered. John jumped to attention, but was silent.

Frankie sat down at his desk and said, "Sit down, Johnny."

John did so, and looked at the man who had been his boyhood friend ... the buddy with whom he had smoked his first cigarette in the basement ... the informal classmate whom he coached to pass a stuffy tutor's history quiz. They were in the same room, but separated by worlds of custom, power and wealth.

Lieutenant Bartlett broke the tense silence. "What happened out there a little while ago," he said, nodding toward the larger office, "was bound to happen some time."

"Request the Lieutenant's permission to speak, sir," the Apprentice Seaman said.

"Johnny, I'm going to forget the military formalities just for this meeting. Anything you want to say, you better get it out now. Once you leave this office, we will be strictly military from then on. You are an enlisted man, and I am an officer. There's no use pretending that I'm not the boss's son. Dad is a Rear Admiral and he is responsible for the relations between the United States Navy and the British and Australian Forces in the Pacific, in case you didn't know."

"My mother told me in a letter," John said.

"That's the other thing. The only reason you are here is because your mother prevailed upon Dad to do something about your case. I understand they weren't training you to do anything at Great Lakes except mop the head."

John nodded.

"Even in civilian life I would have gone to work in my father's office. It's a given that someday I'll take over the company. You would have probably taken over your father's job." He hastened to add, "You still can after the war."

"I guess I could become the faithful old family retainer," he said sarcastically.

Frankie ignored the tone. He leaned back in his swivel chair. "I just came from my father's office. He told me he was afraid something like this would happen. Dad is not very happy about this whole thing."

Francis X. Bartlett IV lit a cigarette, without offering one to John. He blew the smoke out in a long stream. "I'm not too happy, either. I am an Annapolis graduate and expected to set the example for the rest of the officers — especially the 90-Day Wonders. That 'Frankie' shit you pulled out there today didn't do me any good as far as prestige is concerned."

"I'm sorry," John said. "I was so glad to see you, I just forgot myself."

"Well, don't forget yourself in the future. And when you see my father, don't even let on that you know him in the presence of others — officers or enlisted men."

He let the swivel chair snap into the forward, upright position. "Now, we have to find something for you to do. As far as the Navy is concerned, you are a deck ape ... an anchor clanker. You have no skills. I thought of putting you in the Admiral's galley, but the Filipinos and Samoans have that part of the Navy pretty well sewed up."

John leaned forward and said, "I wanted to be a gunner. I requested gunnery school, but I was ignored."

"Forget it, Johnny. You aren't going to be a part of any gun crew. My father insists that you stay with us. He's going to have quite an entourage. His appearance is always to be above reproach. Because of his Flag Rank he is authorized to have a couple Personal Aides. Admirals don't press their own uniforms, and do their own laundry as you might have guessed.

"Dad also doesn't like strangers too close to him in his personal quarters, as you may well remember." Lieutenant Bartlett smiled. "You would be perfect for the job."

"You mean as your old man's valet?" John said, disbelieving. "Did I join the Navy so I could follow him around like my father did back in Marblehead?"

With some impatience, Frankie said, "You will be a Personal Aide to a Rear Admiral, *Apprentice Seaman Bartlett*. If that does not suit your fancy we can have you mopping up puke at the base hospital for the duration. What is it, Johnny? Get it out in the open now — or forever hold your piece."

"When you see your father, ask him why we have the same last names — Sir!"

"Can that shit, sailor. Get out of my office and report to the Admiral's living quarters," he snarled. "We're shipping out in the morning for the South Pacific."

Johnny picked up his gear and moved out smartly.

Lieutenant Bartlett wrung his hands in anger and frustration. His father had told him about the name business for the first time less than a half hour before. The weight of the knowledge was nearly unbearable. Suppose Johnny went around telling that story to other people.

***

During the next few days, Dr. McDuff became aware that something was going on, and he didn't know what. Yani slept at the camp, but when McDuff woke up in the morning he was alone. Yani would be back at the site in time for the morning radio transmission, but had no comment or explanation as to where he had been.

He always came up from the direction of the beach, and it could have been assumed that he had a secret lady friend or he was simply taking his daily community bath. But Yani had stopped wearing the local, sticky insect repellent that needed to be washed off. They slept above the bug line. The white man decided he would follow Yani when he heard him leave the next morning.

At first light, Yani got up from his pallet and made his way down the path. Moses forced himself awake, and slipped down the mountain at a safe distance behind him without being detected. He saw Yani go to the water's edge and kneel with his back to the rising sun. The American positioned himself behind a clump of bushes and watched.

The young Chase Islander folded his hands in the manner the missionary had taught him so many months ago, when he was an apprentice churchboy. In a loud, clear voice complete with the pauses and pronunciations taught at The True Church of God Seminary he heard Yani call out:

"Our father who art in Heaven,
Hallow-ed be thy name.
Thy kingdom come.
Thy will be done on earth, as it is in Heaven..."

The failed missionary felt tears well up in his eyes. He was overcome by emotion. He was not a failure. This is what all the questions were about while they were on the *Wombat*. Here was a convert who was a private Christian — even a secret Christian. His conversion had been so deep that he saw it as a personal relationship between him and God that did not need public celebration. He apparently felt so strongly about it that he did not even share his passion with the very man who brought him to Christ. Here, every morning, he had been coming down alone at the break of day to kneel beside the sea and recite the Lord's Prayer in a forceful manner.

Once more he felt like *Reverend* McDuff, and wanted to jump out of his hiding place, run to Yani and embrace him. It took all of his willpower not to do so. He realized that if he were to disclose his furtive behavior, he might upset a delicate balance. Instead, he crept backward on his hands and knees, keeping the covering bush between him and Yani. When he reached the edge of the denser growth, he stood up and hurriedly made his way back to the camp. Yani would never know he had been followed.

However, had Moses McDuff stayed at the beach a little longer, he would have heard Yani recite a backup prayer in Pidgin, which he had also taught him: "Big name watchem Sheepy-sheep; watchem black fella. No more belly cry fella hab...."

And if two prayers were powerful, Yani thought, three would be irresistible. Using his gift of language memorization in much the way children sing *"Adeste Fideles"* at Christmastime without knowing what the Latin words mean, he remembered Big Man Duff's magic formula for making ships appear: "Oh, most merciful God ... He who provided manna for the children of Abraham, hear our pleas. Send us the shipload of supplies we so desperately need. Help us to do your great work of conversion. We ask this in the name of Jesus Christ. Amen."

Yani remained in the kneeling position in silence as he had been taught. Then he stood up, removed his Policeboy/Coast Watcher shorts and plunged into the blue waters of the lagoon for his morning swim.

Chapter 29

Lieutenant Saburo Sakai was one of Japan's three top-scoring aces. He loved to fly. He was not above fabricating reasons to keep his Mitsubishi fighter plane airborne when the rest of his unit had returned to the carrier. Today's excuse was to check out the little island on the horizon for evidence of enemy activity. He had flown over it a few days before and had seen nothing suspicious, but he persuaded his commanding officer that it would be no trouble to be certain.

As the sun was setting, he chose to make a wide circle of Chase Island to study it from all angles since that would take the most time. After his first circuit, he then flew straight over the island's volcano. Even when he was a little boy he had always wanted to look straight down the center of a volcanic crater — now he would get his wish. He flew precisely over the center and tipped the wing so he was at a 90-degree angle to the ocean.

It was beautiful, despite of the deepening shadows. He could see the steam bubbling out crevices in the walls of the living mountain. He remembered all the stories his grandfather had told of the spirits who lived in Mt. Fuji and wondered what the old man would say if he could see him now 500 feet above an active volcano, peering down its throat like a doctor examining a patient.

Once was not enough. He flew out to sea again, and did a roll that brought him in at right angles to his first flight. This put him in direct line with the sunset, making it a bit hard to get a clear view. He dropped his altitude 100 feet to get a closer look at the scenery. He was grinning at his own cleverness in arranging this reconnaissance flight. No danger — just pleasure.

Then he saw it! It couldn't be, but there it was. Perched on the edge of the volcano was a small, single engine plane.

Sakai could not believe his eyes. This was impossible. There was no landing strip on top of the volcano. In fact there was no landing strip anywhere he could see on the island; even the beach was too short.

He pulled back hard on the stick and roared into a steep climb. He leveled off and flew out to sea. He was flying under radio silence, so dared not call the carrier. He was on his own. He had been training for more than two years, and had recently been part of the attack on Hawaii.

The Imperial Navy does not need officers who need to ask instructions constantly, he told himself. *If I break radio silence I will be asking for trouble. What do I do?*

Another circuit of the island was in order, while he made up his mind. *It cannot be one of ours. If someone had crashed, I would surely have heard about it. Besides, it's too small. In fact, it's the smallest plane I have ever seen*, he reasoned. "If it is not Japanese," he said aloud, "then it is an enemy plane and must be destroyed."

Only the top ten degrees of the sun was above the horizon, now casting very dark shadows on the spot where he saw the aircraft. However, using the top of the sun as a guide and centering on it, he knew exactly where the grounded plane was, even if he could not see it clearly.

He sighted on the spot and began a long dive, exceeding 200 miles an hour. While he was still a half-mile out to sea, he began firing his two 7.7mm machine guns. He allowed a least 500 of the slugs to rain at random on the jungle on the outside of the volcano, and sprayed as many inside the cone. The bullets ripped through the fuselage of the target plane, tearing off one wing totally. Tracers showed him he was successful. One of them ignited the body of the plane and it began to burn.

One more pass at the lip of the crater, this time spewing 20mm cannon rounds, showed Lieutenant Sakai the burning outline of the unidentified airplane. It would offer no threat to the Imperial Navy.

Performing a victory roll, contrary to Naval regulations, he sped toward the distant carrier to proclaim his unexpected victory.

***

He couldn't explain it, but a restlessness had overtaken Moses McDuff late in the afternoon. For lack of something else to do, he hiked down to the village with Yani to talk to Ooma about trading tinkens for fresh coconuts. The American had developed a taste for a fresh coconut milk drink his island companions prepared. More and more he preferred it to the rainwater he collected almost daily, and pretended not to know that it was half tuba wine. It took a great deal of selective perception not to be aware that Yani had several palm trees from which he was collecting fermented sap.

Everyone was just getting comfortable. McDuff was sipping his coconut drink, and Ooma, Yani and the other men involved in the trade negotiations were drinking kava. Yani was sitting in a position that let him gaze out toward the ocean. When a movement caught his eye, he pointed and asked McDuff, "What?"

Never leaving the camp without his binoculars, he trained them on the object. "It's a Zeke," he said. "It's like those airplanes that flew over the island last week. Remember?"

A quick discussion went through the group. Yani said, "Ooma still wants to catch one. He thinks they would make him very strong."

"I think you would kind of have a tiger by the tail," McDuff laughed. "They are rather hard to tame."

"I think John Frum, he come in plane, maybe," Yani suggested.

"John Frum isn't coming in anything, Yani," McDuff said angrily. "That's a Japfella plane and it's certainly up to no good." He watched it pass out of view and was quick to figure out that it was scouting the island.

A few more sips of kava and the powerful coconut cocktail allowed the conversation to come back to how many coconuts should be traded for each tinken.

When the Zeke made its appearance again, there was no ignoring it. It flew low over the island in the direction of the volcano at 150 miles per hour. The prop-wash shook the tops of the palms. "My God, I hope he doesn't see our antenna," McDuff shouted in alarm, and jumped to his feet. The others were in no condition to stand up, much less jump. The kava had done its work, and the natives would not leave the clearing where they sat for a number of hours. Their legs were asleep for the night; Yani's included.

Foolishly, McDuff decided to return to his camp. What he would do when he got there was not clear, but he felt his presence was required. But the tuba wine had taken its toll, and he lost his footing in the dense undergrowth. He slid down the hillside, away from the path and had to crawl up the rough slope, pulling himself forward bush by bush. It was getting dark quickly, since the sun was going down on the other side of the volcano. Then he heard the Japanese fighter shrieking in his direction. Its machine guns were blasting a path through the trees about 100 yards to his right.

"He's seen the antenna, damn him!" the ex-minister said in the strongest language he dared. "He's strafing the camp. The dirty son-of-a-bitch." McDuff even surprised himself. He had never used such language before in his life. War and wine evoked strange behaviors.

He lay there panting in the heat. Partly the climb, but equally the excitement of the attack had raised his pulse and breathing rates. Keep cool, he thought. Yani is down below, and there is nobody at the camp. This is just an exercise in noise and violence. He closed his eyes and began praying aloud.

When he had repeated the Lord's Prayer for the third time, he heard the plane making another run. The tracer bullets had started small fires in the jungle, but the vegetation was so moist most of them went out for lack of fuel. This time, he could tell the guns were even bigger and louder. He heard a few trees fall when the cannon fire cut them in half. His prayers got more specific and he begged to be out of the line of fire. He was.

A few minutes later he heard the plane's engine getting further away. It apparently decided to return to its carrier. *More than ever, I have to get back to the camp …send a message to Headquarters to report the hostile engagement. But who's gonna run the generator?* He was on the path now, trying to regain his strength. *I just need to relax and close my eyes for a few minutes,* Moses told himself. *Then I'll be able to climb the rest of the way.*

The next thing he new, Yani was returning from his morning bath, and had found him sleeping on the soft grass next to the trail.

***

McDuff examined the campsite quickly, checking mainly to see if his radio equipment had been damaged by the strafing. He sighed deeply and his shoulders relaxed. "It was a tale told by an idiot, full of sound and fury, signifying nothing," he said to Yani, who plainly did not quite understand the comment.

"It means there was a lot of noise, but little damage. The first thing we need to do is take that aerial down. He probably saw the crossbar and guessed what we were up to," McDuff said.

While Yani was moving the antenna wire to a more concealed place along the rock wall, one of the warriors entered the clearing. He was coming down from the top of the volcano and wanted to talk to Yani immediately. They conferred amid a great deal of gesticulating and arm waving.

"What is he saying?" McDuff wanted to know.

"He say Japfella shoot duck at top of volcano. Duck burn up, sir. All gone."

"What ducks. I didn't see any ducks up there. In fact, I didn't see any kind of birds up there."

"You come with Yani, sir. I show you," the young man said.

"No. First I need to send a message to report the Japfella plane to headquarters. I have to tell them we have been attacked." He motioned to Yani to start the generator and tapped out his code sign and message: "Attacked by Japanese Zeke last night. Heavy strafing of camp. No injuries or serious damage. They know we are here. I await instructions."

A little while later he received: "Anticipate landing party to seek and destroy. If Japs land take to bush. Seek native help."

McDuff responded: "Natives friendly. No problem. Is Les Gale there?"

A few minutes later: "Hi, Mo. Read message. Take care."

"Having wonderful time. Wish you were here. Yani will be my lifeline."

"Bad news. Percy traitor. Convinced Japs are John Frum's soldiers. Tried to kill Wembly. I had to shoot him. Watch out."

"Sorry to hear. Will beware."

"New code shortcut. Zeke is now Zero. Use long dash for symbol. Out."

The Coast Watcher put down his earphones and was bewildered. *Percy tried to kill Mr. Wembly?* he thought. *Does Les think Yani would be a traitor,* too? What's all this "John Frum" business about anyway? I refuse to think that Yani can't be trusted. Yani is my friend. He has even saved my life ... But, that was before he got friendly with Percy. But he seemed to be our friend also.

Seeing that McDuff was finished transmitting, Yani stopped the cranking. "We go and see duck now?" he asked.

For a moment the Witman did not understand the question, then remembered the conversation that took place just before he sent his transmission. "O.K., Yani, let's see the duck that the Zeke — excuse me — the Zero shot down."

When they reached the summit, McDuff stood on the path that ran around the top and said, "Which way?"

Yani pointed across to a spot where the ground was a different color. There was a pile of ashes from a fire that had spent itself during the night. At first he thought it might have been a hot boulder shot out of the boiling mud pit, but as he reached the spot it took shape. It had the rough outline of an airplane.

"What on earth?..." he said. "What is this? It looks like an airplane." Examining the unburned portions he added, "but it must have been made out of bamboo and leaves."

"We build duck-coy, like you say," Yani said.

"Decoy?"

"You say Witman catch ducks in America with wooden decoy ducks. We make decoy airplane. You say 'set out decoy' and Ooma can catch Japfella plane. We make decoy from bamboo and reeds from lake. It work. Make plane come."

Understanding came like a flash. "That's what all you fellas were doing coming up here with the tools and bamboo and stuff the other day."

"Yes. But we not catch Japfella plane. He plenty angry. Not like decoy. I think he want real girl-fella plane."

"No, Yani, no. They are not birds. They are flown by Japfellas. Just like Witman who flew the plane to Brisbane you were on."

The technology escaped the Chase Islander. He was still convinced that the Zero was a disappointed avian lover, who had not found what he wanted.

McDuff guessed pretty closely what had taken place. And said, "Better throw pieces into volcano. He will be plenty angry if he comes back and sees decoy again. He send Japfella soldiers." The white man picked up a small, unburned piece of wing and examined it. *Pretty good job, considering*, he thought, and sailed it out into the void.

Chapter 30

As the sun came up over the mountain behind him, Yani finished his recitation of "*Big name watchem Sheepy-sheep...*" Like makers of prayers around the world, he was becoming bored with the constant iteration of the same words. He was racing through "*Send us the shipload of supplies we so desperately need...*" when his eye caught a speck on the horizon. He stopped the litany in mid-sentence and lifted his sunglasses. They had become so scratched it was difficult to see anything clearly through them any more, especially something far away.

There were two specks out on the sea, not one. His first impulse was to abandon his prayers and race up the trail to tell Big Man Duff to send a message to Port Moresby. In fact, he was in the process of getting up when he stopped. It was as though a voice called out "Stop! Maybe this is the answer to our prayers. Maybe this is John Frum coming to the island!"

Yani sank back into the kneeling position. He closed his eyes, folded his hands in the classic supplicant position, and said very slowly, "*Help us to do Your great work of conversion. We ask this in the name of Jesus Christ. Amen.*" When he opened his eyes again he focused on the rapidly growing shapes at sea.

It was not long before he could make out that the lead boat was very similar to the *Wombat* in its form; perhaps even larger. The other boat was a boxy affair of a kind he had never seen before. Judging from its shape, it could hold a great deal of cargo. *Yes! This must be what I am waiting for,* he told himself.

Other men and women from the village were coming down to the water's edge for their morning baths. As they joined him Yani said, "John Frum, he come! John Frum, he come!" and pointed at the two boats coming toward the beach. Before long everybody in the village was assembled. All the warriors held their shields and two or three throwing spears.

Ooma asked, "Witman Patrol boat again, or Captain West comes back?" The latter worried him. The old man was concerned that he might have returned after all this time with reinforcements.

"No," Yani insisted. "John Frum, he come!"

Never-the-less, the excitement was growing. The prospect of battle was something the men were not afraid of. For years there had been no opportunities to test their virility and valor against an outside aggressor. If it wasn't John Frum, it was at least a chance for young men to earn reputations for daring and bravery.

***

Two young officers stood on the bow of the Imperial Japanese Navy torpedo patrol boat and surveyed Chase Island. Ensign Ogata Ishikawa and Lieutenant Junzo Mitsumo looked through their binoculars at the mass of black bodies that were gathering on the beach. Mitsumo turned to his Chief Petty officer and said, "Fire a burst of six rounds into the cliff behind those trees ... about ten meters above the water line."

"Yes, sir," the man answered smartly and passed the order on to the gunner, who sent a half dozen 20 MM armor-piercing shells arcing into the rocks on the cliff face near the beach.

The senior officer grinned with satisfaction when the explosions had the desired effect. Everyone ran from the strand to the palm trees that edged the sand.

"No disrespect intended, sir," Ishikawa said. "But I think that we might have better luck with another approach with the natives."

Ishikawa's father had operated a small fleet of trading vessels out of Sasebo for 35 years. Ogata had worked on the island-hopping boats since he was a teenager, and was quite familiar with life on the islands of the South Pacific. In fact, he had been sent to this part of the world mainly because he spoke Booga-booga and Pidgin rather well. Normally, he was attached to the Admiral's flagship, now anchored off Guadalcanal.

However, it was decided that his linguistic skills would be useful in investigating the report of enemy activity on this small island.

Mitsumo, a graduate of Eta Jima, the Japanese Annapolis, had a low opinion of this man who was loaned to him for this operation. However, he came from the flagship staff, and the same dynamics were at work here that operated in anyone's navy. He deferred slightly to the young man and said, "What do you propose to do — *Ensign?*"

Ignoring the emphasis on his lowly rank, he said, "Perhaps I could take a small boat and a few men and go ashore to talk to the chief. I have looked at the charts, and the lagoon appears to be locked in by reefs. However, I am sure there is an opening somewhere in the chain. Invariably they have a low spot somewhere that connects with the open sea."

"And then what? Will you have tea with the chief, and ask him if he has seen any British or Australian airplanes landing on the island?" Mitsumo mocked.

"Essentially, yes," Ishikawa said, coolly. "I don't see any reason to risk the lives of any of our men, or to just slaughter the natives, for that matter."

Lieutenant Mitsumo could not stomach this butterfly approach to warfare. "We are not on a trading mission, Ensign. You are here as an interpreter, not a strategist. Our men are not afraid to die, but I doubt if a handful of natives offer much of a threat to a landing barge loaded with 40 combat-trained soldiers of the Imperial Army. I don't care if we have to kill every spear-chucker on that island to fulfill our mission. Which — since you missed the briefing last night — is to determine if there is an enemy installation anywhere on the island."

Mitsumo pushed roughly past Ensign Ishikawa, and went to the bridge of the torpedo boat. He laid out a map of the island and examined the recent photographs of the lagoon. "Two torpedoes here," he said, pointing to a point on the map, "should open up a channel large enough for the landing craft to enter the lagoon."

He spoke on the radio to Captain Nagama, who was in charge of the infantry company on the seagoing tug that guided the barge full of troops. "I will blast an opening in the reef for you to use. Let me speak to the captain of the tug." There was a brief silence while the other Navy officer took the microphone and put on the headset.

"Line up behind me," Mitsumo told him, "and prepare to push the landing barge through to the spot where you see the torpedoes detonate."

The helmsman of the second boat positioned his boat as directed.

***

Moses McDuff awoke with a start. The six 20 MM shells going off on the cliffs below his camp jolted him out of his half-awake state. He jumped to his feet and foolishly ran to the edge of the cliff where he could have been easily spotted. Below were two Japanese boats, roughly in the same place the *Wombat* had occupied when it delivered him to the island. However, all eyes were on the beach and he escaped notice.

He ran back to his radio equipment and wondered where Yani was now. He hoped he had not been harmed by the shooting, and needed him to run the generator. Fortunately Pee-wee, the 10-year old assistant generator operator who knew the drill came racing up the trail. He chattered away in Booga-booga, telling the obvious tale of the Japanese Navy's arrival. McDuff pointed to the generator and made a circular motion with his hand.

In a matter of minutes he was clicking off a message to Port Moresby: "Japs here. One torpedo boat. One landing barge under tow. I am leaving base camp. Will transmit when able."

McDuff picked up his pre-arranged escape gear, generator, transmitter, and his rifle. Pee-wee watched him take the trail for the top of the volcano and disappear.

***

There were two massive underwater explosions spaced about ten seconds apart at the low spot on the reef. After delivering her deadly tin sharks at the target, the torpedo boat swerved off to the right. The officer in charge of the tug revved his engines to the maximum rpm to get a high speed run at the opening in the reef marked by churning froth. The distance from the starting point to the entrance to the lagoon allowed the tug to propel the barge at a speed of better than 20 knots.

Captain Nagama had climbed on to the barge. He told his infantrymen that once their craft shot through the narrow gate it would continue to accelerate. The maneuver was to skim across the shallow tidal basin and come to a decisive stop at the beach. The men would then drop over the sides into the shallow water. Forty screaming soldiers with fixed bayonets would charge toward the cowering natives, shooting their weapons at anything that had the misfortune to be in front of them.

Fed constantly by the news of victories in Hong Kong and the Philippines, their propaganda officer had convinced them that they were "The Japanese Gods of War" and were invincible in battle. Nothing could stand in the way of their victory over this tiny volcanic island in the middle of the Pacific Ocean.

Reality set in when the landing craft was one-third of the way through the new opening. The barge was three feet wider than the newly blasted gate, which caused it to rear up on a 30-degree angle and stay there. Many of its brave, battle-ready soldiers fell over the side into the churning surf around the reef. The landing barge itself, just hung there on the reef, looking to all the world like a large, ungainly and paralyzed fish.

The soldiers on board were not ready for the direction the deck beneath their feet took. The fixed bayonets were already unsheathed, causing some nasty injuries. There were several accidental discharges of rifles in the hands of soldiers who had never been in combat before, which also took their toll.

Captain Nagama was thrown from his perch at the rear, and landed on the deck. As soon as he could reach the radio he spoke to Lieutenant Mitsumo. He threatened the Navy officer with a painful form of castration, and demanded that he do something to keep his soldiers from drowning. Water was pouring through a gash in the bottom of the assault boat. Some who were already in the deep water had the sense to let go of their rifles and unbuckle their combat packs. Others drowned before they realized the bottom was a good twenty feet below them.

***

Ensign Ishikawa maintained perfect facial control, and said how much he regretted that the accident had happened. Mitsumo was shaken. The loss of the landing craft was clearly going to be blamed on him, and decided that the final failure of the mission should fall on the hapless Ensign.

Swallowing hard, he said with a quaver in his voice, "Do you have an alternate approach to achieving our objective?"

"I am afraid you will find my actions extreme, sir," Ishikawa said.

"Extreme!" he shouted. "How much more extreme do you think things can get? We are about to lose 40 men without even engaging the enemy."

"Then allow me to take one man in a small boat to the island, and talk with the tribal chief. The only problem is we will have to go completely naked, and it may take time," Ishikawa said.

"We don't have time. That boat is sinking and I can't fit more than half of the men on to this one. What do you think you can do by going in naked?"

Ishikawa explained that during his years on his father's trading boats he had learned the native languages, and their customs. He was planning to employ the same tactics the Australians had witnessed when Yani and Negeb went ashore. The only problem being that he was not a native.

Mitsumo had no choice but to agree.

**

Yani and Ooma watched the Japanese dinghy make steadily for the beach. "This is John Frum?" Ooma asked.

Somewhat chagrined, Yani replied, "No. I think these are Japfellas. I should go tell Big Man Duff."

"No. You stay here. Ooma needs you more. We will talk with the Japfellas."

Several warriors threw long, javelin-like spears at the Japanese soldiers who had tried to swim to the shore. Now they aimed for the approaching boat, but it was too far away for them to reach. Ooma told them to stop trying until he had a chance to hear out the emissary who apparently knew the island customs.

Both Ishikawa and his companion held their oars above their head to demonstrate that they bore no weapons. "I wish to make a circle in the sand," the

Japanese said in perfect Booga-booga. It took both Chase Islanders by surprise. Neither expected to hear a Japfella speak their language.

"How do you speak our tongue?" Ooma asked.

"My honored father traded in these islands many years. I was fortunate to spend much time with him. He taught me the ways of the island people."

"We cannot make a circle with someone who has tried to kill us with powerful weapons," Yani said. "I believe you are bringing your war with the Witman to us."

Ishikawa got down on his knees and pressed his head to the sand. "I humbly beg the forgiveness of the chief of the island. As you have warriors who throw spears without being told, so we have people who do not know how to be a friend of the Blackfella."

"Why does the Japfella come to Chase Island?" Yani asked, as several of the warriors came to stand next to the shamans to hear what was going on.

The Japanese looked them over and made some mental notes. "Our ship is trapped on the reef. I am afraid that our men will drown in the surf. We ask permission to allow the men to swim to shore. They will set up a camp on the island until we can send another boat to take them away."

Ooma allowed Yani to conduct the discussion because his contact with the outside world was greater. Yani chose not to raise the question of why they were trying to breech the gap in the reef in the first place. The islanders seemed to have the advantage now, and he wanted to see what gifts the Japfellas might offer them as compensation for letting the endangered soldiers come ashore.

Yani and Ooma walked off a few yards and turned their backs on Ensign Ishikawa. They talked it over and decided to allow him to evacuate the landing barge. There was still the danger that the torpedo boat might do them serious damage with its guns, and force a landing anyway.

When they returned to the Japanese, Ooma said, "We will expect you to show your gratitude with tinkens and knives."

***

On his way back to the Torpedo boat, Ensign Ishikawa boarded the seagoing tug. In spite of the desperation of the situation, the other men were amused by the sight of a naked naval officer. Ignoring them, he spoke to Captain Nagama, "I have negotiated safe passage onto the island for you and your men. Take as many men as you can hanging on to the dinghy until we reach a point where the water is shallow enough for them to walk. I will tell Lieutenant Mitsumo to give you as many life rafts as possible to transport your weapons and equipment ashore."

"Do you think there are enemy soldiers on the island?" Nagama asked.

"I don't know. But I did notice that all the men wear strands of telegraph wire around their wrists. They didn't make that themselves. One of the Big Men, the younger one, wears a Christian cross and sunglasses. He must have had close contact, or he took them from the body of a flier."

"Good work, Ensign," Nagama said. "Tell that arrogant fool, Mitsumo, that this is not over. I will report his stupidity to the highest command."

***

In a very short time life rafts from the tug and the patrol boat were put over their sides. Once they were guided to the sinking barge, guns, packs, and other equipment were stacked on them. Injured soldiers were transferred to the tug to be returned to their home base. Lieutenants Eisaku Harunobu and Isoroku Shakaru, the platoon leaders got into two larger lifeboats. Soldiers who could not swim were allowed to hang on the sides until the water got shallow enough for them to wade ashore.

On a second trip, radio equipment and food was transferred from the larger ships to the rafts and lifeboats. When all the equipment was stacked in random piles, the mildewing "Japanese Gods of War" were assembled in military ranks.

The natives were immediately curious about what gifts they had brought, and advanced cautiously. Guards were assigned to the equipment piles, and young Japanese privates stood at port arms with bayonets glistening at the ends of their rifles.

The Chase Islanders found their new visitors of great interest. With long slender spears in their hands, the natives gradually encircled the landing party. Ten of the warriors gathered around a stack of boxes full of sake, the property of the officers. They poked at them tentatively while the frightened soldier on guard watched.

"What did you bring us for a gift?" one asked in Booga-booga. He jabbed sharply at a box. The soldier took a defensive pose, ready to defend his post.

"Sergeant of the Guard," he yelled. "Sergeant of the Guard!"

A Sergeant came running with his sword drawn. He charged into the crowd of natives, swinging. When he cut one of the islanders on the arm, a spear was thrust between his ankles, making him fall. Before he knew what was happening, he was on his back with a spear skewering his wrist to the sand. There were six other spear points at his throat.

Ensign Ishikawa, now wearing a pair of shorts, raced to the scene. "Wait!" he said, half pleading, half commanding. "There are presents for you. I will give them to Ooma and Yani." He looked up just as the two men came on the scene.

"We have presents for Ooma and Yani," he said, pressing his forehead into the sand in front of the two shamans. "Please tell your men not to kill my Sergeant."

Ooma told the men to back off, and they complied.

Ishikawa broke open the nearest wooden case containing small ceramic flasks of sake, and gave each of the leaders some of the rice wine. He showed them how to take the cork out of the bottle and sip the contents. There was no time to indulge in any kind of ceremony. Ooma pulled out the cork on his jug and poured the contents into his mouth. He immediately spit it out, and said "Hot water! Burns the tongue!"

The Ensign demonstrated a more proper way to sip the contents, and Yani followed. He laughed and said in Pidgin, "Japfella Scotch!".

"*Hie*! Japfella Scotch," Ishikawa repeated in the same language. "Blackfella hab Witman Scotch? We trade?"

"Churchfella no likem Scotch. We no hab," Yani said without realizing how much information he had unwittingly given away.

The Ensign said, returning to Booga-booga, "Japfella soldier cook rice. You bring fish. We have feast. We be friends. Blackfella go back to village now. We make feast when sun go down."

The warriors withdrew from the beach, and several soldiers helped the sergeant to a sitting position. The spear had to be broken off about four inches from the entry wound and pushed through the opposite side of his forearm. Native spears had barbed points that were not intended to be removed.

Captain Nagama was beaching his lifeboat with another load of supplies as the natives were leaving. He ran up to where the bloody sergeant sat keening in pain. "What is going on here, Ensign. What happened to Sergeant Ubo?"

The old battle-hardened soldier struggled to stand at attention and answer for himself. "We were defending the Officers' rations when the natives attacked."

"Then why do I not see any dead natives?" Nagama demanded.

"I intervened," Ishikawa said. "As acting intelligence officer, I thought it best to settle the matter without a battle."

"That may be a strategy in the Navy, Ensign..." Nagama started to say.

"Begging your indulgence, Captain. How many men do you have left on the beach?"

"Thirty-two," he said suspiciously.

"It is my guess that there are at least 200 armed warriors behind that green wall of a jungle you can see from here. We would not be able to achieve our objective if they all threw their spears at one time," he said. "We would all look like Sergeant Ubo."

"Hmph!" the Captain replied.

"However, I am certain they are harboring a missionary here on the island. The younger chief said as much. He also speaks Pidgin fairly well and he is wearing a cross. So, he has been in close contact with the Australians."

With a deep sigh, the Infantry officer said, "What do you propose we do?"

"We will cook up a large amount of rice, and give them some more sake. I have persuaded them to provide the fish, and we will have a native feast. I think there is a missionary, and we can find out where he is. If there are any military types on the island, we should be able to find that out, too. We'll be out of here in a day or so if we play this right."

Chapter 31

The Japanese cooks had set up a field kitchen. By persuading Captain Nagama and the two other infantry officers, Ensign Ishikawa had gathered enough specialty food items for the feast. They had been intended for the officers' mess for the duration of the mini-invasion. By experience, the Captain had learned that warfare was difficult in the extreme, and compensation for leadership was hard to come by. His officers knew that no matter what else they might face, fine dining could be achieved behind the lines with a little planning.

A couple months earlier Nagama, Harunobu, and Shakaru had been present at the fall of the Philippines. As luck would have it, their company had taken the Governor's Palace — and its kitchen. When word came that they would be ordered to the larger Pacific Campaign, the Governor's pantry was combined with theirs, and some of the booty had been taken with them to Chase Island. Little resistance was anticipated, and the exercise was regarded as an opportunity for Rest and Recreation. Finding a downed enemy flier on a flyspeck island could be drawn out to take a week or more. It was better than life aboard a troop transport. They had come prepared to enjoy their stay. But that was before they came out second best in their battle with the coral reef.

The plan now was to cajole the natives into surrendering whatever white men might be found on Chase Island. Ishikawa assured the Army officers that feasting was the most effective way to deal with this problem. Most of the infantry company's rice ration was cooked up, and numerous dried and canned items were prepared. Native women brought raw fish wrapped in large green leaves, and disappeared.

When the moon rose, Ooma, Yani and a large number of warriors approached the area marked by kerosene torches stuck in the sand. Yani began the feast by scooping up a handful of the high-grade white rice and stuffing it into his mouth. Most of the islanders had never seen rice before, and found it interesting. They took quantities of it between their fingers and examined it closely. There was excited chatter, and the mess sergeant asked Ensign Ishikawa what they were saying.

He laughed and answered, "They want to know what kind of grubs they are, and where did you find so many?"

All the fancy items were tasted, and often cast aside to the irritation of the Japanese officers. "What is wrong with the expensive items we have offered as presents?" Lieutenant Harunobu hissed at Ishikawa.

Somewhat ill at ease, he answered, "They want to know where the sago palm is, and why there is no taro?"

"Ignorant savages!" the Captain said angrily. "We waste all this good food on them, and they look for something I would plaster a wall with. Let's get on with this meeting. I want to know where the Australian or American pilot is they are hiding."

The Ensign, Captain Nagama, and the two Lieutenants sat in a small circle with Ooma, Yani and several elders. Ishikawa wanted to go through the traditional small talk that such a meeting required, but Nagama said, "Ask them where the white man is."

Using some discretion, Ishikawa started out saying, "The Japanese man is the friend of the Blackfella. The White man is his enemy. He only wants the Blackfella to be his slave."

The natives looked to Yani for an answer. McDuff was his wizard. He had brought him to the island with promises of what he could do for them. Now they had all these foreigners with guns here, looking for him.

"We welcome the Japfella as a friend. But we do not have war with the Witman, either. Some Witmen are bad. Not all bad," Yani answered.

"We know a Witman crashed his plane on the top of the volcano. One of our pilots saw it and shot it."

Yani smiled. "That was not a plane. It was a duck. We have duck on top of mountain ... no Witman plane."

"Well, what does he say, Ensign. You are doing an awful lot of talking, and I am waiting for an answer. Where is the white man?" Nagama said.

"He says there was no plane on the volcano. It was a duck."

"You may think it is amusing, Ensign, but I do not. You sit there and let this black idiot make a fool of us."

He turned to Yani again. "The Captain is very angry. He does not believe in ducks. He wants to know where the white pilot of the plane is."

"There is no pilot. Blackfellas built the duck on the top of the mountain to catch girl-fella duck. Japfella come set fire to duck. Volcano people now have it."

Ishikawa's efforts to translate what Yani said only infuriated Nagama more. He jumped to his feet. "Pick him up," he yelled at the two Lieutenants. "I'll get some answers out of him."

The movements of Shakaru took Yani by surprise. With a few deft motions he had twisted both his arms up behind him and Nagama kneed him in the groin. The solders who had been on guard only a few feet away kept the rest of the elders seated by threatening them with their bayonets.

Yani's body slumped. "Where is the white man?" the Captain shouted, and nodded to Ishikawa to translate.

An angry but stubborn Yani refused to answer. Nagama punched him in the face, and the young man lapsed into unconsciousness. "Tie him up. He will talk or wish he never saw a white man."

Ooma defied the bayonets and struggled to bring his old, overweight body to a standing position. In the process, he felt a sharp pain in his chest. His first thought was that he had been stabbed, but the pain extended to his left arm, up his neck and to his left temple. He crashed to the ground, and the other elders crawled to his side. His breathing stopped almost at once. When they saw he had no wound, they pointed to Captain Nagama and almost as a chorus they yelled. "*Bis, bis!*"

They ignored the armed soldiers and scrambled toward the jungle. The other natives quickly picked up the shout, dropped what they were eating, and backed away from the infantry officer's little circle. Soon it seemed everyone was yelling: "*Bis, bis, bis.*"

Ishikawa examined the old man, and said "Ooma has had a heart attack. He is dead."

"What are all the natives yelling? What is it that they are saying?" Lieutenant Shakaru asked.

"Whenever someone dies of natural causes, they believe he is killed by a sorcerer, or wizard. They call these people '*bis*' — They won't come near them. That's why they are running home. They fear Ooma's spirit and Captain Nagama's power."

Nagama liked that. "Good. A little fear is good for the soul. It's about time they found out who is in charge here. Let the old man lay there. They can claim him in the morning."

Ishikawa tried to warn him, that tomorrow morning would also bring retribution. In the night it was easy for ghosts and spirits to walk abroad. The sun and the daylight would change that.

As Nagama's soldiers dragged Yani to their camp, no one noticed Ensign Ishikawa quietly launch one of the lifeboats and row out toward the anchored torpedo patrol boat.

***

As darkness settled on Chase Island, Moses McDuff settled into a clump of bushes, where he could look down on the trail. During his training back at Port Moresby, he recalled the officer told them that when the situation had reached what was now its present condition, he was supposed "to melt into the jungle like the natives do. Don't let the Japs know you exist, much less where you are hiding."

That's easy for him to say. He probably grew up on one of these miserable little islands. I never even belonged to the Boy Scouts. I have no more idea how to melt into the jungle than lead the Boston Symphony Orchestra. And frankly, right now I would rather try the latter.

He was wearing shorts and mosquitoes were tasting his bare legs. Insect repellent was not one of the things he remembered to stuff into the emergency pack. He leaned forward to get a better view of the trail. He was almost at the lip of the volcano, and had avoided going that far in daylight. He did remember to stay off the ridge lines, so his training wasn't a complete loss.

He felt the ground shimmer under him as the volcano belched. Like Yani, he had become accustomed to the frequent movements of the ground. He wondered if Yani's "volcano people" were really the more savage natives he believed lived in the thick brush of the mountains of the inner island.

He stilled his own breathing for a few seconds to listen for noises that might indicate a Japanese patrol coming up the slope to look for him. He wondered where Yani was and if he was all right. *I hope the Japs don't do him any harm. They might torture him into revealing my hiding place. They'll find the base camp easily enough. All they have to do is climb the hill.* He thought of Percy and his betrayal. *Yani would never do something like that,* he assured himself.

He listened some more, concentrating on sounds to determine if they were natural or man-made.

***

Ensign Ishikawa climbed aboard the torpedo boat. Lieutenant Mitsumo greeted him with, "I was just wondering how to get in touch with you in a hurry."

"Why, sir? What is happening?" He had already noticed that the patrol boat's engines were idling and the sailors had weighed the forward anchor. "Are we going somewhere?"

"Yes, Guadalcanal. I have orders to maintain radio silence and leave this area as quickly as possible. There is an enemy task force headed this way — It's believed to be American," Mitsumo said, with a worried note in his voice. "If we stay where we are, we will be directly in its path."

"What about the soldiers on the island?" Ishikawa said. "Are we going to try to get them off?"

"That, Ensign, is the Army's problem. They can send a boat back for them at a better time. Besides, I certainly have no room for a company of Infantry on my ship. Do you have a problem with that?"

When John Frum Came

Ishikawa looked toward the island, as the engines roared to life. "They will all be dead men in the morning, anyway," he said sadly.

***

In spite of his fear, McDuff dozed briefly. He was having a frightening nightmare of trolls coming out of the depths of the volcano when a sound woke him up. The nearly full moon had come up, and disoriented from his dream, he looked around slowly. He jumped when he saw two glowing eyes staring at him from a stand of gnarled trees. He froze. *Uh, oh,* he thought. *I don't like this. Is this one of the volcano people?* He didn't move. The eyes stayed fixed on him as he felt his skin rise in goose bumps and the hair on his neck stand up.

Features started to form around the eyes as he stared back. *It could be a human face with a lot of war paint on it*, he thought. *No. It looks more like a monkey face ... maybe a little more pointed. Wait! It's got ears — I think.* Suddenly it moved and came toward him. As it entered the moonlit clearing, words burst from his mouth involuntarily, "My God, it's a troll!"

Without thinking, he pointed his rifle and pulled the trigger. The sharp report of the weapon startled him back to reality, as the little creature fell dead on the ground. He took out his flashlight, which he had been reluctant to use for fear of being seen. He shined it on the furry body. His troll turned out to be a cuscus — a jungle marsupial the size of a small dog.

But the real damage was done. He had fired his rifle in the middle of the night. He knew the Japanese must have heard it.

***

At the base of the mountain two Japanese soldiers were smoking and talking as they stood guard on the outer fringes of the beach. They were nervous since the aborted feast earlier in the evening. Every click and swish of a branch filled them with visions of wild black men pouncing from the darkness.

To keep up their courage they discussed their macho fantasies. "I don't care if you are from Kure," said one young man, "that's a Navy town. All the women are worn out from constant use. In Osaka we still have a few virgins." They both laughed.

There was really no mistaking the echo of the rifle shot up the trail. If they were to investigate, it would mean going into the jungle. Both were city boys who missed their quiet, peaceful streets. Silence hung heavily between them, as they looked at each other. The private from Kure said, "It is strangely quiet tonight. I have not heard any unusual sounds all evening."

"I agree," said the other.

Chapter 32

After shooting the cuscus, McDuff was certain that the jungle would be swarming with Japanese soldiers. At first light, he crept up the path to the top of the volcano, and moved as quickly as he could toward the opposite side. He wondered which would be worse, being captured by the Japanese or by the unknown savages. The original plan called for Yani to go with him into the jungle to deal with the *kanakas* who lived there. He fancied Ooma's people virtual pussycats by comparison with what he unconsciously termed the "volcano people."

Once he was about one quarter the way around the rim, he stopped and looked across the huge crater at where he had started. No sign of soldiers or natives could be seen. He decided that this was as good as anywhere to stop for now, perhaps even to make a stand. Down below him the floor of the crater bubbled like a witch's cauldron. He could see huge methane bubbles form in the thick mud, occasionally even bursting into flame. *If ever there was a preview of Hell, this is it,* he thought to himself. *I wouldn't be a bit surprised to see Satan's imps dancing along that ... that Stygian lake.*

As though in reply, there was a violent shaking of the cone of the volcano. Although he was lying flat, he could feel himself leave the ground like a flapjack being carelessly tossed in a frying pan. He traveled a good ten or twelve inches into the air, knocking the wind out of him when he landed. There was a bright flash inside the crater followed by a peal of earthbound thunder. He covered his ears and head with his hands, and felt a series of stings on the back of arms and legs. His first thought was that he was being attacked by some kind of fire ants, but when he swatted the bites, he found hot little cinders searing his skin.

"*Lapilli!*" he said in his best Harvard accent, examining the hot spots. He had taken a semester in Natural History and Science, during which there had been some lectures on volcanoes. *Lapilli* was Latin for "little stones" which is what he was frantically brushing off his clothing before they could ignite his cotton shirt.

The crater glowed much brighter than it had before, but the light was suffused by the steam forced from the fast-baking mud. The cinders had been blown hundreds of feet in the air but were still hot as they came down.

Keeping his sense of humor in the face of disaster, he said out loud, "I guess the volcano people are angry."

***

Yani had spent the night hog-tied to a post driven into the ground at the center of camp. There were four guards watching him and the dark beyond the campfire. No one made any heroic attempts to rescue him.

He looked up to see Captain Nagama approaching. He looked very angry. "You black pig," the officer yelled at him in Japanese. "You think a few dozen savages will intimidate the Japanese Army. My men are ready to die for their Emperor and their country. You will tell us where the white man is."

Naturally, Yani did not understand a single word, but he had no trouble understanding the rage in the man's voice. He wondered what became of the pleasant young man who spoke his language. Without his help, there would be no communication with this outraged beast of a man.

Yani could see that Ooma's body still lay on the beach where he had fallen. These ignorant people had not even made any preparation to build a funeral pyre.

Two soldiers dragged Yani to his feet, and he was afraid the Captain would give him another knee to the groin. He did not. Instead, they tied his hands together in front of him, cut the ropes around his ankles, and put two nooses around his neck. There were two strong men holding the ends of the ropes, and it became clear that he was going to be led or dragged somewhere.

"You will take us to the white man," Nagama stated bluntly. And in the universal manner of making black natives understand a foreign language the Captain enunciated the Japanese words and said them very loudly. Yani guessed what they wanted him to do, and decided that his best chance of escape was to lead them up the slope through the jungle. Even an uninitiated child would realize that the path to the top of the volcano was the best place for an ambush. He led them willingly.

***

Lost among the convoy of U.S. Navy ships steaming toward their destiny at Guadalcanal was a freighter named *The Great Snitkin*. In the wardroom, Rear Admiral F.X. Bartlett III, talked privately with his son in his capacity of Operations Officer.

Looking at the orders, he said, "Well, Frankie, I trust you've made the arrangements for moving into our new home. I just got the confirmation orders. That island out there doesn't look very large, but it's ours."

"Yes, sir. There's an LSM pulling alongside as we speak. It will be assigned to us permanently after it finishes its chores."

"Officially, it's Island Number 321. I think it might be a nice gesture if we named it *Bartlett's Island*. Maybe the name will stick after the war — sort of our own personal signature on the success of the war."

Lieutenant Bartlett looked at the map. "I like that," he said. "I'll make sure that we get all our communications equipment ashore. Uncle Bill's promise to make sure we would have what we need has been taken care of. The stuff he sent to Port Moresby is already on the island. We will not be lacking for creature comforts, sir. I also supervised the loading of our goods back in San Francisco. Don't worry about anything. It's all under control."

"Good." The senior Bartlett ran a few things through his mind and then said, "What's the latest on Johnny?"

"I've tried to get him transferred to this ship as his duty station when we get off. But they claim they have no place to quarter a single Negro sailor, short of giving him a private room. Meanwhile, I put him in charge of off-loading our personal possessions to make sure they find their way to where they belong. I had a detail of men get everything up on deck in a staging area."

Chapter 33

At daybreak, ill tempered from his lack of sleep due to his injured arm, Sergeant Ubo formed up the soldiers. He selected the guards who would relieve those who had spent the night on the perimeter of the encampment. After a quick breakfast of rice left over from the feast, ten men marched out of the camp in a column of twos. When they reached the beginning of the trail that led up the volcano the privates from Kure and Osaka should have been waiting. They were not.

Sgt. Ubo swore out loud at the missing men, and dressed down the replacements as though it were their fault. He left two men and proceeded to the next guard post further down the beach. Again there were no guards, and no sign of where they might have gone. He began to worry, and looked more carefully at the sand. It showed signs of two bodies having been dragged into the bush. Everyone figured out the obvious at the same time.

He gave each of the guards two extra packets of ammunition, and told them to stand at the water's edge with their backs to the ocean. It was unlikely that the natives would swim up from behind. If the guards saw anyone in the jungle, they were to shoot him without a challenge.

The story was the same at the remaining three posts, and Ubo returned to the camp alone.

When he reported the situation to the officers, who were just shaving, they were alarmed. "We need that idiot, Lieutenant Mitsumo, to rake the whole village with machine gun fire. It is time to show these savages that the Imperial Japanese Army is not to be trifled with," Captain Nagama blustered.

His Lieutenant tried to raise the torpedo boat on the radio with no luck. They strained their eyes looking out to sea and could not spot its silhouette. Captain Nagama also noticed that the life boat was gone, as was Ensign Ishikawa.

***

A large, amphibious landing craft had been drawn up alongside the *Great Snitkin*. John could never keep straight the difference between an LCM, LCVP, and a LCT. All he was certain of was that this was a fairly big one, and had a small crew who lived on it. At the moment, that entire crew was on a scrounging mission. Every time they unloaded a larger freighter, they bought and traded all kinds of luxuries: movies, books, magazines and liquor primarily. Some was for re-sale and some for their personal use.

The greatest commodity they had to trade was rapid service. None of the freighters liked to sit still where they were targets for submarines and air attacks. Twenty-five pounds of frozen beef could set records in unloading a cargo. So far, however, the green crew of the *Snitkin* had only offered a one hundred-pound sack of potatoes and three cases of beer — Hardly a big enough tip "To Insure Promptness."

John Bartlett watched the other sailors hauling things up from below deck. Every time he saw a red tag on an item, he told them to put it in the LSM's crew's quarters, with "The Old Man's stuff." Admiral Bartlett liked being called The Old Man. It sounded like he had been a Navy man for a long time, instead of less than a year. When all the official cargo was secured on the landing craft, John made sure the red-tagged items were safe. He could only guess what Frankie might have brought along for Daddy's comfort. In any event, he climbed down to the LCM by the cargo net hanging over the side. He jumped from one massive stack of equipment to another. Much of it was C-Rations. From the looks of things, they expected to stay there for a long time.

Once the work party returned to the *Snitkin*, and the landing craft's crew were still out haggling, John realized that he was the only soul on the amphibious boat. He found a secluded corner out of the sun and stretched out for a nap.

***

The soldiers guarding Yani were strung out single file on the path up the mountainside. One led him by a rope around his neck, a second followed with a similar rope behind. If he tried to make a break for it, they would strangle him until someone shot him. Not trusting subordinates to accomplish such a vital mission, Captain Nagama, pistol drawn, led the small group. Lieutenant Shakaru followed with three other men with rifles. They were supposed to be looking for a white pilot, but all they could think about was the guards who disappeared during the night. The dense greenery might conceal dozens of natives with long, sharp, barbed spears.

When the search party reached the clearing that McDuff had used for his base, the soldiers poked their bayonets into everything he had left behind. It was clear that he had gone. They stayed close to each other during the search, although they saw no signs of life in the bush. When they reached what had been the food stores, Yani knew his tribesmen had been there, and were most likely very nearby. There wasn't a single tinken left anywhere.

Lieutenant Shakaru said something ugly and threatening to Yani, and he nodded toward the path. They strung out the procession on the narrowing path again, and resumed the climb. When a fissure opened within the crater the whole side of the mountain seemed to slide. Loose rocks above and below them began tumbling down in an avalanche of crumbling pumice and basalt. Terror struck. Earthquakes were common in their own country, and they knew there was nothing they could do but pray. The last man in the little column was struck by a boulder the size of a football, and disappeared over the edge and into the ocean below. The rest fell to the ground, and waited out the tremor. The rain of hot ashes had cooled somewhat by the time it reached the lower level where they were, but everything smelled like rotten eggs.

"Keep going," Captain Nagama urged. "Let's get to some level ground, and off this damned sliding gravel pit!"

The pace picked up and they reached the relative safety of the platform of level ground forming the top of the cone. Nagama reached the top first and the two men holding Yani on the ropes spread out to either side of the Chase Islander. Lieutenant Shakaru guarded the rear — but only for a few moments.

One of the men seemed to suddenly grow a spear out of his chest, and slide off the path. Another was struck with a war club thrown by a man who blended with the black basalt outcroppings. The Lieutenant ran back down the path, propelled by sheer terror. No one was pursuing him; he was running from his own fears. All eyes were on Yani, and his captors.

Captain Nagama pointed his pistol at his captive, and the two men with the ropes had now unslung their rifles, and pointed them at Yani. They stood at the edge of the crater, looking down at the glowing center.

The army officer evaluated the situation from a military standpoint. Perhaps he could use Yani as a shield and a hostage to get back down the mountain. Through his body language, which included pointing into the crater, and his tone of voice he made it clear to Yani that he would hack his head off and throw him into the fire if he did not help them down the mountain.

It was a standoff. No one did anything but stand there for a full three minutes. Each waited to see what would happen next. The natives knew that with Ooma dead, they would be without a shaman if something happened to Yani, and the tribe would perish.

Nagama's desperation was on a personal level. This was not the way he saw the war ending for him. He was furious. He drew the Samurai sword his father had given him when he became an officer, and waved it menacingly at Yani. He railed at the island warriors who now allowed themselves to be seen.

"I was never intended to be run through with a filthy, wooden spear wielded by a cave man. I am an educated man. I am the son of generations of Samurai. I deserve to die on a field of honor, in battle with someone more my equal. I am ready to die honorably with a bullet in my chest for the Emperor and my Country."

Three seconds later, the once Reverend Doctor Moses McDuff, now turned guerrilla, granted his wish.

***

Although the archipelago known as the Volcano Islands, lay considerably further to the north of Island 321, the name could have applied to any of the green dots in the South Pacific. For the most part they were the tops of volcanoes rising thousands of feet from the ocean floor. The advance party that had gone ashore on Island 321 felt seismic activity from the first day. However, the Navy command did not want to hear such complaints. The sailors and Marines were ordered to consider such rumblings as normal, and go about their duties as assigned.

It was also a geologic fact that many of the volcanoes were connected to each other along a fault in a huge tectonic plate. When one burped, they all hiccupped. In fact, all the islands over a wide range were joined by a plateau-like shelf that made the water too shallow for something the size of a freighter to get very close. Amphibious craft were the only way materiel could be ferried ashore.

John Bartlett was stirred from his brief nap by a sudden commotion at the rail of the *Snitkin*. A growing crowd of men were yelling and pointing toward the island. He sat up and turned his head toward where the men were looking. He was just in time to see a fireball of gas, lava and smoke burst skyward. A few minutes later he heard what sounded like hail coming down on the boxes, crates and cartons stacked around him. They were little, hot, black marbles of obsidian, volcanic glass. He scrambled to his feet and almost dove into an open doorway of the crew's quarters.

As the stones clattered on the metal roof of the conning-tower-like structure he looked again toward the island. What he saw was horrifying. A large portion of the beach was sliding into the ocean amid much hissing and steaming. He could see Marines trying to outrun the encroaching waves, then disappear in the surf.

Aboard the *Snitkin* panic was breaking loose. The public address system blared. "General Quarters. General Quarters."

In the shallow waters off the little atoll, gentle swells were taking on the aspect of roller coaster dips. The captain wanted to get out to sea and away from the shelf that magnified the ocean's movement.

Marine Lieutenant Bartlett realized that there was no one on the landing craft to steer it to safety. Not that he was sure where "safety" was. Heading into the sinking island did not seem to be an option. If the truth were known, he was more concerned about the loss of his father's red-tagged possessions. If they lost this boatload of equipment, they would be forced to live on standard Government Issue.

He scrambled onto an empty cargo net, hanging over the side from a crane. "I'll hang on to the cargo net," he yelled to the deck officer. "Lower me onto the boat. I'll handle it."

Clinging to the net he dropped to the LCM, but found it difficult to maintain an upright position. Although they were right next to each other, the freighter rose and fell at a different rate than the lighter boat. The pallets started to shift to starboard when the hawser connecting the two ships was pulled taut by the action of the sea.

The relative positions of the two ships changed so rapidly that the cargo net first lay limp on the deck, then virtually jumped into the air. On the first try, Lieutenant Bartlett fell off the net and thumped hard onto a wooden case.

Unsympathetically, the deck officer called "Give it up, Lieutenant. God damn it, get back so we can get the hell out of here."

As the rope to the cargo net tightened, Lieutenant Bartlett got a foot tangled in it and rose into the air, hanging by one leg. The crew reeled him in like a marlin that had broken the surface. If they didn't get him up fast enough, he would be dropped back into the deck head first.

John watched the procedure from below with an idiotic grin. His old pal, Frankie, rose rapidly to the end of the crane and they swung him aboard. He was dropped unceremoniously on the deck of the *Snitkin*. His steel helmet kept him from getting a fractured skull, but his neck was in pain. The deck officer said again, "We want to get out of here as fast as we can. That God damned island is sinking, and we don't want to get sucked in after it. This is the South Pacific. We're gonna get ripped apart, capsized or blown away if we don't get rid of the damn landing craft."

"You can't cut it loose. All our equipment is on that boat."

In the meantime, two Marine sergeants and the Chief Petty officer who piloted the landing craft out to the supply ship were panicking also. They had come aboard the larger vessel loaded with money from the men back on shore. Their objective was to buy as much liquor of any variety as they could put their hands on. The chief was now sitting on four cases of Old Grand Dad, while they rigged the cargo net to swing them over the side.

"Belay that shit," the deck officer screamed, trying to sound nautical. "You guys aren't going anywhere with that cargo net…"

The *Snitkin* took a sharp drop, like an elevator slipping two floors. In spite of the officer's orders, the cargo net swung out and lowered the cases of whiskey down toward the smaller boat. However, it was on a downward trip and the cases crashed into the rapidly ascending steel deck amid the heart-rending sound of breaking glass.

Apprentice Seaman Bartlett was on the net in a flash. He cut the rope with a bayonet before it could be yanked up into the air again for a second dashing. With no counterweight, the rope reeled back up like a window shade. The hoist looked like a yardarm. If he had his way, Chicken-shit Lieutenant Frankie would be swinging from it.

The precious fluid from the broken bottles spread out across the deck as John watched.

***

The sudden shot that felled Captain Nagama took everyone by surprise. One of Yani's tormentors, the one who had held the trailing rope, raised his rifle above his head, and in a grand gesture of surrender threw it into the underbrush. He stood with both hands above his head, smiling and chattering about bearing the Blackfella no ill will. The Chase Islander nearest him ran forward with an ornately carved war club, and hit him squarely in the face.

The second guard took a defensive position for hand-to-hand combat with his bayonet-tipped rifle as he had been taught. In a half crouch, he challenged the bearer of the war club. The black man smiled and obviously relished the opportunity to demonstrate his proficiency with his massive weapon. Almost in a wrestler's stance he circled his opponent, and moved in closer.

The position assumed by the Japanese solider also proved a springboard for a quick sprint. Converting all his adrenaline to energy, he darted to the right and chose to do a modified swan dive into the steamy volcano's throat rather than allow himself to be either defeated or captured by the fierce natives hemming him in on all sides.

Yani took the ropes off his neck and threw them to the ground with a display of showmanship. McDuff stood up almost immediately after it was clear the soldiers were surrendering. He seemed to be ready to use his rifle again, if need be, but after the scuffle was over he carried it by its sling, almost dragging it behind him.

He and Yani walked briskly. When they reached each other, the two men embraced in a show of true emotion. He had saved his friend's life, finally returning the favor Yani had performed back on Christ's Despair. Tears of joy and relief streamed down their faces.

A rhythmic noise caught McDuff's attention. All the warriors were thumping the butts of their spears on the ground or against their shields, and were banging war clubs against outcroppings in unison. Then, almost like a referee in a boxing match Yani raised one of McDuff's arms. He turned to the agitated men and shouted, *"Pooja! Pooja!"*

The men thumped louder and faster and chanted together: *"Pooja! Pooja! Pooja! Pooja!"*

In addition to his Harvard Bachelor of Science Degree and his Doctorate of Divinity from The True Church of God Seminary, Moses McDuff was now a warrior of the *Pooja* totem. He was a crocodile.

Chapter 34

No one on deck saw it coming. All eyes were on the drama of the broken booze bottles. The rising and falling of the *U.S.S. Great Snitkin* up to this point might have been compared to a gentle rocking compared to what happened next.

The ship's Captain, Carl V. Stoepel, standing on the narrow deck alongside the bridge, saw it through his binoculars. About five miles astern, it looked like one of the breakers that were consuming the beach of Island 321 — except it was between forty and sixty feet high and was as wide as the limited horizon.

The Captain had never seen one, but he knew its name … It was a *tsunami — a tidal wave*. He knew how the captain of the Titanic must have felt … except this was no iceberg. Captain Stoepel gave a blast on the ship's whistle and yelled over the intercom to the engine room: "Ahead Full! — Flank speed!" He really didn't think he would be able to outrun it, but he had to at least give it a try. When the huge propellers engaged, the big ship gave a shudder and started to move forward.

But Stoepel could feel there was something wrong. Instead of going in a straight line, the ship was pulling to port, as if it had left an anchor in the water. He realized in a moment what it was … he was dragging the LCM along with him.

He got on the horn. "Attention, all hands. Cut loose the landing craft on the port side. Cut loose the landing craft on the port side — On the double!"

Lieutenant Bartlett ran to the gunwale and shrieked, "Wait, we're not on it. We're not on it."

"Look to the stern, Lieutenant," the Deck Officer barked. "Cut that son-of-a-bitch loose before we all drown together."

The Marine looked to the rear of the ship and saw the *tsunami* gaining on them rapidly. "Jesus Christ," he said. "Cut the hawser immediately," he told the nearest sailor.

"With what?" the sailor answered. The cable was three inches thick and was as taut as a rubber band. The Lieutenant ripped a fire ax away from its bracket on the bulkhead, and began whacking away at the huge rope.

Suddenly he noticed that the line was going slack. The LCM was sliding down the face of a wave, and was about to collide with them side to side. It hit them with the jar of two bump cars in an amusement park. The wave preceding the *tsunami* lifted the huge ship's stern out of the water. Its screws were no longer submerged and they came out of the water turning at full speed. The entire ship vibrated like a gong. Rivets popped on its sides where the steel plates had been weakened by rust.

Prayers for salvation went up from the crew in a body. When the hull smashed down again into the water, its propellers whirred faster than they had ever been designed to go, the *U.S.S. Great Snitkin* surged ahead.

The landing craft slid down a wave in the opposite direction snapping the weakened tether. John Bartlett watched the rows of cargo start to shift. He stayed in the crew's tiny quarters above the diesel engines, and quickly sealed the watertight doors. He felt the boat creak and groan as it strained on the leash that held it to the large freighter. Then in an instant the LCM seemed to leap out of the water as the line broke with a whip-snap.

The lurch knocked him off his feet and he hit his head on one of the supporting beams in the little compartment.

Unconsciousness was the best thing that could have happened to him. Had he been awake, he might well have died of fright as Landing Craft (Mechanized) #666 rode the biggest tidal wave since Krakatoa went skyward 60 years before.

***

Lieutenant Shakaru, his pistol in one hand and his sword in the other reached the end of the path. The two guards were still where they had been posted earlier, but now they were headless. He took only fleeting note of their condition and called out as he ran, "Sergeant Ubo! Sergeant Ubo, where are you?"

"Here, Lieutenant. Here, down by the beach. Be careful. They're all around," he heard someone call. A ten-foot spear thunked into the sand next to him, missing him only by inches. A burst of machine gun fire erupted from a clump of bushes on the beach. He could see one of his men waving him toward the camp they had set up the night before, and ran for it while the soldiers laid down covering fire.

What was left of the Japanese infantry company had retreated to a small peninsula that jutted out into the water. From this promontory they had a view of the entire beach.

Lieutenant Shakaru threw himself into the sand behind some convenient rocks, panting furiously. "Report!" he said to Sergeant Ubo.

Crouching behind the machine gun, and not taking his eyes off the beach, he said, "As soon as you left, they sent out a bunch of old women to get the body of their chief. Some of the men thought they would scare them, so they fired into the air. The women scattered, and we thought it was over."

He hesitated. "A few minutes later the air was thick with native spears and arrows. They looked like a swarm of mosquitoes. Any of the men who were not here inside the camp were nailed."

The officer looked over the top of the sheltering rocks. He saw men in uniform strewn across the beach. Some had as many as three spears in them.

"How many men did we lose?" he asked.

"The question is how many are left. There are only six of us here, counting you, sir. I have little hope for the guards on their posts."

"I'm sure they're dead," Shakaru said, remembering the bloody corpses he passed when he ran down from the mountain. He looked out to sea, and remembered that the torpedo boat was far from Chase Island by now. "What about ammunition, and supplies?"

"We used most of the rice for the feast last night. Our ammunition is in boxes out there on the water's edge," Sergeant Ubo said despondently.

Suddenly the palm trees danced in unison as if they were animated by what seemed to be an inner spirit. Some swayed to such a degree that their coconut clusters were tossed 30 feet from the tree. Yet others just snapped in the middle, allowing the tops to crash to the ground.

There was a rumble coming from beneath the ground, and Lieutenant Shakaru was amazed to see a wave coming toward them. It was not coming from the ocean — there was a three foot swell of sand on the shore. It behaved like an ocean wave, but in reverse. Its movement continued out under the lagoon, and made the placid surface dance. He was speechless.

Sergeant Ubo watched the geologic display with him and said at the end, "What are your orders, sir?"

"There is nothing to do but wait," the officer said.

"Wait for what?" the sergeant asked.

"I shudder to think," Shakaru said.

***

John Bartlett was vaguely aware of a rumbling feeling. His head hurt sharply and it took a great deal of effort to open one of his eyes a crack. All he could see was cold gray light that had a slight tint of yellow to it. With both eyes open he made out a compartment in which everything was painted gray. He felt like he was lying in the back of a pickup truck bouncing down an unpaved farm road.

As his head cleared he realized that he was in the crew's quarters of the LCM, and was looking up at a pair of bunks built into the bulkhead. He was surrounded by boxes and bags with red tags.

Painfully, he raised himself up on one elbow and reached for the nearest crossbeam to try to get himself off the deck. He had the oddest feeling of being drawn down to the corner of the room. It was painful, but he slowly brought himself far enough into an upright position to see out the closed porthole. He was looking *down* at the surface of the ocean. It was no illusion — the LCM was at a 45-degree angle to the horizon. It was traveling sideways at a high rate of speed, and he was looking at the backside of what he thought must be the largest wave ever seen by a living man.

He climbed up the sharply inclined deck and looked out the other side. Contrary to what logic and reason told him, there was nothing to see. A hazy sun was no more than a bright orange circle in the midst of a gray cloud. He had the sensation of sailing through the air. The frightening part of the event was that it was more than just a sensation of flight — he was actually riding a 110-foot surfboard that would most likely wipe out on an atoll without notice.

Fighting gravity and the angle of the boat, John worked his way over to the bottom bunk. Whoever slept here had made a mattress out of a modified inflatable, yellow life raft. Most likely it had been salvaged from a downed plane. It was deflated to just the right pressure to make it a comfortable little nest. He dropped into it, closed his eyes and tried to convince himself this was some kind of weird dream.

***

Yani led the way back to the trail down the mountain. As they passed the bodies of Captain Nagama and the dead guard, the American averted his eyes. He had no desire to see the face of the man he had killed. Regardless of the natives' acclamation of his heroism, he took no joy in ending another man's life. He felt sure he would go through the rest of *his* life with the burden of having killed another human being uppermost in his mind. The only justification would be that he had saved his best friend from imminent slaughter in the process.

Yani respected his silence as they descended to the plateau of their old camp. As soon as possible he would have to recover the radiotelegraph and generator from where he had hidden them. Port Moresby needed to know what had happened. He was sure they would tell him he had done well, and make a big fuss over his role in the shooting.

"What about the rest of the Japfellas down on the beach?" he said to Yani. "We will have to deal with them now."

Yani laughed. "I think there are no more Japfellas on the beach. I think they all dead fellas."

"What do you mean?"

"I think *pooja* in village kill all Japfellas by now," he said.

With that, the rest of the warriors came down from the volcano rim. McDuff gagged at what he saw. The heads of the two Japanese who were killed at the top of the mountain were mounted on the war spears of two of the men. They also were carrying the heads of the other unfortunate soldiers who died on the way up. One of the native leaders stood before McDuff and Yani offering the new *pooja* his trophy.

"Tell him to take it away," McDuff yelled at Yani, turning away so he would not throw up. Yani shrugged and motioned the warriors to take their prizes down to the village.

As the men left the clearing and headed home, Yani and McDuff were knocked to the ground by a loud explosion, and a furious shaking of the ground. As they lay there dazed for a few moments, watching the trees doing their strange dance, small stones began to pelt them from above. They scrambled to their feet and sought the shelter of a shallow cave in the side of the hill. McDuff's Harvard training identified the stones streaming from the sky as tektites.

"Big wave come from ocean soon, climb mountain. I think we see Jesus today," Yani declared.

"I realize the situation is serious," the minister said, "but it doesn't mean we will be killed."

Since numerous volcanoes on other islands had already blown their tops, large gray clouds of ash had been building in the upper atmosphere. The sun's light was being gradually blocked out. McDuff was just too busy to notice. Yani had, however, observed the changes and drawn some conclusions.

Without prelude Yani said, "Our father who art in Heaven, Hallow-ed be thy name. Thy kingdom come."

"Considering the situation," McDuff smirked, "I think the prayers of the congregation are in order."

Back on *Wombat* you say, "When Jesus comes back to earth, there will be a Day of Judgment ... 'Thy Kingdom come' means there will be a terrible day. This is a terrible day, is it not?"

"Terrible day?" McDuff said. "I can't think of a worse one."

"But it will be wonderful for the true believers who have accepted Jesus Christ as their savior. We will be with him in Heaven. You say so. The Bible tells us so."

McDuff was embarrassed to be told his business by a native convert. *This man is a better Christian than me*, he thought. *All I have been doing is feeling sorry for myself. He sees us going to Heaven.* McDuff reached into his backpack and took out his Bible.

Both men jumped when a wild sow and three piglets came squealing out of the jungle, and ran across the clearing toward the top of the mountain.

"You find the part about Sun, and raining stones," Yani begged eagerly.

He ran his finger down the page. "The sun shall be darkened in his going forth, and the moon shall not cause her light to shine..."

Yani pointed to the fading outline of the sun without comment.

"And the wild beasts of the islands shall cry in their desolate houses..."

"Pigs know ocean come ... climb mountain. Some children not get up hill ... houses spoiled. You see. Trees tell story already.

He turned to Revelation 16. Verse 18. and read: *"And there fell upon men a great hail out of Heaven, every stone about the weight of a talent..."*

Yani was quiet and thinking while the tektites continued to fall near them. "I remember you say, 'All things are possible in the Kingdom of God...'"

McDuff simply nodded his agreement.

"I think we will see Jesus today..." Yani said. "Kingdom come." Then silently, since he knew McDuff did not like to hear him say it, Yani thought, *And John Frum, he come!*

***

A mile ahead of John Bartlett's private toboggan was yet another *tsunami,* considerably smaller than his. The residents of Chase Island, directly in its path, had felt the same ground tremors as the Japanese. However, they dropped whatever they were doing and snatched up the nearest small children. They had felt the ground shake and they knew instinctively from the behavior of the palm trees that a giant wave would be upon them in no time. Everyone headed for higher ground, even though the mountain was a volcano that just might blow up. No one stopped to save a single possession. Time was the only thing worth saving.

The Japanese soldiers saw the mass exodus of people from the village, and knew that something was happening, but had no idea what. They, too, had felt the vibrations but the only thing they knew to do during earthquakes was to lie flat in an open field. They were already doing that.

Looking in the direction of the ocean, Lieutenant Shakaru's men saw a wall of water 30-feet high that spread as far to the left and right as the shape of their peninsula allowed them to see. He panicked.

Those soldiers whose prayers asked that the gods find a way to remove them from this terrible, living hell got an immediate positive response. Those who had not prayed for deliverance were delivered anyway as the water surged over the rocks.

The wave crashed through the village and jungle, knocking over houses, palm trees, pigpens and anything natural or man-made that stood in its path. The people on the mountain screamed and continued pushing their way up the trails as far and as fast as they could go. The warning had been in time for practically all the able-bodied men and women, most of them carrying children. The aged who could not navigate under their own power were left to be claimed by the flood. Tidal waves had been passing over this and similar islands for thousands of years. The priorities of who got saved had been determined several hundred waves ago. There would be a proper ceremony honoring the victims at a later time. Right now survival beat sentimentality in the homestretch.

The fluid dynamics of the wall of water meeting the volcanic mountain resulted in a slowing down in the rush of water. Following the laws of physics, the mountain sent a good portion of the water back in the direction from which it had come. When John Bartlett's wave met the churning surf from the first one, the net result was for the undertow to neutralize some of the forward momentum of the second *tsunami*. Not that it made much difference since the first wave had moved most of what was moveable.

***

John edged from his stupor and heard noises mere words could not describe. He was sure that anyone else, who had heard similar noises before, did not live to discuss them. The dropping-elevator feeling meant that the LCM had been launched from the crest of the wave and was now airborne. He pictured himself as a flat stone being skipped across the surface of a pond by a colossal ten-year old. The flight lasted an eternity and when the LCM touched down on the sea's surface, it was with such a thud, that the only thing that kept him from being splattered on the deck was the partly-inflated, yellow life raft he was wearing like a cocoon. Water surrounded the boat and from what he could see through the porthole, the surface seemed somewhere above the cabin.

The watertight door had been properly secured and successfully held out the sea.

The LCM aquaplaned the full three-mile length of the lagoon. If the boat were submerged the outcome was inevitable. But he felt the landing craft come to rest on the bottom.

Can I get loose and swim out the door? he thought. He was struggling with his rubber straight jacket, when it seemed as though someone had pulled the stopper out of the bathtub. The water outside rushed away, leaving the decks. Sitting upright he worked on regaining his equilibrium. Finally, when most of the water was off the decks, he stood up and looked around. Most of the Bartlett family's possessions were in a logjam near the foot of the bunks, a tangled mess.

He went out on the elevated deck and looked over the side. The water was receding from the lagoon where the LCM had come to rest. The water was still rough, but it was clear that he had been lifted over a coral reef that ringed the island. It would not allow him to get out again even if the boat had working engines.

Shakily, he took stock of the situation. He was not a religious man, but it is not just in foxholes that there are no atheists. He looked skyward and called out, "God! If you're out there ... Thanks."

Chapter 35

From McDuff's camp to the rim of the volcano, and for as far as he could see in all directions there were refugees from the tidal wave. Children ran after each other in games that only they understood, but the adult population of Chase Island virtually sat in silence. The ocean had climbed the mountain as Yani predicted it would, and now an hour later had receded back to from where it had come.

McDuff was stricken by the quiet orderliness of the people. There was no wailing and crying. There were no hysterical demonstrations of grief. Everyone seemed to be looking his way. *Do they expect me to do something?* He thought. *I would share the food I had left before the Japanese came, but they've already taken that. Do they expect me to pull some kind a rabbit out of a hat? Jesus may have been able to feed the multitudes, but I am kind of shy on miracles right now.* He smirked. *Is this the White Man's Burden? Do they really think there is anything I can do?*

He was nudged out of his reveries by Yani. "Japfella kill Ooma. Yani must go down the mountain and clear the way through the spirits so his people can return to the village."

The words came as sort of a shock to McDuff. The people were not looking at him. They were looking at Yani. He felt like a fool. No one was looking to this presumptuous white man to take over their problems. They were looking to their new spiritual leader, their shaman, the "man who really knew."

"Blackfella afraid to go back to village. Spirits make too much *simka,*" Yani said. "I learned formulas from Ooma to send spirits back into sea. I go now and see village."

Incredulously, McDuff said, "Yani, do you still believe that black magic business that Ooma held over these people's heads? I thought you were a Christian, now. I know you say the Lord's Prayer every day. How can you go back to the old ways?"

Yani was confused by his words. He saw no conflict in believing in the spirit world of his people and the Witman's Jesus. "Blackfella have no food now. Big Man Duff come with me to call ships to come with tinkens for people. You call ship to old island when we have no food. We say Our Father together. We ask Sheepy-sheep to help. If we call ships from Heaven together maybe we get tinkens sooner."

McDuff was flustered. "I believe in the power of prayer, but it's not as simple as you seem to think. Just praying for ships to deliver food isn't going to do it. I think we'll get better results if I fix my radio and we call Port Moresby for some kind of relief aid."

Yani wondered what had happened to Big Man Duff. He had always been ready to pray before. But, he did not have time to waste on a reluctant partner. His people were depending on him to come to their rescue, so he sniffed the breeze and decided the wind was right for exorcism.

Yani thought it over and decided that it would be appropriate for him to start calling the ships as he walked down the trail, since he needed to be on the actual site of the village to drive the spirits out.

He was reciting, "...Thy will be done, on earth as it is in Heaven..." in a loud voice as he came upon the high-water mark. This was the point where the wave ran out of steam. However, it was not before the water had pushed everything in one direction, broken off fully grown palm trees, loosened rocks, and then drew all the debris back again like a giant broom, scraping the topsoil and loose gravel down to the sea.

He stopped praying. It took all his concentration to pick his way down the last fifty feet or so to the island's sea level. His eyes were riveted on the ground, to pick out the safest foothold for the next step. When he reached the sandy floor where the jungle stubble ended, he finally looked up.

He was stunned.

There in front of him was a massive ship shaped like a box. It was at least as big as the *Wombat,* maybe larger. It was hard to say, since it was shaped more like the wooden Japanese boat that sank on the reef. But this one was apparently made of iron, and was partly submerged in the sand dune the receding tide had stacked against it.

He rubbed his eyes, and looked again. It was still there.

Since the tide was out and the lagoon was filled with sand, Yani was able to walk around the whole thing — at a distance. He wanted to touch it, but chose to look at it for a while longer before making so bold a move. He sat down on a fallen palm and allowed his senses to return.

I've done it, he thought. *I've really done it. I have called to Heaven for a ship, and Jesus sent me one. I hope it is a good one and not full of Japfella soldiers or bad men like Captain West.*

***

Aboard *U.S. Navy LSM #666* John Bartlett was recovering from his ride. His primary thought was that he had no idea where he was. When he looked over the side earlier, all he could see was a lot of muddy water, and a devastated tropical island. He thought it unlikely that anyone on it had survived the huge wave.

So, what am I — a modern Robinson Crusoe? At least I won't starve to death. I don't even have to go ashore. Everything I need is right here on the boat. I'll just sit tight until they come looking for me.

The next thought was whether or not the *Great Snitkin* had survived the tidal wave itself. It might have gone down. It could have capsized.

Suppose the Japs find me first. Now that's a really scary thought.

He had found a War Department pamphlet one of the crewmen had in his quarters. It was titled *"Pidgin English for Americans."*

He opened it at random and read a sentence or two:

"The native is nearly, if not quite, as good a man as you are. Don't underrate his intelligence. Don't curse and swear at him — and don't make fun of him. Joke with him by all means ... but don't deliberately descend to his level.

"...Don't beat a native drum without first asking ... as often as not the village drums are under taboo...

"...Remember three things in any village — gardens, pigs, and women. Interference with any of them will bring trouble for you and your mates."

John flipped to the glossary of commonly used words and phrases.

"It is estimated that there are more than 700 languages spoken in the islands of the South Pacific. Because of the absence of communication until the 19th Century, each island developed virtually its own language. However, Pidgin was developed by island traders and is understood in many places. It is a combination of English, German, and local languages. Following are some words and phrases American Servicemen might find useful.

He looked over the lists of words and realized that they were largely phonetic pronunciations of words that resembled English. More interesting were the penciled in notes made by the Marine who had owned the pamphlet. He had compiled a list of local obscenities and insults.

Suddenly, in a fit of anxiety John sprang from the bunk and went out on deck. He was frightened by the prospect of truly being alone. Having no one else to talk to was unique. *Maybe there are some natives alive on the island. Yeah, and maybe they'll have you for dinner if you get off the boat.*

He leaned over the armor plating that shielded the walkway around the outer edge, and let his eyes wander along the shoreline. Any sign of life, human or animal, would make him happy. Then his eyes fell on something bright red on a palm tree, half laying in the water. He squinted and it took shape as a black man wearing a red bandanna around his head. John ducked down to keep from being seen back. Anxious as he was for human company, he wanted to make contact on his own terms.

Staying below the edge of the bulkhead, he scurried back to the crew's quarters. He had seen a carbine lying in a corner, under some red-tagged boxes. He dug it out and found it had a clip of ammunition in place. He slid a cartridge into the chamber and went back outside, still keeping himself out of sight.

How do I do this? he asked himself. *Do I fire off a bunch of rounds to get his attention? No. I might scare him into the bush and I'd never see him again. What do I say? ... "Hey buddy, how's it hangin'?" How about "Hey, you!"* He just didn't know.

Finally, he reasoned, *You're in the Navy, right? How about Navy talk?* He felt foolish but he stood the rifle against the bulkhead, and raised himself up on a step. With his head and shoulders above the edge of the armor plate he cupped his hands in front of his mouth and yelled, "Ahoy, on shore. Ahoy, on shore!"

The startled Yani stood up and froze in position. He was taken completely by surprise. He was beginning to think that the boat was abandoned, but wondered about the wisdom of trying to board it alone.

John waved his arm as a greeting. Yani waved back. He became excited and began to run back and forth in the ankle-deep water in a little pattern no more than ten feet wide. He couldn't make up his mind if he should run out to the boat or wait for the man in the white sailor's hat to call him. He knew from the Australians that you did not go aboard someone else's boat without an invitation.

John wished he had studied the Pidgin booklet a little more. He didn't know what to say next. Pointing to himself, he said, "Me friend." He pointed to Yani and said, "You friend?"

Yani understood and said, "Yani friend. I go boat?"

John waved his arm in a gesture of welcome, and Yani ran out to the LCM. He climbed up a welded ladder on the front of the craft next to the drop-door, and threw his leg over the edge. As they stood on the narrow walkway, the two men surveyed each other.

John saw that Yani wore a piece of red calico around his head, and had on cotton shorts. Around his neck he wore a mahogany cross suspended on a leather lanyard. *Thank God, a civilized native.*

Yani, on the other hand, almost did a double take. He saw a man as dark-skinned as himself wearing white man's clothes. He had seen many natives wearing khaki shorts and shirts, but this one wore blue clothes that covered his legs. He was unfamiliar with U.S. Navy dungarees. Furthermore, this man had shoes on his feet. He held a rifle loosely cradled in his arms.

Yani took it all in and summarized the answer in a few words of Booga-booga.

"I don't understand? You speakee English?"

Yani repeated himself in English. — "You kill all Witmen on board? Take clothes? Take cargo?"

John was shocked. He was speechless for a minute, than said. "No. I didn't kill anybody. This my boat."

Yani looked around warily. "Witman let you speak English?"

"What the hell are you talking about? I'm an American. I always speak English. This is an American Navy ship."

Almost afraid to ask, but not able to resist, Yani said, "What is your name? What island you live on?"

"I'm John Bartlett. I don't live on any island. I am *from* America."

Yani heard only what he wanted to hear. "You are John? You are John Frum, American?"

"Yes. Damn it. I am John from America," he enunciated clearly and slowly.

Yani fell on his knees and pressed his head to the deck.

"John Frum, he come! John Frum, he come!" he said, sobbing.

John leaned his rifle against the bulkhead again, and went forward to help Yani back to a standing position. Tears streamed down Yani's face. He looked at the American and said, "I tell Big Man Duff today, John Frum, he come…"

***

John felt like he had gotten on a moving train. He was confused by Yani's behavior and wondered how anyone could have known he was coming. He only found out a few hours ago himself, and it certainly wasn't anything he had expected to happen.

He sat Yani down on a crate and let him get control of his emotions. "Where did you get that cross?" he asked, pointing to the mahogany pendant.

"Big Man Duff give it to me. He is a *bis* who knows how to call ships. He taught me how to call this ship."

Bartlett's imagination had a flare for the dramatic. He was an ardent movie fan. He had a mental picture of the islands and their inhabitants based on movies like "*White Cargo*" and "*South of Pago-Pago*" from the 1930s. From the name, John pictured Big Man Duff as a strapping, white, 260-pound sailor left

When John Frum Came

over from the furnace room of a tramp steamer that ran aground. Although they had been sailing in Pacific waters, this was his first landfall since San Francisco. Yani was the first real native he had encountered.

"Who is Big Man Duff?" he asked.

"Him churchfella. Yani churchboy. He come to Christ's Despair to convert ignorant savages. He teach me magic formula for calling ships." As John listened, to his dismay Yani recited *"Big name watchem Sheepy-sheep; watchem Blackfella.."* right through to the end.

The American guessed that this was a prayer of some sort in Pidgin. "You mean he was a missionary?" John said, brightening with hope. "Is he still here?"

"Yes, he is in camp on top of volcano. He come from America, too."

"An American missionary? Here, right on the island?"

"Yes, he come from island called Boston. We Coast Watchers now. No more churchfella."

"Boston?" he shouted, "So am I."

"You from Boston Island. He from Boston Island. Maybe you know him."

"I doubt it. Boston is a pretty big place. But I have to talk to him. You take me to him?"

Yani suddenly remembered his original mission, and turned very serious. "Yani have to go back on island, now. Sea spirits destroy Blackfella village. Ooma is gone. Yani have to drive out spirits first. Everyone is waiting on top of mountain for Yani to come back."

"You can't leave now. I have to see your missionary and find out where I am. I have to contact my ship and let them know I'm alive," John argued.

Yani stood up. "I come back. We talk more." He looked over the cases and guessed their contents. "You bring cargo? You bring tinkens?"

"Tinkens?"

"Yes, tinkens. Open box. Yani see if tinkens O.K." He tugged at the paraffin impregnated cardboard carton he had been using for a seat. It did not yield to his fingers.

"These are C-Rations. Food for American soldiers and Marines," John explained.

Then, not waiting for John, Yani took out his knife, and slit the corner open. He could see the small olive drab cans crammed into the waterproof box.

"Yes, tinkens. Many, many tinkens," he said excitedly. He pried two out and opened the larger with his knife while John admired his speed.

Some of the contents of the can spurted onto Yani's arm, and he licked at it. "Taste good," he said. He poked into the can with his knife, looked at the contents and said, "How you call … worms?"

John couldn't stifle his laugh. "No. Spaghetti in tomato sauce." He took one of the noodles out and put it in his mouth. Yani did the same.

"Worms good," he said and scooped out a few more with his fingers. He downed the contents of the can in no time. "All tinkens have worms?" he asked.

"No," John assured him. "Each one has something different in it. Some good — some not so good."

Yani held up a can. "No have picture on side. How you know what inside?"

"I read the printing on the side. The words tell me what's inside."

"You read words like Witman?"

"Of course. All Americans know how to read."

"I never see Blackfella read. Even Negeb not able to read. Always have to ask Witman." He digested the thought for a minute. Then he decided a test was in order. "You know 'Our Father huartin Heaven' formula?"

"Do you mean, do I know the Lord's Prayer? Of course."

"You say?"

John recited it in its entirety.

Yani's respect for John was magnified tenfold. Now he *knew* this was John Frum, … that he knew how to call ships … and no doubt knew many other things yet to be discovered.

***

Yani waded ashore, continually looking back over his shoulder to make sure that the big steel box of a ship was still there. Finally, he had to force himself to direct his attention toward the devastated village that lay just inside the tattered ring of palm trees. It was only recognizable by the basalt outcroppings that had served as sort of a village square. From there he could more or less establish where things used to be. Not even the bamboo skeletons of the flimsy houses were anywhere to be seen.

He wandered through the rubble, trying to remember the magic words Ooma had told him a long time ago. These were the word formulas that would drive the sea spirits off the land and make it again habitable for men. He stood atop the rocks and called the names of the monsters that lived in the water — the Hevehe. These creatures had been around since the days of Kilibob and Manup. There were tales of the combat that took place between them and the founders of the human race. The humans had won and claimed the dry land for men. Hevehe could only live in the deep water of the ocean. But now, they had built a mountain of water and climbed the mountain of land.

The Hevehe had taken the oldest inhabitants of the island out to sea with them. They were also in possession of Ooma's body now, since the Japanese had kept him from being cremated. The sea monsters had certainly captured the old shaman's spirit as well. This troubled Yani a great deal. He wept for his father and said the formulas that might help release him from Hevehe control. When the tribe was once more established in the village they would build body-masks eight-feet high and perform the ceremony that would keep the monsters away for many more years.

***

John Bartlett stood on the deck just outside the crew's quarters, and watched Yani disappear inland.

This is truly strange, he thought shaking his head in disbelief. *How the hell did I wind up 12,000 miles from home talking to some strange, little guy who thinks I killed all the white men on board and took over the boat? He looks like a Negro, but the only thing we have in common is the color of our skin. He's from another world. The worst part is that he says he was expecting me. He knew I was coming. He thinks I'm somebody named John Frum.*

John paced back and forth, looking at the tumbled boxes of food and government equipment. The stacks had shifted and in some cases had collapsed. Judging from the condition of the island, the most logical thing he could do with all this stuff was give it to the natives. *Chances are that the tidal wave wiped* out their food supplies. I couldn't have arrived at a more opportune time. They can probably use every last can on this tub. What would Lieutenant Frankie and Mr. Francis say to that.*

He laughed out loud. "You snooty sons of bitches," he yelled out to sea. "I'm gonna take pleasure in giving all your shit to a bunch of colored folks that can't even speak English!"

If the Navy objects, I'll just say they overran the boat, and took everything. But what about this American missionary, Duff? The native said that he's up on the mountain. No doubt he's white. Once he sees this load of stuff he'll probably claim it for himself — especially once he sees that there's just a li'l ol' colored boy in charge of it.

He bit his lower lip thoughtfully. Talking out loud again to himself, he said, "I guess there's no two ways about it. I better find out what he knows about where we are. He might have some way of getting in touch with the Navy.

"Shit," he mumbled, "I don't now if the *Snitkin* is still even afloat. If they are, do they care where I am?" He pondered that a bit. *No, they don't care where I am, but you can bet your ass they're worried about the Admiral's LC-whatever-it-is.*

***

After a couple hours had passed and he could think of no other ritual actions to take, Yani returned to the beach. He could no longer keep his mind on his work as a shaman.

After months of going down to the beach and performing the proper rituals every morning, it had finally happened — **John Frum had come.** In spite of the Hevehes, this was the greatest achievement of Yani's shamanistic career. He wished Ooma could have lived just another day longer to see that he had called a ship full of tinkens. He had to admit to himself, even *he* had not expected to attract such a vast cargo of canned food. He was hard pressed to acknowledge its reality when he saw it all in one place.

What will Negeb say when he hears that John Frum has come to my island? But at least one point of the controversy had been finally cleared up — John Frum was a Blackfella. The surprising thing was that he was an American Blackfella. He had no idea such people existed.

Chapter 36

To the surprise of just about everyone on board, the *U.S.S. Great Snitkin* survived the *tsunami*, but it would be at least a day and a half before the Captain could determine just where they were. The only thing he sure of was that this was the Pacific Ocean. The ship was bobbing about like a cork in a sunfish pond since its main drive shift had broken. The problem was to contact help without letting Japanese subs know it was helpless in the water.

While Lieutenant Bartlett was lying on his bunk trying to imagine what to do next, he was summoned to the Captain's quarters. He knocked on the Captain's door and was told to come in. He always went through a dramatic little show of proper military bearing, snapping to attention and almost shouting, "Second Lieutenant Francis X. Bartlett the Fourth, reporting to the commanding officer as ordered, sir."

"At ease, Lieutenant," the Captain said.

"For Christ's sake, Frankie, we know you are a Marine and went to the Academy," his father said. "Save it for the God-damned troops. We have real problems."

"Ease up, Lieutenant," the Captain said. "I've told you any number of times, we're not big on military formalities on this ship. Just about all the officers are 90-day wonders, pressed into service to fight the Japs. We get along pretty well here as long as everybody does his job."

"Yes, sir!" he answered a little less crisply.

"Sit down. We better get this landing craft business straightened out," the Captain said with an air of finality. "Now, were you charged out with the LCT?"

"LCM, sir. I was assigned to off-load food and other supplies for the communication station on Bartlett's Island"

"Bartlett's Island? I thought it was Island 321. How did it get that name?"

"My father — er, the Admiral — thought it might be more appropriate."

The Admiral grinned sheepishly.

"What was the matter with the original name, *Merdsot Isle*. That's what the natives called it. I think it sounds romantic," Captain Stoepel said, as his mind filled with bare-breasted native girls in grass skirts.

"Begging the Captain's pardon, sir, but I think *Merdsot Isle* translates roughly into 'Dumb Shit Island,'" the Lieutenant said.

"Oh," said the Captain. "Let's get on with the story."

"While the LCM was being loaded, its regular crew were on board your ship to buy non-regulation items that are not available on the island. One of our men, Apprentice Seaman John Bartlett, stayed on the LSM to oversee the loading of the cargo, sir. When the seas got rough, he was swept away with the tidal wave."

"Yes, and lucky you got aboard this ship when you did." He added, "Is everyone in your unit named Bartlett?"

"No, sir. There's just the Admiral, myself, and the lost sailor."

"Well. I fear the Navy has lost a good man, Lieutenant. I am reporting LCM 666 as having gone down with only one man on board. We'll hold a service for him on the fantail after lunch," Captain Stoepel said, and looked as sad as he knew how.

"Well, that brings us to a bigger problem. All the equipment for your communications station was on the LCM. Worse than that Island 321 seems to have gone down as well. The last we saw, the local volcano had become active and was swallowing everything in sight."

"What all this means, Frankie," Admiral Bartlett cut in, "is that I am an Admiral without a command. Once we find out where we are, I am planning to resign my commission and go back to Marblehead. I'm too old for all this shit. I'll leave this war up to you younger fellows. I think I can contribute more to the War Effort by running Xavier Shipping Enterprises."

The Marine was stunned. "But, sir. I'm the Ops Officer for the British-American Liaison unit. What will happen to me?"

"The BAL unit never was activated. As far as I'm concerned, it never existed. Captain Stoepel, here, has agreed to take you on as a staff officer on the *Snitkin*. This looks like a fairly safe place to spend the war. He'll take care of all the paperwork."

"But, Dad, I shouldn't be expected to pull freighter duty. I'm a graduate of the United States Naval Academy." He turned to Captain Stoepel and said, "You are a senior officer, sir. Certainly you understand military traditions. I respectfully request that I be put off on the next island with a Marine Unit, sir. I want to get out there and kill Japs."

"We were short-handed when we left San Francisco, Lieutenant. I need you as part of my officer staff. You can start pulling watches with the rest of the officers starting tomorrow."

Captain Stoepel looked at him admiringly. He stood up, saluted and said, "I'm glad there are men like you, Lieutenant. Men, who are willing to risk their lives in combat. But I think it is only fair to tell you that the name of my last ship was the '*Utica*.'"

"Wasn't that one of the destroyers that went down in the Battle of the Coral Sea?" he asked, preparing to be proud of his comrade-in-arms.

"No, Lieutenant, the *Utica* was one of the New York Central System ferry boats that ran between Weehawken, New Jersey, and 42nd Street in New York. I'm one of the 90-Day Wonders I mentioned before."

***

Yani picked his way through the rubble-strewn part of the trail up the mountain slowly, but moved more quickly as he reached the part that had not been submerged. By the time he was within earshot of the camp he was almost at a dead run. "John Frum, he come! John Frum, he come!" he began calling.

McDuff heard him and was annoyed. His first reaction was *How can I disabuse him of this ridiculous notion that some miraculous being is going to bring him all the fruits of Western Civilization.* He stopped working on the ash-clogged generator disassembled before him, ready to reprimand the young man when he came into the camp.

Nor was McDuff the only one growing tired of this constant talk of John Frum. The Elders were not receptive to everything that appeared on the horizon being construed as the arrival of some marvelous Witman. Some of them felt that Yani was responsible for the recent invasion. The Japanese were mistaken for the arrival of John Frum, too. In the end they were a problem and the cause of Ooma's death. In fact, they were an outright disaster. Two of the elders agreed that the introduction of this new idea Yani and Negeb brought with them had somehow strengthened the Hevehe to the point where they could build their mountain of water.

As Yani came into the camp area, he encountered the council of elders. They had been waiting for him to bring the news that the Hevehe had been dispersed, and the people could come down the mountain. Instead he came yelling his familiar "wolf cry" about John Frum.

"We do not want to know about your Witman stories," one of the older men said angrily.

"We want to know if the Hevehe are back out to sea," said a second. "Is there anything left of the village?"

A third said, "What are we going to do about food? Has the lake been filled with seawater? What will we drink?"

He told them, "The giant wave left an iron ship full of cargo for everyone. When I reached the bottom of the mountain, there it was — waiting. John Frum was on the deck wearing strange clothes. The boat is full from one end to the other with boxes of tinkens. There was nothing to worry about."

A serious debate ensued. They seriously doubted his story. Believing in miraculous explanations of things that happened beyond the memories of living men was acceptable. Even wonderful things happening on far away islands were believable. But this was a different matter. The cold practicality of survival colored their willingness to accept the story.

Unfortunately, the lagoon was not visible from the cliff at the edge of the camp. They could not just look down and see the ship full of cargo.

"If there is anything down there," Aboo, one of the leaders said, "how do we know it is not just a trap set by the Hevehe to capture our bodies and our spirits?"

"I agree," said another. "It doesn't seem to me that you were down there long enough to get rid of all the Hevehe. If Ooma were still alive, I think he would have spent all day there making sure they were driven off the land."

Yani was shocked and hurt. This was his first big test as Ooma's replacement, and he was not doing very well. Bewildered, he walked away from the elders. Immediately, he saw Moses McDuff watching the proceedings. He smiled and walked across the clearing to him.

"Big Man Duff!" he said. "John Frum, he come. He is in the lagoon with his ship full of tinkens and the elders will not believe me."

Since the discussion had been in the island dialect, McDuff had no idea of the nature of the controversy. But he could tell that they were unhappy with Yani. "Did you tell them that John Frum was here?"

"Yes."

"Yani, you have to stop this nonsense. Your people are in a serious situation right now. What are you going to do about food? It's going to be a few days before you can even get things together enough to catch any fish. The pigs that didn't drown are running wild. I'm sure all the gardens have been washed out. You might be able to dig up some taro or yams, but hardly enough to feed all these people."

"John Frum have plenty food. He have a whole boat full of tinkens. We never have to raise gardens again. No need to catch pigs. Plenty cargo for everyone."

McDuff reached forward and took Yani by the shoulders, as he had on other occasions, and shook him slightly. "Yani," he said sternly, raising his voice, "listen to me. There is no John Frum. He is just a story made up by natives on other islands looking for free handouts."

Yani scowled. He reached into the pocket of his shorts and felt the second, smaller can he had taken from the C-Ration box. It was about the size of a tuna fish can. He smiled a triumphant smile, and handed the can to the American.

"You read words?" he asked.

McDuff stared in disbelief for a long minute. Then he took it in his right hand and read the label:

U.S. ARMY C-RATIONS.
HAMBURGERS IN GRAVY. CANNED 1/5/41

***

On the way down the hill, McDuff said, "Tell me again. Where did he say this ship came from?"

"He say it belong U.S. Navy. John Frum say he come from Boston island, just like you."

"Are you sure? He said he was from Boston? That's too good to be true," McDuff said almost stumbling in his haste to get down the mountain. He was giddy with excitement, and asked Yani the same questions a half dozen times, not allowing himself to fully believe the answers. If it were not for the C-Ration can, he would not have believed a word the Chase Islander told him.

Finally, they came in sight of the grounded landing craft and McDuff started laughing like an idiot as he ran across the flat beach toward the LSM.

They ran to the edge of the water, and McDuff yelled, "Hello, on board the Navy ship! Hello, on board the Navy ship!"

Bartlett had taken off his work clothes and was lying on the bunk in his skivvies. He was reading the pamphlet on Pidgin English again, trying to memorize some of the words. He heard a voice calling in English and raced to the deck. Mounting the drop-door, he looked to see where his visitors were.

McDuff saw him climb to the top of the forward structure and said, "It looks like someone has beaten us to it. One of your people is here already."

"No. That is John Frum."

McDuff could taste the disappointment. "You told me he was an American ... from Boston. He's a Blackfella."

"John Frum is Blackfella," Yani said, not seeing any contradiction.

Bartlett scrambled down the ladder on the outside of the bow, and dropped the last five feet to the shallow water in his haste to meet them. McDuff stood at the edge of the water, as the other man approached with his hand extended. "Hi," he said, "I'm John Bartlett. You must be Mr. Duff."

For a minute, McDuff did not say anything. "You *are* an American," he said. "I'm sorry I didn't know you were a Negro. Yani said you were from Boston, and I assumed..."

"All Negroes don't come from Alabama, you know," Bartlett said, and dropped his hand.

McDuff was flustered, and his right hand darted out. "I'm sorry. That was very rude of me. I'm Dr. Moses McDuff of Cambridge, Mass." Bartlett shook hands with him. "What part of Boston are you from?"

"Actually, I'm from Marblehead," John smiled.

"Marblehead?" McDuff said, with a note of surprise, remembering only expensive homes.

"Don't worry, doctor, my family are all servants. They've lived there since the Civil War ... Underground Railroad, and all that ... if you're familiar with that sort of thing."

"Why, yes. I'm quite familiar with it."

They stood on the beach seeming to have run out of conversation. Bartlett broke the tension by gesturing toward the LCM. "Would you care to come aboard my yacht for lunch?"

The two Americans laughed and Yani did, too. He did not get the joke, but he was happy, even overjoyed. His dreams were all coming true.

They climbed up the ladder and McDuff looked in awe at the numberless boxes of food crammed onto the vessel. "Where did you get all this?" he asked.

"I didn't *get* it anyplace. I was just on this boat, loading it. We were going to take this stuff ashore when that monster wave came out of nowhere. The fact that I'm still alive is only a matter of luck."

John told the *tsunami* story in detail as they hopped from stack to stack. While he was talking, he reached into the case of C-Rations Yani had opened, and each man carried as much as he could back inside the crew's quarters.

"Can you tell me what all this talk is about somebody named John Frum?" Bartlett asked. "Like I say, my name is John Bartlett."

"It's rather hard to believe, but you are the fulfillment of a prophecy."

"A prophecy? Me?"

"It doesn't do much for Christianity, but I'm a witness to it," McDuff said.

John Bartlett looked confused, to say the least.

"For months Yani, here, has been telling everyone that John Frum is coming and he will bring a shipload of cargo for the natives. It's all part of what they call a Cargo Cult, very complicated…"

"So here I am with a load of canned food and stuff … and my name happens to be John."

"…*from* America. Don't forget that," McDuff said.

They took boyish delight in deciding what their menu would include. There was a 20-gallon thermal water cooler Yani and McDuff tapped to slake their growing thirst.

This indulgence caused the minister to say, "Here we are having a picnic, when there are hundreds of people who need this food worse than we do."

Bartlett stopped him from making a dash for the outside. His apparent reaction was that he would grab a case of canned food and carry it on his back up the mountain. "I attended some medical corpsman sessions on the *Snitkin* on the way here. They emphasized the importance of corpsmen staying healthy and free from injuries themselves if they're going to do their job. If you're going to help anybody, Dr. McDuff, you're not going to do it on an empty stomach.

"The other thing is that we can't go running off in all directions. Even in the movies, the good guys make plans how they can beat the guys in the black hats. Which reminds me — what's the Jap situation?" John asked.

Yani described what happened to him during the past couple days, and McDuff told all he knew, including his great guilt feelings about shooting the Japanese officer.

"It's a war, Dr. McDuff. If you didn't kill him, he would have killed Yani, and probably you, too, if he got the chance. How did you wind up here, Reverend," he asked.

He told John a little about Christ's Despair, and how he came to meet Yani. While putting away two cans of "ham and lima beans" McDuff explained the role of the Coast Watchers. He stopped in the middle of his description and said, "Oh gosh, I left the generator in pieces up at the camp. I hope no one has taken any of the parts. They love little machined things. They make jewelry out of them and wear it in their noses."

"I guess we had better get our act together," John Bartlett said, "and figure out how we are going to distribute this stuff where it will do the most good."

"One more question, John," McDuff said, "What do you know about how the war is going?"

"They played radio broadcasts over the bitch box — er — excuse me, the P.A. system on the ship. What comes to mind is that the Japs took the Philippines and we lost a lot of guys ... maybe 36,000 ... on Bataan."

"36,000?" McDuff said, not being able to visualize that many people."

"And you worry about shooting one lousy Jap officer? On the plus side, some of our planes got to drop some bombs on Tokyo."

"What about this part of the Pacific?"

John told about his being the Admiral's valet and hearing things that not everyone else knew. "I know that a couple months ago they had what they're calling the Battle of Coral Sea. That stopped Japs from landing at Port Moresby."

"Our communications with our friends in Port Moresby have been kind of scarce," McDuff said. "I've been worried about them."

"It looks like the Japs are massing for a big show at Guadalcanal — some coconut farm near New Guinea. That's where most of our task force was heading. We were going to set up a communications station on an island, but all that crap is in some of these big boxes."

Chapter 37

John went to the control bridge of the LSM where he found some of the latest examples of modern military technology. The boat was built only months before, and was transported to the South Pacific aboard an LST. It was loaded with the newest U.S. Navy equipment.

However, he gave up on the idea of making the engines run even before trying. Where would he go if they worked? John readily admitted to himself that he had not the slightest idea how a diesel engine ran. All he knew was that they burned oil instead of gasoline. The engine compartment was "aslosh" in greasy bilge water, so he just kept the door to that area closed.

But there was one set-up he did manage to figure out — the public address system. The boat had a massive bitch-box meant to urge G.I.s to run out the open end of the craft into direct enemy fire or neck-deep surf. It had a waterproof electric circuit, powered by a battery, and charged by an emergency generator. The generator was shorted out by sea water, but the battery light still flashed green when he flipped the toggle switch. The same circuit also controlled the power-rewind winch for the drop-doors.

Hey, he thought, *Dr. McDuff said he was repairing the generator for his radio. Maybe he could fix this one, too.*

He switched it on and hit the button for the Public Address system. Green lights again. He spoke into the microphone in front of him and said, "Attention on deck. Attention on deck, this is the Captain speaking."

When John Frum Came

The loudspeakers boomed so loudly that McDuff was startled and lost his footing. He and Yani, fell off the pile of boxes they stood on. Bartlett was amused, but ran outside to help them up off the deck.

"I'm sorry I took you by such surprise. I didn't think they worked that well."

McDuff brushed himself off and said, "Now there's a little toy that'll impress the natives."

"It sounds like the voice of God — if you'll forgive the expression, Reverend," John said.

Yani, who had seen loudspeakers on the *Wombat* and in Australia agreed. "We tell them John Frum speak. They pay attention."

John told them about the generator and the three men went to look. The power plant, which was little more than a two-stroke outboard motor engine, was hooked up to a truck-sized automotive generator by a fan belt.

"It doesn't look much different than the Bartlett's 1939 Packard," John commented. "I was just getting used to it back home. They wanted me to become the family chauffeur, so they thought I should know how the car ran."

"I think it just needs to be dried off," McDuff said, and he found some rags for Yani to do the job.

As they returned to the deck, McDuff said, "You know, talking about generators, I think I better run up the hill and get mine and the radio. I'll bring the pieces back here and assemble it. Maybe we can get off some kind of message."

"Gee, I haven't even been ashore on your tropical paradise, and you are trying to get rid of me already," John said, only half joking. "I'm not that anxious to get back to the Navy. It wasn't very friendly... but that's a long story for another time." *God only knows what the Admiral and Lieutenant Frankie have planned for me next,* he thought.

McDuff was all apologies. "Don't get me wrong. I find it's great to have another American to talk to..."

"...Even if he *is* colored," Bartlett finished the sentence.

McDuff told Yani he was going back to the camp for the radio and generator, but Yani chose to remain and finish his work. Without realizing it, he was really worried that John Frum would disappear if he let him out of his sight. He would feel more secure waiting on the LSM.

***

When he reached the camp clearing, Dr. McDuff felt that there was something in the air. He sensed that there was tension, and even the children, who usually greeted him with pleasant smiles, did not come up to him in their usual manner. Everyone hung back as he picked up his equipment. Fortunately, it was all there and he stuffed the pieces into a canvas bag.

He looked up and prepared to go back down the mountain, but saw that there was a group of men blocking the path. They were behind Aboo, Yani's chief antagonist in the Council of Elders.

He raised his hand to the Witman and said in his own language, "You stay here. Yani is making a big problem. He is angering the Hevehe. We see the boat, but we do not see any John Frum. We do not see any tinkens. I think Yani will keep the boat for himself."

While McDuff recognized that he was being upbraided, he did not understand what was being said. In all the time he had been in the islands, he really made no attempt to learn Booga-booga. He felt it was the obligation of the natives to learn English, or at least Pidgin.

He went forward as if to walk through the group blocking the way. To his amazement, one of them struck him on the forehead with his shield, knocking him to the ground.

"You are not *pooja*. You are a trash man," the man who hit him said.

Not understanding that he was just insulted and given a challenge that could cost him his life, McDuff said. "I have no quarrel with you. I am a man of peace." He rubbed his head, examined his bloody fingers, and continued to sit there.

Without realizing it, he had acknowledged that he was a trash man by not fighting back. And, having such a lowly status, there was no valor for the warrior to treat him as an adversary. Instead, the man put his foot on the Witman's back and said, "This is Yani's trash man. We will take him to the beach and trade him for a coconut."

The men in Aboo's group laughed. One of them grabbed him roughly by the hair and another tied his hands together with a vine.

Chapter 38

A spear rattled along the deck. A second one hit the center of a cardboard carton squarely and penetrated an inch or two.

"Yani!" John yelled. "They're attacking. Get up here and do something."

Yani appeared in a wink and climbed the drop-door. He could see Aboo and his men standing on the beach. He was disconcerted to see his *bis* being led by a vine rope around his wrists. "Quick, John Frum. Look at beach. Aboo has Big Man Duff tied like pig."

Bartlett grabbed his binoculars and brought the war party into view. McDuff had blood on his face, apparently from an injury to his forehead. "What do they want, Yani?"

Yani called to Aboo and told him to let Big Man Duff go.

He refused, and said he would trade him for John Frum and all the cargo Yani had promised. Yani refused, and said that John Frum had come to him — not Aboo.

Aboo was angry and the men headed to the site of the old village, dragging McDuff with them.

***

A little later the drumming began. Apparently the village's slot drum, made from an immense hollow log, had been found. It was dragged down to the beach. At first the *pooja* struck single notes. About every thirty seconds a different warrior approached the log with an immense club and struck it as hard as he could.

"What does that mean?" John asked Yani.

"*Poojas* call spirits of ancestors to help them be *pooja*. Not fear any man if spirit with you when fight begin."

"Do you think they'll attack the boat?" John said.

"In morning. This night dance, sing, make great fire."

While Yani was talking John noticed that large numbers of gooney birds began to circle above the beach. Some of them had a wingspan of ten feet. John looked up and said, "What brings the birds now?"

"Aboo bird-fella," he said pointing to the *kanakas* on the beach, meaning that the albatross was their totem. They were chumming the water with scraps of dead fish they had found on the sand. The birds were normally drawn to the lagoon where schools of minnow-sized fish came close to the surface. Now, the large birds swooped down and made numerous forays to feed on the chum.

"Big bird name Ak-ak. Ancestor of Aboo. They come. Stay with Aboo for fight. Ak-ak taboo. Bird die — Aboo die."

So, John thought, *the Gooney Birds are called Ak-aks. The natives think they are their ancestors, and they want them around to protect them if a fight breaks out. What am I sayin if — the word is* when. *That's not a fire drill those guys are putting on out there.*

The frequency of the drumbeats had changed. Now each of the *kanakas* was striking the log twice. As the day wore on they progressed to the point where they each struck it five times. Their mathematical concept had reached its limit — five was the number of fingers on a hand.

When that phase came to an end, the beat became steady and frantic, the work of one dedicated man. This time it was clearly someone of skill. He also had some other drums besides the hollow log. As he beat out a variable rhythm John said, "Sounds like they brought in the union guys. Whoever is playing the drums is a professional."

"Him called Koko. Him make drums for wedding, funeral, feast. Koko fall off sailboat long time past. Ooma give him food, Mary, house. Koko no have to fish ...no grow garden. Him no *kanaka*. Him taboo. Koko make *pooja* strong — call ancestors." Yani was truly agitated. He was impressed with the power this drummer had to make the warriors powerful.

Peering through the binoculars, John could see a huge man on the beach who easily weighed 300 pounds. From his features, he was clearly Hawaiian.

The large birds were becoming thick in the skies. John watched them and said, "They look like God-damn buzzards circling a wagon-train in the desert."

"Buzids?" Yani asked. "Dezsit?"

"Sorry," John answered. "It doesn't translate. A desert is place with no water."

"Big Man Duff say Hell have no water."

"Well, if he's right, by this time tomorrow we might know that for sure. I damn well better pull some kind of Houdini."

Although Yani thought he understood a lot of English, but John Frum used words neither McDuff nor any of the Aussies ever did. But then, he was a special kind of man — Blackfella American from Boston Island. Part of his magic no doubt came from the secret words he knew.

***

John Bartlett was an educated man, in spite of the lowly circumstances from which he had recently emerged. At the Bartlett mansion he had read books on his own that Frankie only read under pressure from the hired tutors. He was familiar with the historic and literary heroes who had been in similar predicaments — Robinson Crusoe, Swiss Family Robinson, Young Jim Hawkins in *Treasure Island*, and Fletcher Christian.

This whole damn island castaway business is taking on the aspect of living in a "B" movie, John thought.

Yani listened to the drumbeats. "Aboo not give up, John Frum. He drum *poojas* all night. Sun come, *kanakas* come. Maybe now time shoot Aboo with big rifle?"

"No. I don't want to kill him or anybody. I want Aboo to be our friend. Not hurt Dr. McDuff. Let me think. I will find some way of saving him."

Yeah, just like in the movies, he said to himself. *Too bad I'm not Douglas Fairbanks. He'd go ashore wielding his trusty cutlass, felling savages left and right, freeing the missionary and carrying off the lovely native princess in his arms.*

He continued thinking about the fantasy for a few more minutes, reminding himself that there were no lovely princesses to be rescued — but what about just plain lovely native girls? There must be a bunch of those around. He just hadn't seen any yet.

John jumped to his feet, looked straight into Yani's eyes, and said in a loud voice, "What the hell! Why not? If I don't make my move now, I can just sit out here on this barge and wait to be murdered in my sleep."

John went to the bridge again and flipped all the switches for the loudspeakers. The feedback squawked for a few seconds then he said what only one man on shore could understand. "Hang on McDuff, and damned be him who first cries 'Hold, enough!'"

He climbed rapidly over the cartons until he came to a wooden box. He had opened it once before, and found that it contained an assortment of expensive toys that had belonged to the Admiral. Among them was a chrome-plated sporting piece, complete with a box of 12-gauge shotgun shells. Apparently he planned to shoot a little skeet. It must have been the most envied gun at the country club.

He stopped next to an ammo box opened by mistake. He picked up a hand grenade very gingerly. He had seen these in the movies too, but had never been to basic training, so it was his first. He was really quite scared of the damned thing. Overcoming his fears, he palmed it and climbed up to the edge of a gunnel.

Without knowing what he was going to do next, John pulled the pin out of the grenade. "Count to ten, they always said." He counted up to five and said, "Screw this..." and hurled it like a football as far out into the lagoon as he could. His caution was rewarded when the grenade exploded on what would have been the count of eight just as it touched the lagoon's surface.

The resulting noise and geyser of water got the attention of the people on the shore. Some dropped to the ground at the noise, having seen the Japanese soldiers using similar weapons. Shrapnel fell far short of the beach, but Yani and John heard some of it ping off the side of their boat.

When John Frum Came

Everyone was looking out toward the landing craft and wondering what was happening.

It was twilight, and the gooney birds were settling down on the lagoon, not far from the landing craft. In Aboo's eyes his ancestors were surrounding his enemy. They were quietly bobbing along, dipping for fish swimming near the surface. John mounted the side railing of the boat and apologized to the seabirds. "I realize that this could get me thrown out of the Hyannis Gun Club, but then again, this ain't Massachusetts."

Aboo's men could see John had something bright and shiny in his hand, but had no idea what. He raised the Admiral's custom-made, repeating shotgun to his shoulder and pretended he was in a beachside shooting gallery. Two of the birds swimming next to each other were the first to disappear in a flurry of feathers and blood with one shot.

The other birds, startled by the noise, took off as a group. He fired into the midst of the slow, low flying birds and two more fell. He kept firing until he had used all the shells in the magazine. There were dead birds floating everywhere. He reloaded and peppered the dumb creatures who didn't fly away because they had never been shot at before. At this range, John could not miss.

When the shotgun was empty, John waved at the men surrounding Aboo. The old man was too nearsighted to see anything in detail, but he knew that he had lost a large number of protective ancestors in the last few minutes. He was scared of this John Frum, after all.

Yani had perched himself at the highest point on the landing craft, where he could observe the goings-on through John's binoculars. He reported that Big Man Duff was stretched between two palm trees from vines around his wrists. "Please, John Frum, you shoot Aboo."

"I'm afraid that his people outnumber us, and they would just overrun the boat," he argued.

"You do *something*, John Frum. Maybe Big Man Duff die waiting for you."

"Good point," he said while he made one more inventory of what alchemy was onboard his enchanted vessel that could be used to reverse the situation.

A frontal assault using the carbine to pick off natives on the beach would only result in their staying out of sight. "If I shoot Aboo, they'll kill McDuff."

Since his arrival John had been taking items out of the stack of red-tag specials. The most unexpected item was Lieutenant Frankie's portable wind-up phonograph and a small selection of Big Band swing records.

Yani watched John rapidly assemble the things he needed to create his Douglas Fairbanks drama. The most awesome artifact by far in Yani's eyes was the ceremonial sword. He had never seen anything this beautiful. It's silver blade sparkled in the sun and its gold hilt bespoke wealth beyond reason. No doubt, up to this point it had been polished with a reverence due a sacred object. The only thing he could not understand was the absence of a cutting edge. Of course, it was never intended to be used in battle, so for safety's sake Lieutenant Bartlett had never sharpened it. Besides, it would have scratched the chrome plating. Now, John Frum put an edge on it with a grind-wheel he had found in a miniature machine shop next to the engine room. He regretted defacing it, but it would be useless in its pristine condition.

Yani watched in amazement. John said, "Yani, come with me." They ran to the bridge and he pointed to the microphone. "This strong magic from U.S. Navy."

John cranked up the emergency generator, and it caught on the second try. A green light lit on the control panel. He flipped on all the switches for the public address system and the drop-door.

"Who is your most powerful god on the island."

"Kilibob … but him leave island."

"I think he's about to come back."

Yani wondered if John Frum knew something he was not telling him.

"How do you say 'Kilibob angry' in native words?" the American demanded.

Caught between fear and excitement, Yani squeaked out "Kilibob *pagow!*"

He picked up the microphone and brought it near the amplifier. The resulting screech of feedback was music to his ears. John spoke directly into the microphone in the deepest tones he could muster. The crackle and boom of the amplifiers reverberated in the natives' ears. From the center of the lagoon they heard "Kilibob *pagow!* Kilibob *pagow!* Kilibob *pagow!*"

There was a cry of terror from the men on the beach. This had to be the voice of Kilibob. Many ran frantically into the surrounding bush. John turned off the P.A. system and thought about his next move.

***

Aboo was rattled by the display, but he was not fooled. He remained in control of his senses, and through the binoculars John could see him emerge from his observation post in the jungle.

I must show my people that I am not afraid of noise, Aboo thought to himself. *If John Frum wants a war of noise I will have my drummer make a magic drumming like he has never heard. That will instill bravery and strength in the men.*

The old man went to the fat drummer and said, "John Frum makes a fool of you. He makes sound with White Man's tricks. These sounds have no power. It is not drumming — it is only big noise. You make drumming greatest ever. You make drumming all night."

The most loyal *kanakas* returned to the beach and began to dance as the sun sank below the horizon. The drummer dredged up some syncopated beats never before heard on Chase Island.

Chapter 39

John climbed down from the control bridge and crossed to the living area. With the frantic drumming going on as background music, he went over the plan three times with Yani until he was certain the Chase Islander knew *what* he was supposed to do *when*. He assembled the pieces in the order they were to be used.

He wound the spring in Lieutenant Bartlett's portable victrola and placed the record on the turntable. "As soon I release the drop-doors, you start this playing." He showed him how to place the needle in the record groove. The phonograph was positioned so its speaker was next to the open microphone. "Don't move anything," he warned. He rehearsed the magic words Yani would say, just before he started playing the record. Yani had mastered them after two tries, and John Frum began to get dressed.

When the sun had set completely, the drumming had settled down to a monotonous and oppressive beat. "Now is the time," John told his assistant. "What this party needs is some fireworks."

He pointed a flare pistol skyward, inclined it slightly toward the island, and fired. The projectile streaked upward and with a muffled bang the sky was filled with a red glow.

The drum stopped in mid-beat and faces tilted upward. He could almost hear the natives gasp in astonishment. No one had ever seen a red star fall from the Heavens before. Surely something terrifying was going to happen. Everyone was frozen in place, even Aboo. John fired a second red flare just as the first was about to sputter out. It was more fear-inspiring than the first.

John operated the manual release mechanism for the big door at the prow of the landing craft. He allowed it to drop with a loud splash that broke the stillness invoked by the red lights.

On signal he heard Yani say into the microphone, "*Kilibob pagow!*" It was followed by the scraping and hissing of a needle finding the groove at the beginning of a record.

John fired his flare pistol into the air one more time, and there was a tracer-like streak over the heads of the people on the beach. But this time it ended in a loud "pop," followed by the brilliance of a phosphorous flare. To the utter astonishment of the assemblage the bright light seemed to hover over the beach. They could not see the little parachute that slowed its descent, nor would it have made any difference if they did. They were only aware of the bright blue-white light that banished the night and left them looking wide-eyed at each other in disbelief.

Immediately, like a school of fish executing a turn in unison, they all fell on their knees or bellies in the sand, cringing in dread. The flare would last just about five minutes, and John had another loaded flare pistol, which he stuck in the back of his belt.

While the loudspeakers blared Gene Krupa's version of "*Stompin' at the Savoy*" at full volume, Kilibob emerged from the darkness of the landing craft on to the ramp. He was fully illuminated by the scintillating glare of the U.S. Navy issue Roman candle.

He stood at attention dressed in Lieutenant Bartlett's bright white Annapolis graduation uniform, with white hat, belt and gloves. His gold buttons sparkled. In front of him he held the ceremonial sword by its handle, vertically with both hands. The bright, chrome-plated blade caught the light in such a way, that he seemed to be holding a beam of light in his hands. He looked neither to the left nor the right, but stared straight ahead at his sword and the beach in front of him.

The tide was all the way out, so there were only inches of water in this part of the lagoon, he walked as though he were the honor guard at the Tomb of the Unknown Soldier in Arlington. The flare floated on the evening breeze and he headed straight for McDuff tied between the bamboo poles. The missionary's arms were now stretched out from his sides, held tautly by the vine ropes.

John quickened his steps as soon as he was on dry ground. No one moved a muscle. There was hardly a twitch on the beach. The phonograph record reached its end and there were the usual scratchy noises. No one noticed.

Everyone saw Kilibob stand before the helpless Big Man Duff. He raised the sword and with two strokes, he cut through the rope-vines effortlessly. The man fell to the ground just as the parachute on the phosphorous flare caught fire and it fell into the sea.

The missionary was conscious but weak. "Go to the boat, now!" John commanded. He helped him to his feet in the darkness. With both the drumming stopped and the flare gone, the *kanakas* began to recover their senses. There was a murmur of confusion and Aboo was giving orders. John was sure they were going to be pounced upon. He pushed McDuff in the direction of the boat and reached around to the back of his belt for the flare pistol.

In the darkness Aboo thrashed about with his walking stick. It struck John's hand just as he pulled the trigger. Instead of going skyward, the projectile ripped into Aboo.

Aboo clutched at his chest where a great pain had suddenly developed. He fell to the ground, atop the flare, with his eyes and his pandanus leaf clothes ablaze.

During the chaos that followed, John and McDuff made a run for the water. A huge figure raced toward them in the darkness. It was Koko, the giant Hawaiian drummer. With a cry of surrender he threw down his immense body at the water's edge. He was prostrating himself with arms outstretched to where the echoes of Gene Krupa had been pulsating only moments before. His timing, however, was such that John and McDuff tripped over his huge carcass, somersaulting them ass over teakettle into the shallow water.

It was a moonless night, but the two of them managed to get back on their feet, and then safely back on the landing craft. Yani was waiting and he pushed the button that winched the landing ramp on battery power to the closed position.

John Bartlett collapsed out of breath. He looked up at his two smiling companions and said, "How the hell does Fairbanks do this so often, and stay alive?"

Chapter 40

There was no one on the beach when the sun came up.

Yani stood atop the drop-door and strained his eyes for signs of people hiding among the trees, but there was no one. McDuff joined him and said, "You really didn't think they were going to come down here after last night's show, did you?"

"Nobody swim. They afraid Hevehe still in water."

"My guess is that they are afraid of Kilibob. Even I had my moments with all the sound effects, and..."

"Busby Berkeley lives!" said a voice to their rear. "I tell you I am missing my calling. Hollywood needs me," John Bartlett laughed.

"I have to hand it to you, John. That was Broadway at its best." He rubbed his scraped wrists as he spoke. "And I want to thank you again for saving my life. I really think they would have killed me if you hadn't come to the rescue."

"That's what white hats are for," he said. He was still wearing the Annapolis Middy's cap. "How's your head?"

"We must drop Admiral Bartlett a thank you note. I enjoyed that Old Grand Dad. I'm afraid I am undergoing a religious revision — I'm beginning to understand why some people drink."

"The thank you note should really go to the guy who owns this fatigue shirt," he said pointing to the decorations on the sleeve. John was wearing a Marine Sergeant's fatigue shirt with a corpsman's red cross on the sleeve. "He was the one who bought the booze from some swabees on the *Snitkin*. Most of the bottles broke when they hit the deck during all the excitement."

He looked at the empty beach. "Well, where is everybody?"

Yani climbed down from the door and got on to the ladder. "I go tell Blackfella O.K. to come down. We give everybody tinkens. They very hungry now. No water on island. They find coconuts."

"Go and tell them to come down, Yani," McDuff said. "John and I will open the boxes and get ready for them."

With that, the young shaman went to pursue his cultural responsibilities.

"How long can they last on coconuts?" John asked.

"No problem. It rains here just about every afternoon," the minister told him. "They have ways of collecting the rainwater as it runs off the trees. It's amazing the way they adapt to nature. You and I would die in no time if we were left alone here — I almost did on the other island."

"What happened?"

"Yani saved my life," he said, and as they worked, he filled in the details he had omitted the day before.

John lowered the door and the two Americans began cutting open cartons. Bartlett described how he visualized forming a long line of natives, and handing them each two cans as they passed.

McDuff laughed. "Boy, oh boy. Have you got a surprise coming."

"How's that?" John said.

"People do not get on line in this part of the world, John. The best thing we can do is open as many cases as we can ... stack them on the ramp ... and get out of the way."

"You think they'll just grab?"

"Our biggest job will be to keep them from swarming over this boat like a bunch of locusts. Yani has promised them that John Frum would bring them enough food that they will never have to plant another garden as long as they live."

John started to laugh, until it almost became a howl.

"What's so funny," McDuff asked.

"Wait 'till they find out what's in some of these cans." He found a tin of Beef In Gravy, and held it up. "They'll probably think this stuff is great, but the G.I.s call it 'monkey meat.' It's the stringiest cut of beef the government could buy. But that's O.K. What are they going to think of tuna and noodle casserole? You haven't lived until you've had the government's version of beef stew — 80% potatoes ... 15% carrots and 5% gravy."

McDuff joined in chuckling, and said "John, once you have lived on one of these islands for three months you will think those are gourmet meals!"

***

The people retreated from Yani as he came into the camp clearing. His reputation as a shaman, and perhaps more accurately as a friend of Kilibob and John Frum, had been firmly established. None of the elders challenged his authority after the terrible end to which Aboo had come the night before.

He mounted a rock and motioned the people to come forward. "John Frum wishes to be our friend. He has told me to invite everyone to come down to the beach. The behavior of Aboo and his friends will be forgotten."

"Aboo is dead," one of the elders said. "We have cast his body into the sea to please the Hevehe. We wish to be friends of John Frum. He is stronger than the Hevehe."

"John Frum has come because Yani has called him. He is my friend. He comes from the island of Boston, like Big Man Duff. He is a stronger *bis* than Big Man Duff. They are friends. They do not choose to speak to you in our language. They ask me to tell you what they say."

There were no dissenters.

"Everybody will get a tinken for each hand. Take them to the place of the old village. I will teach you to open the tinkens with American magic called *G.I. canopener*." He showed them the tiny device that hung next to his cross on a string.

He jumped down from the rock and began his descent to the beach and the great gifts from John Frum had brought from God in Heaven.

A few minutes later they appeared on the beach, chanting on cue, "John Frum, he come! John Frum, he come!"

***

McDuff had an idea before the crowd came down from the mountain. "John, I think we are going to have to bring you down to earth. Last night, in the eyes of these people you were a god. You were really Kilibob. You sure as heck didn't look like any American sailor I've ever seen."

"I've been told that," he smiled.

"What I mean is, you won't be able to function with these people on a day to day basis if they think you are Kilibob."

"So? What do I do?" John said.

"Get rid of the white officer's cap. Just wear the Sergeant's shirt. They'll be surprised to find out that you are a Black man like they are. My guess is that they'll be more kindly disposed to you as a result."

He tossed the hat up on the narrow walkway. "What next? Should I shake hands with them?"

"Good point." McDuff reflected on it. "I'll tell you what. Suppose you just stand on the deck outside the bridge and wave to them as they come for their tinkens."

"Tinkens?"

"Pidgin. Comes from 'tin cans."

While they were talking the column of Blackfellas started to come onto the beach. John Bartlett swung up on a nearby railing. "You know them better than me, Doctor. I'll take your advice and bless them from afar."

***

Yani came out to the landing craft alone to confer with John and Dr. McDuff, and to see if everything was ready. They talked about the situation, and he agreed with the idea that John Frum should stay on the upper deck for now.

When he signaled the crowd to wade out to the boat, they charged forward as predicted. Yani stood at the open door with his hands raised to stop the rush. Pointing to the figure on the upper deck he said, "This is my friend, John Frum. He brings much cargo for the Blackfella on Chase Island. If anybody makes him angry, he will call Kilibob to come back."

There was a shudder among the group. For those not on the beach, the events of the night before had been magnified in the retelling. Kilibob had become a doomsday figure.

When John Frum Came

"Now John Frum will live among us as friend. He says you can take one tinken for each hand. We will open them back in village." He gave a nod and there was a frantic scramble of shoving and grabbing. No one knew what he was getting, so they took the first thing that their hands touched. When all the men had theirs, the women and children squabbled over their portions. There was no need for the minor riot — it would be a long time before they could use up all the boxes on the boat.

When Pee-wee, the ten year old, and his friends continued to hang around the open door, even after everyone had gone back to the shore, Yani had an idea. He showed the children how to open the cans with the G.I. can-openers. It was no problem for them, the kids caught on immediately. Each case had several silver colored cans without labels. Yani had discovered that these all contained fruit cocktail. They were an immediate hit. He let them open one can each and consume the contents. Then he told them he would give them each three cans of fruit salad if they went to the village and opened the C-rations for the adults. The deal was struck and a problem was solved.

Chapter 41

McDuff began to think of the removal of the stacks of boxes right in front of the drop-door as sort of a mining operation. The analogy held because he would find things like mess-hall-sized cans of peaches in a box that simply turned up at random.

When he had removed the first tier of empty cartons, he came across a huge pallet-load of something named 'SPAM.' He called John and said, "What does S-P-A-M stand for?"

"What? Spam is Spam," not understanding the question.

"Well, what in blazes is Spam?"

"It's canned pork. Lunchmeat. It's the big thing back home in the States, and the Navy's greatest discovery. It serves Spam for breakfast, lunch and supper. You get Spam and eggs, Spam without eggs, Spam sandwiches, Spam and noodles, Spam and gravy. You name it, they serve it with Spam."

"I've never heard of it," Dr. McDuff said. "Can we get some out of a carton?"

"Sure. I've sort of lost my enthusiasm for it, but we can fry some up. How about you, Yani, would you like some Spam? It's pig meat."

They found a mess kit and a primus stove in the crew's quarters. John pulled a couple of the odd-shaped cans from a box and Yani watched with eager anticipation.

He tossed the rectangular can to Yani, who showed promise as a first baseman if they over got an island baseball team together. "Open it!" he said as if there were nothing to it. The G.I. can-opener did not quite fit. Yani's puzzlement was written all over his face.

He saw the key soldered to the bottom of the can, and a tiny protrusion of metal at the beginning of a concealed strip of metal, but made no connection in his mind between the two. He studied the can for ten minutes, as John watched him shift it from hand to hand, and even tried to chew at a corner. Finally, he handed it back to John. He smiled and said humbly, "This fella no have magic. I think John Frum have magic open can. You tell this fella magic."

In Yani's world nothing worth doing was done simply as a matter of logic and convenience. There was significance in everything — even opening a can of Spam.

McDuff watched the interplay and intoned his words carefully, trying to telegraph a message to John that Yani might not fully understand. "I've found that anything having a technological skill requisite, also necessitates the invocation of magic in the eyes of island acolytes. That reinforces loyalty and insures his assistance. If John Frum wants to maintain his image as a Big Man, he had better share his magical formulas with Yani."

John caught the drift of the message, and said, "Yani, John Frum is going to initiate you into the Sacred Order of Key Twisters."

Using his best stage magician flourish, the American took the can in his left hand and turned it upside down so the key was exposed. With the fingernail of his right index finger he pried the key up and bent it back and forth until it came loose.

Holding the key in his right hand he showed Yani how to thread the little rounded end of metal at the top of the can through the hole in the key.

"Now you say 'Cin-cin-nati.'" He whispered the words slowly, and as he finished saying the word he twisted the key. There was an audible hiss as the vacuum broke.

Yani cocked his head much like the RCA Victor fox terrier, Nipper. "What is ssssss?" he asked.

Thinking fast he said, "It is the spirit of the pig in the can. Now he has left. The meat must be eaten before the sun goes down or it becomes poison. When pig spirit gone make a fella very sick if not eat same day can open."

This made perfect sense to Yani and it saved John the hopeless task of explaining the rapid growth of bacteria in a tropical climate.

Now the real magic of opening a Spam can began in earnest. John showed Yani how to turn the key ever so slowly and evenly so that the metal strip came off in a rigid little coil wrapped tightly around the key. When the entire strip was only a quarter of an inch from the end, John whispered, "O-hi-o."

Yani repeated "O-hi-o," and there was a '*ping!*' as the top became separated. John handed the watch-spring coil of metal wrapped tightly about the key to Yani, and said "You keep."

Yani accepted it with reverence and held it in his hand as John removed the lid. He turned the can upside down on a metal mess kit and the tiny monolith of pig-meat stood in pink splendor, dripping salty gelatin. Yani examined the can and saw that the edge was cut absolutely even all around the top, and was sharper than any native knife. In fact, John used the can for a knife and sliced the Spam into six evenly spaced slabs.

Yani's face held an expression of awe. Here were slices of pig-meat ready to be eaten with no further preparation necessary. But John was not satisfied with eating the meat 'as is'. He took three slabs and laid them out in the mess kit, using it as a frying pan. Over the primus stove the meat browned quickly and the smell was tantalizing.

McDuff thought it was delicious. John withheld his opinion, pleading overexposure, but Yani declared it the most delightful food he had ever tasted. He had previously been in love with British corned beef, but now he begged to practice his key-twisting skills on another can.

John could not believe Yani's reaction. He looked like his mother's cat on catnip. He turned to McDuff and said, "How much of this stuff did you find out there?"

"I think the word 'unlimited' would describe it," he said. "No disrespect intended, but if the other natives like this as much as our man, Yani, I think we might have founded a new religion," John quipped.

***

In the evening, the natives were allowed to make another raid on the C-Rations. This time everyone took an extra minute to get a look at John Frum up on the bridge. He waved to them and some even got up the nerve to wave back.

John took Yani aside after the evening food frenzy, and said, "Yani, when do I get to meet the people. Especially some of the girl people. I see some women who are pretty attractive."

"John want Mary?"

"Oh, do you have someone in mind? Who is Mary?"

"All women called Mary in Pidgin. Yani find Mary for you tomorrow."

"How about tonight?" John said.

"You wait. I bring Mary here to boat." He started toward the open end of the craft, but John caught him by the arm.

"No. I don't think Big Man Duff would like it. Ministers are funny that way. I'll go ashore with you while he's taking a nap."

"Yes. Churchfella Duff no like Mary. Him never take Mary all the time I know him."

"I don't know how they do it," John said.

"Him like Patrol-fella Gale. Him only like boy-fella."

When he finally figured out what Yani meant, John said, "Well, I'll be God-damned. He's a fairy ... All the more reason I think I'll spend the night on shore."

***

Yani and John came back to the LSM in the morning. They both looked like they hadn't slept, but John was on the point of collapse. He made it to the bunk bed and fell into it. He mumbled to himself as he surrendered to sleep — "Who the hell would have thought you could catch up on three months in one night? She was ... was ... zzzzzzz."

At about noon, McDuff woke John up. When his eyes opened the older man said, "I was worried about you and Yani last night. I woke up and found you were gone. I was afraid something might have happened to you."

"It did," John said. "If I ever get back to the Navy, I will have the shore leave story to end them all."

"I'd rather not know, if you don't mind, John," McDuff said stiffly. Discussion of sex with strangers was still more than he cared to undertake. "Yani wants to take some Spam to the village elders. It could be a way to break down the barriers."

***

After John was introduced as John Frum, a great but friendly *bis* from the island of Boston in America, each of the elders placed a hand on his chest to feel his heart beat. They were satisfied that he was human and not a spirit.

Yani picked up a can of Spam and opened it in the manner he had learned. The mess kit was placed on the embers of the fire set up in the middle of a newly built palm-frond hut. In seconds it was sizzling and after a few minutes, it was thoroughly browned and crisp on both sides.

Outside the hut a small band of people had formed, drawn by the smell of the frying Spam as well as plain curiosity. Among them was Poon, whom John had correctly assessed as the oldest man in the village. He had proved his right to the position of tribal wise man by having started climbing the mountain two hours before anyone did to avoid the tidal wave. He was toothless, and his body was shrunken to about two thirds of its original size.

It did not take much imagination to realize he desperately wanted a piece of the Spam. Saliva was dribbling down his chin. John took pity on him and gave him a slice of the cooked delicacy, served on a large green leaf.

The old man devoured the piece of strange meat hungrily. The others watched him eat the crispy morsels and savor the taste. They were silent while he gummed the foreign treat. He rolled his eyes and said, "*Natum, geko. Natum geko.*" Some of the villagers made a face of disgust but the older men made questioning noises.

"*Geko?*" one warrior asked.

"*Natum geko,*" the wise man answered.

John looked at Yani. "What did he say?"

"Poon say taste like long pig. The other men want to try some."

John broke the pieces in half and gave them to the outstretched hands. Some turned away, choosing not to try the fried Spam. However, those who took pieces seemed to agree with Poon. "*Natum geko,*" was the prevailing opinion.

John opened another can and cooked all the pieces that were not eaten uncooked. Yani reported that there was general agreement that Spam tasted like long pig.

When the economy of the island returned to normal, John was thinking of opening a trading business. Spam could be traded for fish, breadfruit, coconuts, bananas and other jungle fruits — even Marys. Spam was the currency and he would be the banker.

Yani held the official position of "Spam can-opener." He would never allow anyone to take away a sealed Spam can. He was the only one who was authorized to open them, complete with the invocation of Cin-cin-nati, O-hi-o.

Chapter 42

The next great mining discovery was the K-Rations. These were the dehydrated foods combat soldiers were supposed to carry with them into battle. They were so unpalatable, that even the natives were not anxious to have them. The only edible items the two Americans could handle were nicknamed "sawdust biscuits."

"I think these are what old time sailors used to call hardtack," McDuff said, trying to bite down on one," ... with the emphasis on 'hard.' No wonder they mutinied."

"Fortunately, they come with these little tins of grape jelly," John said, picking up a small disk that looked like a shoe polish can. "I think I'll just eat the jelly and forget the biscuits. There aren't any dentists around here."

What made the K-Rations valuable was what else they found in the packages. They had made a table of one of the crates and had several empty cartons on the deck. Into these John and McDuff tossed certain valuable cultural items money could not buy in this part of the world. They agreed they would be totally wasted on the natives — toilet paper packets, cigarettes, and coffee.

When the treasures had been removed, Yani carried the boxes to a waiting party of natives and they gratefully received the Big Man's gifts. But they made no movement toward leaving the beach. They were apparently waiting for something.

"What's the problem?" John called to Yani seeing an animated discussion in progress.

"No problem. *Kanaka* greedy fella. Want more."

When John Frum Came

"We have plenty. What do they want?"

One of them shouted to John over Yani's protests. "*Tinken geko! Tinken geko!*"

He listened to the words and recognized that the man was saying, "Tin-can geko." Recalling the episode with Poon, g*eko* was long pig.

"Do they want some cans of Spam?" John called.

"Yes," Yani answered.

"Give them two hands Spam cans," meaning ten cases, enough for the whole village. "Hell we've got tons of the stuff. But Yani chose to misunderstand and fetched up ten cans of Spam from his treasure trove, instead. When he gave them to the waiting collection party John could not see Yani peel the little keys off the bottoms of each of the odd-shaped cans. He would charge the villagers later to open them.

***

The speed with which the jungle grew back was amazing. Some of the gardens were uncovered from the layer of sand that had been deposited on top of them. Yams and taro seemed to have survived the inundation. The fish returned to the lagoon, and two weeks after the *tsunami*, it was hard to tell there had been one.

McDuff preferred the clearing on the mountain, where he continued to work on his generator and radio. John passed the days walking along the beach, smoking his K-Ration cigarettes and reading the books he found among the "Red Tag Specials" as he called the Admiral's personal possessions. He found a War Department circular and used it for a bookmark. He read it as he stood on the beach:

"Ironically, the South Pacific with all its beautiful beaches affords little good ocean swimming. Coral reefs are everywhere to gash unwary toes, sharks and barracudas lend doubts to the stoutest hearts, and the tropic sun adds a further hazard. So, on many of the forest-covered islands swimming is centered about shaded streams."

"I gotta get Yani to take me and the Marys for a picnic inland at the lake Dr. McDuff mentioned," and sat with his back leaning against a boulder embedded in the sand to read more comfortably. In a matter of minutes, Yani came running up the beach toward him, carrying something.

"John Frum!" he yelled, "John Frum!"

John closed the book and stood up. Apparently something had happened Yani thought he should know about.

When he was about ten feet away, he said, "*Kanakas* hunt for wild pig, find Japanese solider. Him not die in Hevehe water mountain. Him hide on volcano."

"What do you have there," John asked, pointing to the object he was carrying.

Wrapped in a Japanese officer's tunic was a Samurai sword. If John were able to read Japanese he would have found it belonged to Lieutenant Isoroku Shakaru, who had left his men to follow the natives up the mountain.

"Wow!" John said handling the sword. "This is neat."

"Kill last of bad Japfella. Blackfella have own island again. We have big feast…"

"Sort of what Americans call an Independence Day Celebration!" John suggested.

"Yes, Independence Day," Yani said liking the sound of the word. "Yes, also funeral for Ooma, Blackfellas taken by Hevehe." Then remembering he had a message, Yani said, "*Kanakas* say I bring John Frum. We celebration *John Frum, he come.*"

"Well, I can't very well stay away from my own party, now can I," John smiled. "Will Marys come to the party, or is this a stag affair?"

"Stag affair?" Yani asked?

"Is it just men, or do women come, too."

Yani frowned in disbelief. "No women. No Marys. *Geko* feast make women sick."

"Oh," said John, a little disappointed.

***

McDuff and John made a point of having lunch on board the landing craft every day. Today, the Coast Watcher's excitement was evident in his grinning face. He had a surprise. When John saw him unpack the generator and radio he knew immediately — he had it working.

"I know the tubes are broken in the ship's radio, but the aerial certainly must work," McDuff said. "Let's try hooking it up to the mast antenna."

John made the connections and began turning the handle on the generator. They were rewarded with a blue spark on the telegraph key. McDuff checked the proper date-code information and tapped out: "Mo/Exodus 14," three times, and waited for a response. Just when he was about to declare the effort a failure a message came through.

"Mo. Good to hear from you. Feared Japs had caught you."

McDuff tapped back, "Japs all dead from tidal wave. Have American LSM #666 beached here in lagoon. One survivor. American sailor named John Bartlett. Can someone rescue him?"

"Will contact U.S. Navy and report back. Any Jap ship activity?"

"None seen since tidal wave."

McDuff sent along a personal message to Leslie Gale, who was out on patrol at present. There was a little more chatter back and forth, and radio contact time was set for the next day.

Moses McDuff took off his earphones and said, "They're contacting the Navy and will send us a message tomorrow. I guess you can start packing."

"Do you really think they'll send a ship just to pick up the likes of me?"

"I should think so," McDuff said.

"Yeah, maybe at the end of the war."

Chapter 43

A group of elders waded out to the LSM with Yani acting as interpreter. They were here to see Big Man John who was now clearly the wealthiest man on the island. He was a Big Man among Big Men. He was expected to make a substantial contribution to the community feast.

Having been burned by this tradition because he did not understand it, Dr. McDuff was now in a position to advise John Frum of his duties. "You're obliged to be very generous by native custom. Ordinarily an island Big Man would provide at least a couple pigs for the feast. Most lowland pigs were drowned in the flood, but they know you have pigs in cans — Spam."

"How much should I give them?" he asked. "What do they expect?"

"The Big Man must not ask," he was told.

"We give plenty gift for John Frum," Yani said holding up three fingers on his left hand. "I give this many C-Ration." Then holding up his right hand, "Give one hand K-ration."

"I think Yani spent too much time with the white man," John said. "Give them two hands cases C- Rations and one hand cases Spam."

Even Yani was impressed with John Frum's generosity, but he did not think it was necessary to go to such extremes.

"I don't know how much longer I'm gonna be here," John said to McDuff, "But after I leave, they aren't gonna say John Frum was a cheap bastard."

When John Frum Came

When the sun went down the Americans could see the brightness behind the palm trees that was obviously the central bonfire. The sound of agitated drumming also filled the air. They could not see Yani, and guessed he had most likely gone ashore to open Spam cans.

Again McDuff had some words of advice, "Stay on the ship, John. You don't know what you might run into at the feast since you don't know their customs."

The drums built to a crescendo and stopped dead. The collective silence became collective babble from the site of the feast. John saw a lone figure running down the beach, followed by a group of somewhat eager islanders.

John saw the movement on the shoreline, and called, "Yani! Is that you out there?"

"Yani here," he called out. "Island fella want see John Frum."

"John Frum happy to see them. In my country we call this celebration Fourth of July."

The tide was out and the water was no more than a foot deep in the lagoon. In the bright moonlight John could see three figures start to wade out toward him. One of them was clearly the ancient one — Poon.

Yani spoke with the other men as he approached. John listened and tried to make sense out of the exchange. The most he could understand was an occasional "John Frum" and a definite "*geko.*" *Geko* was mentioned several times and from Poon's body language he appeared to be offering a gift of something wrapped in banana leaves.

"Yani, what is going on? What do they want?" he called into the darkness.

"Poon fella say he make present John Frum. Him fella, *kanaka* fella bring long pig for Big Man Frum."

John waded out to meet them. "Are you saying that Poon wants to give me some long pig from the feast?"

"Yes. I say Yani no eat long pig. John Frum no eat long pig."

John thought *can it be that some of them know about trichinosis? Has experience taught some of them that pig meat can be dangerous in the tropics?*

Not wanting to offend the old wise man, John said, "Yani, bring long pig to John Frum. I taste."

Reluctantly, Yani took the banana leaf package from Poon amid a great deal of approving clamor. It sounded like "John Frum *pooja*, — John Frum *pooja*." The younger men waded back to the strand, leaving Poon to follow as best he could. When they hit the beach they broke into a run back toward the bonfire, yelling "Jon Frum *pooja*!"

John and Yani sat on the beach. The American unfolded the large green leaves and found a piece of meat inside. It was burned more than roasted; charred on the outside; more raw than rare in the middle. He held it up to Yani and said, "You eat?"

Yani made a face of disgust and said, "No eat long pig. Only *kanaka* eat *geko*."

John theorized an explanation: *Long pig was a description of the skinny pigs that ran wild on the island. Yani had been exposed to civilization too long and had lost his taste for the primitive food of his people.*

He took a knife and sliced into the charcoal covered meat and hit a bone. It ran lengthwise through the meat and he severed it from the mass. The meat around the bone was fairly rare but he gingerly bit into it. It was sweet to the taste, and he turned to Yani who was watching in morbid fascination.

"It needs salt, but it's better than Spam," John said, holding out the meat toward his island friend. Yani grimaced and spat vigorously.

John laughed and said, "Who would have thought I'd find an Orthodox Jew ten thousand miles from Jerusalem." He gnawed the bone he asked, "Why don't you eat *geko*, Yani? Spam is made of pig."

"All fella eat pig. Only *kanaka* eat *geko*."

There was apparently some fine line of distinction that was escaping him. "You eat pig, but not long pig."

"Yes," his face brightened. At last John Frum understood.

John examined the meat again and tested his knowledge of porcine anatomy. What part of the pig did this come from? Judging from the bone he was holding, it would probably be one of the front legs.

"This pig's front leg?" he asked Yani.

Yani shook his head negatively, and volunteered a piece of information to this very dense American, "Long pig not *pig*."

"So that's it. Long pig isn't a pig, but some other kind of animal." He didn't now what else was native to the islands. He asked his friend, "If it isn't a pig, what kind of animal is it?"

Yani thought the American was teasing him. He thought the answer was rather obvious. "Long pig Japfella!" he said. While John cautiously considered the revelation, he recognized that the gift in the banana leaf had toes. It was a human foot. In a spasm of anguish John Frum was violently ill.

Chapter 44

John had given Yani some tin snips from the boat's little work shop, and a long term project was just beginning. After taking both the tops and bottoms off the C-Ration cans, John showed him how to cut them along the seam, and flatten them out.

Using wood and nails salvaged from some of the crates, the outline of a small shack was constructed. The flattened cans were used like shingles, and the only tin roof on the island took shape. Sides for the hut were optional due to the heat. Yani finished the roof just in time for the daily downpour, and the three men sat beneath it out of the rain.

Watching the water cascade off the roof into yet-uncut cans, conversation had drifted off to nothing.

John had mixed emotions about the radio report from the Coast Watchers in Port Moresby. He had not really thought the Navy would make any effort to take him off the island, but a seaplane was on its way.

He had not fully recovered from the episode with the long pig the night before. He still gagged occasionally as he talked, although there was nothing left to expel from his stomach. He had the "dry heaves" most of the night.

"They'll probably want to reclaim the LCM," John said. "Yani, I think your people better take everything off the ship they can carry and hide it in the jungle. You never know what kind of a prick you might get for a Navy officer in charge."

"I think they already have," said McDuff. "But I agree, Military types are liable to throw an armed guard around the landing craft."

"Well, so much for The Emperor Jones," John said sardonically.

"Who?" said McDuff.

"The Emperor Jones. He was the chief character in a play by Eugene O'Neil about 20 years ago. I never saw it, but I've read it. It's about a Negro from the United States who takes over a little island — I think in the Caribbean."

"Oh, yes. I remember. It caused quite a controversy at the time," McDuff said. He faltered for a minute and added, "You weren't thinking of something like that here ... were you?"

In John's weakened condition, his guard was down. "Why the hell not. The Navy treats me like shit. I'll always be some kind of servant to guys like Frankie Bartlett and his daddy, the Admiral. I could live like a prince with these people. You said it yourself, I'm almost a god to them."

"John, be realistic. Once the food on the boat is gone, what will you do? You don't have anything in common with these people. Look at what happened last night."

While Yani had renounced eating long pig in light of his new-found civilized point of view, he was at a loss to account for John's severe reaction. "John Frum ask if Mary go to feast. I say no. Women eat get sick from eating *geko*."

"Please!" John exclaimed. "Let's not talk about it any more. How about you, Dr. McDuff? Are you going to spend the rest of your life here? Do you think you are going to make these *kanakas* into Bible thumpers. Even if they understood English, or you learned to speak Booga-booga do you think you could change them at all?"

"Strange you should say that. I've been thinking about the problem off and on for months, but once I contacted Port Moresby and they said they'd call the Navy I haven't been able to think of anything else."

John said nothing.

"You know I came out here because in spite of my age, my father treated me like a naughty child. Maybe at the time I was. And if you will forgive a little Bible thumping on my own behalf, Paul says in Corinthians 13, Verse 11: "When I was a child, I spake as a child, I understood as a child, I thought as a child: but when I became a man, I put away childish things."

From his own youthful church training, John wanted to say "Amen to that," but held himself back.

"If you and I have not learned enough to call ourselves men at this point in life, after what each of us has been through, we might as well just sit on the beach here for the rest of our lives and see what the next tidal wave brings."

"Are you saying I should gladly go back to the Navy and put up with the bullshit they've been dumping on me," John said.

"That's your decision. If you want to stand up for yourself, you can do that, too. Either way it won't be easy."

"So, are you going back home to tell your old man off?" John asked.

"I am going to see if the Navy will take me along, when they take you. But I'm not going home to tell anyone off. I'm going home to be myself."

They both smiled, and John offered his hand. "Shake on it?" he said. They shook hands.

Yani listened to his two friends talking and realized that his world would be changing drastically without these two men. "You go back to America, Yani have no *bis* to protect him and tribe."

"Yani, you are as strong as Ooma. You know all he did," McDuff said, "… and more."

"Yani know how to call ships full of tinkens," he beamed. "Big Man Duff teach him how."

"After the war is over, I'll make it a point to come back for a visit to your island, Yani," John told him. "Who knows what I'll bring the next time."

***

Yani saw the plane first, as it came in slowly and circled the island for a place to set down. McDuff had told Port Moresby that the only possible spot was the lagoon, but the pilot needed to make sure for himself.

"Egg from Heaven come to get Dr. McDuff and John Frum," Yani told the natives who were pouring on to the beach. John was wearing his blue dungaree uniform again. McDuff wore his usual khaki shorts and shirt. He no longer had a "well-fed" look and his once-smooth chin was now covered with a full beard. He held a small bundle of things he wished to keep.

"I've never flown in a plane before," John said.

"No problem," Yani offered. "I fly to Heaven in this egg once. I saw Sheepy-sheep there. Heaven strange place."

When John Frum Came

John looked to McDuff for clarification. "They flew him to Australia for Coast Watcher training," he said without further elaboration.

Fortunately, the landing craft was at the end of the lagoon, leaving enough space for the Navy PBY to put down safely. It was low tide and the retractable wheels were only in about six inches of water when it taxied to where its passengers were waiting. A door popped open and two sailors and a Marine Second Lieutenant climbed out.

"Oh shit," John said to McDuff. "Enter the famous Lieutenant Frankie Bartlett, stage left."

He approached the Americans, now surrounded by Chase Islanders, and John stood at attention. "Apprentice Seaman John Bartlett reporting for heroic rescue, sir!"

Frankie returned the salute. "When are you going to stop being a wise-ass, Johnny? We were worried about you." He addressed the only white face in the crowd and said, "Second Lieutenant Francis X. Bartlett the Fourth, sir. I assume you are Dr. Moses McDuff?"

"Yes. For a minute I thought you were going to say, Dr. Livingstone, I presume."

Frankie smiled. "I thought about it," he said. "I see you have a little baggage. Are you planning to come with us? This is a Navy aircraft, you know."

"Well, I'm an American citizen waiting to be evacuated from a war zone. I plan to go wherever you are going."

The Lieutenant turned to look at the LCM. "Is it still seaworthy?" he asked.

"Haven't the foggiest," McDuff said.

"It's resting on the sand, so we don't know if it will float, sir," John said.

Lieutenant Bartlett walked down the beach to get a better look inside. Through the open drop-door he could see into the boat. "Where's the cargo? It's less than half full."

"The natives stripped the vessel, sir. We were helpless to restrain them." John whispered to Frankie, "Get a load of those spears. They know how to use them. It's best to get the hell out of here while we can."

The Marine rested his hand on his .45 and said. "O.K., gentlemen, let's get aboard the plane and return to base."

Yani hugged McDuff heartily and then did the same with John Frum. "You go to Heaven, now. You tell Jesus I come sometime. Big Man Duff in-tro-doots me to God."

**

The Chase Islanders held their ears as the PBY revved up its engines for a take off, leaving them with an image that would last a lifetime and be subject to many variations in the retelling.

They were airborne in only a short time, staying fairly close to the ocean. Yani watched their profile growing smaller as it finally approached the horizon.

Lieutenant Saburo Sakai, the Japanese ace who shot down Yani's decoy plane was returning to the site of his great kill. He had heard the Imperial Army had screwed up badly on the same island. The report was that there were only natives on the island. He wanted to do a fly-by to check for himself. His Mitsubishi was cruising at 10,000 feet, when he saw a U.S. Navy PBY taking off from the island's lagoon. He was right, it was an American military base.

He climbed almost to the Zero's maximum altitude and circled the big lumbering plane. When he approached with the sun at his back, the pilot of the PBY was unaware of his presence until the 20mm shells ripped through the starboard engine. The flying boat did a cartwheel into the beautiful azure crystal waters of the South Pacific.

Yani stood on the beach, but was unable to see what had taken place beyond the horizon. He spoke to himself in a quiet voice as he looked at the sky, "John Frum, he come back."

Epilogue

If you have enjoyed this story, you may be interested in my other books available wherever eBooks are sold.

In Der Fuehrer's Face.

During WWII President Roosevelt spent $100,000 to produce a deck of dramatic, colorful, propaganda poster playing cards that never saw the light of day.

In a bold propaganda move in 1944, President Franklin D. Roosevelt launched an anti-Nazi program. Antonio Bernal, Mexico's foremost political

Bill Schroeder

cartoonist, was commissioned to create a deck of playing cards to be distributed throughout Central and South America. The idea was to persuade Latin-American countries to openly declare war on Germany and Japan instead of just supporting us verbally.

Bernal created 55 posters based on the theme of a deck of 52 Poker playing cards with three Jokers and a design for the back of the deck. The original paintings were on unbound sheets (15-1/4" x 113/8") in folio form.

Just a few weeks before the posters were to go to press as playing cards; Roosevelt had a stroke, Hitler committed suicide, and Mussolini was strung up on a street lamp. World War II was over. There was no further use for the propaganda cards so they were never printed.

They remained virtually forgotten until 2002 when I obtained copies of the original posters from the Library of Congress. I was the first to request them since 1946. With the help of the Library of Congress, I wrote *In Fuehrer's Face* and privately printed 500 decks (of which only five mint-sealed decks are known to exist).

EBook version, illustrated in full color, is available for only $7.99.

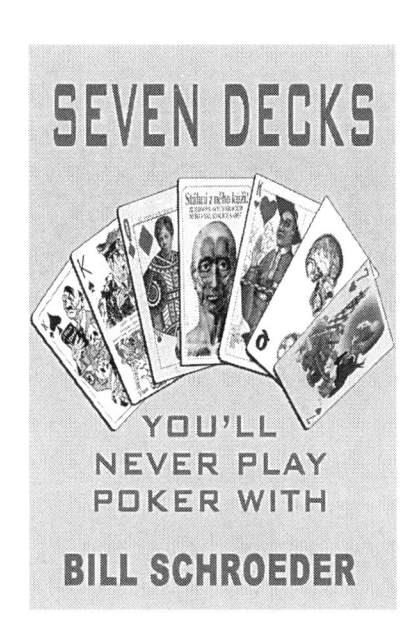

When John Frum Came

SEVEN DECKS

YOU'LL NEVER PLAY POKER WITH

BILL SCHROEDER

My second book on rare and unpublished playing cards is ***Seven Decks You Will Never Play Poker With.***

This is an illustrated wonderland of playing cards that you may not know ever existed. The book displays seven decks of cards that are either very rare or were never published after they were designed. Each has its own exciting story. The 1933 Chicago World's Fair barred the USSR from exhibiting anything after trying to distribute their Anti-Religious deck.

In 1934 FDR prevented the printing and publication of the "Roosevelt for King" deck and spent $100,000 on another deck that wasn't printed (In der Fuehrer's Face). Thousands of Nazi soldiers died in the Siege of Leningrad while two decks of Russian propaganda cards (One in 1939 and another in 1941) rained from the sky.

From 1978 there are two Italian "off-the-wall" 40-card decks known as the Under Your Skin decks. They were designed for Italian medical students in Milan to study for anatomy exams. Both are well illustrated; one deck deals with muscles and the other with bones.

While you may never own any of the actual decks, you will be able to see what they were like. A Kindle and e-Book version, illustrated in full color, is available for only $7.99.

The Innocent Assassin — How a Schizophrenic Changed American History. This novel full of factual information you never heard before, presented in an exciting narrative form with illustrations.

To schizophrenic Charles Julius Guiteau his Divine Inspiration to "remove" President Garfield was real to him, even as he dangled from a rope. Garfield's agony is chronicled elsewhere. This focus is on the delusional world of his shooter. Some actions are fictionalized to dramatize the actual story. It took Guiteau five tries to shoot Garfield and there were at least seven attempts on his own life.

(Disappointed office-seeker, indeed!)

An e-Book version, illustrated in full color, is available for only $5.99.

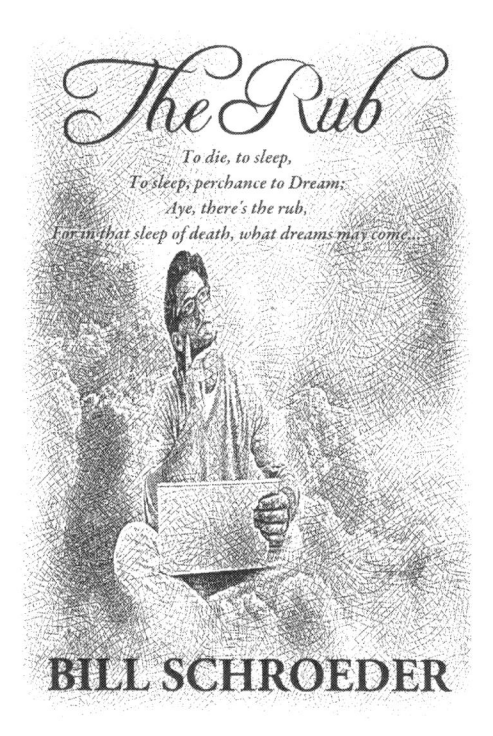

HAMLET
...To die, to sleep.
To sleep, perchance to dream—ay, there's the rub.

Part 1:

The Rub derives its name from Hamlet's question regarding the nature of existence after death. The primary character, Jack Richards, is a Rush Limbaugh-type, ultra-negative TV personality who refuses to accept his own death. He experiences numerous possibilities regarding what comes after crossing over.

Part 2:

Short Stories and Observations consists primarily of a variety of short stories and the author's memoirs covering in the 1940s up to the present. The observations underscore that one's life need not be limited to a single straight line of events. Special attentions is given to the concept of Synchronicity.

Paperback version, $11.95, Kindle and other e-Book versions, illustrated in full color, available for only $5.99.

Bill Schroeder's Author Bio

Bill Schroeder ... Was the kind of geek kid in your sixth grade class who wrote the science page in the school newspaper.

He could see the Empire State Building from his bedroom window on the Jersey side of the Hudson River, and went to New York City every chance he could. Usually, it was to the many museums on weekends.

He never missed a football or a basketball game ... never went to one and never missed it.

Bill loved black and white television in its infancy. He was both envied and ridiculed in high school when he appeared with a friend on the John Reed King Show with their pet ducks in 1950. But no one else did anything similar at the time.

He became an office boy in New York just because it put him a half a block from the New York Public Library. He spent all his lunch hours there reading and doing his homework from Rutgers University Evening Classes.

He built a genuine log cabin without power tools on weekends in the woods of central New Jersey with two friends, using a book he borrowed from in the NY Public Library.

Bill lost his student exemption from the Korean draft after dropping a college course. The Army taught him to type and take shorthand for a job in the CID. They shipped his ass to a remote base in North Korea to write reports for men who could not write declarative sentences.

He returned to Rutgers full time on the GI Bill to major in English and Creative Writing. He appeared on the Rutgers educational TV channel, representing the student body.

Bill Schroeder became an advertising copywriter, public relations hack, and executive speechwriter for a major Defense Contractor.

He married Pat Christopher, a woman of genius intelligence, who won college scholarships in Music, Art, and English. Their union resulted in six gifted and talented children.

Schroeder assumed the role of what *The Wall Street Journal* calls a "Corporate Gypsy." He worked as Public Relations Director for several Blue Chip Companies until contracting a near-fatal illness, forcing his ultimate return to the company where he started out.

There he had a change of life goals and sought new areas of expression. He was offered the position of Producer/Director of The Maryland Renaissance Festival's Shakespeare Program. He doubled as a Tarot card reader. First he was billed as The Mad Monk, later he became Prince Ali-Ba-Boon (Knows nothing tells much!)

Bill pursued "life upon the wicked stage" as a hobby for the next few years in local theater groups. He played a variety of roles: Lt. Brannigan (Guys and Dolls), Mayor Shinn (The Music Man); Merlin (Camelot); The Prime Minister (The King and I); the Arab Sheik (Don't Drink the Water); and The Chinese Detective (The Butler Did It!).

For a change of pace Bill took early retirement from the Defense contractor to go into the retail business. Harking back to his childhood love, in Washington DC's Restored Union Station he recreated a small museum named *Schrader Scientific* where he "sold the things The Smithsonian displayed (Dinosaur bones, Fossils, Gems, Taxidermy, Anthropological Artifacts)." At the same time he opened playing card stores both in DC and Baltimore.

However, he found that as much fun as it was, retail stores were not profitable. So, he moved on to running a "Welfare to Work" program in Maryland for three years. He was asked to leave after his unsuccessful unionizing attempt.

After officially retiring again, he took this opportunity to pursue his most deep-seated desire ... to write books. The first was *When John Frum Came*, followed *In Der Fuehrer's Face, Killing President Garfield, Seven Decks You Will Never Play Poker With,* and *The Rub*.

Most recently he has turned his attention toward developing the Genuine American Flag Movement after discovering that China has sold us more than $69 Million dollars worth of inaccurate copies of Old Glory. The only authentic design Old Glory is the Eisenhower Flag that became legal on August 21, 1969. He has established a detailed, informative website www.genuineamericanflag.com.

Made in the USA
Columbia, SC
24 April 2025